ONE FALL

ONE FALL

Spencer Baum

iUniverse, Inc.
New York Lincoln Shanghai

One Fall

iUniverse, Inc.

For information address:
iUniverse, Inc.
2021 Pine Lake Road, Suite 100
Lincoln, NE 68512
www.iuniverse.com

ISBN: 0-595-32675-7

Printed in the United States of America

CHAPTER 1

▼

There is an instant of clarity right before the pain. Joey had felt it before. The world slows down and is more brightly lit. Muddled noise becomes distinct, separate sounds. Skin is a circuit board, alive with current at every switch.

Joey took advantage of that clarity to let his colleague know that everything was okay. Just before falling to the ring floor, as if knocked unconscious by the violent chair shot to his skull, Joey winked.

Normally a wink wasn't necessary. In most cases a wink would be frowned upon, lest the audience saw it and the illusion was broken. Normally a chair shot hurt, and sounded good, and left you with a headache the next day, but didn't require any reassurance that the match could continue.

But this chair shot wasn't normal. This chair shot snapped all the way to the upper deck. The sound was so vivid that it might have been Joey's spine snapping like a wishbone.

Maybe the wink wasn't a good idea. Someone might have seen it. Joey hoped he hadn't ruined what was potentially a great moment in wrestling history—the nastiest chair shot ever.

Then the clarity was gone, washed out with the pain, and any second thoughts about the wink would have to wait. The pain pressed against his entire head at once, as if his brain had grown too big for his skull and would squeeze its way out of his ears. Joey lay motionless on the ring mat, knowing that this spot would be most effective if he appeared totally unconscious. But it took all his will not to grab his head with both hands and scream in agony.

He hoped the crowd was buying it. Judging by the noise, they were. Or was that just the ringing in his ears? He wouldn't know until he watched the tape tomorrow morning.

Joey Mayhem was a new face in the Global Wrestling Association, and tonight's match was his first appearance on their flagship television program, *GWA Burn*.

Joey's opponent tonight, Rob "Jumbo" Sanders, was a familiar face on *Burn*, having wrestled for the promotion for the past eight years. As a television character, Jumbo was among the nastiest of villains, and always drew some decent venom from the crowd. A muscular black man with a 70's-style afro, Jumbo was half way between six and seven feet tall (but always introduced as a "Seven-Footer") and dwarfed Joey by comparison.

That size disparity made the chair shot all the more sinful. Jumbo was already a foot taller than Joey, and had been systematically beating him into mush for ten minutes. Why did he need to pound Joey in the head with a steel chair?

18,000 people had crammed into Ford Center in Oklahoma City on this night to watch the live taping of *GWA Burn*. They had come from Tulsa, Denton, Shawnee, and Wichita. Some of them had kids. Some of them were kids. Some of them had paid upwards of sixty dollars for their seats. Many of them would call in sick to work tomorrow. After the chair shot, all of them began chanting, "JUM-BO SUCKS! JUM-BO SUCKS!"

Still sprawled on the powder blue rubber of the ring mat, Joey heard the referee yell at the timekeeper to ring the bell, ending the match. In professional wrestling, punching, biting, eye-poking, hair-pulling, body-slamming, and choking were all allowed, but hitting someone over the head with a steel chair was not. Hence, this match was officially over, with Joey Mayhem pronounced the winner via disqualification.

But just because the match was over didn't mean the fighting had to stop. According to plan, Jumbo grabbed Joey's long brown hair and pulled him from the mat. Acting dazed, but feeling alert, Joey opened his eyes and let Jumbo lead him to his feet.

"You up for this?" Jumbo whispered.

"Yeah," Joey whispered back.

Jumbo pushed Joey's head down like he was dunking him in a bucket, then wrapped his arms around Joey's waist. Knowing that "The Jumbo Bomb" was coming, the crowd booed. Like a bulldozer carrying a mound of dirt, Jumbo lifted Joey high over his head, then dropped him. The seven-foot fall was impressive, exclamated with a mechanically enhanced thump when Joey's back collided with the ring. Jumbo took a second to tug on his sagging silver tights, then pulled Joey up by his hair to repeat the entire routine.

Two Jumbo Bombs later, the crowd was thoroughly incensed.

"You Suck you slow pile of shit!" shouted a young woman from the front row. Jumbo showed her his middle finger. Another second to pull up his tights, then Jumbo bounced himself off the ropes and completed a body splash, dropping all four hundred pounds of himself on top of Joey's lifeless body.

The ring bell sounded five times, following a strange wrestling tradition of ringing the bell repeatedly when wrestlers were fighting outside the confines of a sanctioned match. A troop of referees appeared from backstage and ran down the entrance ramp to the ring, supposedly to bring order. Jumbo, now in a state of manic rage, picked up the referees one at a time and power slammed them in an assembly line of carnage.

The ring bell continued to sound. The crowd continued to boo. Joey felt like he might black out. He couldn't have been happier with how things were going.

Heading into tonight's match, Joey and Jumbo had two goals: 1. Anger the crowd with an extended pummeling of Joey, including a vicious chair shot. 2. Surprise the crowd with the finish.

As Joey lay on his back, surrounded by fallen referees, listening to the jeers of the fans as Jumbo's heavy rap music began to play, he was certain that Goal Number One had been accomplished. Now it was time for the surprise.

Jumbo's music was the cue from backstage to move the segment forward. Following that cue, Jumbo left the ring, stepping over the top rope then descending two metal stairs attached to the ringpost. As Jumbo slowly walked up the ramp toward the exit, taunting the fans along the way, Joey jumped to his feet and worked his eyes into a wild gaze. The crowd thundered in approval.

Feeling a rush from the crowd's energy, Joey sprinted to the edge of the ring (hurdling two fallen referees on the way), and leaped over the top rope. The crowd was now making so much noise that only a fool wouldn't turn around to see what was going on, but Jumbo continued walking up the entrance ramp, as if he didn't hear the fans and didn't notice that his theme music had stopped playing.

Joey ran up the ramp, careful to ensure that he looked into the nearest TV camera so the home audience could see his crazy eyes. Jumbo turned around just in time to get punched in the face. He fell back from the force of Joey's fist. This powerful monster, seemingly invincible just minutes before, was now fodder for Joey's rapid kicks and punches, which were delivered in sets of five or six, each set separated with a look at the crowd to show off the wild eyes and maniacal laugh that were to be Joey Mayhem's gimmick in the GWA.

Jumbo curled up in the fetal position on the floor. A merciful character would have left him there. But Joey Mayhem had an edge of psychosis. Joey stomped and punched Jumbo for an unheard of sixty seconds uninterrupted, before another troop of referees appeared from the back. The referees tried in vain to stop Joey, but he continued his violence until his theme music (upbeat hard rock) came on, allowing the scene to end gracefully. Joey stepped over his victim and strode to the back, all the while looking into the camera. When he reached the top of the ramp he turned for one more look into the audience. Then he disappeared behind the black curtain as the crowd chanted "JO-EY! JO-EY!"

The television viewers saw Jumbo, all seven feet of him, curled up on the floor, as the last shot of the night. The commentators encouraged them to tune in next week, and the screen faded to black, ending the show.

On the other side of the curtain, Joey descended six steps into a tight corridor that led to an open atrium. He had hoped the other wrestlers would be waiting there to congratulate him on the success of his first TV appearance.

The only person to greet him was Rashann Sanders, Jumbo's wife.

"Hey," she whispered. She gave him a nervous smile, then looked over his shoulder, as if he were in the way of something.

"Well that went over pretty well, didn't it?" said Joey.

"Yeah," she said. Once again she flashed the nervous smile and looked past him, this time stepping to one side and craning her neck as if Joey was blocking her view of a movie.

Joey took the hint and stepped out of her way. She found what she was looking for when Jumbo appeared in the corridor.

"Hey there," she said to her husband. Jumbo ignored her and walked straight to Joey.

"What was up with that wink?" he said.

Wink? Joey's mind rewound past the standing ovation, the chants of his name, the adrenalin rush of it all, the pain of the chair shot…

"Oh yeah. Sorry. It was just—that chair shot was killer and, I guess I wanted to let you know that, even though it was such a good one, I was fine."

Jumbo shook his head. "The camera could have seen it. Man, why would you think I needed to know you were alright? I know how to do a chair shot."

"Oh no, I didn't mean anything like that. It was a mistake to wink. I guess I was just in the moment." Joey wished he was wearing more clothing than his wrestling tights and boots. He felt awkward; he had no comfortable place to put his hands.

"Damn right it was a mistake. God I hope the camera didn't see you."

"I didn't know it would be such a—" Joey turned to Rashann, "Did you see the wink?" he asked her. Her opinion meant nothing to him, but she seemed a safe place to turn. Joey wanted to appear properly concerned for Jumbo's sake, but he knew this wasn't a big deal. The crowd had eaten him up. Who cared if he broke character for a second?

"Yeah, I saw it," said Rashann.

"Ah fuck," said Jumbo, now completely in a huff. Joey wondered what he could say to end this conversation. Deeply sorry? Won't happen again? Why are you acting like this is the end of the world?

He could hear the movement and chattering of people from the shadowy corridors in the back. When would the other wrestlers came out to congratulate him?

As if on cue, Jack Branson, a veteran wrestler who had performed earlier in the night, stepped into the atrium and walked toward them. He had showered and was wearing street clothes, his short black hair wet and neatly combed. This was good, Joey thought. Jack Branson was one of the most respected people in the company. He would make it clear that Joey's performance tonight was cause for celebration, and this stupid conversation about his wink would be over.

"Hey Branson," Jumbo called out to him. "Did you see the wink?" Jumbo's voice, familiar to Joey from years of watching him on television, echoed in the open space with accusation.

Branson nodded his head as he approached. "Camera caught it dead on," he said.

"Shit," said Jumbo, using a snap of his head to accentuate the word.

Joey opened his mouth to speak, but had nothing to say. He was torn between defending himself and acting contrite.

"Don't worry about it kid," Branson said, then patted Joey on the chest. "Otherwise, you did fine."

Fine? He needed to watch the tape. If Branson said it was fine, maybe it was only fine, instead of great, and that was why Jumbo could get away with this shit. Maybe the fans sounded more responsive than they actually were. Maybe he misjudged the whole thing, and it really was just fine. And since it was just fine, a mistake, like winking at your opponent in view of the camera, was a big deal. Maybe Joey's first match on national television was going to be remembered solely for that wink.

"Thanks," he said to Branson. Joey realized that a year ago, maybe even an hour ago, he would have been thrilled to hear Jack Branson tell him, 'Your match was fine.' Jack Branson was a legend, someone Joey had watched since he was twelve.

That was the catch. Tonight Joey Mayhem had not only introduced himself to the world, but to his heroes, and, apparently, he had screwed up.

CHAPTER 2

▼

GWA Burn ended its live broadcast from Oklahoma City at eleven central. Ten hours later and six hundred miles away, three middle-aged men sat around a buffet table in a luxury hotel room in Worcester, Massachusetts, discussing what they had seen on the program.

They analyzed the production, noting with pleasure that the show continued its recent streak of mishaps, from the wrong camera angles being aired to inexcusable difficulties with the ring announcer's microphone.

They analyzed the writing, and were again pleased that last night's broadcast was less than perfect. The first ninety minutes were disorganized and made little sense. No storylines were created or advanced, and wrestlers who should have gone over did not.

They analyzed the wrestling. These three men loved wrestling, and loved to talk about wrestling, spending more than an hour going over the technique of each wrestler who appeared on *Burn*. Every suplex, every punch, and every body slam were examined, and, in their opinions, the wrestling on last night's show was sub-par.

But most important to these men was the response of the live crowd. They were interested in who got cheered, who got booed, and who got nothing. The live crowd was the most accurate barometer of the response of wrestling fans worldwide.

The men were in agreement about the lesson to be learned from the crowd's reaction to last night's show. *Burn* had found a new superstar. His name was Joey Mayhem.

The three men were the Head Booker, Talent Manager, and President of Revolution Wrestling, the GWA's primary competition. This Tuesday morning meeting was a repeat of their meeting a week before in Providence, and the week before that in Hartford. For them, *GWA Burn* was for Tuesday-morning viewing and discussion, because Monday nights were spent producing their own live show, *Revolution Riot*, which aired directly opposite *Burn* nationwide, in an intense competition for viewers known in the wrestling world as the "Monday Night Battle."

For the past two years, *GWA Burn* consistently garnered higher ratings than *Revolution Riot*, but wrestling fans knew the tide was changing. While *Burn* was growing tired and complacent, *Riot* was taking off, stealing a growing chunk of the GWA's viewers every week. Because of *Riot's* recent success, these Tuesday morning meetings of late were little more than congratulatory sessions, giving the three men an opportunity to pat themselves on the back while their competition floundered.

The good cheer continued this morning, until they watched *Burn's* main event and the way the crowd reacted to newcomer Joey Mayhem.

"What do we know about Joey Mayhem, and how soon can he be working for us?" said Max Zeffer, President of Revolution Wrestling.

It was well known in the wrestling world that Max Zeffer saw employment contracts and company loyalty as minor inconveniences on his path to assembling the ultimate wrestling promotion. A multi-millionaire by birth, and the youngest major player on the North American wrestling scene at only thirty-six, Max had built Revolution Wrestling into the second largest promotion in the world by the brute force of his money. The majority of his staff, from the wrestlers to the production crew to the men sitting with him this morning, were former GWA employees whom Max had personally bought out.

"He's just a couple months into a standard developmental deal over there. He'll be up for negotiation next year, but not before," said a short balding man with a whiney voice. The man was Larry Jenkins, Revolution's talent manager, responsible for finding and cultivating new stars. "I honestly don't think this kid is that big of a deal. We marked him as a prospect the first time we saw him do a match in Memphis. Good enough to keep an eye on, but not good enough for our developmental program. We thought he was a risk. He was unfocused and careless in the ring."

"We thought he was a risk, or you did?" said Gene Harold, Revolution's Head Booker. A giant of muscle and fat with a bushy beard, Gene was unique among the three in that he was once a professional wrestler himself. His angry tone openly condemned Jenkins for passing over this hot talent. Gene Harold and Larry Jenkins had a dislike for each other dating back to the early seventies, when both men worked as road agents for The Mid-America Wrestling Alliance, which would eventually be purchased by the GWA. Back then, Gene and Larry both had ambitions of becoming the major wrestling promoter in the Midwest. Had they not been trying so hard to climb all over each other, the wrestling landscape might not have been such easy pickings for Duke Correlli to create the GWA and run all the regional promotions into the ground.

"I thought Joey Mayhem was risky when I saw him in Tennessee," said Jenkins. "I take full responsibility for letting him go. As far as I'm concerned, he still isn't a good prospect."

"Not a good prospect?" said Gene. "You're right, he's not a good prospect. He's not a prospect at all anymore. As of last night, he's the real deal."

"I'm telling you guys, I've seen him wrestle a real match, not like the made-for-TV blip he did last night, and the kid's reckless and unfocused," said Jenkins. "He might make it to the top, but he's going to hurt someone doing it."

"That wink was reckless," said Max. "But it showed spunk. I bet the Internet fans are already excited with him."

"I don't get it, Larry," said Gene, ignoring Max's comments. "If you know he can wrestle, you put him in the ring with the right people and let him wrestle. Who else are you letting slip through the cracks?"

"This is one guy Gene, relax," said Larry.

"Gentlemen, come on," said Max. "This argument is pointless now. The kid's a star and we don't have him. The fans loved him last night. They're going to talk about him. They're going to tune in to see him. If we can't have him on our show for a year or more, then what are we going to do to make sure people watch us rather than him?"

Gene and Larry looked at each other to see who would speak first. They both had plenty of ideas for the show, ideas they would love to express to Max in private when the other wasn't there to criticize.

Jenkins turned to Max and spoke as if Gene wasn't at the table. "I've been thinking about a hot shot angle to open up the show next week," he said.

"Out of the question," said Gene. "None of the angles, none of the storylines, and none of the booking will be changed. We've been planning next Monday's show for seven months. It's the very best we've got to offer. If Duke can come up with something better than what we've got, then so be it."

"I disagree, Gene," said Larry, his intonation one of forced civility. "I think we need to let it all hang out right now. This Joey Mayhem kid could become a tidal wave or he could wash out next week. If we get people talking about us instead of him—"

"Oh, so now the kid's got potential. You just said—"

"I just said that the kid's reckless and wasn't a good prospect for us. I don't deny that he was a hit last night, and because he was a hit, we should put on our very best show next week."

Gene shook his head and sighed.

"We are putting on our best show, Larry. I will strongly oppose any changes to next week's script because they will, by definition, be inferior to what we already have. Next week's show is the climax of a seven-month long story and it has been thought about and planned for since last January. We can't abandon a winning plan just because our competition may have finally gotten their act together. The best we can do is stick to the script."

Larry threw his hands up and turned his head to look out the window.

"What about defections?" asked Max, bringing Larry back into the conversation. "Zeke Thunder's still holding out for a better contract over there. Maybe we should snatch him up."

Revolution Riot had made its greatest leaps in the television ratings when a series of high-profile wrestlers defected from the GWA and showed up unexpectedly on *Riot* the next week. The GWA responded by putting all of its big-name wrestlers on extended, big-money contracts. The competition for big-name wrestlers between the promotions had resulted in a huge increase in average salary for professional wrestlers in the two promotions, and had put a sizable financial strain on both companies.

This competition for wrestlers made free agents out of big names whose contracts came due for renewal. Most notable of the existing free agents was a veteran performer named Zeke Thunder, who had demanded a large raise from the GWA last month. When Duke Corelli refused, Zeke chose to hold out for more money, thinking that if the GWA didn't give him a nice raise then Revolution would. The aging wrestler had since been off television for almost a month, with neither promotion offering anything close to what he demanded.

"Yes," said Larry. "That's exactly what I'm talking about. We don't need to change existing stories, just find ways to hot shot the ratings and keep the buzz on us rather than Joey Mayhem. I'm all in favor of renewing talks with Zeke right away."

"We've already decided we don't want Zeke," said Gene. "He's locker room poison and we don't need him."

"Dammit Gene. Even if he adds nothing to the product as a whole, he still carries enough weight to get people talking. We just need some rumors from those Internet kids," said Larry.

"So start some rumors," said Gene. "We really don't need another politicking old-timer in our locker room. Besides, even if you were able to pull something off, those Internet kids wouldn't care. You should never book something with them in mind."

Max quietly stood up and left the table, as if he had nothing to offer until this argument worked itself out.

"Typical old fashioned hogwash," said Larry. "You're still living in a world of cartoon heroes and cauliflower ears Gene. Wake the fuck up. These Internet kids you hate so much are the lifeblood of our business. They're the ones buying the pay per views and spreading the good word. When little kids in the school bus and big kids in the office talk about our business, it's the Internet geeks who speak with authority. More than anything, it's their loyalty that will decide who wins Monday Nights."

"That's great Larry, have you ever visited one of the wrestling web sites?" said Gene. "These kids are cynical know-it-all naysayers who will turn to a comic book or a video game the minute we piss them off, and if we start pandering to them we will piss them off, because we will never make them happy. We're gaining viewers because we've stuck to our guns while Duke's been floating in the wind. Good storytelling can't happen if you don't tell a story, and people tune in to see where we're going to take them, not where they're going to take us."

"You're such a windbag Gene," said Larry, giving up. "What are you thinking Max?" he called toward the kitchen.

Max walked out of the kitchen sipping on a mug of coffee.

"I don't like our options," he said in a soft voice.

"I don't either," Larry agreed.

Max sat back down at the buffet table and began speaking like a teacher addressing two debate students.

"The thing is, neither of you are saying what I want to hear. I agree, Gene, that next week's script is our very best effort and will only be made worse by tinkering with it. But I very much disagree with the idea that we do nothing to quell the buzz that is certain to surround Joey Mayhem and his performance last night. I will not sit back and let Duke beat us in the ratings during May sweeps, that's just not an option this time."

"What's the big deal with the ratings?" said Gene. "If we stick to plan we'll have our biggest pay per view ever next month."

Max put his coffee cup on the table, freeing his hands to wave about as he spoke.

"I don't care so much about the pay per view this month," he said. "May sweeps is the bigger fish to fry right now. Duke's already on the ropes with ITN. Now is the time to move in for the kill."

Gene decided not to argue the point. He didn't completely understand all the ins and outs of the TV business like Max did, and guessed that Max probably knew what he was talking about. *GWA Burn* had been a ratings winner for Imagine Television Network (ITN) for ten years, but was still disliked by the network's executives, at least according to the gossip. The execs at ITN didn't care much for the fact that their number one show regularly featured half-naked women wrestling in pools of muck, or monstrous men beating each other over the head with sledgehammers and steel chairs. With ITN already reticent about *Burn*, a ratings victory for *Riot* in May would be invaluable. The month of May was a crucial time for television networks, because advertising rates for the next quarter were calculated based on May's ratings. As such, it was common for both wrestling promotions to put on bigger, better shows throughout the month.

"What exactly did you have in mind, Max?" asked Larry, now in full eager-to-please mode.

"I don't know. I'm thinking I might go down south and knock around."

"What does that mean?" said Gene.

"I'm going to go snoop around the GWA tour and see what I can dig up that might be useful," said Max.

"Just what do you hope to accomplish?" said Gene, with a tone of skepticism.

"Well, I want more options than I presently have, so I'm going to go down there and see if I can find some."

"That sounds like a good idea," said Larry.

"It sounds like a shitty idea if you ask me," said Gene.

"You know," said Max, "it's no wonder Duke beat you guys to the punch all those years ago. You both play it way too safe to make it to the top."

"Oh go to hell, Max," said Gene. "How are we supposed to know what the fuck you're talking about when you say you're going to go snoop around the GWA tour? If you weren't my boss and this wasn't your own god-damned company I'd tell you that's the dumbest idea I've ever heard. No one from the GWA is going to talk to you. If they're even seen with you they'll be suspected of defection. Hell, if anyone sees you down there the Internet geeks are gonna go hog wild."

Max chuckled as he stood up and left the buffet table. He walked to the kitchen and dumped out his coffee cup in the sink.

"I'll call from Dallas tomorrow night," said Max. "Gene, you'll need to run the production meeting on Thursday. Tell the production team I went home to visit my daughter, and if anyone needs to contact me for any reason, they can do it through one of you."

"You're going alone?" Larry asked.

"Yes, Larry. I'm going alone."

"Yes Larry, he's just going to head off to Dallas, find someone from the GWA, and convince them to give him some juicy gossip." said Gene sarcastically.

"Professional wrestlers are ambitious people," said Max. "You give them what they want, they'll give you what you want."

"That's a nice little cliche, Max. If only it were so easy," said Gene.

Max smiled. "Hey, it worked with you two, didn't it?"

CHAPTER 3

▼

Taken from www.wrestlinghotline.com

Greetings slugs.

Today is Tuesday, April 18th, and this is your Tuesday Morning Hangover, the weekly scorecard of the Monday Night Battles.

Last weekend, I was called upon to go into the crawl space underneath my grandparents' house and look for Friskers, their missing cat. I didn't find Friskers, but I did find an old Schlitz can that had been opened with a can opener. You know, the pointy-nosed, cut-into-the-metal can openers where you'd make a big triangle hole on one end to drink from and a little triangle hole on the other to let air in. Insane. How old is that can?

Then I started thinking about the progression of beer cans over time, and realized that we've been through several stages of beer-can-opening systems in my lifetime alone. Right now, we're in the wide-mouthed-can poptop stage, which recently replaced the regular poptop stage. But the poptop isn't that old. As recently as the 80s, there was the peel-away tab. Remember the peel-away tab? You'd pop the lid and get that burst of carbonation, then you'd actually peel off the tab and have to throw it away. In the eighties, there were used peel-away tabs from beer cans everywhere! In the gutters, on the streets, in your yard. Where did all those tabs go? Kind of makes me think it's perfectly okay to litter. After all, the peel-away tabs from the 80s are completely gone!!

Old beer cans and missing peel-away tabs are what keep yours truly moving forward in the dark doldrums of wrestling's downtimes (like the 1990s). Fortunately, things are looking up.

We begin with an overnight ratings report:

GWA Burn pulled an overall 4.3, with a 3.9 in the first hour, a 4.4 in the second hour, and a 4.5 in the overrun. These numbers are roughly comparable to last week's, meaning the television ratings slide for *Burn* might be over, or at least abating. This is especially significant considering the big buildup for this week's *Riot*.

Speaking of which, *Revolution Riot* got an overall 4.2, with a 3.8 in the first hour, a 4.3 in the second, and a 4.5 in the overrun. Once again, comparable to last week, and the second week in a row that the shows are statistically tied at 4.2–4.3, which roughly translates into 4.3 million homes tuning in to each show.

The News:
Rumors are running more and more rampant about Zeke Thunder's imminent return. Last week in an interview with Chandler Dresby of wrestlingdailytribune.com, Zeke said he is anxious for an offer from either major promotion, and implied that he may be willing to accept less money than he's been asking for. Zeke would be a welcome addition to either roster at this extraordinarily competitive time, and could quickly fit into the main event scene on either side. With the May sweeps upon us, I expect him to show up on television sooner rather than later.

In other news, the Family Television Group has intensified their all-out assault on *GWA Burn*, which is now listed at Number One on their list of the top 10 most family-offensive shows on television. From a press release dated April 21st titled "Wrestling Show Tops FTG 10 Worst":

> Wrestling program *GWA Burn* tops the Family Television Group's updated list of the 10 most family-offensive shows on television. The wrestling program, now in it's twelfth year on Imagine Network Television, had an average of 138 instances of family-offensive content in a two-hour show as measured by FTG's Offensive Index. Clocking in more than one offense per minute, *GWA Burn* was by far the worst offender on prime time television.

> "Families need to be aware that *GWA Burn* is not appropriate for children or teenagers," says Sonia Katzenberg, FTG Chairwoman. "The show is littered with acts of graphic violence, inappropriate sexual content, foul language, and degradation of women. We have named the program Public Enemy Number One, and will initiate a boycott of their sponsors unless they clean up their act immediately."

The press release goes on to call *Burn* an "American Embarrassment" and says that *Burn*'s sponsors are "shameless money-grubbers" for choosing to support the show.

Interestingly, *Revolution Riot* is never mentioned in the press release, and doesn't even make the FTG Top 10. This shouldn't be a complete surprise, since *GWA Burn* has garnered higher ratings for years, and is quite a bit raunchier than *Riot*. Still, I don't know how I would take this if I were Max Zeffer. On the one hand, Revolution seems to have escaped the wrath of the goody-goody censors, at least for now. On the other hand, FTG's apparent ignorance of *Riot*'s existence is kind of an embarrassing snub, suggesting that the mainstream still thinks the GWA is the only game in town.

As of yet, there has been no official response from the GWA, but we shouldn't expect Duke to take this lying down. As we speak, Duke and his minions are likely preparing for a massive legal battle, the likes of which we haven't seen in wrestling since the drug scandals a decade ago.

As far as I'm concerned, the FTG can go to hell and deserves the legal jihad Duke and his thugs are sure to unleash. More on this story in future reports, I'm sure. For now….

The High Points:
GWA Burn—Those of you who missed last night's show are probably reading this because of the deafening buzz created by GWA's newest face. Joey Mayhem, formerly Maniac Joey Hamilton from the Southeast Wrestling League, made his television debut last night, in the main event no less. Although the match itself was a squash, the events after the match were the most surprising I've seen all year.

Just a quick recap: *Burn* opened last night with Duke offering Jumbo a main event slot against an opponent of his choosing. Then, after a mostly forgettable show, Jumbo came to the center of the ring and announced he would face anyone brave enough to come out and challenge him. When Joey Mayhem came out, the crowd was silent, most of them having never seen him before. And when Jumbo squashed Joey for ten minutes, the crowd got pissed off.

But after Jumbo left Joey Mayhem (and four referees) in a heap in the middle of the ring, Joey jumped to his feet, sprinted after Jumbo, and beat the shit out of him. It was totally surprising and sweet as all hell for those of us who think

Jumbo is about as interesting as maple syrup on a pizza. The crowd dug it, the announcers put him over, and we have ourselves a new star.

About damn time, too. When was the last time the GWA tried to create a new main-eventer? Right now, the only person in the GWA main event scene who debuted with the company in the past three years is Goliath, and even he's getting passe. Duke's uncharacteristic decision to push a newcomer is just what the company needs and couldn't have come at a better time. Revolution has been putting on killer shows for months now, while GWA has continually dragged out the same old faces doing the same old shit.

So, here's to Joey Mayhem. May he bring some much needed change to the GWA upper card.

I shouldn't let this discussion pass without mentioning "the wink." Last night everyone was talking about the wink and what it meant. For those who missed it, right after Jumbo flattened Joey Mayhem with a chairshot, Joey winked at Jumbo before falling to the floor. Everyone has their theory about the wink. Was it was planned? Will it be part of his character? Was it an inside joke? Was it unscripted? Was it Joey's way of accusing Jumbo of being soft? Who knows?

My personal hope is that the wink was planned and has some deep and interesting significance that we'll find out about later. Hey, a fan can dream.

On the other side….
Revolution Riot—Lots of high points here, as usual.
1. Flash Martin vs. Edgar Hoover. Flash's solid, steady push continues, as he goes over clean against the wily veteran. The Flash Martin push thus far has been nothing short of a clinic in good booking.

2. Crystal Waters promo. Finally, something interesting happening in women's wrestling. Memo to Duke: This is what we want to see. The Crystal Waters/Marian feud has been based on good wrestling and good backstory. If you have good wrestling surrounded by a good story, people will tune in to watch a women's division, even if the women aren't watermelon-chested toothpicks. While the GWA is doing its bad Skinamax impersonation, the women on Revolution are actually WRESTLING. Funny, actual wrestling on a wrestling show is going over in the women's division, go figure.

3. Lucifer vs. Jerry Senika—No. 1 Contender's Match. Well, it lived up to the hype. The wrestling gets four out of five stars in my book. Lucifer's long march to the top of the world takes another step forward, after he beats the living legend in a grueling 20-minute epic.

I can't wait for next week's title match.

Speaking of which, onto...

The Big Picture:
Despite the GWA's best effort to put on an interesting finish to this week's show, the talk of the upcoming week will be *Revolution Riot.*

Lucifer vs. Red Jackson for the World Title is the biggest match I can remember being given away on free TV, and it's now just a week away. This match will be the culmination of Lucifer's seven-month-long push from obscurity to superstar. I've got to give props to Max, Gene, and Larry for their patience in slowly building up Lucifer, in what has to be one of the most magnificent rises to the top in wrestling history. What a brilliant way to bring this push to its culmination. Wrestling's biggest young superstar against its greatest active legend for the title. That's what everyone will be watching.

I, like always, will tape both shows and give you the definitive review of what goes down. Until next time, this is Steve Garcia. Peace.

CHAPTER 4

▼

Joey took seat number 230, in row EE of the United Spirit Arena in Lubbock, Texas. On the floor, twenty-nine rows down, Jumbo and Jack Branson were running their spots in the ring. They would be performing together in a little over six hours. Standing around the ring, watching and giving advice, were three veteran wrestlers: Crusader, Deep Six, and Lord Mayberry.

At this time last year, Joey would have emptied his savings account to sit and watch these megastars of the wrestling world rehearse spots and work out together in the ring. Now he was here, not only to watch, but also to get in a few minutes of practice time himself. Later tonight, in a non-televised house show, he would wrestle Bret Stevens, a performer he'd admired for years.

Joey's interest in professional wrestling predated his earliest memories. On Saturday mornings, while other kids watched cartoons, Joey and his older brother Mark watched wrestling. By the time Joey was a teenager, he and Mark were imitating their favorite wrestlers in their parents' basement. The floor strewn with pillows, they would re-enact Red Jackson vs. Shane Walker, or Chuck Campo vs. The Great Santos, move for move, with a recliner, a coffee table, and a toy chest as the ring posts.

When they were in high school, Joey and Mark founded the Memphis Backyard Brawlers, a group of ten boys who met every day after school to act out their wrestling fantasies in Joey's backyard. Each boy had his own character and they all took turns as the World Champion, (the champion wore a brown leather belt with a large silver buckle that belonged to Joey's father). It was in the Memphis Backyard Brawlers that Maniac Joey Hamilton was born.

As the group became more advanced in their skills, they also became more daring, and on one cloudy afternoon in late March, Mark decided he would attempt a moonsault from the lowest branch of the maple tree in the backyard. With his opponent (Joey's best friend Tito), bravely and patiently lying on the grass, Mark climbed the tree, set himself up on the lowest branch, and leaped. He landed perfectly across Tito's chest. The group cheered in approval. As Joey, the acting referee, was squatting to do the three count, Tito and Mark simultaneously screamed in pain. Mark rolled off Tito's chest. Their match was never finished. Mark had broken his right leg and left Tito with two broken ribs and a punctured lung. That afternoon an ambulance came to the Hamilton house. The Memphis Backyard Brawlers never met again.

After the accident, Mark lost interest in professional wrestling, but Joey, much to his mother's chagrin, continued to watch, if no longer imitate, the Saturday shows. His senior year, Joey saw a documentary on cable that described the inner workings of a professional wrestling school and the life of a wrestler in an independent promotion. That night, using his parents' 166 megahertz computer with a 56K modem, he got on the Internet and found the web site for Victor Blakey's school of pro wrestling in Nashville. The next night, at dinner, he told his parents that he wanted to enroll in wrestling school after graduation.

"Absolutely not," his mother said.

Three months of pestering and pleading passed before Joey's mother acquiesced. In June, she accompanied him to Nashville and signed a six hundred dollar tuition check for a year of wrestling school.

That year, thirteen people, including Joey Hamilton, enrolled in "Beginning Professional Wrestling" with Victor Blakey. At the end of the first week, the thirteen was down to ten, after two people quit and one tore his ACL. At the end of the first month, only six remained, after three more quit and one poor kid broke his neck on a failed back body drop. By Christmas, Victor Blakey had kicked two more kids out of the program after discovering they were addicted to painkillers, and another young man fell to injury, this one tore his right bicep. When the program finished in May, Joey was one of three who received a certificate of completion. Of the three, Joey was the only one to receive Victor Blakey's coveted recommendation to the Independent Wrestling Promoters Association. In June, the Southeast Wrestling League offered Joey a spot on their tour. He took it, and Maniac Joey Hamilton, dormant since the demise of the Memphis Backyard Brawlers, was re-born, this time as a bona fide professional.

Joey's first real match was against Oscar Esquivel, a long-time wrestler in Mexico who had recently begun the American "Indy" circuit in hopes of landing a job with one of the major companies. Joey and Oscar wrestled for thirty minutes, in front of one hundred and fifty people, in a rodeo arena in Little Rock. By the time Oscar hit a shooting star press for the win, Joey was already over with the fans. Their thirty minute match generated lots of buzz in the burgeoning Internet Wrestling Community. Word started to spread that there was a kid in the Southeast Wrestling League who had "It."

Three nights later, Joey and Oscar wrestled again, this time in Memphis, with the old Backyard Brawlers and Larry Jenkins from Revolution Wrestling in the audience. In front of the home town crowd, knowing a big money contract was at stake, Joey's second ever pro match was a disaster. He tried to go too fast, and missed his spots. He tried to be too flashy, and botched a missile dropkick, barely grazing Oscar's shoulder. After thirty minutes of mistakes, Joey, a bundle of nerves, misplanted his foot for a superkick, and nailed Oscar straight in the face, breaking his nose and his front teeth. Joey went over that night, but he didn't get a contract with Revolution. He lost the respect of his opponent, he scared the hell out of his mother, and he earned a reputation of being dangerous in the ring.

It took a year and a half to recover from the Memphis disaster, but with persistence, realistic expectations, and some financial assistance from home, Joey's stock slowly rose again. On New Year's Day, Joey received a call from the Global Wrestling Association, inviting him to their headquarters in Chicago for a tryout. Two weeks later, he signed a one-year developmental deal with the GWA for forty thousand dollars.

For the next two months, Joey wrestled in Rosemont, Illinois, in the GWA farm league, under the tutelage of the great Shane Walker, one of his childhood heroes. Shane told him if he kept his head down, his mouth shut, and his eyes open, great things would happen for him one day.

One day turned out to be soon. On April 11th, Joey was invited to perform a "dark match", a non-televised warm-up match, before the taping of *GWA Burn* in Kansas City. He wrestled against Benjamin Grant, his sparring partner from the farm league. In front of fifteen thousand people, he put on his best performance ever, earning accolades backstage and a lunch date with Duke the next day. At the lunch, Duke asked Joey if he felt he was ready to appear on television. Joey said yes. The next week was his match against Jumbo Sanders on *Burn*. A nasty chair shot, a buzz-causing wink, a post-match surprise beatdown of the main event heel, and Joey was a star.

And in the three days that followed the notable confrontation with Jumbo, the wrestling world had crowned Joey Mayhem its new prince. The Internet sites talked about him incessantly. His family, friends, former colleagues from the

Southeast Wrestling League, and veteran wrestlers from the GWA, were asked to give their thoughts on him in interviews for web sites and newsletters. A Joey Mayhem T-shirt, complete with trademarked logo, was in production, to begin selling at GWA shows next month. Even an old home movie from the Memphis Backyard Brawlers surfaced on the Internet and was downloaded across the world.

Against that background of overnight sensation, Joey looked across the empty arena, where in hours he would wrestle his first match as a superstar. He thought about the last time he had wrestled with expectations this high, the night he had kicked Oscar Esquivel in the face. He really wanted to get in the ring and work out the spots with Bret. Was Bret even here yet?

"Are you always this early?" said a female voice from behind him.

Joey turned and saw Jade Wilcox, who wrestled under the name Jade Sleek, descending the stairs toward him. She was wearing sinfully tight jeans that somehow fit over her black boots, and a long-sleeved white T-shirt. Her jet black hair fell over her shoulders but couldn't completely cover the enhanced breasts that were a staple of women's wrestling.

"Well, I don't know. I guess. I was hoping to get in some practice time in the ring."

Jade dropped her gym bag and sat next to Joey. "Really? Did one of those guys invite you to work out with them?" she said.

"No, I was actually going to wait for them to finish, then see if Bret wanted to go over our spots."

Joey hoped he didn't sound as intimidated as he felt. Jade had wrestled for the GWA for six years, longer than any other woman on the roster. She had been women's champion five times, and at one time was the premier women's wrestler in the world. In addition, she was a worldwide sex symbol, having appeared in *Playboy* and *Sports Illustrated*. Joey was a little surprised she was talking to him.

"So you're wrestling Bret tonight," she said. "Have you ever worked with him before?"

"No, I haven't. I've actually never even spoken to him."

Jade laughed. "Well, you'll get your chance tonight."

"What do you mean?" Joey smiled, not sure if he understood the joke.

"My guess is you won't get to work out with Bret before your match. He doesn't like to do practice sessions, and those guys aren't going to give you any ring time. You will get to talk to Bret though, during your match. He likes to call every spot, and at the house shows, he'll even give you criticism when he's got you in a rest hold. He's a total trip."

Joey felt his muscles tighten, an instinctual nervous response for him. He didn't like the thought of going into a match without any preparation at all.

"Why won't those guys give me any ring time?" Joey asked.

"Because you're new. New guys don't get ring time, especially new guys getting pushed."

There was a whiff of smugness in her voice that made Joey defensive.

"What does that mean?" he asked.

"What, that you're getting pushed?"

"No, that guys getting pushed don't get any ring time."

Joey knew full well what a push was. In the wrestling world, a push was the term used to describe the shine of the company spotlight. If a promotion wanted to make someone a star, the bookers would give him more television time, and larger parts in the stories. They would have him win matches, or at least lose matches with more flair. They would intensify and focus his gimmick, and give him a catch phrase. The sum total of this attention from the bookers was referred to as a push, and it was the most sought-after prize in professional wrestling. And there was no doubt that, following his debut in the main event of *Burn*, Joey was getting pushed.

"I know, it doesn't make any sense," said Jade. "You'd think that, since you're new, the company would get you in the ring before the shows so you could get your legs under you and be ready to run with the ball when it's yours. But that's not how it works here. Here, practice time before a show belongs to a privileged few, and they guard it like gold. Those guys down there have all been in the company for a long time, and they all have one thing in common. They've never been, and they're never going to be, number one. Those guys have worked as far up the ladder as they can get without getting to the top, and they're scared and resentful of new people who might have a chance to go further than they did. Someone like you comes in here and can be packaged and presented to the fans as a winner from day one, and before you know it, you're doing the headliners at the pay per views that could have been theirs. They'll do everything they can to hold you back, and that includes keeping you away from the ring where you can practice and improve."

Jade's voice had taken on a familiar teaching-the-rookie tone. Joey found that professional wrestlers, from all walks of life, in the biggest or the smallest promotions, loved to find a rookie and chew his ear off with their knowledge. He knew it was best to shut up and listen, and as he looked down at the guys around the ring, he wondered if what Jade was saying wasn't right on. These guys had all been in the company forever, and had never been the number one guy.

Crusader and Jumbo had both joined the GWA at a time when everyone had a silly, cartoonish gimmick. They both debuted as comic book characters, with bright costumes and larger-than-human personas. Unfortunately, wrestling changed, but the memories of those gimmicks stuck with their owners. Crusader, a Canadian wrestler named Scott Rollins, originally played a ridiculous knight of the round table character, chivalrous and morally righteous. He'd long since abandoned that character, but the name and the memory stuck with him, and despite the fact that he was skilled and had a good look, he probably would never be the top guy in the company.

Jumbo's past was even worse. He was brought in as a demented circus freak character, who was led to the ring on a leash by an animal trainer. The name Jumbo was supposed to remind people of a trained elephant, and his silver tights originally were supposed to be reminiscent of a circus performer's outfit. Like Crusader, Jumbo dumped the lame character when wrestling outgrew it, but remnants and memories of his past prevented the fans from ever taking him too seriously.

Deep Six and Lord Mayberry likewise were talented wrestlers trapped by the gimmicks that once got them over. Deep Six debuted as an odd, cowboy/ghoul creature that at one time was the most exciting performer in the company. Now he wore a black leather jacket to the ring and cut long-winded promos, but otherwise had no discernable personality. Lord Mayberry had come into the company playing a variation on the classic British snob character that was in every wrestling promotion at the time. He still played the snob, only now his accent was gone and he wanted to be taken seriously as a tough guy.

"So how does a new guy, with no sway backstage, become one of the people who can work out in the ring before the show?" said Joey.

"I don't know," said Jade.

She looked like she had more to say on this topic, but a cell phone ringing from inside her gym bag interrupted the conversation. After unzipping her bag and fumbling through it for a few seconds, she pulled out the phone and cringed when she saw the name on the digital display.

"Just a second Joey," she said as she flipped open the phone. "What is it Tony?" she said into the receiver.

Joey sat quietly as Jade had a telephone conversation with someone she obviously wasn't fond of. He silently cursed the phone for interrupting this surprising little rap session.

"Sorry, that was my lawyer," Jade said as she stuffed her cell phone back in the bag.

"Your lawyer? Is everything cool?"

"Yeah, I've just got a prick of an ex-husband who wants my money and has been trying to get it for two years."

Joey nodded silently. He knew all about this story; everyone did. Jade's divorce and its aftermath was genuine celebrity gossip, made all the more juicy because of persistent rumors of an affair between her and the current GWA champion, Goliath, while she was married to her personal trainer. Joey chose not to say anything about it; instead he looked at her as if he were ready to listen.

"Anyway, where were we Joey? Oh yeah, the guys who get to work out in the ring. It's like high school. The popular kids run the show. They have access to all the stuff everyone wants. And for a freshman like you, the best way to go somewhere would be to buddy up with the popular seniors."

"And those guys in the ring are the popular seniors?"

"You got it."

"So, you know those guys. How do I get them to, you know—"

"To like you?" Jade laughed at the silly turn the conversation was taking.

"Yeah. I guess that's it. How do I get them to like me?"

"Oh Honey, I don't think you can."

"Why not?"

"I've already told you, you're being pushed."

"I guess I don't understand why that's such a big deal."

"Of course it's a big deal. You're the freshman, remember? How do you think the seniors would react if some freshman came in and snatched up the homecoming queen?"

"Okay, yeah, I get that part. I just, well, the fans liked me on Monday night. If the fans like what I'm doing, then it's good for business. If it's good for business, then I'd think those guys would get over themselves."

Jade shook her head. "Let me tell you how it works now that you're in the big leagues," she said. "Loyalty to the company doesn't exist. These guys could care less if the GWA grows, shrinks, sinks, or swims. If things don't work out here, they'll go to Revolution. If things don't work out there, they'll go to wherever things do work out. I think the fans like to think that it's all about the promotions in these Monday Night Battles, but it's not. It's about the stars. Whoever becomes a big star will have it made. He can wrestle for whoever has the most money to give him. Over in Revolution, Lucifer has become such a huge star that he'll be the World Champion in whatever promotion he wants to wrestle with for the next twenty years.

"And when he gets tired of wrestling, he can go become an actor, or retire on all the money he made from television commercials. That's what those guys down there want. That's what everyone in the business wants. There's big fame at stake in wrestling nowadays, and even the most passionate wrestlers are seduced by it.

"Think about it, kid. Why are you a wrestler?"

Joey had answered this question a thousand times to himself, his friends, and his mother.

"I just love it," he said. "I've always loved it. I couldn't do anything else."

"Great. That's great," said Jade. "And I totally believe you. Now think about what it was like on Monday night, when the whole crowd took to you like you were going to lead them to the promised land. They started chanting your name. How did that feel?"

"It felt great. It was the most exciting moment of my life."

"Exactly. Now that you've tasted that, it's going to be tough for you to go back. Sure, if you have to, you'll wrestle for peanuts again, and do it for the love of the sport. But, given the choice, how can you not want that moment of fame, that moment when everyone in your world adores you?"

"I don't understand what you're getting at," said Joey. "Of course I'd choose the big crowds and the adoration, given the choice. I still love wrestling. It doesn't mean I'd want to leave it to become a movie star or something."

"No, but maybe you'll find yourself doing things, making compromises, things you wouldn't be doing if you were in this for your love of wrestling more than your want for fame."

Joey was about to ask her what she was talking about, but before he spoke, he realized what she was saying. Images of Jade wrestling other women in a pit of muck wearing only a bikini popped into his head. He remembered a skit she did last year where the audience was led to believe that Duke peed on her after she lost the Women's Title. He didn't know if he wanted to talk about this anymore.

"I'm sorry Joey," she said. "I didn't mean to bring you down with all this. I just got on my soap box, and…the thing is Joey, I can tell you've got a big future ahead of you if you play your cards right, but I'm worried for you, being thrown right into the spotlight in your first match. And I just hate the way things work around here. I guess all I'm saying is you need to watch your back. There's nothing you can do to avoid the politics. Just don't get hurt or frustrated if the old guys give you the cold shoulder for awhile."

"I won't," said Joey, but he wondered. This conversation had made him aware of how little he really knew about this business, of how green he really was.

"What about you?" Joey asked. "Where do you stand in all this? Do you care about the politics?"

"I don't know anymore. I used to, but, well, I don't know." Jade reached down and started fiddling with the straps of her gym bag. A few seconds of silence made it clear that Jade apparently had no interest in talking further about herself.

"Do you have someone to travel with this week?" Joey asked, surprised at his own boldness.

Jade continued to look down at her gym bag. "Safire and I are driving the circuit this week, and don't even ask, because the answer is no. You and I can't travel together." Her voice was sullen as she delivered the rejection, almost as if it hurt her more than him.

"Okay," said Joey. What was he thinking? An American sex icon takes a few minutes of her time to talk to him and he spoils it.

"Here's your last tip, Joey. Don't try to be friends with any of the women around here, because to the guys backstage, and all the geeks on the Internet, you and a woman can't be friends, you can only be an item. Trust me, I know. I…"

She was distracted by something on the arena floor.

"Shit. Look who's here," she said, almost to herself. "I'm gonna go get something to eat. It was nice talking to you Joey."

Jade was looking across the arena at two men in matching gray Armani suits who had stepped onto the floor from the service area. One was a giant of a man, with long blonde hair and muscles that bulged through his suit. Next to him, looking like a midget by comparison, was a bald man with a round torso. They both were wearing sunglasses. The two men, Patrick French, better known as Goliath, and Michael "Duke" Correlli, had spotted Joey and Jade.

"Joey, come down here," yelled out Goliath. "We need to talk to you."

"Nice to see you too, Champ," Jade said under her breath. "Well Joey, good luck."

"Aren't you coming down?" asked Joey.

"Of course not. He only invited you, kid. Go on. They'll keep on pretending like they never saw me."

"Why don't you just come—"

"Shut up and get your ass down there."

"Okay, okay. Listen, thanks for the advice. I'll see you around?"

"Go on already," said Jade, waving him off like he was a fly.

"Well, can we eat dinner together sometime or something?" *What the hell am I doing?* he thought.

"I…whatever…sure…just get down there. Goodbye."

Joey waved awkwardly at her before turning to head down the stairs. He felt giddy. He'd just asked Jade Sleek out on a date, and she had said yes, well, maybe.

"Glad to see you here early, Joey," said Goliath, extending his hand in greeting as Joey reached the bottom of the stairs.

Joey could think of nothing to say as he shook Goliath's hand. The two had never formally met, but Goliath was acting like they were old friends.

"It's nice to spend some time in the arena before the fans arrive," Goliath said. "It always helps me feel at home."

"Yeah, it's really nice," said Joey. Why had Goliath not even acknowledged Jade? Goliath and Jade had a rocky past together, and Joey was overcome with the feeling that he was somehow now in the middle of it. He was reminded of the time his mother caught him watching porn. She knew she had seen it, he knew that she'd seen it, but they both acted like it never happened. Goliath was treating Jade the same way Joey's mother treated porn.

"Joey Boy, you're just the man we need to see," said Duke Corelli. Duke smiled and extended his hand. The arena lights glimmered off his gold-capped teeth. Duke had lost his two front teeth three years ago when a disgruntled former wrestler named Bishop Brock punched him in the mouth after a show. It was well known in the wrestling world that simple dental surgery could have put Duke's teeth right back in his mouth, good as new, but Duke instead chose to get two gold-capped implants. The implants made him look like a deranged mafia boss every time he smiled, adding a new quirk to the greedy, self-serving boss character he played on his own TV show.

"We need to talk to you about the next few shows, so come with us if you've got a minute. Have you got a minute?" said Duke.

"Yes sir," said Joey.

"Great, I use an office on the concourse," said Duke. "Let's go."

As Joey followed Duke and Goliath up the stairs, he realized that the guys working out in the ring, "the seniors," were watching him, "the freshman," head off to a private meeting with the World Champion and the boss.

*   *   *   *

"Joey, they loved you," Duke said from behind the oak desk. Duke, Goliath, and Joey had made their way to a business office on the arena concourse. Goliath had closed the door behind them. Duke was sitting in the leather chair as if he came to this office every day. Joey sat directly opposite Duke, with Goliath crowding him on his right. There was one overhead fluorescent lamp and no windows. The gray lighting made the room look like a home movie.

"Believe me, Joey," said Goliath, "the reaction you got on Monday night was something special. Most people in this business will never hear something like that. I hope you allowed yourself to enjoy it."

"I did. It was a great night for me," said Joey. He believed every word of what Jade had said to him, and knew that whatever this meeting was for, it might be better for his standing backstage if it wasn't happening. Still, he enjoyed the praise.

"We're going to jump on this right away," said Duke, who was breathing heavily from the walk up the stairs and around the concourse. "These opportunities only come once in a great while, Joey. You're the hottest thing on the show already. Goliath and I think you're ready to take the next step."

"Thank you, I really appreciate that," said Joey. He wished Jumbo were in here to listen to this praise, to hear that Joey's wink wasn't a big deal to the boss.

"You'll have your scheduled matches with Bret through the house shows, but come Monday night, we're going to put you in a new program," said Duke.

"We're in the process of re-scripting Monday night, specifically because of you," said Goliath.

"Here's what's planned," said Duke. He cleared his throat, making a disgusting, turkey-baster sound. "Tomorrow morning we announce on the web that the next episode of *Burn* will have a tournament to determine the number 1 contender for the GWA World Title. Then, every hour between noon and eight on Saturday, we announce on the web site one of the wrestlers who will be competing in the tournament."

"It's going to be Crusader, Jumbo, Lord Mayberry, Gordy Goodnow, Jack Branson, Deep Six, Zombie, and you," said Goliath.

"You'll be announced last," said Duke. "Then, on Sunday at noon, we'll post the tournament brackets on the web. Your first match will be against Lord Mayberry. He'll cheat, the ref won't see, the deck will be stacked against you, you know the routine, but you'll be going over. You, Crusader, Jumbo, and Branson will all advance to the second round. You can imagine that you'll be seen as the underdog among those four."

"Sure," said Joey. They were going so fast he didn't completely understand, but figured he'd catch up as they went along.

"The underdog is the most natural babyface in wrestling," said Goliath. "You'll be the underdog in every match. Every match will be scripted for you to go over against impossible odds. By the time you make it to the finals, the crowd is going to be nuts for you. It will be the ultimate Cinderella story."

"And in the finals," interrupted Duke, "you'll meet Jumbo in a rematch of last week's classic. The script will be the same, only this time you're going to take even more of a beating. It's going to be insane when you pull out the stops and win the match. And, of course, that will be what sets you up to go against Goliath in the main event the next week. How do you like it so far?"

"It sounds great," said Joey, overwhelmed. A program for the World Title? Was this for real? "Who all knows about this storyline?" he asked.

"No one yet," said Duke. "Goliath and I just finished concocting it on the drive over here. I'm going to tell the other guys in the tournament about the whole plan as soon as they get here. The rest of the roster will hear about it when it goes on the web."

"We thought it would be better if only the participants in the tournament knew," said Goliath. "We're going to be really careful about leaks. We don't want any of the Internet fans getting word that you're going over in the tournament."

"I have to admit," began Joey, "I'm a little nervous about the reaction this will get in the locker room. I'm getting a major push here, and—"

"I can understand your concern, Joey," said Goliath. "Believe you me, there's been a lot of politicking in this locker room in the past. But I've gotta tell you, when the ratings come in and we wallop *Revolution Riot*, the guys are gonna love you like a brother."

"You think so?" said Joey.

"Oh yeah," said Duke. "This is a big month. We need ratings to pay the bills. The other performers aren't going to care that you're getting pushed if your success pays their salaries."

"Trust me on this one, Joey," said Goliath. "Guys care about the pecking order, and about paying their dues, but when it comes down to it, we all know that none of that means squat if no one's watching. Ratings have been down for months now. All of us are anxious to try anything that might work. I was hanging out with Crusader and Zombie earlier this week, and they're excited about the reaction you got on Monday. And they're not the only ones. Guys here really want us to do something that will get people to watch. Whoever gets people to watch is going to be a popular man in the locker room."

Joey relaxed into his chair. Goliath, Crusader, Zombie, and Duke—these were big, powerful names that apparently were in his corner. He was particularly surprised to hear Goliath say that Crusader was on board. "That makes me feel better," said Joey. "I was talking to someone earlier, and I thought that maybe…well—"

"Was it Jade?" said Goliath.

Joey hesitated. He didn't want to rat out his new friend and future date, especially not in front of Goliath.

"Don't worry about Jade," Goliath continued. "She's a great wrestler, and a great woman, but she's also a gossip. Wouldn't you agree Duke?"

"Oh yes. Love her to death, but don't listen to a word she says. That gal's always out to start a ruckus. It's just her personality. Some people are like that."

"Seriously Joey," said Goliath. "I wouldn't worry a bit. If the angle works, and people watch, the guys backstage will love you. If the angle doesn't work, and Revolution kicks our ass this month, the guys backstage will understand. We all know we've got to try something different than we've been doing."

"I completely understand your concern Joey," said Duke. "If this angle doesn't work, we'll gently put you back in the midcard and try something else. But I don't think that will happen. I think this will work. People are going to start talking once we get word up on the Internet."

They were speaking so fast, and every word was one of reassurance. Joey felt like he was among friends. "So what happens the next week when you and I have our title match?" Joey asked Goliath.

"I'll win," Goliath said. "But I'm going to have to cheat like hell. You just aren't going to go down easy."

"And of course that will lead to a rematch," said Duke.

"A rematch at the pay-per-view?" said Joey.

"No, not this time," said Duke.

Joey nodded his head, as if to say, 'Of course not this time, I'm just a rookie, it was a stupid question.'

"We're really going to let it all hang out on television and clean up in the May sweeps," said Duke. Joey nodded some more as Duke continued. "I have plans for an extended feud over the course of several weeks between you and Goliath. The details aren't all worked out, but you know the routine, some cliffhangers, some teasers, a bloody beatdown by the heel. It will all build to a World Title Match on the last episode in May."

Duke stopped there, as if his sentences had winded him. This time Joey was able to sit quietly and wait, even though Duke had left out an important detail. After a few seconds of silence, Goliath answered the obvious question.

"May sweeps will end with you winning the World Title, Joey." Goliath smiled as he spoke, delivering the news like a nurse speaking to a new mother.

"Are you up to it?" said Duke.

Joey was speechless. He couldn't believe this was happening. He was going to be the GWA World Champion. It had been his dream since he was a teenager.

"Yeah, I'm up to it," he said.

"Good. I'm glad we're on the same page Joey," said Duke. "This will be the beginning of great things for you."

"This will be the beginning of great things for all of us," said Goliath.

CHAPTER 5

▼

James "Lucifer" Duvall was born in Manhattan on April 4th, 1979, the only child of Linda Duvall and Martin Gorman. He was conceived while his parents were both undergraduates at Columbia University, where they were active in what remained of the New Left on the campuses of the northeast.

Knowing that Martin would think a child an obstacle to his long-term plans, Linda kept her pregnancy a secret until it was too late to terminate it. At the beginning of her third trimester, Linda came home from class to find Martin naked in bed with a freshman English major. Martin, apparently consumed with guilt, was insistent that he should leave. By the time James was born, Martin was living in San Francisco. James was never to meet him.

James's early youth did not include time spent with playmates and toys. Instead, Linda carted him around as she continued the rebellion of her university days. James attended his first political protest meeting in his mother's arms when he was six months old. By the time he was two, he was riding the train from Baltimore to DC with his mother every morning so she could participate in whatever hippie regalia was taking place on the mall that afternoon. When he was four, he sat in the hallway outside the Chancellor's office at Winston College for seven hours (along with his mother and sixty other people), in a successful attempt to shut down the school until a particular European history professor was fired.

The year of James's fifth birthday, his absent father was named editor-in-chief of the radical magazine, *Proletariat Activist*, where he wrote a highly praised piece about the continuing oppression of women. Linda wrote a letter to the magazine calling Martin a deadbeat dad. The letter was never published, but Martin began sending a monthly check. Linda quit her waitressing job and became a full-time volunteer activist.

With guaranteed money and a stern hatred for all men, Linda renewed her radical spirit and took up the cause of oppressed women everywhere. She paid increasingly less attention to her son, who, in her mind, had driven Martin away, and was predestined to become an oppressive monster by nature of his penis.

His father gone, his mother inattentive, James grew up on his own.

At school he was a whipping post for the kids with social skills and confidence, becoming a regular in the nurse's office with black eyes and bloody noses. At home he was a nuisance to his mother and her friends. So he withdrew from interest in the real world, and instead spent his time in daydreams of superheroes and adventure. Early one Saturday morning, while his mother was asleep, James discovered the professional wrestling programs that aired on network television. After watching two hour-long wrestling programs back to back, James ran into his mother's bedroom and awakened her to excitedly relay all that he saw. He told her about the matches, the characters, the managers, and the spectacle, with an excitement he had never displayed before. Linda had never seen wrestling, but knew that it was violent, disrespectful of women, and insensitive about racism, and in a rare moment of parenting, she declared that James was never to watch it again. On the next Saturday, when she caught James watching wrestling in secret, she moved their only television into her bedroom. Wrestling was never spoken of in the Duvall household again.

When James began ninth grade at Ulysses S. Grant High School in the fall of 1991, he was five feet four inches tall and weighed 120 pounds. Two years later, when he finished the tenth grade, he was an even six feet and weighed a solid one-eighty. The schoolyard beatings promptly came to an end.

The next year James grew another three inches, placing him in league with the tallest students at school. He accepted an invitation from Mr. Garrison, the varsity basketball coach, to try out for the team, and found, to everyone's surprise, that he was a decent athlete. His academics improved, and he found his own niche of friends. He took to exercising, and convinced Mr. Garrison to let him have a key to the school weight room, where he worked out every morning for at least an hour before school started.

On his graduation day, James drove his mother's Saab to Hastings Arena, where the ceremony was held (she didn't attend, calling graduations "pompous celebrations of the ruling class"). When James left the arena that afternoon, he didn't drive home. Instead he got onto I-70 West and drove for ten hours. At one in the morning, he pulled into a rest stop off the freeway just inside the Kentucky border and slept in the car until dawn. Then he drove into Lousiville, parking the Saab in front of Pruitt's Wrestling School, an unmarked red brick building in a seedy neighborhood outside of downtown. He went inside and paid $900 cash, money he had saved for three years, to Jack Pruitt, buying himself 10 months as a student in one of the South's premier schools of professional wrestling.

Two days later his mother tracked him down with the help of a private investigator. She took her Saab back to Baltimore, and James never spoke to her again.

For the next year, James waited tables from morning until mid-afternoon, attended wrestling school in the evening, and worked out in the gym at night. He lived in an empty studio apartment within walking distance of his job, his school, and his gym. He didn't own a car or a telephone, but he did own a television and a VCR, which were exclusively used for study. He watched *GWA Burn* and *Revolution Riot* every week. He borrowed tapes from Jack Pruitt's library and caught up on all the wrestling he had missed in his youth. He studied the greatest matches, sometimes staying up all night or calling in sick to work so he could watch the masters of the sport for hours at a time. He never socialized with anyone, lest he lose even one more minute of life that could have been spent with his passion.

By the end of the year, he was Jack Pruitt's prize student, and had been invited to join the Southeast Wrestling League, the largest independent wrestling promotion in the country. Two days before his first match in the SWL, he bought a used Toyota Camry, which would become his home for the next two years.

His first gimmick in the SWL was a mysterious gothic man named Scorpion Mace. He wrestled five nights a week, every night in a different city. He owned one suitcase, one gym bag, two pairs of shoes, one pair of wrestling boots, and a clear plastic jug that was always filled with water.

On most days, breakfast was a piece of fruit, and lunch and dinner were peanut butter sandwiches, made with ingredients purchased at whatever gas station could provide them. Showers happened in high school gym locker rooms, YMCAs, and one time at a homeless shelter. When he traveled through the Carolinas, where the shows were usually well-attended and the pay was better, he shared motel rooms with other wrestlers. Otherwise, he parked his car at rest stops and public parks and slept in the back seat.

Wrestling venues in the Southeast Wrestling League were as nice as the brand new 2000-seat arena at the fairgrounds in Greensboro, and as dreary as the abandoned airplane hangar in Jackson. Pay for a night's work in the SWL varied from nothing to six hundred dollars, depending on the venue. If a show was cancelled due to poor attendance, the performers weren't paid. If a show was poorly organized by a fly-by-night regional promoter, the performers weren't paid. Grocery store shoplifting and gasoline pump driveaways were common practice among SWL performers.

After a particularly long stretch without pay in December of that first year, James asked a college kid who attended all the Kentucky shows if he was interested in buying the black T-shirt James wore in the ring. The kid paid twenty dollars for it, money James used for gas to get to Charlotte. In Charlotte, the promoter told James that he could not wrestle shirtless, that the black T-shirt was part of Scorpion Mace's gimmick. James asked around backstage if anyone had a black T-shirt he could borrow, and received an old heavy metal T-shirt from the trunk of Frankie Dice's car. The shirt was faded black, plain except for one word in red lettering on the back: Lucifer. That night James wore the shirt while he wrestled a popular babyface named Gunner Brown.

The next night in Raleigh, James wore the shirt again. A group of teenage boys who had traveled from the previous show in Charlotte held up a poster with the word "Lucifer" on it. A large section of the audience chose to cheer for James's character.

Before the next show, James purchased a bottle of black hair dye at a drug store off the Interstate. He paid $4.00 for it. In a grungy bathroom at a gas station in rural South Carolina, James dyed his hair black. That night in Charleston, James asked the promoter if he could be introduced as "Lucifer Scorpion Mace." During his match, the black hair dye began to bleed. The match turned into a gooey mess, with black muck all over James, his opponent, and the ring. The promoter was furious and James was only paid half. As James headed for the shower, he saw himself in the mirror with his shirt off. Black streaks of hair coloring swirled down his neck and shoulders. James imagined he had thick veins filled with black blood. He left the building without showering and found a tattoo parlor down the street. He paid all the money he had, forty-three dollars, to have the black streaks of hair coloring turned into permanent tattoos.

The next show was in Jacksonville in a high school performing arts center. Three scheduled performers no-showed this small venue. To fill time, the promoter asked James to cut a promo before his match with top babyface Clubber Brody. Having never done a promo before, James nervously agreed. As he walked to the ring, he tried to think of what he might say, but came up with nothing. When he took the microphone in the center of the ring, he just opened his mouth and said whatever came out. "Do you people want to see a beating tonight?" A small chorus of cheers came from the seats. "Is that all you've got, people? Don't tell me you came out here and paid your hard-earned money to watch a bunch of no-names pussyfoot around. You people want to see a beating. And I'm going to give it to you. Now, do you want to see a beating or not?" A few more cheers came from the crowd. "Do you want to see violence?" More cheers. "Do you want to see blood?" The crowd grew louder. "Who wants me to hit Clubber Brody over the head with a steel chair?" Now the crowd was getting excited. James dropped the microphone, jumped out of the ring, grabbed a steel chair, and hopped back in. "If you want to see me smash this steel chair into Clubber Brody's skull, let me hear you!" The crowd screamed in approval.

When Clubber Brody's music played and he stepped out, he was booed by the audience. The audience cheered wildly when James clocked Clubber Brody over the head with a steel chair, and booed when Brody eventually won the match as planned. As soon as they got backstage, Clubber Brody punched James in the mouth.

"That's for stealing my heat," Brody said.

"There's nothing I hate more than a wrestler who won't play the part. You were supposed to be the heel out there," the promoter said. "Don't expect to work for me again."

James didn't get paid that night. But his spontaneous babyface promo earned him far more than the $100 the promoter withheld. The show that night was broadcast on Jacksonville community access cable. A man named Stanley Mushnik was watching. He was impressed with the way James worked the crowd, so much so that he called his old friend, Gene Harold. After the next SWL show in Orlando, James met up with Gene Harold and Larry Jenkins backstage, and signed a one-year developmental contract with Revolution Wrestling.

Two months later, on October 26th, James made his national debut in Grand Rapids, Michigan for Revolution's *All Hallows Eve* Pay Per View. He was a well-hyped "Mystery Opponent" for a mid-carder named Adrian Smoke. His ring entrance was a frightening combination of shadows and fire, set to crass heavy metal guitar music. The ring announcer introduced him only as "Tonight's Mystery Opponent" and the television announcers made a big deal of his anonymity. In a four-minute squash, the nameless wrestler defeated Adrian Smoke. The crowd was confused. The announcers were aghast.

For the next three weeks James plowed through the undercard on *Revolution Riot* as an anonymous wrestler. His matches were booked more like a circus act than a sporting event, as James was encouraged to show off his cruiserweight-style repertoire and handle his opponents like crash test dummies. By mid-November, James was more over than any wrestler in the company. On the November 24th edition of *Riot*, James gave his first interview on Revolution television, and told the world his wrestling name, Lucifer.

Lucifer became an instant ratings sensation. At the *Last Man Standing* pay per view in November, he defeated veteran wrestler Miller Wilson and delivered Revolution's highest buy-rate ever. On the next *Riot*, he defeated Revolution mainstay Edgar Hoover in a critically acclaimed 23-minute epic. The match was a mature showing of ring psychology, high spots, and mat wrestling, and featured the debut of what would become Lucifer's trademark finisher, a variation on the Scorpion Deathlock submission hold. He called it The Devil's Trident. The Internet wrestling community pronounced Lucifer as their new hero. *Riot*'s overnight television ratings went up a full point from the previous week.

January began Lucifer's first ever extended feud in Revolution, when mat technician Tony Campbell laid him out backstage with a sledgehammer. A match between Lucifer and Campbell was announced for the *Massacre* PPV, and for the next three weeks, the two men put on an old-school style feud, highlighted by Lucifer's first in-ring promo on the January 13th edition of *Riot*. Lucifer repeated "I'm coming for you Campbell," as a mantra throughout the promo. It played more like an historic speech than a wrestling interview, and the Internet began comparing Lucifer to the greatest performers in the history of wrestling.

At *Massacre*, Lucifer and Campbell wrestled for sixteen minutes before Campbell landed in the Devil's Trident and tapped out. It was the first time in Tony Campbell's career that he had submitted.

Heading into February, Lucifer was Revolution's biggest star, getting monster pops and selling hordes of merchandise. He appeared as a guest on *SportsTalk*, and spoke quietly and eloquently with legitimate sports journalists about the line between sports and entertainment. His interview was well-received by the mainstream press, and the television ratings on *Revolution Riot* reached new heights.

In February, Lucifer was booked in his first main-event-level feud with Butterfly Johnny Grace, a wrestler who might have been pushed to the very top had Lucifer not taken off like a missile. Lucifer and Grace stole the show at the *Aggression* PPV and had a rematch on the February 24th edition of *Riot*. Lucifer went over clean both times, solidifying him with the fans as a championship-level contender.

Rolling into March, ratings for *Riot* were closing in on *Burn*, and the Internet proclaimed Revolution Wrestling as the future of the industry. Max Zeffer announced on Revolution.com that March and April would be spent determining a ranking list for the number one contender for the Revolution World Title. A complicated round robin tournament was set up to take place over the next 6 broadcasts of *Riot*. Lucifer was given the chance to go from bottom to top on the entire roster again, and did so impressively, leading up to a critically acclaimed Number 1 Contender's match between Lucifer and Jerry Senika on *Riot* in Worcester, Massachusetts. Three days later he made a nationally televised appearance on *The Late Show With Reggie Foster*. Lucifer's appearance gave the talk show its highest ratings ever. He went to bed that night aware that he was on the verge of becoming an international superstar.

The morning after his talk show appearance, James awoke on the sixteenth floor of the Hyatte in North Brooklyn, feeling rested for the first time in many months. His schedule for the upcoming week would allow him to skip all the Revolution house shows over the weekend to do publicity in New York for the Monday episode of *Riot*, live from Madison Square Garden. It would be his first weekend off from wrestling in three years.

James rolled out of bed and walked to the window. Looking east, he could see Madison Square Garden, where on Monday Night he would wrestle Red Jackson for the Revolution World Title.

He thought of his childhood, and his mother. When he left her house three years ago, he had nine hundred dollars and a borrowed vehicle. In two days he was scheduled to win the World Title and solidify his place as the premier wrestler in the world. He wondered where he could go from here.

CHAPTER 6

▼

On Friday night, just a few hours after learning he would be the next GWA Champion, Joey defeated Bret Stevens in Lubbock. The crowd treated him like a war hero, exploding in noise, camera flashes and homemade posters when he entered. During the match, they cheered whenever he was on offense and they booed whenever Bret had the upper hand.

On Saturday morning, GWA.com announced there would be a tournament for the World Title on Monday night's *Burn*, with the participants to be announced the next day. As the wrestlers gathered in Amarillo for the Saturday-night show, there was a growing buzz regarding the recent announcement on the web site. No one knew who was going to be in the tournament, or who would win. Company leadership was strangely silent regarding the announcement. Joey avoided anyone who might ask him if he knew about the tournament. That night, after wrestling Bret again, in front of another hysterical crowd, Joey rushed to his hotel.

On Sunday, as promised, GWA.com gradually posted the names of those who would be competing in the tournament. At noon, the web site announced Crusader as the first participant. At one, Jumbo. At two, Jack Branson. At three, Deep Six. At four, Zombie. By four-thirty, wrestlers were arriving at the Fort Worth Convention Center for the Sunday night house show. They had been traveling all day, and were unaware of whose names were posted on the web. Joey and Bret put on the same show, to the same response. After the match, Goliath slapped Joey on the back and said, "You're our hottest commodity right now."

By the end of the Sunday-night show, after word had gone around about whose names were posted on the web, the tournament was all anyone could talk about backstage. As the wrestlers learned that Duke wasn't giving away any of the booking, curious speculation turned to giddiness, and then anxiety. Who would win? Why were they putting a tournament on free TV with such little notice? Why wasn't Duke telling them who was going over?

As far as Joey could tell, most people assumed the finals would be between Crusader and Branson. He didn't know about the whisper campaign that had started in the locker room. He didn't hear the jealousy, the vitriol, the angst in the voices of Jumbo and Deep Six, who told their admirers that Joey had disappeared with the boss and the champion for a private meeting before the Lubbock show.

"Hey Joey, do you have a second?"

Joey was on his way to the showers after his third match with Bret in three days, lost in his own world of fan adoration and television tournaments. The gravelly voice that had disturbed him belonged to Shane Walker, GWA road agent, former World Champion, and Joey's trainer from the farm league. Shane was sitting by himself in a folding chair against the wall, leaning on his cane and not about to get up. Joey went to him.

"You're getting quite the response these days," said Shane.

"I know, it's unbelievable," said Joey.

Joey had grown up watching Shane on *Pro Wrestling All-Stars*. At that time, Shane had long, flowing blonde hair and an outrageous physique that no longer was possible in pro wrestling following the crackdown on anabolic steroids. Today, Shane was bald and slim, with skin that could have been removed from a hot dog. He leaned on a cane, even while sitting, and his body shook, as if he were riding a bus.

"How do you feel about the reaction you're getting?" Shane asked.

"I love it," said Joey.

"Do you think you deserve an ovation like that?" asked Shane.

Joey's instincts told him to end this conversation immediately and leave. The last thing he needed was for his idol and teacher to tell him he was stealing the spotlight from more deserving players.

"I don't know if I deserve it, but I don't have any control over that," said Joey.

"You're right," said Shane. "You can't control the fans."

Joey nodded his head, knowing there was more listening to do. He had spent many an afternoon listening to Shane's patient speeches.

"You know, Joey, my first TV match was on *Pro Wrestling All-Stars*. I was twenty-two. I had been wrestling for Clyde Gallagher's promotion in the Midwest for three years and got noticed by Larry Jenkins. Larry was barely a teenager back then. He invited me to come on *All-Stars* and be a jobber for a fellow named Igor who wrestled by the name Polar Bear. Igor was a hairy monster who couldn't wrestle worth a shit, but was tough as nails. Back then, if you were a jobber you were expected to take a beating. A real beating. I let that Igor fellow beat the shit out of me for six minutes, and it hurt. The guy was stiff as a board on me. I finished that match with a broken finger and a black eye. Two weeks later I got invited back to *All-Stars* to be a jobber for Wrangler Billy Black. Broke my nose in that one.

"For my first two years on TV, every time I stepped in the ring, I had to do the job to some established star who beat the crap out of me. Someone had done it to them, now they were doing it to me. It was tradition. It was a way of making sure that the young crop coming up didn't make it to the top unless they really wanted it.

"And you know Joey, even though it was painful and frustrating to let those guys pound me like that, I'm thankful they did it. I'm thankful because it gave me an opportunity to pay my dues. It was a chance for me to earn respect from the veterans, one beating at a time. It's a shame that tradition's fallen out of favor. Wrestling's changed. It used to be that it took the fans awhile to warm up to somebody new. They wanted to see familiar faces win the matches. They wanted courageous, good-hearted heroes to defeat the bad guys. Now it's harder. Now it seems like they want something different every week. Duke's got to give these fans what they want to see or else none of us get to perform. Right now the fans want to see you. Next month they might want to see someone else. Who knows?"

Joey stood silently, unsure of how to react. Was this advice?

"If you ask me," Shane continued, "I think you should just enjoy it while it lasts, and quit worrying about what the other guys think. They might get angry if the crowd takes to you and not to them, but when push comes to shove, they'll do whatever Duke tells them to do. In the end it will all wash out. Your fifteen minutes of fame will be over and some new kid will take your place."

Joey was saved by a deep, rhythmic beating sound that trembled through the concrete floor under his feet and distracted Shane from his spiel. It was Zombie's music playing out in the arena.

"Zombie wasn't supposed to go over tonight, was he?" Joey said.

Shane's eyebrows tightened into a puzzled look. "Not that I know of." They both turned toward the arena entrance.

While Joey and Shane had been talking, Jack Branson and Zombie had been wrestling. They had performed together two times in two cities leading up to tonight's show, with plans to get a feud between them on television soon. Branson went over every time, and was surely supposed to go over tonight. It would be an odd booking decision to let Branson, one of the company's biggest stars, lose to Zombie, even at a non-televised event. But the music out there was not Branson's blues guitar theme. It was Zombie's tune, an unmistakable heavy metal riff with a thick percussive beat.

Zombie came through the black curtain, breathing heavily and shaking his head. He made a left turn to head toward the locker room. Outside, in the arena, the fans began applauding, a rare form of recognition in professional wrestling. Amidst the applause were scattered "Bran-son" cheers.

"Did you guys hear what happened?" said Jade. She was approaching from down the hall, dressed in the black rubber outfit that served as her wrestling attire.

"No, what's going on out there?" said Joey.

"Branson's hurt," said Jade. "Something happened when he went for a clothesline."

Joey wondered if he'd heard correctly. Although it was common to get injured when on the receiving end of a clothesline, it was definitely not common to get injured when delivering one.

"I think he planted his foot wrong," said Jade. "Looked like his left knee buckled under him. He totally missed the move and fell to the ground, holding his knee. They had to improvise the finish. When Zombie figured out what was going on, he grabbed Branson's neck in a choke and held it until he could be disqualified. The crowd was pissed. For some reason, Tony fired up Zombie's music and that was the end. It was a total mess."

The three of them watched the curtain, listening to the crowd cheer. Branson's familiar blues theme came over the stadium speakers. A few seconds later Branson hobbled through the curtain with the help of Victor Pardo from security. As soon as he stepped through, a team of sports trainers and paramedics swarmed and lifted Branson onto a rolling gurney. Branson's face was contorted in an expression of pain that looked very real. The trainers grabbed at his kneecap, asked him where it hurt, tested his movement, and yelled at the other wrestlers to get out of the way. A crowd of wrestlers and entourage followed the medics as they rolled Branson through the locker room area and out to a loading dock, where he was lifted into an ambulance.

"Do we know if he's going to be okay?" Joey asked Jade.

"I have no idea," she said. "I'll go talk to Zombie and see what he knows."

Joey watched the ambulance leave the parking lot and disappear into the dark of an unfamiliar city. He thought about the main event-level spot that would be left open in Branson's absence. Maybe the locker room would be more accepting of a new star now that an old one was out.

Then he cringed at his own opportunism. Branson had worked tirelessly for years to achieve his dream, and tonight a freak injury might have taken the dream away for good. It was no time for Joey to be thinking of personal gain.

What a crazy business. One misstep in a non-televised match in a forgettable town and a career could end.

With the ambulance gone, the crowd of onlookers dispersed into ten different conversations. Joey, thankfully, was part of none of them. He seized the moment to escape to the showers, alone.

When he finished cleaning up and returned to the backstage area, he found it mostly empty. Everyone who was available to leave had gone to the hospital to visit Branson. Everyone except Jade.

"There you are," she said when he stepped into the main atrium of the backstage space. "I've been looking for you."

Jade Sleek was waiting backstage for him? His ego swelled.

"Shane and I are going for a bite," said Jade. "You wanna come?"

Joey's balloon popped. Why did Shane have to come?

"Yeah, I'd love to go," he said, and, though he really wanted to go with Jade alone, he wasn't lying. This was the first time he'd been invited to do anything with people from the company.

Five minutes later, they were in Jade's rental car, driving the streets of Fort Worth. Joey sat in the back seat. In the passenger seat was his childhood idol. In the driver's seat was an international sex symbol. Two days ago he was told he'd win the GWA World Title. It was as if Luck herself was giving Joey a push.

CHAPTER 7

▼

They landed at the Cattleman's Steakhouse, a kitschy restaurant in the historical district. The place was nearly empty when they were seated.

Shane ordered "The Heffer", a 64-ounce cut of sirloin that was free if he finished it in an hour. When the waitress brought it, she also dropped off a digital clock that counted down from sixty minutes. It took Shane only ten minutes to plow through the first half of the steak, but with a good 30 ounces left to go, he started to look tired. Jade ate two helpings from the salad bar. Joey had a chicken breast.

Shane's endless stories from wrestling's past took up the first part of the evening. Joey and Jade patiently listened as Shane went from one year to another between bites of steak.

And then Jade took the conversation exactly where Joey didn't want it to go.

"So Joey, what can you tell us about the tournament tomorrow night?"

Joey nodded as he swallowed a bite of baked potato.

"I don't know what I'm allowed to tell you," he said. "This whole thing's so weird. Duke wants me to keep it secret from everyone who absolutely doesn't need to know. I don't know how I feel about that."

"It's not that unusual," said Shane. "Used to be the case that no one but the two in the ring knew who was going over and who was doing the job, and even they didn't know sometimes until they got going and played the crowd a bit. I wouldn't be surprised if we got back to that sort of thing, what with the Internet kids always lurking about and spreading gossip."

"It's put me in a tough spot," said Joey. "The fact that I'm in the loop when so many veterans aren't, it can't be sitting well with some of the guys in the locker room."

"Well I know one veteran wrestler who is safe to tell," said Jade.

"Who?" said Joey.

Jade's face creased into exaggerated disappointment. "Me, of course," she said.

"Oh, sorry." Joey shook his head and tried to laugh off his mistake. Jade wasn't laughing with him, although he couldn't tell if the anger on her face was real or playful. He knew a full confession would more than cover for his goof.

"How you comin' on the Heffer big fella?" said a waitress as she cleared a nearby table.

"Still working," said Shane. He smiled at her and cut off another piece of meat.

"You're not going to try to finish that are you?" said Jade.

"Why not?" said Shane. "I'm not performing anymore. If I finish, I get my picture on the wall over there." Shane pointed with his fork to the opposite wall, labeled "Hall of Fame." The wall was covered with framed 3 x 5 pictures of cowboys who had apparently finished The Heffer. They all had a smug "Now-I'm-gonna-puke" look on their faces.

"It'll clog your arteries Old Man. A heart attack will hurt more than a few knife-edge chops," said Jade.

"Listen to Ms. Salad over here," Shane said to Joey. "She wouldn't even order a baked potato. I'm sorry to say Jade, that unlike you, I don't have to keep up a million dollar figure, and couldn't even if I tried. You keep eating your carrots and celery, I'll keep eating my cow."

Jade rolled her eyes then turned back to Joey.

"So let's have it. Who's going over?" she said.

Joey tilted his head back to drink the last of his water. When he put his glass down he noticed that he had Shane's undivided attention for the first time since "The Heffer" had been put on the table.

"I'm going over," said Joey.

There was a brief pause. Jade's expression was guarded, as if she didn't know if he was teasing or not. Joey took a breath and went on.

"I'm going over Lord Mayberry clean, then I'm going over Crusader clean, then I'm going over Jumbo clean."

"You're serious, aren't you?" said Jade.

Joey nodded. The table was quiet again.

"So Branson and Crusader…" said Jade, more as a question than a statement.

"Branson and Crusader were both going to do the job early. I have no idea who's going to replace Branson, but whoever it is, well, it's my hope that with Branson out it won't be so shocking when I win the tournament," said Joey.

"So what happens next week, do you know?" said Jade.

Her unspoken question was, 'You're not winning the title are you?' Joey was worried that Jade felt threatened by all this, which was the last thing he wanted.

"Next week I lose to Goliath, but, in Goliath's words, he'll have to cheat like hell to beat me. That will begin a three-week feud between us that will end on May 24th with me winning the World Title."

Another second of silence at the table. Joey wondered if he was saying too much. After all, no one knew. What if he was mistaken? What if plans had changed? With Branson out, plans would have to change, at least a little.

"Well congratulations to you," said Shane. That's fantastic. You're headed for super-stardom much faster than you ever thought, I bet."

"Oh yeah. I never pictured myself as a 22-year-old GWA champion," said Joey.

"Are you worried?" said Shane.

"Yes. I'm worried about how everyone backstage is going to react. I wish Duke would lay out next month's booking for everyone like he did for me."

"Don't worry Joey. Everyone will know everything soon enough," said Jade.

"You all aren't going to tell anyone, are you?" said Joey.

"Relax, kid. We won't let anyone know you leaked Duke's secret plans," said Jade. "Will we Old Man?"

"I make it a point not to engage in any backstage gossip," said Shane with a confident smile. "That being said, Joey, we've got to know, where and when did Duke tell you all this, and who else was there?" Shane chuckled at his own nosiness.

"I know the answer to that," said Jade. "It was in Lubbock, when Duke and Goliath met up with Joey before the show. They called him down from the stands where he was having a nice conversation with a sophisticated, older woman. A woman, I might add, who Duke and Goliath conveniently ignored."

"Ah, so Goliath was there also," said Shane. "That's a good sign, Joey."

"Why's that a good sign?" Joey asked.

"Because these days Goliath is in on all the decisions regarding the upper card," said Shane. "When you told me what was planned, it sounded like something was amiss, because it didn't sound like something Goliath would agree to. After all, he's going to give you quite the rub if the next month plays out like you say it will. It just isn't like him to put over the hot new star, and I can tell you, no matter how bad Duke wants you to go over, if Goliath isn't in on it, it ain't happening."

"That's the most surprising thing about all of this," said Jade. "You're the first person Goliath will put over in a big way since he got here."

"Well, they both were eager to tell me about the plan," said Joey, thinking back to the meeting. Goliath didn't seem at all hesitant to proceed.

"That's good," said Shane. "There's something about you and the way the fans connect to you that even Goliath can't deny."

"I don't know about that. This whole situation is as much a surprise to me as to anyone," said Joey.

"Well, for whatever reason," said Jade. "Your number's been called. I guess keeping your head down isn't much of an option anymore, now that we know you're being pushed to the ceiling. I see some tough times ahead for you backstage, Joey Mayhem."

"Ah, it doesn't have to be that bad," said Shane. "Listen Joey, Jade is right, some of the boys are going to be bitter about you getting the title belt, and you'll need to watch out for that. If this business is about anything, it's about politics. But there's another side to this, an upside. You're a player now. You've got Duke and Goliath's ear. The guys will recognize that, the smart ones, anyway. You have to remain a player. Now that you're in the circle, you need to make sure you don't get knocked out."

"What do you mean?" said Joey.

"I mean, don't screw this up. By next week, your star will be one of the brightest in the wrestling world, everyone will be watching you. Your promos, your look, and your wrestling need to be flawless. If they are, people will quickly forget the shortcut you were given. But if you mess up now, well, there's a whole pack of ravenous wolves on the Internet who feed on the mistakes of wrestling's biggest stars."

"Wow, that's some pressure," said Joey.

"Yes it is," said Shane. "Yes it is," he repeated, as if there was a story in his head.

Shane grabbed his glass of cola and raised it in the air. "Enough talk about backstage politics and Internet fans. I propose a toast to the next GWA World Champion, Joey Mayhem."

"Here, here," said Jade, raising her glass of water.

Joey picked up his own glass and clinked it with the others. If nothing else, these two were accepting of him as champion. That was a start.

Shane finished off his cola and looked down at a plate full of meat scraps. "I feel awful just leaving all this steak to be thrown out," he said.

"You could get a box," said Joey.

"A box. Hm. I don't remember the last time I asked for a doggie bag at a restaurant," said Shane.

"Just leave it," said Jade. "They won't mind throwing it out now that you have to pay for it."

"Maybe I could scarf down the rest of this, there's still time," said Shane, holding up the digital clock for Jade, as if his meal was a time bomb in an action movie.

"You're gonna be sick if you do," said Jade.

"I'm going to be sick either way. If I finish it, at least I won't have to pay. Plus I'll get my picture on the wall."

"We know," said Jade. "I'm going to ask for the check, and I'm going to have them charge us for that steak. It's on me."

"Oh no. You're not paying for—"

"Waitress, could we get our check?" Jade called out. "He's not gonna be able to finish the Heffer."

The waitress strolled to the table and pulled the check out of her apron.

"I knew you weren't going to finish that when you ordered it," said the waitress. "Don't sweat it. It's on the house. But," she turned to Joey, "I'm supposed to ask for your autograph."

"My autograph?" said Joey.

"Yes. The manager says you're a professional wrestler. His kid loves that shit. Autograph that check for me and the meal's free."

"Actually," said Joey, "we're all professional wrestlers."

"Really? Would my kid know all of you?"

"Just sign the autograph, Joey," said Jade. "You're the big star now. Shane and I would only lessen the value if we put our names on the same paper."

Joey shrugged, signed the check and handed it back to the waitress.

"Thank you much, you all have a good night," she said.

"Thank you," said Jade. "And thank you for dinner Joey. We should go out with this guy more often, huh Shane?" said Jade.

"You betcha. Good conversation, insider gossip, picks up the tab—you're quite the dinner companion Joey."

Joey couldn't tell if they were being sarcastic. He considered asking, but decided he'd had enough serious conversation for one night.

"You're welcome," he said, and left it at that.

CHAPTER 8

▼

"…3…2…1," from inside the press box atop Reunion Arena, GWA's technical director spoke into his headset to signal that the live feed had begun. *GWA Burn* was on the air. 200 yards away, in a van in the parking garage, a 23-year-old woman pressed an unmarked white button on the console in front of her, cuing the opening video package, an 18-second montage of wrestling footage set to hard rock music. The package played on 3 million televisions across America.

The opening package also played on the 20-foot television screen inside the arena, where thousands of fans cheered the start of the show. From the press box, the technical director watched the giant screen, looking for the close-up of Crusader, his cue that there were five seconds of footage left. When he saw it, he spoke into his headset, "Cue pyro in 5…4…3…2…1…cue pyro."

From backstage, in a makeshift booth nicknamed "The Hobbit Hole," the visual effects coordinator pulled a lever on his switchboard display, initiating a series of rapid-fire explosions that began at the ceiling, advanced to the ring, went up the entrance ramp, and finished with a fiery burst at the stage. The technical director watched the final detonation and said, "Cue announcers."

"You're looking live at Reunion Arena in Dallas, Texas, where tonight, by decree of Duke Corelli, we will have a single-elimination tournament to determine the number one contender for the GWA World Title. I'm Clive Silver, I'm joined tonight by Johnny The Monster Dupree, and have we got a gutbuster of a show for you."

"That's right Clive. Tonight we start with eight men, the top eight in line for a title shot. By night's end, we'll be down to one."

"Cue entrance," said the technical director.

Back in the production van, the same woman who started the show pressed another button, triggering two hundred decibels of guitar riff in the arena. As the guitar bellowed, Joey Mayhem's face appeared on the giant screen.

Joey had been standing behind the black curtain that separated the arena from backstage, thinking about what Shane had told him the night before. Just don't screw up, and the politics will take care of themselves. Just don't screw up.

When he heard his music, he pushed aside the polyester cloth, revealing fifteen thousand eager fans. They were already chanting his name.

The politics, the doubts, the nerves—they all evaporated when he stepped into the arena. Joey Hamilton, the rookie in over his head, was left on the other side of the curtain. In the arena, in front of these people, there was only Joey Mayhem, the cocky, charismatic, unpredictable superstar.

Fans reached for him as he walked down the entrance ramp. Those who touched his arm or his back would tell their friends, and would remember that moment for the rest of their lives.

Joey stepped into the ring and took his first look at the entire expanse of people. Fifteen thousand sets of eyes looked at him in adoration. He wondered how many people ever experienced something like this, and why he was so lucky.

The snooty trumpets of Rule Britannia played over the speakers, shaking Joey from his daze. Lord Mayberry stepped into the arena and waved to the crowd like he was the homecoming queen at the end of a parade. They responded with boos and middle fingers. He trotted to the ring and gently climbed the stairs. From the edge of the ring apron, he turned his back to Joey and waved again. This was Joey's cue to attack. Joey ran and hit Mayberry with a forearm to the back of the head. Mayberry fell off the ring apron and Joey followed him out of the ring. The crowd approved, the announcers were stunned, and the show was on.

The script for this match required Joey to take the early advantage and never lose it. The television announcers had been instructed to promote Joey's early attack as a smart strategy, while making sure the audience at home knew Joey was a long shot to win even one match in tonight's tournament.

Joey threw Mayberry head-first into the steel ring stairs, then kicked him in the stomach while he was down.

The action outside the ring gave the front row ticketholders an opportunity to pan for the TV cameras and interact directly with the stars.

"Kill him Joey!" shouted an overweight woman in a yellow T-shirt.

"You suck Mayberry!" screamed a little girl of no more than ten.

Joey grabbed Mayberry by the tights and threw him back into the ring. Then Joey took a minute to pose for his fans, which, in the wrestling world, was always a grave mistake. His two-second delay before re-entering the ring was just enough time for Mayberry to recover and greet Joey with a fist to the face.

With both wrestlers in the ring, the bell sounded and the match officially began. For the next six minutes, the two men exchanged blows and offensive maneuvers, each gaining and losing the upper hand more than once.

"Let's do the ref bump and take this home," whispered Mayberry while squeezing Joey's head in a chinlock. Following his instructions, Joey allowed Mayberry to swing him towards the corner, throwing him head-on into the referee, who (as referees often are) was right in the way.

The ref, being too weak to possibly withstand a collision with a wrestler, lay face-first on the mat, apparently unconscious. Following standard wrestling logic, with the referee out, the rampant cheating began. First, Mayberry unwrapped the athletic tape on his left hand and used it to choke Joey. Joey responded with a mulekick to Mayberry's groin.

As the referee's stupor stretched on for more than two minutes, the experienced members of the crowd turned toward the ring entrance, aware that this scenario required another wrestler to run in and join the action. Sure enough, Tyson Turner, Lord Mayberry's best friend, came running down the entrance ramp with a steel chair. When he got to the ring, Tyson swung the chair at Joey's head. Joey ducked just in time and the chair hit a perfectly placed Lord Mayberry in the face.

The fans went nuts. They loved the chaos.

Joey clotheslined Tyson Turner out of the ring, then covered the fallen Lord Mayberry. The referee, now out for a good three minutes, came to his senses just in time to see the cover, and counted 1...2...3.

"Oh my God, Johnny! Joey Mayhem has upset Lord Mayberry!" said Clive Silver to the television audience.

Joey's music played over the speakers. The fans cheered like Teamsters at a strike rally, and *Burn* took its first commercial break of the night. Joey stepped out of the ring and walked up the ramp. When he reached the curtain, he turned back to the fans for one last pose. Flashbulbs popped from every corner of the arena. In that moment, Joey was a god.

He pushed through the curtain, hoping that his next match would go over as well as this one.

Martha Tanner, the stage manager for all televised events, greeted Joey as soon as he stepped backstage.

"Well done, Joey. Duke wants to meet with you and Crusader right away to discuss the booking for your next match. They're in Salon A, down the hall and to your left." She handed him a bottle of water then ran off.

"Good match, kid," said Pit Bull Brody, slapping Joey on the back. Joey smiled and said thanks, registering the compliment as Pit Bull's first ever for him.

His walk down the hall was a tour of similar ego-enhancers.

"Good job, you really got them fired up," said a veteran agent named C. David Frye.

"You nailed it out there," said Gordy Goodnow.

Joey opened the door to Salon A to find Crusader smiling with his hand extended.

"Good match, Joey," said Crusader. "You set us up to put on a killer show when we get out there."

"Joey, have a seat," said Duke. There were three chairs in the otherwise empty room. The floor and walls were concrete, and Duke's voice echoed in the small space.

"Well gentlemen, your match tonight is one of the most important ones we've ever had in this company. In a few months, when we're back to our old highs in ratings and attendance, people will point to your match tonight as the turning point that shifted momentum away from Revolution and back in our favor," said Duke.

Joey nodded his head in agreement. This little pep talk was a final check to ensure Crusader was buying into the match tonight. Joey appreciated that. And judging by Crusader's warm greeting, and the nice things the other wrestlers were saying, it looked like everything was going to be fine.

"Crusader, tonight is your night to give our new star the rub he'll need to take us to the top," said Duke.

Joey didn't like Crusader's reaction. His face held a look of surprise, confusion, and anger. Crusader opened his mouth to say something but changed his mind. Then he looked at Joey, the way a man might look at someone who slept with his wife, and Joey understood. Duke hadn't told Crusader that he was putting Joey over. And if Crusader didn't know, then surely no one else knew either.

"So here's how the match is going to play out," said Duke, ignoring Crusader's obvious distress. Duke went into a short spiel about a standard singles match. Crusader would play the heel, he'd get the early advantage, he'd call the match from the ring for five or six minutes, dominating the whole time, then he'd perform his finisher on Joey. The crowd would assume the match was a squash right until the instant when Joey kicked out of Crusader's cover at two.

Then Joey would wake up, seemingly charged with adrenaline, and "Go Mayhem," leading to a clean win a few minutes later.

"Are there any questions, gentlemen?" said Duke.

Were there any questions? Duke had let the air out of the room, replaced it with poison gas, and now was asking if there were any questions. Joey wanted to stand up and run. He wanted to run back to Tennessee and wrestle in the indies again. He wanted his old dream back, his dream of becoming the GWA champion, his pristine dream, where the title belt was his crowning achievement, not his burden to bear. He wanted someone to explain to Crusader that this was Duke's plan, not his. Someone please just tell Crusader and Jumbo and Branson and all the other guys who deserve this belt more than little Joey Mayhem that it wasn't his idea. He was still the wide-eyed rookie. He was just doing what he was told.

"Yeah, I've got a question," said Crusader. "Why am I just hearing about this now? None of us have heard a word all week, and now, 10 minutes before we go on, you're telling me this kid's gonna kick out of my finisher and I'm gonna do the job to him? I guess I'm stupid, but, since I hadn't heard anything, I assumed that I'd be winning this tournament tonight. We all assumed it, Duke. I'm next in line for the belt."

"Scott, you're still very much in the main event scene," said Duke, referring to Crusader by his real name. "But tonight Joey's going over. We need to get people talking, you understand that don't you? Our competitors are riding our butts and we need a buzz to get people to tune in next week. Joey's win will surprise our audience. Trust me on this one, friend. It's best for business, and best for your wallet."

"I disagree," said Crusader.

"I don't pay you to disagree," said Duke, instantly changing from a happy peacemaker into a frightening kingpin. "Now, you can get out there and do the right thing, or you can leave." Duke spoke with the authority of a man who once owned the entire wrestling world.

"Jesus Christ," said Crusader under his breath. He rubbed his eyes and sighed heavily. "I'll do it. I always do it, you know that Duke. I just wish...oh never mind."

Without a heartbeat of transition, Duke returned to the compassionate father figure. "I'm sorry it panned out this way," he said. "Trust me. This is going to help all of us, a lot. You have an important job to do tonight. In two months you'll be thrilled that you were involved in this match. This job isn't about you passing the torch, it's about putting on a good show tonight, when we need it.

Rest assured that your place in line is safe. But right now I need you to do business. We've got to put on an interesting, surprising show, and we've got a kid here who the fans like and will talk about all week."

Crusader didn't seem convinced. But he didn't argue.

"Well Joey," he said, "I guess this is your night to shine." His voice was angry, but controlled. "Let's go do this."

Joey nodded silently and followed Crusader out the door. They would be on next.

*   *   *   *

"Knife-edge chops," Crusader whispered.

Joey obeyed, and let himself get tossed into the corner and bitch-slapped across the chest ten times. Joey's chest would be a blistered mess of welts and bruises tomorrow morning.

Per Duke's booking instructions, Crusader was calling the match, and squashing Joey. He was also putting on a clinic of the most legitimately painful moves allowed in professional wrestling.

He had opened the match with a few smacks to the chest, followed by an irish whip into a hard clothesline. Then he picked up Joey and delivered a sidewalk slam with all his body weight behind it. After a few seconds of filler, Crusader locked his arms around Joey's waist and dealt out three consecutive German suplexes, followed by the knife-edge chops in the corner.

To sell the move, and in hopes of getting a break, Joey fell face-first to the mat after the tenth chop. Normally, Joey's flop to the mat would be a signal to his partner to put him in a rest hold. He hoped Crusader would oblige.

Crusader stepped across Joey's back, and wrenched Joey's left arm backwards, pulling it into a simple yet painful hold. Joey considered breaking the hold and punching Crusader in the face for this stiff match that was bordering on dangerous, but instead he gritted his teeth and let the real pain help him sell the move. Perhaps this beating would earn Joey some respect backstage.

"Other corner. Super-plex, then the Iron Sword," Crusader whispered.

Thank God, Joey thought. The Iron Sword, a combination suplex-bodyslam, was Crusader's finisher, and was the spot they had picked for the momentum shift and the end of this torture. Of course, before they got there, Crusader had called a super-plex, one of the more dangerous moves in wrestling.

Still holding Joey's arm behind his back, Crusader allowed Joey to stand, then pushed him into the corner, where he threw four punches to Joey's head before scooping him up and dropping his butt right on the top turnbuckle. Crusader climbed to the second turnbuckle until he and Joey were both crouched in position for the move.

"One...two...three," Crusader whispered, and he swung Joey over his head. Both men soared through the air like a giant sledgehammer, then crashed down to the ring floor. The wind rushed out of Joey's lungs. A sharp sting ran through his shoulders. He wished he could lie on the mat and go to sleep.

Crusader was immediately to his feet. As if the super-plex was no more than a simple take-down, Crusader scooped up Joey again, held him upside down for a minute, and slammed him in the Iron Sword. Then he went for the cover.

When Joey kicked out at two, the crowd's reaction was so loud that his ears popped. Now it was his turn to call the moves. In the swirling haze of his thoughts, he briefly considered working Crusader as stiff as he'd just been worked. He considered beating the crap out of him and taking away all his heat. He envisioned a half-hour beatdown that would make Crusader's character look so weak that he'd never main event again.

"Throw me to the ropes," Joey whispered.

Crusader followed the instructions. He dragged Joey's carcass from the mat and flung him to the opposite corner of the ring. Joey bounced off the ropes and leaped into a flying cross-body block that landed him in a cover of Crusader.

"Let's trade some punches," Joey whispered while the two men were down for the cover. Crusader kicked out at the referee's two-count. Both men jumped up and started trading punches to the face. Joey hit the first one. Crusader hit the next. Four times they traded blows before Crusader followed the script and let Joey get the upper hand. The crowd went wild as the traded blows turned into a Joey Mayhem trademarked beatdown. The energy of the fans was the most Joey had ever felt. They were not expecting him to go over, and they loved it.

Joey went into his full "Going Mayhem" routine, pummeling Crusader into a corner and stomping and punching him like a lunatic. Then Joey picked him up, threw him over his shoulder, and ran to the center of the ring for an authoritative power slam. Joey covered Crusader, the referee counted to three, and the fans went ballistic. Young Joey Mayhem had just gone over one of the GWA's most prominent stars.

His body screaming in pain from every joint, Joey was oblivious to the ovation he was getting. To the fans tonight, Joey was a bona fide superstar. But their cheers were just white noise in his head, drowned out by pain and disorientation. He focused himself enough to step through the ropes and walk toward the back. Halfway up the ramp he realized that in ten minutes he would be out here to wrestle again. And before he came back out, he'd have to face the thirty wrestlers behind the curtain who had expected Joey to lose this match. Fuck them, he thought. If they couldn't appreciate the shit Joey had just taken from Crusader, then fuck them. As his head cleared, Joey became aware of the cheers he was getting. Unconsciously, he stopped walking, and turned around to face the fans. They cheered even louder to greet him. Joey wished he could stay out here in the arena, among friends—fifteen thousand people who adored him so much they chanted his name. But this was wrestling, and what happened in the arena was just for show. Reality was behind the black curtain. Joey turned around and finished his trek up the ramp.

Martha greeted him on the other side.

"Joey, back to Salon A for another meeting with Duke," she said. "Jumbo and Deep Six," she called out, "Curtain in two minutes!"

Joey walked down the same hallway where, twenty minutes before, the other wrestlers had showered him with compliments. On his way, he passed Pit Bull Brody, Bandit Thompson, Bigfoot, and Henry Dexter, four wrestlers sitting together who were not performing on tonight's television broadcast. They all ignored Joey as he passed.

Joey opened the door to Salon A, where Duke was waiting for him. Duke congratulated him on a successful match. Then Duke ran over the booking for Joey's match with Jumbo. The match would be a duplicate of the one he had just finished with Crusader, only this time Joey would get squashed for even longer before he found the super-human might to shift the momentum.

"Do you have any questions?" Duke asked after he had explained all the booking.

"Yeah," said Joey. "Is it alright if I hang out in here to rest until match time?"

"You bet, kid," said Duke.

CHAPTER 9

▼

Taken from www.wrestlinghotline.com

Greetings slugs.

Today is Tuesday, April 25th, and this is your Tuesday Morning Hangover, barely 6 hours removed from the biggest bender we wrestling fans have ever had on a Monday night.

This morning's hangover isn't one of those drink a bottle of Evian and all is forgiven types, nor is it one that can be fixed with some pancakes and a nap. No, slugs, it's going to take a morning of prayer to the porcelain god and 6 ibuprofens to get past last night's soiree, which started with a classy gin martini and ended with a bad batch of tequila. After the fourth dry heave, we'll all swear never to do it again, but come next Monday, we'll be back where we started.

Well, let's get this over with…

Ratings Report:
GWA Burn pulled an overall 4.4, with a 4.4 in the first hour, a 4.3 in the second hour, and a 4.5 in the overrun. These numbers are way up from last week. If the rumors we're hearing of backstage trouble for Joey Mayhem are true, he can rest assured that if he keeps popping the rating, everyone will be nice as southern peaches. Unless they care that….

Revolution Riot got an overall of 4.5, with a 4.2 in the first hour, a 4.7 in the second, and an astonishing 4.8 in the overrun.

Statistically, the rating is basically tied. But on the chart this week, *Revolution Riot* is going to appear a spot higher in the ranks than *GWA Burn*. This will be a first.

What can we learn from last night's historic victory for *Riot*? Let us begin with…

The High Points:
GWA Burn—Where to start? Last night's edition was probably the best episode of *Burn* since Gene Harold left for Revolution. The tournament was surprising, exciting, and fresh. The best matches were:

1. Crusader vs. Joey Mayhem—Unbelievable. What a great story, and a great way to get the new guy over. Crusader puts Joey through the ringer for ten minutes before Joey kicks out of the first cover and eventually comes back to win the match. Simple, elegant, no-frills wrestling. What made it work so well is that we all were sure Crusader was winning the tournament, and the shift in momentum had me genuinely surprised, creating a nice mark-out moment. Joey Mayhem's stock has risen in my book just for taking that beating, and Crusader gets huge props for doing the right thing and lying down.

2. Joey Mayhem vs. Jumbo—This is what wrestling should be, stories told out in the ring. Last week's melee between these two set up this rematch nicely, and since it was the finals of the tournament, with a shot at the GWA Championship in the balance, the stakes were high enough that even Jumbo's plodding style couldn't ruin the fun. The rumors that Joey Mayhem is getting shit backstage for his huge push make this match even more interesting. Was it just me, or did Joey take an awful beating in this match and the one with Crusader? Wouldn't it be interesting if these rumors were all a work, and the stiff matches were just part of the ploy? Of course, that kind of subtlety isn't Duke's style.

3. Joey Mayhem vs. Lord Mayberry—Without question, Joey Mayhem was the star of last night's show. With three good matches and a tournament victory, Joey has instantly established himself as a credible main-eventer. The match with Lord Mayberry was formulaic but fun. When Tyson Turner began winding up that chair, we all knew what was going to happen, but that didn't stop the crowd from loving it. A great way to open a great show.

On the other side….
Revolution Riot—Only one match from last night's show makes the high points, but what a match it was.

Lucifer vs. Red Jackson for the Revolution World Title—Those of you who missed this match are fools! We knew it was going to be great. We told you it was going to be great. Guess what—it was GREAT!

Forty minutes they went. By the way, that's a record on free television. And they kept it interesting the whole time. Lucifer is the most creative, skilled, unbelievable athlete I have ever seen. Last night he was in the ring with the legend, and what the two of them did was just magical. That high rating in the overrun comes from the blockbuster final eight minutes of the match, during which there were nineteen attempted pinfalls. The spectacle was so breathtaking I couldn't sleep, and I wonder if it will ever be topped.

Congratulations to Lucifer, the new Revolution World Champion.

The Big Picture:
Slugs, if there was a lesson to be learned from last night, it's this. Neither shocking spectacles nor puddles of blood nor funny sketches nor near-naked women can substitute for good wrestling. Last night we had some great wrestling, and the ratings were up on both shows because of it.

The News:
The Family Television Group appears to have made some inroads in its all-out war against *GWA Burn*. Last Wednesday, Fresha Cola announced it would pull all its advertising from *GWA Burn* in response to the FTG's concerns. Electronic Artistry, makers of several popular PC games, is expected to follow suit.

I don't know about you, slugs, but to me, this is downright horrifying. This seemingly harmless little group of fascists, who have been a nuisance for years, but never a real threat to our favorite industry, all of a sudden has major corporations pulling the plug on their sponsorship of *GWA Burn*? This development scares me to the core. We all know that it won't be long before Duke is cleaning up his show just to please these pansies.

And don't think that just because *Revolution Riot* is flying beneath the radar right now that it won't be next. I suspect the FTG is leaving *Riot* alone solely so they can concentrate all their efforts on one big target. But as soon as they've decimated *Burn*, leaving it a shell of its former self, rest assured they'll turn their guns at *Riot*. Also don't think that these do-gooders will go away if *Burn* cleans up its notoriously raunchy second hour. The FTG won't be done until professional wrestling is off the air entirely or relegated exclusively to late-night cable and pay per view. That's why I've taken it upon myself to provide…

A Call to Action:

Slugs, it's down to us to speak up against the evil of the FTG. They started the battle, but we have to finish it. Contrary to what we might believe, this is not a battle of words and ideas, it is a battle of noise. The winner of this battle will be the one who makes the biggest stink. The FTG is already organizing boycotts and negative publicity campaigns against the sponsors of *GWA Burn*. It is now our job to organize negative publicity against the sponsors of the FTG. As such, I am gathering a list of the FTG's largest financial supporters and I intend to publish it on this web site. Next Tuesday, after I have completed collecting the information I need, I will post the list in next week's Hangover. Once the list is up, it will be your job to dig in and start fighting.

Get ready. We've got work to do.

Until then slugs, this is Steve Garcia. Peace.

CHAPTER 10

▼

Joey stacked his styrofoam plate with barbecued chicken and moved on to the potato salad. More so than the big crowds or the big pay checks, the real perk of wrestling for one of the majors was the backstage catering before the show. The Texas-style barbecue at the Alamodome before tonight's non-televised show in San Antonio wasn't the most extravagant meal, but it was good enough to bring out most of the performers and staff for a late lunch.

This Friday-night show was the first time the GWA locker room had re-convened since Joey's tournament victory on Monday. Joey had flown to San Antonio from Memphis, where he had spent his days off fishing and drinking with his brother Mark. He was glad to return to the tour. The time off had been agonizing. He feared what the locker room might have said in his absence, and wanted to be in the thick of things in case his social standing backstage needed some damage control.

He topped off his plate with a roll, grabbed a lemonade, and scanned the tables set up across the loading dock in a makeshift cafeteria. As he looked at all the little cliques of wrestlers sitting together, and wondered which table would invite him to sit, he felt like he was back in junior high, trying to stake out his place on the popularity chain.

He saw Shane sitting at a table of veterans, and considered pulling up a chair next to him, but Crusader was also sitting at that table. Joey and Crusader hadn't spoken a word since their match ended on Monday night. There was an empty chair at Jumbo's table, but it was just Jumbo and his wife—that didn't seem like an appropriate place for Joey to go either. Goliath was sitting with Duke, Joey would be accepted at that table, but sitting there would send the gossipers swarming that Joey was hanging out with the top brass again. There were several empty tables, he could sit at one of those. Of course, doing so might make him come across as aloof.

At the very back of the room, against the brick wall, Safire stood up, tossed her trash, and left, leaving Jade alone at a table. That was the one. Joey went straight for Safire's vacated chair.

"Mind if I sit here?" he said.

"Fine by me," said Jade.

From behind Jade, Bandit Thompson turned and watched Joey sit down. Joey ignored him.

"Did you get some potato salad?" said Jade. "There's something spicy in it. It's really good."

"Yes, I got a good helping. How were your days off?"

"Not too bad. Yours?"

"They were fine. I went home to Memphis."

"Do you have a woman back home?"

"No. I haven't had a girlfriend since high school. Tried dating a few times since then, but the travel and the schedule, well, you know."

"Yes, I do. Well, now that you're a big star, maybe more dates will come your way."

"That's what I'm afraid of."

His mind shot back to the morning before, on the lake, in a rented fishing boat he'd paid for. Mark had been pushing for a fishing trip for weeks. After an hour of awkward pauses and forced conversation, Mark dropped a bomb. He needed money. He'd taken out a second mortgage on his house the year before and was in no place to pay it. He had eighteen thousand in credit card debt. If he didn't get things under control he was going to have his car repossessed. After an hour of awkward financial talk, Joey agreed to give Mark ten thousand dollars, banking on good sales of his new T-shirt and a few pay per view performances that could spike his income. Mark didn't seem to believe that Joey Mayhem, the superstar wrestler, was only making forty thousand dollars before incentives this first year on his contract.

Jade broke Joey's daydream. "What, are you looking for someone who loves you and isn't starstruck?" she said. "Cause you're not gonna find anyone like that anymore."

Tell me about it, he thought.

"Do you speak from experience?" he said, wanting to turn the conversation back on her. Thus far, his relationship with Jade had been one of him talking and her listening.

"Oh yeah. You can ask anyone in here and you'll get the same story. There aren't a lot of storybook romances in professional wrestling. We're all married to our careers, and anyone who comes along learns quickly that they play second fiddle to the squared circle. People who really love you won't put up with it forever. The people who stay are the ones who love what you give them, money and freedom. If you can accept that you're forever a sugar daddy now, at least you won't feel guilty."

"That's good advice. I'll take it to heart," said Joey, trying to sound empathetic. He stuffed a dinner roll in his mouth.

Jade grinned and put her fork down.

"Kid, you're too nice to be where you are," she said.

Joey let the compliment pass, acting like his mouth was too full to respond.

"So, I saw on the board that you're doing another match with Bret tonight," said Jade.

"Yes. Same program as last week, and the week before."

"Be thankful for that. I think it's good for you right now."

"How's that?" Joey knew the answer to his own question, but he asked anyway. It was good for him to continue wrestling with Bret on the house shows because it wasn't threatening to anyone. He and Bret had both been low mid-carders just a month ago. Now Joey was a main-eventer, and there just happened to be a main event slot open on the house shows since Branson was injured. Joey had suspected that he might replace Branson in his matches against Zombie, further solidifying him as a top player in the company. He was glad that wasn't happening.

"I think you know why it's good for you," said Jade. She was smiling at him, telling him without words that now, with half the locker room within earshot, wasn't the time to talk about backstage politics.

Joey nodded and changed the subject. "I see that you've got another mixed tag match tonight," he said.

"Yes," She lowered her voice, "It's shit, but we do what we have to."

Jade's match tonight was a tag match in which she and Danny Jackson, a sound wrestler with a boring character, were going up against Safire and Lord Mayberry. On the house shows, mixed-gender tag team matches like this were common. The women's division in the GWA wasn't known for great wrestling. It was there strictly for sex appeal. On television, there were all sorts of things the women could do (usually requiring them to wear next to nothing and humiliate themselves), but on the house shows, the women's matches quickly killed the crowd. Hence, they were often stuck with the men in a tag team match not at all related to any stories currently brewing on television. Worse, the men were often wrestlers who couldn't get over with the crowd without the help of a sexy woman. For a woman like Jade, a decent wrestler with a lot of experience, the mixed tag model was an insult. But unless Duke began hiring actual wrestlers to populate the women's division, the mixed tag matches were a necessity.

"I was thinking," Joey began, not sure why he was bringing this up, "I believe you still owe me a date."

Jade smiled. "Our dinner with Shane last week didn't count?"

"It could if you want it to, but I was hoping to take you out after one of the shows this week."

Jade looked down at the table and thought for a minute.

"I don't know if this is a good idea Joey," she said.

"Why's that?" he asked, feigning ignorance of the answer.

Jade's demeanor became more serious. "Do you know about me? Do you know about my reputation here?" She looked around to ensure no one else was listening before she continued in a lower voice. "You're just breaking into the big time and the way I see it, you already have some political problems. You might not want to start something with the company skank right now."

"The company—what are you talking about? No one thinks of you like—"

Jade held her hand up both to interrupt Joey and let him know he was speaking too loudly.

"Joey, I have a lot of history in this locker room," she said, leaning in closer to him. "I'm not ashamed of any of it. There are things you have to do if you're going to make it as a woman in this business. Thankfully those days are in the past for me now. But I've been around here a long time and I know how things are and I know how I'm thought of around here. Take it as a compliment that I want to protect you. It's not just the locker room stuff either. As soon as you and I are seen out together someplace those Internet kids will go hog wild. And next thing you know they're saying you became the GWA champion because you slept your way to the top. And ten years from now, when you're the biggest name in the business, you'll have this black cloud over you, and you'll wish you could shake it. These are all things you have to think about now. The choices you make right now will define you and your career."

Joey leaned in even closer.

"You know, Jade, the more you talk like this, the more I'm determined that we're going out tonight."

"Oh, that's just great kid," she said. "Now I'm your rebellion against the system. To hell with them, I'll show 'em. I'm taking out the whore."

"Why do you call yourself those names?"

"Enough—" Jade raised both hands in surrender. "Why don't you think about it some more? We'll be seeing each other all week. If you're still interested—"

"I'm still interested," Joey interrupted. "Unless you have other plans, real other plans, I'm taking you to dinner after the show tonight."

Jade sighed and threw her hair back. "Okay Don Juan. I'm on first tonight, so I'll be in my hotel room early. I think we should leave from there. I can see you're keen on telling the world that we've got a date, but I still think some discretion might be in order. I'm in room 218 at the Hilton right next to the arena. You can pick me up."

"Great, I'm staying there as well. I'll be there after my match is over."

"You'd better take a shower."

"Of course I'll—"

"And you'd better take me someplace nice, and come dressed up."

"We're gonna have a great time."

Jade chuckled, then stood up from the table. "Alright stud. See you later."

"Good luck in your match tonight."

"Good luck in yours too," she said.

Joey watched her leave, finished his food, and headed to the locker room.

CHAPTER 11

▼

The San Antonio house show was mercifully uneventful. Joey got the biggest fan response of any wrestler. As planned, he went over Bret in a short match. Other matches on the card included Zombie going over Gordy Goodnow and Goliath successfully defending the GWA title against Deep Six.

Joey took a fast shower after his match, quickly dressed himself in blue jeans and a maroon polo shirt, and jogged out to his rental car, a Ford Explorer. He exited the parking garage and turned right, driving the one block between the Alamodome and the downtown Hilton. Leaving his car with the valet, he navigated the lobby to the elevators and found himself standing in front of room 218. He knocked twice.

Jade answered, wearing a black pantsuit and diamond earrings. Her black hair was pulled into a pony tail and her face was made up in light tones that were a far cry from her wrestling look. She slumped her shoulders in disappointment half a second after seeing Joey.

"I thought you were going to dress up," she said. Her tone was serious enough to throw Joey into apology mode.

"I never bring anything nicer than this on the road," he said.

Jade rolled her eyes and stepped out of the room.

"I don't either," she said, "there's a mall just down the street. I bought this outfit right after we ate."

"Oh. I should have thought about—"

"That's okay Joey. I'll just be overdressed. I don't mind."

As they walked toward the elevator, Joey's mind plunged through as many options as he could conjure to remedy the bad start to their date.

"Hey, what if our first stop tonight was the mall where you bought your clothes?" he said.

"I'm not returning these Joey. I like the outfit, and I'm going to wear it tonight, regardless—"

"No, not for you to return your clothes. For me to buy some. It'll be fast, and then we'll match."

The elevator arrived. A young couple stepped out. The man's face betrayed starstruck recognition of both Joey and Jade. Joey shot him a look that said, 'Not tonight.' To his surprise, the man understood, and the couple walked past.

"Okay, the mall will be our first stop," said Jade, as they stepped into the elevator. "Then where are we going?"

"Actually, I hadn't decided. I don't know San Antonio. Is there anyplace you'd like to go?"

Jade smiled and shook her head. "You're not much of a date, are you Joey?"

Joey bit his lip. This wasn't going well at all. A bell rang to signify the elevator's halt. Joey wanted to say something like an apology, something about how he'd turn this around and show her a good time. But the door opened, and a small crowd was waiting to get on. Any one of them might recognize Joey and Jade, and somehow Joey didn't want to say anything in front of them. He could tell this date would be awkward. They would have no privacy as long as they were out in the world.

One hour and a few sentences of conversation later, they landed in a private booth at the Watercress Café, a quaint restaurant near the Riverwalk, recommended by the hotel concierge. Joey's polo shirt and jeans were in the trunk of the car; he was now dressed in a black suit with a white silk tie. Jade had picked out the suit from the rack at Foley's. It didn't fit well enough to justify the price, but there wasn't time for tailoring, so Joey paid cash and they were off.

They avoided shop talk during dinner, and instead spoke about each other. Joey talked about growing up in Memphis, his brother, and his childhood life in the suburbs. He didn't mention the Memphis Backyard Brawlers. She probably already knew anyway. Mark had put together a compilation video of the group's travails and was selling it on the web.

Jade spoke about her family in Dallas. Her father had passed away two years ago. She briefly mentioned that she wished she had seen more of him at the end of his life, then moved on. Her mother now lived in a trendy apartment that Jade paid for. Her older brother disapproved of her skimpy wrestling outfits and her nude photo shoots. He was currently ignoring her. She no longer spoke with any of her friends from youth—things had changed when she became wealthy. She cautioned Joey against making the same mistakes she had.

After dinner, Joey offered to take Jade along the Riverwalk, but she declined, fearing they would be seen and photographed. A movie and a dance club were also dismissed. They ended up just driving around town in Joey's Explorer. Jade wore sunglasses until they got on the Interstate.

Joey drove south until they were out of San Antonio proper. They exited onto Highway 181 and followed the road signs to Calaveras Lake. They parked in an open area next to the water. Joey killed the engine. The night air was buzzing with crickets, but there were no sounds of civilization. Through the windshield, they could see a sliver of moonlight gleaming from the lake. Oaks on either side of them made for a feeling of privacy. They sat in silence for a minute before Jade brought up work for the first time of the evening.

"I bet you're nervous about Monday night," she said.

"I'm petrified," said Joey.

More silence.

"I'm just telling myself that I'm going to nail it, and put on the perfect match with Goliath. If we nail it, there won't be anything anyone backstage can say."

"Do you know much about the booking yet?"

"I know we're getting at least ten minutes. I know Goliath is going over but it won't be clean. Other than that, I haven't heard anything. I imagine there will be a ref bump and I'll be hit with the title belt or a chair."

"It sounds like it will be set up so you can connect with the fans."

"Yeah, I guess so." Joey was surprised at how matter-of-fact this crucial part of wrestling had become in his matches. Connecting with the fans was no longer an issue for him. He was now on six performances in a row, in six different cities, where he was getting the biggest fan response of anyone on the roster. It didn't seem to matter who he was wrestling or how well he wrestled. It was just a given that the crowd would love him.

This week the issue was connecting with the veterans in the locker room. If he didn't put on a great match, a much better match than Crusader or Branson or Jumbo or Deep Six could put on, than his political problems would only worsen.

"What are you up to on TV this week?" Joey asked.

"Just more of the same, I think," said Jade. "I'm hearing that I'll be in a program for the women's title again, maybe as early as next pay per view."

"Well that's cool. They need to put that belt on you and leave it there."

"Thanks, but they won't, and I don't know if I care anyway. The women's belt doesn't mean a thing anymore. We're paying the piper for too many years of vaudeville with the women in this company. Now the only people who care about me or any of the other girls are the little boys who want to see tits and ass. The wrestling fans groan when we come out, and I don't blame them. We haven't done anything that would entertain them for years. It just sucks."

Joey nodded his head in agreement. The women's division was the hopeless slouch in the GWA family. While men's wrestling in the GWA was moving steadily toward athleticism, women's wrestling was flying away from it. It used to be expected that women would go out and put on a cat fight with a few wrestling holds and a lot of attitude. Now a woman in the GWA could expect two bra and panties matches in a giant gravy bowl for every one match in the ring. In the past year alone, Joey had watched Jade wrestle in the mud, in whipped cream, in the shower, on a waterbed, in a kitchen, and in a hot tub. She had to perform skits where she made out with other women, stripped naked in front of Duke, and had cow manure poured over her head. She, like most of the women on the roster, endured this embarrassment because every once in a while she was allowed to have a regular match, in a ring, with rules, and like the men in the company, Jade was a junkie for the drama of professional wrestling. Joey couldn't imagine enduring the crap she went through just to get a shot at an occasional wrestling match.

"Have you ever thought of going to work for Revolution?" Joey asked, boldly breaking an unspoken GWA rule with his question.

"Of course I have," said Jade. "I remember what it was like to work under Gene Harold. He understood what wrestling fans wanted to see out of women's matches. My contract here is up in a little over a year, and maybe I'll finally bolt, but, you know, it's hard. I've been doing this for eight years now. I'm kind of tired."

Jade paused and looked out the window, as if she were seeing a memory out in the lake. The moonlight lit half of her face. Joey wanted to tell her how beautiful she looked. After all, this was a date. Somehow the conversation hadn't been very romantic.

"I don't want to talk about me anymore," said Jade. "You're the exciting one in this company. Let's talk about you."

"I don't know if I'm that exciting," said Joey. "Just lucky, and, for whatever reason, chosen by the boss."

"It's not for whatever reason, Joey. You're a superstar. You need to accept it."

"Well, you're very kind," he said.

"I'm not being kind, just honest," said Jade. There was something in her voice that Joey hadn't heard from her before, admiration. "I think you've got it. I think you're the best foil for Goliath we have in the company, and a good feud between you two will get a lot of people watching. And I think you're going to be a huge star someday. Hell, what am I talking about? You're already a huge star—the reaction you're getting at the house shows, it's…it's unreal.

"And I'll tell you something, Joey. Everyone backstage knows that you're the real deal. That more than anything is why they're giving you grief. Crusader can act upset that he has to put over a rookie, but what really upsets him is that he knows he'll be putting you over from here on out. He knows that you're going to take this opportunity and run to the moon with it, and his dream of being number one is finished."

"You think so? Jade, I really appreciate you saying—"

"I'm not just saying kid, it's obvious to everyone. Listen, I know the backstage shit is really bothering you, and I know that two weeks ago in Lubbock I told you to watch your back, and I know that last week I didn't react well when you told me and Shane that you were winning the strap. But it took just one little push and the fans went ballistic for you. I've never seen anything like it. Do I think you're getting the title too early? Yes. I think Duke is making it really hard for you to put on good programs with the veterans who will be jealous of you from now on. But so what? You're the hottest guy around right now. The fans will love it when you win the belt. I think I see what Duke's trying to swing here. I'm being honest when I say I hope it works out."

"Thanks Jade. That means a lot to me."

"You're welcome."

The conversation reached its destination with Jade's compliment, and they sat in comfortable silence for awhile. Joey wondered if anyone else thought like Jade. Maybe he had more allies in the locker room, and just didn't know who they were. He considered asking Jade if she knew of anyone else who was behind him, but was scared of leading the conversation back to him and his career. He didn't want to come across as self-centered.

"Why did you ask me to come out with you tonight Joey?" said Jade.

There were a hundred reasons. She was beautiful, she had been flirting with him, he thought she'd say yes, he had a feeling, he was attracted to her, she was an icon and a trophy.

"I don't know," he said.

"Well…do you have anything more planned for us to do tonight?"

"I guess I don't." Joey smiled, hoping Jade would understand that he didn't know what he was doing, but he had enjoyed the night.

On the way back to town, they spoke about each other and their interests outside of work. Jade talked about her love for old movies. Her favorite actor was Carey Grant; her favorite movie was *Roman Holiday*. Joey talked about his memories of fishing, hiking, and hunting with his family. He recalled a memorable camping trip in Virginia when racoons stole all their food.

Joey parked in the garage for the downtown Hilton, and escorted Jade back to her room. She thanked him for their date. They said good night. They didn't kiss, or even hug. Just good night and Jade softly closed the door behind her. It was oddly appropriate, Joey thought. Amidst all the sexual charge of the wrestling world, he and the industry's biggest sex symbol had just completed a first date straight out of Dear Abbey. And it felt right. Joey strolled back to his car, feeling smooth as a ribbon. That night he slept little, his mind a bustling mix of excitement and fear.

CHAPTER   12

▼

A phone was ringing. Deafening. Make it stop.

Joey rolled over. He had been dreaming about a Koala bear with peanut butter in its naval whose head exploded when the phone rang. He picked up the phone.

"Hello?"

"Good morning Joey, it's Fran Wallace. I'm so sorry to wake you."

"Good morning," said Joey. Fran Wallace? Where was he? It was dark, and cold.

"Listen Joey, Duke has asked me to get you to Houston today for some publicity work for Monday's show. I've booked a flight for you at nine-thirty."

"Okay." Joey had figured out he was in a hotel room.

"I'll have a cab for you in the lobby in an hour. Do you think you can be packed, checked out, and ready to go at six thirty?"

"Yeah, um…just a second please." Joey sat up in bed, put the phone down on the night stand, and rubbed his eyes. He looked at the digital clock next to the phone. 5:31. What day was it? He flipped through the wrestling matches in his memory and tried to put them in order. He had wrestled against Henry Dexter last night. He was in Corpus Christi, Texas. In a hotel. The Marriot. He had driven here from Austin. It was Sunday.

Now Fran Wallace was calling him. Fran Wallace, she was…Duke's assistant. Joey had spoken to her before. He was supposed to do another house show tonight. Houston was Monday, but it was the big show, and he was in the main event. He would have to do publicity. He should have expected it.

He took a big breath and slowly exhaled. Everything was fine. He picked up the phone.

"Hi Fran, sorry, I just had to get my bearings."

"Well that's perfectly understandable. I'm so sorry I woke you up." She had a heavy New York accent. Joey could picture her now. She was short and skinny, with straight brown hair that went all the way down her back. She wore business suits.

"Would you like me to start over Joey?"

"No, I've got it. Be in the lobby, ready to go, in an hour."

"That's right. Gunther Olson will be waiting for you when you arrive in Houston. He'll take care of you."

Damn it was cold. The air conditioner was blasting like only a hotel unit could.

"I'm scheduled to wrestle tonight," Joey said, hoping that Fran would say his match was canceled. His back was still hurting from Crusader and Jumbo's pounding last Monday. There was ibuprofen in the bathroom. He'd be popping a handful as soon as he got off the phone.

"Don't worry about tonight Joey. We've got you covered. Don't worry about anything. You'll learn that I take good care of my wrestlers out on assignment. Gunther will take you back to the Houston airport this afternoon in plenty of time for you to catch a flight back to Corpus for your show. Be sure to pack everything you'll need."

Great. Two flights, publicity appearances, and he still had to do the show tonight. This was going to be an awful day.

"Alright. So I guess Gunther will know everything I need to know once I get there."

"Right again Joey. You just show up in the lobby in an hour. We'll take care of you from there."

"Okay. Thanks Fran. I guess I'd better get moving."

"Have a good day Joey."

He hung up the phone and headed to the bathroom.

An hour later he was in the Corpus Christi airport, where he boarded a commercial jet to Houston. The flight was forty minutes long. On the way, he used the airplane cellular service to leave a voicemail for Duke. He still hadn't heard anything about the booking in his match on Monday night, and was starting to get nervous. He had hoped to spend the weekend memorizing his spots.

As promised, Gunther Olson, a stocky former wrestler turned GWA gopher, was waiting at the airport. Upon seeing Joey, he took off his baseball cap and waved it over his head. He looked like a fool.

"Welcome to Houston, Joey," he said.

They shook hands. Gunther's palm was sticky.

"Thanks Gunther. Hey, did Duke give you a call? I've asked him to call you as soon as he can. I need to talk to him, and I don't have a phone on me."

"What are you doing traveling without a phone, Joey?"

Joey shrugged. He never could afford to have a cell phone before he signed with the GWA, and since signing, he never had time to get one. Life on the road left him no time to take care of everyday necessities like cell phone shopping.

"Well Duke hasn't called me," Gunther said. "I'll keep my ear out for him. If he doesn't call by noon, we'll see if we can get in touch with him."

"I appreciate it. I really want to talk to him about Monday's booking. I haven't heard a thing yet."

"What makes you think he's already got Monday's booking figured out? This is Duke we're talking about, right?"

Gunther laughed at his own joke. Joey forced a smile. Duke was known for last-minute changes and "booking on the fly." He often made crucial booking decisions as he spoke with the wrestlers minutes before showtime. Joey had hoped Monday night's match would be different. There was enough pressure on him already. He didn't want to improvise his first title match.

Their first stop was a radio station, where Joey answered phone-in questions from fans for an hour, then recorded an interview to be aired later that day on a nationally syndicated rock and wrestling show. From there, Gunther carted Joey to a television studio to shoot a 10-second promotional clip for Monday Night's *Burn*. Still in television makeup, Joey's next appearance was at a bookstore, where he did an autograph signing and an interview for another local TV station. Noon came and went without any word from Duke. While Joey was signing autographs, Gunther called Duke's cell phone, his office, and his home, leaving messages at each.

"Let's leave messages for all the VPs and all the road agents. Someone has to know where he is," Joey said to Gunther while scribbling his name on the back of a little girl's T-shirt.

"You don't make it far in this business by pestering the boss," said Gunther. "We've left three messages. That's enough. Nothing more we can do."

The girl with the T-shirt giggled and stepped out of the way. Her friend stepped up next and asked if Joey would sign her hand.

Joey supposed Gunther was probably right. Duke did things on his own time. No amount of harassment would budge him.

The autograph session ended at two, and Gunther rushed Joey into the car for their final stop, an Internet media firm who wished to tape an interview with Joey for a webcast the next day. They were completely disorganized and after ten minutes Gunther announced that it was taking too long and canceled the session.

As they were driving back to Houston Intercontinental, Gunther's phone rang. Joey sat up.

"Gunther speaking…Hi Honey Bear."

Gunther spoke with his wife for the rest of the drive, stopping the conversation only to shake Joey's hand before dropping him off at the airport.

By the time Joey landed in Corpus Christi, there was only an hour left before the show started. No one was at the airport to pick him up. So much for Fran's promise that he would be taken care of.

It took him fifteen minutes to get a taxi at the tiny airport, and another twenty to get to the arena.

Martha Tanner greeted Joey backstage.

"We didn't know if you were gonna make it, kid. You should have called. Do you have my phone number?"

"I didn't have a phone with me. I was doing publicity in Houston."

"Well it would have been nice if someone had told someone. No one knew where you were. You know you're in the main event tonight, don't you?"

"No. I didn't know that. Am I wrestling Goliath?"

"No, he's not here tonight. Only a half card for this podunk town. You're going over Gordy Goodnow. You should find him. I bet he wants to talk to you about the match."

"Thanks Martha."

Joey took his bag to the locker room to change into his wrestling attire. To his disappointment, none of the other wrestlers confronted him about being late, so he didn't have an opportunity to tell his sap story of plane trips and publicity sessions.

Joey and Gordy Goodnow worked out a simple match with Joey going over. They performed their makeshift script without any problems. The match was one that both of them, and a thousand other wrestlers, had done countless times in countless cities. Corpus Christi ate it up.

✴   ✴   ✴   ✴

Joey woke up the next morning at eleven. He panicked when he saw the time. Less than twelve hours until his World Title Match. He still hadn't heard from Duke. No call from Fran either. As far as he knew, he had no way of getting to Houston. What a shitty job she had done as his travel coordinator.

After checking out of the hotel, Joey took the hotel's shuttle service to the airport, where he caught the next flight to Houston. From the airport he took a cab to the Astrodome.

On the way, he thought back to when he was a teenager, and had watched Red Jackson defeat Shane Walker for the GWA Title at Myers Arena in Memphis. Joey remembered the wrestlers seeming distant, mysterious. They weren't human. They were characters from television, larger in stature than any regular man could be.

Joey had never considered that Red Jackson or Shane Walker might have been nervous that night. From his vantage as a fan, the performers were incapable of human weaknesses like fear. But now he wondered. Did they go out there and improvise their match, as Joey and Goliath were now likely to do? Was Shane Walker worried that he might find himself half-way through the match, out of ideas, throwing his opponent into a chinlock and killing the crowd? Did Red Jackson wonder if he had what it took to be the number one guy? Did either of them have to deal with backstage politics?

A security guard let Joey inside the stadium. The crew was running sound checks and testing the ring ropes. No one had seen Duke yet.

The other wrestlers began arriving at four o'clock. One of the first to come backstage was Jade. Joey was relieved to see her.

"Hey stranger," she said. "How did the Corpus Christi show turn out?"

"It was fine. Crowd dug it. I had fun."

"And the night before that was…"

"Austin. It also went well. Did you enjoy your time off?"

"Oh yeah. It's so rare to get a Saturday and a Sunday off. My sister and I went shopping and to the movies and out to dinner. It was sweet."

"Well cool. Listen, you haven't seen Duke or Goliath around have you?"

"No, but I just got here. I suppose you want to talk to them about your big match tonight. Still nervous?"

"Yes. And I have no idea what we're doing."

"I suppose that would make me nervous too." Jade smiled. Her face said, Don't sweat it, we've all been there.

"Well, I'll be rooting for you, kid," she said. "I'm going to go get dressed and do some stretching. I'm on early tonight."

"Good luck. I'll see you later?"

"Sure. Find me after the show."

For the next hour, Joey paced the hallways of the backstage area. At six, one hour before showtime, Duke and Goliath appeared. Duke was speaking on his cell phone, and he looked frazzled.

Joey pushed through a group of crew members to get to Duke and Goliath right as they stepped into the backstage area. Goliath smiled at Joey and shook his hand. Duke ignored Joey and continued down the hall, speaking furiously into his cell phone. Goliath and Joey followed.

"We've had an issue brewing all weekend that doesn't look good for us," said Goliath, almost in a whisper.

"What is it?" said Joey.

They now were walking through the hall toward the performers' entrance. Right behind the entrance sat the control table, where Duke was stationed during the live shows, able to speak to the commentators and the referees through their headsets.

"Crusader's jumped ship," said Goliath.

Instant joy popped into Joey's gut. He hadn't felt comfortable around Crusader since their match last week.

"Really, he's already gone?" asked Joey.

"Yes. Apparently he's going to show up on *Riot* tonight. Duke's been on the horn with the lawyers all weekend. From the sounds of it, I don't think he can stop it."

Joey felt like the bully was absent from school. But then he wondered if the locker room would blame him for sending Crusader away. He could hear Crusader, with his ridiculous Canadian accent, telling the guys that having to do the job to Joey was the last straw.

"Nothing. We've got nothing. Those god-damned bastards," said Duke, snapping his cell phone shut. "I can't fucking believe this."

They arrived at the control table, which was still being set up by two crew members. Shane Walker was sitting against the wall behind the table, speaking to Monty Monroe, another GWA agent. Shane nodded his head to acknowledge Joey.

"Eight years I've worked with Scott," Duke said to no one in particular. "All he had to do was ask and I would have let him go. That asshole's gonna pay for this."

"They're not going to know what to do with him," said Goliath.

"Damn right they're not," said Duke. "Asshole would be cleaning toilets if it weren't for me. He got pushed because I thought he was loyal. Serves me right I guess."

"Gentlemen, we have a problem," Duke said to Shane and Monty.

"Come on, we'll catch up with Duke later," Goliath said to Joey. Without waiting for Joey to respond, Goliath started walking toward the locker rooms. Joey hesitated. He looked at Duke. All weekend he had wanted to speak with him. Now he was here. But it wasn't the time. Duke wasn't in a mood to talk. Joey caught up to Goliath.

"Do you know what we're going to do in our match tonight?" Joey asked.

"I've got it worked out. Duke might go over some specifics with us later. You're going to get the upper hand, you're going to beat the squat out of me, the ref's going to take a bump, you're going to pin me with no one there to count. With the ref still out, I'll come to and cheat, I might start with a low blow. By the time the ref's up, I'm going to hit you with the title belt and you'll be easy to pin."

"Okay," Joey said. Duke might go over specifics later. So this was it. There would be no script. Goliath had just laid out the standard match for a main event with a heel going over. Getting from spot to spot within that layout would be up to Joey and Goliath in the ring. They would call the spots to each other as they went. Joey hated wrestling that way.

"I'm going to go stake out a quiet place in the back somewhere," said Goliath. "I'll see you in a bit whenever Duke's ready to talk to us."

"Alright. See you later," said Joey. He didn't want to separate. He wanted to cling to Goliath or Duke until the match, to force them to tell him everything they knew. But it was common practice, practically tradition, that Goliath would disappear in the backstage area for an hour or so before his showtime. The official story, the one told to journalists and rookies and snoops backstage, was that Goliath needed private time to focus. After all, Goliath's intensity and focus in the ring, especially on TV and pay per views, was unmatched. That intensity carried out of the ring too. After his matches, Goliath might throw violent temper tantrums and pick fights with the boys backstage. These sorts of incidents had to be covered up to protect the official story, lest the truth escape. Everyone in the company, including Joey, knew that Goliath disappeared before his matches to jack up. Steroids, amphetamines, uppers. The laid-back demeanor that greeted Joey tonight would be gone when Goliath returned. In its place would be a chemically-enhanced wrestling beast.

Joey took a seat in front of one of the many televisions backstage and the show started. Duke sat at the control table and actively spoke into his headset during every match and TV segment. It was apparent that he wouldn't be speaking to Joey at all tonight.

For the next hour and forty-five minutes, the TV announcers hyped Joey's match like the Super Bowl. They talked about it during every segment, ignoring whatever was happening in the ring at the time to promote the night's main event. Clips of Joey winning the tournament were shown before every commercial break. A promotional video package of Goliath training in a gym to heavy metal music aired twice. At the start of the show's second hour, the announcers began a countdown until the World Title Match, periodically announcing the number of minutes left until the match began.

At 9:30, fifteen minutes before their curtain time, Goliath re-appeared from exile. His pupils were dilated, and his face was intense. He slapped Joey on the back as he walked past him.

"Joey, let's get you in place for your entrance," said Martha. Joey followed her out of the locker room area toward the black curtain.

✱   ✱   ✱   ✱

Joey's entrance was first. He stood behind the curtain, listening to Melissa Marcus, the ring announcer, "The following match is scheduled for one fall and is for the GWA World Heavyweight Championship!"

"Okay Joey, you're on," said a stagehand. Joey's music started, and he stepped into the wrestling world.

"Introducing first, weighing in at two hundred twenty pounds, Joey Mayhem!"

Thirty-thousand people filled the Astrodome from the floor to the ceiling, and they were all his fans. Signs bearing Joey's name floated atop the sea of people. Joey's hard rock music blared throughout the stadium. As he walked down the aisle, he could hear the shouts of the fans closest to him.

"Alright Joey!"

"Kick his ass tonight!"

Joey stepped into the ring, then worked the corners. At each ringpost, the crowd responded to him like he was some sort of deity. Hundreds of flashbulbs popped in the darkness. As Joey took it all in, he felt a shudder of fear that one day soon it all would end, and these same people who adored him now would grow to hate him, or worse, become indifferent.

"And introducing the champion, weighing in at three hundred pounds, Goliath!"

The arena lights dimmed, and Goliath's rhythmic heavy metal music started. The twenty foot TV screen above the entrance glowed bright orange with Goliath's black logo in the center. Goliath stepped into the arena, and his fiery orange pyrotechnics exploded around him. The crowd cheered for his impressive entrance.

Goliath stepped into the ring as the arena lights returned and his music faded. He handed his title belt to Nick Gaugin, the referee, who held it over his head and turned to display it to the entire audience. Nick walked to the edge of the ring, handed the belt to the timekeeper, and called for the bell, starting the match.

The crowd was already in a frenzy of anticipation. Joey sensed that these people expected the world from him tonight, and suddenly he felt naked.

He stepped forward for the first lock-up with Goliath. On Goliath's cue, they snapped into a wrestling hold, Joey's left hand on Goliath's right shoulder, his right hand grabbing onto Goliath's mane of blonde hair. Goliath won the lock-up and threw Joey to the floor. The crowd was a mix of cheers and boos at Goliath's initial victory.

Joey stood up slowly, keeping his eyes locked on Goliath's face. The two men circled the ring, staring each other down. The crowd remained hot. Goliath charged and they locked up again. This lock-up had a little more action. Joey instantly fell to one knee, but was able to get up, regain his balance, and push Goliath into a corner, where Nick stepped in and broke the hold. Obeying the ref, Goliath lifted his hands in the air, playing innocent, but as soon as Nick stepped out of the way, Goliath planted a knee right in Joey's abdomen. The crowd booed. Joey groaned and doubled over, allowing Goliath to knock him down and pummel him with fists and kicks.

Joey curled up in a protective stance and Nick pulled Goliath off of him. Goliath stepped to the middle of the ring and held up his hands to pander to the crowd, who were only too happy to boo and hiss. As Joey lay on the floor, doing his best to writhe in agony, he listened to the crowd's venom. The heat for this match was blistering. Everyone in the Astrodome wanted Joey to win.

He stumbled to his feet only to see Goliath charging at him with a vicious clothesline that sent him right back to the floor. Again, Goliath stepped away and pandered to the crowd.

Joey crawled back up and staggered toward Goliath again. As the babyface in peril, Joey would allow Goliath to beat him senseless until Goliath called a new spot. GWA matches usually played out as such. The heel would gain the upper hand and dominate the match until the crowd just couldn't bear it. The babyface wouldn't get in any real offense until the very end of the match, at which point the announcers could point out his stamina and heart.

After two more minutes of general pummeling, Goliath called for a more active spot. "Bulldog from the corner," he whispered to Joey before swinging him into the ringpost. An instant after Joey's back hit the turnbuckles, Goliath splashed right into him, then grabbed the back of his head and pulled him to the ground in a well-executed bulldog. Goliath rolled Joey over and covered him.

"One more near-fall after this," Goliath whispered.

Nick swept to the floor and pounded out one…two…then Joey used his feet to kick out of the cover.

Acting frustrated, Goliath grabbed Joey's hair and pulled him to his feet, only to deliver a hard punch to the face that sent Joey right back to the floor. Goliath lifted Joey again and whipped him off the ropes into a clothesline. Then he went for another cover.

One…two…Joey kicked out again.

The crowd was pleased that Joey was kicking out of the near-falls. Even though it appeared that Goliath was dominating the fight and was near a victory, the crowd knew well where this match was going. For the most seasoned fans, the fact that Goliath was in complete control of the match in the early-going was all the more reason to believe that Joey Mayhem would be the victor when the night was over.

Again, Goliath used Joey's hair to raise him from the mat.

"Ref bump, then you hit a superkick," Goliath whispered.

Joey looked to Nick to see if he was ready to take the obligatory "ref bump." Nick nodded his head once. Joey allowed Goliath to swing him into an irish whip. Goliath followed through and swung Joey toward the corner. On the way, Joey caught Nick and sandwiched him into the ringpost. As Joey reeled out of the corner, Goliath charged at him to deliver another clothesline. Right as Goliath swung, Joey ducked out of the way, and Goliath walloped Nick, who fell back in a blur of stripes. Nick landed on his back, rolled over to his stomach, and lay still as if unconscious. Goliath hesitated in surprise. Joey collected himself to prepare for the big kick that would switch the momentum of the match. Goliath turned around and Joey stepped forward to deliver a high kick right to his chin.

The kick connected.

Goliath snapped to the mat with the impact, making a loud slap as he fell. The crowd went crazy. Joey stumbled and fell on top of Goliath for the cover. Of course, with Nick face-first on the mat, there was no referee to make the count.

The crowd knew their job here, and counted in the referee's absence.

"One…two…three…four…five…six…" they yelled.

"Wesley Bunt," Joey whispered, signaling a classic wrestling spot. Wesley Bunt was a GWA wrestler in the 80s who became famous for losing his matches due to distraction. Whether it was a manager, another wrestler, a valet, or the fans, Wesley always paid attention to something other than his opponent and got walloped when he wasn't looking. Hence, in the GWA, if you wanted to have a spot where your opponent hit you from behind while something else distracted you, you called for a Wesley Bunt.

Joey rolled off Goliath and walked to the corner of the ring where Nick was laid out. Leaning down, he shook the referee as if trying to wake him. As he did this, Joey braced himself for a kick to the back of the head.

He continued shaking Nick.

"Wake up," Joey said aloud for effect. "Come on."

Nick lay still, as he was supposed to. A cardinal rule of refereeing was to remain unconscious if the babyface was in a position to win.

"Wake up ref," Joey said, frustrated that Goliath was taking so long.

The crowd was growing quiet. Joey was getting angry. In professional wrestling, a few seconds of downtime could ruin an entire match.

"What's taking so long?" Nick said discreetly.

Joey chose not to respond, since the television camera was pointed right at his face. He turned around. Goliath was still down on the mat with his eyes closed, unmoved from where he had landed. He was too experienced to miss a spot. He must have knocked himself unconscious when he fell to the mat, Joey thought. Now, with thirty thousand fans in the arena, and another million watching on television, Joey was going to have to fake his way through this mess until Goliath woke up to finish the match.

Joey looked around to assess the situation. Goliath was down in the middle of the ring, Nick had wisely chosen to remain strewn out in the corner. Nick wore an earpiece through which Duke could speak to him while the match was in progress. No doubt Duke would keep the ref down until Goliath got up. It was Joey's job to figure out how to entertain the fans and keep the match going until that happened.

And suddenly it was all familiar. He had been here before. His second professional match ever, in his hometown, against Oscar Esquivel, with his whole world watching. He had messed up a superkick and knocked out Oscar's front teeth. It was the worst mistake of his career, and now he had done it again, only this time he had left his opponent out cold.

And this time it was on national television, for the World Title.

No, he couldn't have done it again. He'd mastered the move since then, probably better than anyone else in the business. He knew what a well-executed superkick felt like. Just light contact after your leg is fully extended. He had done it hundreds of times. Tonight was no different. And he would never forget that jolt of face-smashing inertia that came after the botched kick. It wasn't there tonight. The kick was fine. Goliath had taken the bump wrong.

Stay in character, Joey told himself. What would Joey Mayhem do if this were all for real? Joey Mayhem wants to win the World Title. His opponent is unconscious on his back in the ring. All Joey needs is a referee to count to three.

Joey stepped under the ropes and walked to the ring announcer's table. He grabbed a microphone and rolled back into the ring. Putting one foot on Goliath's chest (a legal cover for a pinfall) Joey said into the microphone, "Can we get another referee out here?"

The crowd went nuts. They loved this sort of chaos. As they began their own pinfall count again, "One...two...three...four..." Joey thought to himself that this wasn't turning out all bad. The crowd was very much into it, and they were still on the side of the babyface. Joey had done his part, Duke would send out a new referee to make this look like it all might have been planned. Maybe Goliath would wake up. If not, Joey was scheduled to win the belt down the road anyway. Everyone would understand. Beneath his foot, Joey could feel Goliath's chest moving up and down. If Goliath could just pull himself together, this all would turn out fine.

"Seven...eight...nine..." the crowd continued to chant. And then Dr. Ernie Trott, a long-time GWA physician, came out from behind the curtain and ran to the ring. The crowd popped for his entrance like he was a wrestling superstar. Dr. Trott slid into the ring and waived his arms at Joey, asking him to get off Goliath. The crowd booed. Dr. Trott knelt down next to Goliath, and took his pulse off his neck. As he did so, the crowd's boos faded to silence as they realized the injury might be real.

A hand touched Joey's left shoulder from behind. It was Nick. He was standing, and out of character.

"Let's get out of the ring," said Nick.

No, Joey wanted to say. No, he's going to be alright. This is a terrible idea; the match will be ruined. The stupid lug just took a bad bump. Maybe if he weren't so drugged up he'd be more careful.

But still aware of the TV cameras all around him, Joey said nothing, and followed Nick through the ropes and to the timekeeper's table, where steel chairs for skull-bashing were always kept. Nick and Joey each unfolded a chair and sat.

In the ring, Dr. Trott was holding smelling salts beneath Goliath's nose. Goliath's eyes opened, and he tried to sit up, only to fall back again.

The crowd remained quiet. In recent years, professional wrestling had blurred the line between real injuries and fake ones, making it difficult for fans to determine if they were being worked or not.

The television audience went to commercial. When they came back, they saw a team of paramedics sliding a straight board under Goliath, and, on a 3-count, lifting and carrying him out of the ring. They gently slid him under the bottom rope and onto a stretcher. With cameramen following, the paramedics rolled the stretcher out of the arena, through the backstage area, and onto an ambulance. The crowd applauded as Goliath was rolled out. The television announcers spoke in hushed tones to the home audience, using platitudes like, "This is bigger than the show. We all hope Goliath is okay. He and his family will be in our prayers."

For the fans watching at home, the last shot of the night was the ambulance driving into the darkness.

"Okay Joey, we're off the air," said Nick, holding his hand over his earpiece. "They're going to play your music. Make a quick exit."

And, right on cue, Joey's music began. He stood up, faced the crowd, and raised his hands. He got very little reaction from the confused fans. Quickly, he walked to the ramp and headed out.

CHAPTER 13

▼

No one greeted Joey when he stepped through the curtain. The backstage area was empty.

He needed water. Usually one of the trainers or a stagehand had a bottle of water for him when he came through the curtain. He turned left to go down the corridor to the locker rooms, where he remembered a fountain on the wall.

Safire came out of the women's locker room with wet hair, wearing jeans and a T-shirt.

"Did everyone go out to the parking lot?" Joey asked her.

"Why would they? What's going on?" she said.

"Goliath got knocked out in our match. They put him in an ambulance and took him out."

"Really? What happened?" Her tone had gone from curious in the first question to accusing in the second.

"I don't know, I...it was...weird," Joey was tired and didn't care to explain.

Safire walked past him, into the corridor that led to the parking lot. He followed her.

As they reached the end of the hall, they encountered a herd of wrestlers, all of whom were coming in through the back door.

"Is everything okay?" Safire asked Deep Six, the first of the pack.

"I hope so," he said. "What happened out there Joey?"

"I don't know," Joey said. "He must have taken the bump wrong. He was out cold."

"Is he awake now?" Safire asked.

"He's conscious, but he's really woozy," said Deep Six. "He couldn't even sit up. They're taking him to a hospital just a few blocks down. I got directions from the driver, and a few of us are gonna head over there in a minute if you want to come."

Deep Six was now speaking only to Safire, as if Joey wasn't there.

"Yeah," she said. "I'll grab my bag and meet you in the parking lot."

Duke appeared from behind Deep Six and stopped walking when he saw Joey.

"Joey, hi. Let's take a walk," he said. Without waiting for Joey to respond, Duke put his arm on Joey's shoulder and led him back down the corridor toward the locker rooms.

"How are you doing?" Duke said.

"I'm fine," said Joey. "How's Goliath?"

"He was awake and coherent when they took him away. He's in good hands."

Duke said nothing more as they continued walking. Joey knew he was being taken someplace private for a tongue-lashing.

They stopped when they came to a corner, in front of a storage closet. Just behind them, wrestlers were walking in and out of the locker room as they got themselves dressed to leave. Joey wished he was getting dressed with them. He wanted to know what they were saying.

"Listen, Joey. I don't know what happened out there. No one will know until we've watched the tape and spoken to Goliath, but you were way out of line grabbing a microphone and calling for another referee."

Well maybe I'd have known better what to do if you'd given us any booking directions, Joey thought, but knew better than to say.

"Some of the guys who were watching have their panties all in a tizzle now, and it's going to be hard for me keep up your push," said Duke. His face and voice reminded Joey of a soccer coach from childhood, who always finished his sharpest criticism with a fatherly slap on the ass.

"I understand," said Joey. His push was over. Maybe this was for the best. Maybe now he could start at the bottom and work his way up, like a normal rookie.

"Anyway, as soon as we know if Goliath can perform next week, we'll re-work the story and just make this a part of it. We'll talk this week about where we'll take the story from here."

"Okay," Joey said, not exactly sure what Duke meant.

"But until we know more about Goliath's condition, we have to be careful. I'm thinking he's okay, which is good for you, because maybe after another match next week, a better match, some of the guys around here will forget about what happened tonight."

"You're thinking of running a re-match next week?" Joey asked. This didn't make any sense.

"Oh yeah. I think tonight's match will make for a good story going into next week. It'll make the stakes that much higher for when you eventually win the belt."

"I'm still winning the belt?" Joey said, and immediately wished he hadn't. He couldn't contain his surprise, and had spoken too loudly.

"You've got a lot of nerve kid," said a deep, recognizable voice from down the hall. It was Jumbo. When Joey turned to look he saw an entire gang of wrestlers staring at him, all of whom had probably been eavesdropping.

"Easy big guy, it's been a long night," Duke said to Jumbo, who was now approaching them. Behind Jumbo the entire locker room was watching the burgeoning conversation. Joey could sense their eagerness. Jumbo was going to speak for all of them.

"I can't believe this kid is wondering about whether or not he'll get the strap after he laid out his partner and left him in the cold," Jumbo said.

"What are you talking about 'left him in the cold'?" said Joey.

"I'm talking about you sucking out Goliath's heat, kid. I'm talking about you standing on his chest out there like a god-damned prima donna while he's out cold because you fucked up a kick. Now you're wondering if you'll get the strap. Jesus Christ you've got a lot to learn."

"That's enough Rob, go home and get some rest," Duke said in a volume that communicated to everyone present, not just Jumbo.

Jumbo stood and glared at Joey for a long second before letting out a sassy click of his tongue and turning to leave. The other wrestlers dispersed, except for one.

Joey wished Duke hadn't stepped in—he didn't get a chance to respond. Now it was too late. Now the whole locker room probably thought it was his kick that knocked out Goliath. He needed to tell them that the super kick went off perfectly, that he had done it a hundred times before, and tonight felt no different. Just light contact with the cheek, perfectly safe, he would have known had he messed up. Goliath took the bump wrong. It happens. He let his head snap into the mat when he fell. Didn't he? Didn't they see that? What had they seen? The superkick had turned Joey sideways and he hadn't seen anything. Maybe he had missed the kick. Maybe he had missed the kick and the TV audience could tell. Come to think of it, he had no idea what Clive and Johnny were saying to the audience at home. Maybe tomorrow the whole wrestling world would think, would know, that Joey had botched a kick and injured his colleague.

"I'd like to get dressed and get over to see Goliath as soon as possible," Joey said. He looked down the hall at Jade, the only straggler from the group of eavesdroppers. She approached Joey and Duke.

"I've got a quick meeting right now," said Duke. He lowered his voice as if to purposefully exclude Jade from the conversation. "Why don't we get together in an hour and head over there?"

Joey thought about the other wrestlers already at the hospital, about what they might be saying. He needed to be there. He needed to ask Goliath himself. But if he waited for Duke, who appeared to be his only protection from the raging locker room…

"Actually, if it's okay with you Duke," said Jade, "I'm headed over there right now and I'll just take Joey with me."

No, thought Joey. He had this sudden urge to cling to Duke, like a little boy to his father.

Duke's expression went blank. "Okay," he said. "Joey, you do whatever you need to do."

"We'll see you later Duke," said Jade.

"Alright," he said. "Good night."

The deal was done. Apparently, Joey was going to the hospital now, without Duke's protection, to be thrown to the lions, and he was sure to drag Jade down with him.

As Duke walked away, Jade put her arm on Joey's back.

"You okay?" she said.

"Yeah, I'm fine," said Joey. "Listen, you don't have to go with me. I don't know if it's good for you to be with me right now. I'm thinking that I'm not going to be very popular around here tonight."

"You'll be fine. And if you're not, who cares? I'm not very popular around here as it is."

Joey stopped walking and turned to look at Jade. He wanted to hug her and cry. Minutes ago everyone else backstage had been ready to lynch him. Were it not for Duke's presence, who knows what would have happened? And when the angry veterans dispersed in anger, no doubt to go off and badmouth Joey together, Jade had stayed behind. She was ready to march off with him, the two of them against the world, and that was fine with Joey. It was better than fine. Everyone else could have the approval of the boys backstage and the cheering of the fans. He could have Jade.

But it wasn't fair to her.

"Thanks so much—"

"Don't mention it, Joey. Why don't we get dressed and we'll go. I'll meet you out here in a few minutes. You look drained. Can I get you a bottle of water?"

Joey smiled.

"Yes, I'd like that."

*   *   *   *

"We're here to see Patrick French."

"What floor?"

"I don't know."

"When was he admitted?"

"Tonight, probably less than an hour ago."

"One moment."

Joey and Jade stood in the empty lobby of Houston General Hospital. The lobby was meant to be illuminated by skylights. At night, the purple fluorescent lamps and the soft dentist office music on the speakers made for a creepy setting. At the main desk in the lobby's center sat an old black woman, with silver hair, curvy glasses, and a slow Texas drawl.

"Mr. French was discharged at eleven forty."

"Discharged? So he's okay?"

"I don't know, sir."

"Well, how can we find out?"

"Sir, that's a legally confidential matter. If you're friends with Mr. French I suggest you allow him to inform you of his medical condition."

Joey looked at Jade to confirm that she shared his confusion. She did. Joey was about to ask if anyone was admitted under the name Goliath, but realized that was ridiculous. Goliath insisted that everyone use his wrestling name when communicating to him, but he would use his real name at the hospital, wouldn't he?

"Do you think he'd check in under—"

"I was just thinking that," said Jade.

"Ma'am," began Jade, "could you tell us if anyone was admitted tonight under the name Goliath?"

"Goliath?" The woman broke the syllables so distinctly that they sounded like three separate words.

"Yes," said Jade.

"G-O-L-I-A-T-H?"

"That's right," said Jade.

"And the last name?"

"No last name."

"One moment please."

The woman clicked around on her computer with the care and patience of someone who didn't grow up with computers.

"I'm sorry, no Goliath was admitted tonight."

"Okay, thanks," said Joey.

"You all have a nice evening."

Joey and Jade exited through a sliding glass door and stood on the sidewalk in front of the hospital.

"What do you suppose happened?" Joey asked.

"I have no idea. That's really strange."

A flashbulb went off from behind the bushes. For a brief instant, Joey's mind was back in the ring, with hundreds of fans taking his picture like he was an exhibit at a zoo. A rustle from behind the bushes caught Joey's attention and he saw a young man running away.

"What the hell?" said Joey.

"I bet that picture shows up on the Internet tomorrow," said Jade.

"Shit, you're right. Should we try to catch him?"

"Oh no. You want to be seen right here, at the hospital, so the fans know you're concerned about your fallen comrade. Hopefully you were looking distraught when he snapped the photo. It'll be good PR."

"What about for you? Is it good for you to be seen here with me?"

"Who knows? Maybe I'll get a rub. After all, you are the future world champ."

"Maybe. I don't know if there's going to be any rub for me to give after tonight."

"Don't worry about it Joey. This sort of thing happens in wrestling, the fans know that. And the ones who don't will think it was all a work. Besides, it sounds like Goliath's just fine. He's already been discharged."

"I hope so." Joey more than hoped. He pined, yearned, that Goliath was okay. Part of Joey's mind raced with the idea that Goliath's quick discharge would fly around the Internet, and Goliath would be the one to bear the blame for tonight's fiasco. Joey could see the signs in the stands next week. Neon green posterboard with black marker: "Goliath the Wussy".

The thought, the joy of the thought, made Joey cringe. What was he becoming? Was he so eager for acceptance that he'd take delight in someone else's misfortune?

"I hope he's okay," Joey said again.

"Well, come on. We're not going to learn anything standing here. We'll just be fodder for more paparazzi. You wanna go get coffee?"

The thought of hot coffee late at night after all that had happened sounded awful.

"That sounds good," he said.

CHAPTER 14

▼

They landed at the Green Dragon coffeehouse, one block down from the hotel. When they arrived a little after twelve thirty, the cafe was empty, no music was playing, and Joey was sure the shop was about to close. Fifteen minutes later, the place was filled with twenty-somethings, more employees seemed to materialize, and two folk singers with guitars took up stools in front of the empty fireplace.

"The bar crowd," explained Jade. "As the bars close, they come here. They'll keep this place hopping until four in the morning."

"You've been here before?"

"Oh yeah. We usually hit Houston twice a year. I always stay at the Hyatt, and I always come here after the show. You'll find yourself doing the same. As the tour goes on, pretty soon the cities stop changing. You hit the same places, you start to learn what's where. You'll develop these little spaces of familiarity at each stop."

Joey looked down at his coffee. He didn't want it. Over the years, he'd trained his body to reject anything that was off the path of supreme fitness. He could have ordered juice, or water. But Jade wanted to go out for coffee. Jade stood by him when…he didn't even want to think about the damage she might have done to her own standing backstage tonight. The least he could do was have coffee with her.

"I think I experienced some of that in the indies. The second time through a town, it already felt like home," he said.

"That's right. Just wait until the tenth time through, or the twentieth. Houston's a city we usually hit twice a year. I've lost count of how many times I've been to this coffee house. But I know those paintings on the walls. I know these cups. I know these singers. Next time I'll probably even know their songs."

"Do you get tired of it?"

"Sometimes. Everybody does. Especially when things aren't going well. Last year I had a stretch where I did a gravy bowl match one week, a bra and panties match the next, then was off TV for three more weeks."

"I remember that. I wasn't in the GWA yet, but I remember those two matches, then a long stretch where we didn't see you."

"I hope you're the only one. I sure want to forget it. We had two shows in Vancouver that time around. I just did dark matches, and at the second one I blew a spot, botched a suplex and dropped Barbara Lipke on her head. She was alright, but I could have paralyzed her, easily. That night I decided I would retire when my contract was up."

"Really? It was that bad." Joey wondered if he should be feeling worse than he was about tonight's accident with Goliath.

"Oh yeah. I was sure I was done. It wasn't remotely worth it. Here I was, thirty-one years old, divorced, no kids, lots of money but no time to spend it and no one to spend it on—after that match with Barbara I just knew I'd regret it if I didn't get out and start a normal life before it was too late."

Joey looked at Jade and imagined her as a mother. It fit, and for an instant, everything seemed clear. What he was doing was absurd. He was pretending to beat people up every night in a different stadium in a different city, all the while clamoring for their adoration. He did it because it made him a star. It gave him the riches and accolades that made celebrities superior to everyone else. He was living the dream. But in doing so, he was giving up a lifetime of moments like these. Sitting in a coffee shop with a woman, talking about whatever came up.

"What happened?" he said.

"The tour went on. I wrestled more shows. I got back on TV. Duke put me in a program with Safire that got hot. When my contract came up in February, I remembered wanting to quit, but I just couldn't do it. And, totally in the moment, I asked Duke if he could extend my new contract from two years to three. He did. I thought it was for the best. If that desire to quit ever came up again, I'd have to wait even longer before I could do it. It was a huge mistake."

"Why, because you want to go to Revolution?" Joey said.

"That's part of it. There's other stuff too."

"Like what?"

"Don't worry about it." Jade's voice and body turned rock solid. Joey could tell she didn't like talking about this part of her past.

"I wonder if I'll ever want to quit," he said.

"Don't be surprised or scared if, at some point, it gets to be too much and you want to quit. It happens to everyone. It hasn't happened to you yet because you're still on the upswing. You're chasing the title for the first time right now. You're the new, hot thing going and the fans love you. Even all this shit backstage and tonight's mess isn't going to derail you. What you need to do now, more than anything, is enjoy this. Someday, after you've been the number one guy for awhile, some new kid is gonna come up and the fans will take to him. You'll be asked to change your gimmick and become a heel. You'll play the coward and the fans will boo you. You'll tell everyone you love it when the crowd gets hot, when you've got them all worked up, and a part of you will. But secretly you'll wish they still loved you. Not because you don't like playing the heel, but because you know that some of that hatred you're getting from the stands is real. Some of that hatred is their way of saying they're bored with you."

"Gracious," Joey said, smiling. "That's a fun thing to think about."

Jade's face lit up with the realization that she'd said too much. "I'm sorry, Joey. I don't mean to sound bitter. I should slow down here. I hope you don't think I'm bitter."

"I don't think you're bitter at all Jade. I think you're a realist who's aware of how things are and I appreciate you sharing your wisdom with me."

"God, I feel old tonight," Jade said, then she laughed in an attempt to defuse her seriousness. Joey reached across the table and touched her hand. He gave a light squeeze on her fingers and smiled at her.

"Seriously Jade, I appreciate you sticking up for me tonight in the locker room."

"I didn't stick up for you." Jade had turned her palm and they were now holding hands across the table.

"Yes you did. You stayed around after all the guys went their separate ways and…I know that just by being with me tonight you're making all sorts of trouble for yourself."

"I've already made all sorts of trouble for myself, Joey. Whatever falls out after tonight will be small potatoes. And trust me, I know firsthand how unfair the politics around here can be, and I think it's shit. We'll see what comes of Goliath's injury and deal with it from there. I think this whole thing will blow over by next week."

"I hope so."

Jade took her hand back to grab her coffee mug and finish it off. Joey looked at the wall clock behind the counter. One in the morning. It reminded him that he was supposed to be sleepy.

"You ready?" Jade asked.

Ready to face the other wrestlers in the locker room? Ready to deal with the fallout on the Internet of tonight's title match? Jade had pushed her empty coffee mug to the center of the table. She must have meant ready to leave.

"Yes," said Joey.

CHAPTER 15

▼

Taken from www.wrestlinghotline.com

Greetings slugs.

Today is Tuesday, May 2nd, and this is your Tuesday Morning Hangover, where our headaches aren't caused by freak wrestling accidents.

My fellow slugs, as I write this, it's five A.M. and I haven't slept all night. Judging by the activity on the boards, I know I'm not alone. For those of you who weren't shooting the midnight black with the rest of us, here's a recap of the night's activity on the net.

10:56 pm, On *GWA Burn*, Joey Mayhem superkicks Goliath in their main event championship matchup, sending Goliath to the floor and the crowd to its feet.

10:57 pm, Goliath has been down for almost a minute and the fast-paced match takes on a decidedly 'What's going on?' turn.

10:58 pm, Matrix Bob puts up this post on the Hotline Newsboard: "Does anyone else think Goliath might be out cold?"

10:59 pm, Goliath hasn't moved for more than two minutes, the match has broken down, Matrix Bob's post has 11 responses attached, and everyone watching knows something is wrong.

11:00 pm, Dr. Ernie Trott runs in from the back, waves Joey away from Goliath, and calls in the EMTs. Referee Nick Gaugin breaks character and stands up like he was never knocked out during the match.

11:04 pm, the EMTs load Goliath into the ambulance and drive out of the arena. The match was never declared finished, and no winner was announced.

11:05 pm, *Burn* goes off the air. The final shot is of the ambulance driving away.

11:35 pm, GWA.com posts a mysterious message in the headlines section reading, "Goliath was injured in his match with Joey Mayhem and was taken to a nearby hospital for observation."

11:30pm–12:00am, the Hotline Newsboard lights up, with a record 7800 posts in an hour. Fierce debate erupts as to whether or not the ending of *Burn* was a work.

12:10am, Chandler Dresby of Wrestlingdailytribune.com reports that Goliath is at Houston General and is under observation for head trauma. He does not give a source for his information. The online debate about the legitimacy of the injury continues. One camp swears the injury was real, noting that the finish to the match didn't make any sense. Another camp says that the injury would make for the perfect swerve and would allow the GWA to stretch the Goliath/Joey Mayhem feud all the way to the next pay per view. A third camp argues that the injury was a "worked shoot," i.e. the GWA will pretend that the injury was real even though it was fake. I will weigh in with my own opinion later in the column.

12:30am, Houston-area fans are posting sightings of wrestlers at Houston General. Joey Mayhem, Jade Sleek, Deep Six, and Lord Mayberry have been seen by fans in or around Houston General Hospital. The online debate leans toward the injury being legitimate.

2:00am, the Hotline Newsboard finally starts to quiet down as east-coasters hit the hay. The Net is close to agreement that tonight's finish was real.

4:30am, GWA.com reports that Goliath is under observation for head trauma, confirming what Chandler Dresby reported earlier in the night. The posters on the Hotline Newsboard (and there were still a lot of them, even at this late hour) have the proof they need.

And that brings us here. The sun is about to come up as I write this. I hope to have it on the site in 3 hours or less, so we'd better get going.

Ratings Report:

GWA Burn pulled an overall 4.7, with a 4.5 in the first hour, a 4.8 in the second hour, and a 4.8 in the overrun. For the second week in a row, the numbers are up, and last night's *Burn* was the highest rated so far this year.

Revolution Riot got an overall of 4.9, with a 4.9 in the first hour, a 5.0 in the second, and a 4.8 in the overrun. More on that later, first…

The High Points:

GWA Burn—Well, where do you put it? On the one hand, last night's main event has already taken on an historic feel. On the other hand, the match itself was nothing special, ending with a non-finish. Either way, I'm going to call the odd main event a high point just because it has everyone talking.

Revolution Riot—Scott Rollins. Wow. Didn't see that one coming. They've got to be a little disappointed that last night's *Burn* generated so much buzz when they had a big buzz point themselves. Scott Rollins, formerly known in the GWA as Crusader, made a surprise entrance in the second hour, interrupting Lucifer's promo, and throwing himself right into the main event scene.

The News:

Huge news on the Family Television Group vs. GWA battle front. Wrestlingdailytribune.com is reporting that Imagine Television Network (ITN) is going to make specific contractual requirements of *GWA Burn* before they renew the show, presumably in response to pressure from the Family Television Group. Specifically, ITN will require an outside consultant to sit in on all creative and production meetings regarding *GWA Burn*. This consultant will have the power to nix any storyline or segment idea if deemed inappropriate. *Burn*'s television contract is up for renewal next month, so presumably this new level of network control could start as soon as July.

Slugs, our response to this horrendous idea must be swift and strong.

Hence, the…

Feature:

As promised, I have spent the past week researching web sites and digging through public records (specifically IRS Form 990, a public domain document for non-profits like the FTG), and have collected a definitive list of the Family Television Group's biggest donors.

Rather than beginning an ineffective, uncoordinated spam campaign, I'd like for us to focus our efforts, one donor at a time.

Our first target should be the biggest, and the FTG's largest donor, by far, is some outfit called Americans For Productive & Responsible Entertainment & Media. Total contributions last year: $1,650,000. This group does not have a web site, in fact there is no mention of them on the Internet anywhere. Luckily for you, I'm a scrupulous researcher, and went off to the business library at Northeastern Illinois University, where I found this wily bunch listed in public domain IRS records. Here's what I know: Americans For Productive & Responsible Entertainment & Media was founded two years ago by Andrew Smith and Jonathan Taylor, both from Calgary. Why two Canadians would start a group called Americans for blah blah blah is beyond me, but there you have it. Their headquarters are in Wilmington, Delaware, and their charter declares their purpose to be, "The promotion of psychologically healthy, socially responsible entertainment in the mass media."

Send your hate mail to this address:
Americans For Productive & Responsible Entertainment & Media
3412 North Hanover
Wilmington, DE 74565

Our second target is The Betsy Piper Foundation, whose total contributions to the FTG last year were $890,000. This group does have a web site, albeit a lame one: www.betsypiperfoundation.org. The web site proclaims the foundation as "a monetary advocate for those causes which Betsy held most dearly." No mention anywhere on the web site of what those causes are, where the group is located, who is involved, or anything else that might possibly be of use to anyone. Just page after page about the lovely Betsy Piper, an old-world New England socialite, who apparently was the Martha Stewart of her day.

Once again yours truly found more useful information at the library. Here's where we might be onto something. Like Americans For blah blah blah, The Betsy Piper Foundation was founded two years ago, by two men from Calgary. The founders of this group are named Jeremy Washington and Peter Jackson. And, the Foundation's headquarters are also in Wilmington, Delaware. Coincidence? I think not. My initial guess is that there's a racket of Old School Canadians who want a return to carnie-style wrestling and have put together a huge consortium to shut down the Americanized product. Okay, that might be a little far-fetched. Nonetheless, there's certainly something here worth looking into. Is there a connection between these two non-profit groups? Is there one supreme target to unearth, whom we can shower with hate mail so venomous as to make an actual impact on the FTG's campaign against our beloved past-time? Hop to it slugs!

In the meantime, here's the address for mail to The Betsy Piper Foundation:

The Betsy Piper Foundation
PO Box 1212
Wilmington, DE 75448

And until next time, this is Steve Garcia. Peace.

Return. Click. Send to FTP.

Steve Garcia stood up and stretched his hands to the ceiling. It was now a little after six a.m. His mom would be waking up soon. Maybe she'd make him breakfast before he went to bed.

His eyeballs ached. He had been staring at either his computer or his television for almost twelve hours now. All for that column, for his readers, the slugs.

Steve began maintaining Wrestlinghotline.com in 1996, when the web was for nerds and wrestling was for losers. Back then, the web site was just an offshoot of the actual Wrestling Hotline, a 976 number that fielded 200 calls a day at fifty cents a minute. As a teenager, Steve was a regular caller to the Hotline (his mom allowed him two dollars worth of calls a week) and he was the first to answer the Hotline's advertised request for a web site designer.

Steve expected to work as a webmaster with a boss, posting and maintaining the web site to the specifications of the Hotline's owner, a reclusive New Yorker named Ben Evans. But a week after Steve launched the site, the phone number went inactive and Ben Evans disappeared. That week Steve posted his first column anyway. No one seemed to care.

So the next week Steve posted another column. His phone didn't ring, his email box sat empty, the wrestling world marched forward and no one said a thing.

The next week Steve posted another column. He received three emails from readers, flaming him for his opinions.

The next week Steve posted another column, and his Inbox flooded. He had developed a following.

In 1997, the wrestling boom began. In 1998, the web became mainstream. In 1999 Steve purchased software to follow the traffic on his site. By 2000, he was the most widely read wrestling columnist on the Internet, a title he still held.

And no one thought twice that Wrestlinghotline.com was registered to Wrestling Hotline Associated, a sole proprietorship in the state of New York whose founder and owner had been AWOL since 1996.

Several times Steve had considered trying to get ownership of the domain name, or moving the site to a different location. His readership was in the hundreds of thousands and he never made a cent.

But he never got around to it. Making money with his site would be nice, and it might shut up his nagging mom, but it would require real work. He would have to file papers with the state. He would have to pay taxes. He would have to keep records.

Someday he'd do all that.

For now, he wrote. He also trolled the message boards and chatrooms, swam through thousands of emails, bounced ideas off of friends and Internet contacts, and kept abreast of everything wrestling that was published on the web or in the newsletters. All his work came to a head every Monday night, when he worked on The Tuesday Hangover, his site's centerpiece. For whatever reason, wrestling fans on the Internet had grown to love Steve's random musings and ramblings on the wrestling they had watched the night before.

The universal "computer is done" bell sounded on the speakers. The file transfer was complete. Steve went back to his computer and sat down. The Tuesday Hangover was posted. He opened the web site and quickly double-checked his column for any errors he might have missed. When he got to the last word he felt a strong sense of relief. A whole night of work and play went into that column. Now he could sleep until mid-afternoon. By the time he was up again, he'd have at least 200 emails from his readers.

The little envelope appeared in the lower right corner. Someone already had something to say.

Steve double-clicked on the email icon.

To: Steve Garcia
From: Aaron Culley

Steve,

I was at the Houston GWA show last night. The shit rocked.

But that's not the point. After the show, my friend and I went to Houston General to see if we could get a look at Goliath, and we did! But he was on his way out. Some long-haired dude had taken him on a wheelchair out of the hospital and helped him get in a truck and they just drove off. This was at like, midnight. Goliath looked dazed, but was able to get into the truck without any assistance.

Big deal, right? So he got discharged at midnight. Probably a hundred people snooping around could have told you that.

Here's the shit though. My friend and I raced back to our car and followed the truck. They went to Houston Medical Center! Pulled right into another hospital! Goliath must be totally fucked up. I bet his brains are so scrambled that Houston General didn't even have all the equipment they needed to fix him. Or maybe GWA wanted him to see someone specific at a bigger hospital.

Thought you might want to know.

Aaron Culley.

Steve closed the email. Going back to his web browser, he took a quick trip to the competition's site, www.wrestlingdailytribune.com. He scanned their story about Goliath's injury in last night's match. Taken to Houston General. Concussion suspected. Stayed overnight for observation.

Perfect. He had a scoop.

Steve re-opened TuesdayHangover0502.htm.

At the top of the page, he wrote: "Breaking News: Goliath transferred from Houston General to Houston Medical Center."

Ten minutes later he posted his updated file, complete with an edited version of Mr. Culley's email.

He turned back and looked at his bed. It was so inviting. But now there was a new development. More had to be coming. Steve sat up in his chair, rolled his head around a few times, and settled in for a morning of surfing and digging.

CHAPTER 16

▼

The phone was ringing. Please don't let it be Fran Wallace again.

Joey rolled over and picked it up.

"Hello?"

"Hello, Joey? This is Duke."

Joey sat up, rubbed his eyes, and cleared his head. It wasn't often that you got a phone call from Duke.

"Yes Duke," he said. Then he panicked. He looked over his shoulder, back at the bed, to confirm the source of his fear. It was real. Jade was sleeping on the other side of the bed. This was her room. It was morning and Joey was in Jade's hotel room, awakened by the phone while sleeping next to her. How did Duke know he was here?

"Listen Joey, have you got any plans for the two days off?"

"No," said Joey without bothering to think if he had any plans. His immediate instinct was to just do whatever Duke said. He told himself to act like there was nothing unusual about Duke finding him in Jade's room.

"Good. Joey, I'd like you to stay in Houston if you don't mind. Fran's got some publicity work for you tomorrow, and I'd like to meet with you today."

"Sure. What time?"

"Let's say noon, in my suite. I'm in 2200, just a straight shot up the elevator from where you are. We'll have lunch and discuss some things."

Where you are, Duke had said, with no question or concern in his voice. Joey picked up the alarm clock and turned it violently to view its face. It was almost eleven.

"Alright Duke. I'll see you then."

"Wonderful."

Joey hung up and rolled out of the bed. Jade was still completely asleep. Neither the phone nor the conversation had disturbed her. Probably for the best. Maybe she didn't need to know about that conversation yet. Who else knew he was here?

The night before, Joey and Jade had left the coffee shop, returned together to the Hyatt, and walked to Jade's room, very much intending to say good night. In the comfortable silence of the elevator, Joey had prepared closing comments for the evening, a neat turn of phrase or two to express to Jade one last time how much he appreciated her companionship tonight, how completely he understood the potential fallout backstage she faced for standing by the reckless Joey Mayhem.

And when they came to the door of room 1412, Joey lifted his shoulders and barreled his chest in preparation for the words. But Jade didn't behave properly. She immediately slid her keycard into the lock and opened the door without once turning back for a final goodnight. And as she fluidly opened the door and stepped inside Joey waited, thinking she'd turn back and accept a goodnight from the other side of the threshold. But instead she held the door open. With her back to him still she held the door open, as if they were roommates and there was no question that he was coming inside.

So Joey followed her in. Her room, identical to his, began with a living room area and kitchenette, separated from the bedroom and bathroom by an open doorway.

"Excuse me for one second while I go pee," Jade said, turning to Joey for the first time since leaving the elevator.

"Sure," Joey said back.

Jade went through the bedroom to the bathroom, and Joey took a seat on the sofa in the living room area. Over the silence of the room, Joey could hear Jade peeing. It was two in the morning. A mild coffee buzz and the excitement of the unknown kept Joey wired despite his exhaustion.

The toilet flushed, Jade emerged, smiled at Joey, sat right next to him, and kicked her shoes off. Was he supposed to kiss her? Joey dove into his recently abandoned speech.

"Jade, thank you again for standing by me tonight. I can't tell you how much it means to me."

As he spoke, he could tell Jade was waiting for him to finish. She was looking right in his eyes and was much closer than she needed to be. The prepared speech had three more sentences, one about her friendship, one about her wisdom, one about her courage. Joey abandoned the lecture and kissed her.

A minute later, Jade led him from the couch to the bedroom. And Joey was glad, euphoric, that he had laid out Goliath tonight. And fuck all of them backstage who wanted him to be sorry. Fuck anyone who thought he didn't deserve his spot in the main event. And God help the next person who made some backhand remark about Jade's history with Goliath and her ex-husband. Joey would beat the shit out of them.

And now, with full daylight creeping under the curtains and the alarm clock confirming it was almost the afternoon, Joey wondered what he had done. Sex with Jade was one thing. One beautiful, wonderful thing that Joey hoped would happen again in the next city, and the next, and maybe lead to a house in the Hamptons and 2 kids who had no interest in becoming wrestlers. But Duke's phone call, direct to Jade's room, in the late morning, looking for Joey—that was another thing. The only way Duke could know Joey was here was if everyone knew.

Joey walked out of the bedroom, through the entrance area, and to the door. It stood closed, locked to anyone who didn't have a key card. On this side of the door was safety, and love, dare he say it, yes, love. Two people and a night full of real love expressed in its highest form. On the other side…

Joey looked through the peephole. He was only in briefs, and if the entire world was out there waiting for him to come out and confirm what Duke already knew, that Joey had drunk from the company trough, the same one that Goliath had drunk from last year in a gossip frenzy that lit the wrestling world on fire, Joey would be dressed first. The tunnel vision of the peephole showed an empty hallway. Closed doors and generic hotel wall paper. How did Duke know he was here? There was no answer in the peephole.

Joey turned the doorknob clockwise until he heard a click. He pulled on the door slowly. Light from the hallway appeared on the floor. He continued pulling. The same vision that was in the peephole began to take shape on the other side. No one would be out there. Joey swung the door past his body and was now standing in the doorway of Jade's hotel room, wearing only his boxers, for anyone who cared to look.

No one. At the foot of the door was a newspaper, *USA Today,* in full color, face up, centered like a doormat. Joey leaned down to pick it up.

The flash came from the right. It flickered for a second in red-eye reducer before it exploded into the full and unmistakable flash of a camera, known well to professional wrestlers. Joey turned to the flash and saw a black leather jacket and blue jeans running down the hall. He recognized this run, and this backside. It was the same boy who had photographed him last night at the hospital. He was Duke's informer.

"Hey!" Joey said after the photographer in a half-yell, still conscious of his desire to be discreet.

The boy opened a door to a stairwell and disappeared.

Instinctively, Joey took two steps after him, then realized he was almost nude and stopped. Maybe it was sleepiness that kept him from rushing back to the room, maybe it was stupidity, but Joey stood still in the hallway for an instant too long and heard the sound. Click, click. The door to Jade's room had closed itself behind him. He didn't have a key.

Joey breathed deeply through his nose. There was no need for panic. Every week, tens of millions of people saw him dancing around in underwear and boots, so there was no reason to worry about this one moment in the hall in his boxers.

As if to show himself that he wasn't upset at all, Joey walked slowly to the closed door and paused before knocking softly. Then he waited for what felt like an hour. He knocked again, three times, this time with more snap. After the third knock he counted silently in his head. One…two…three…four…five…he didn't know why he was counting or when he was going to stop…six…seven…now he was getting nervous. No point in denying it. He really wanted to get back inside the room, out of this hallway, lest another photographer showed up and did whatever he did to inform Duke right away that Joey was bonking the company's most popular woman.

Click, click again, this time from down the hall. Someone was opening a door. Joey considered running for it. Maybe a quick exit to the stairwell. Maybe a quick exit out the window and a 14th-floor splat on the concrete. That would give the little shit something to photograph.

Pride kept Joey locked in place. He had nothing to be ashamed of. This was just a funny situation. A cool person would find the humor and share it with everyone. Down the hall, the door finished opening and out stepped Lord Mayberry, wearing jeans and a T-shirt, carrying a suitcase. He took one step away from his room and then saw Joey. His immediate reaction was one of surprise, as if he'd stepped in on Joey's private space.

"Hey, what's going on?" Joey said as he threw his chin up in the classic cool-guy hello.

"Good morning Joey. Nothing's going on. How are you?" Lord Mayberry's real name was Matthew MacDowell. When he wasn't in character, his 'British' accent gave way to a Canadian lilt.

"Oh, fine, just…"

"Are you locked out?"

"Yeah. I came out for the paper and got distracted and now I'm stuck out here in my underwear."

"Well that's quite a predicament, now isn't it?" Mayberry was smiling but not laughing.

"Yeah, I…yeah, this sucks," Joey laughed nervously.

"Well, good luck."

"Thanks," Joey smiled as if Mayberry's behavior was appropriate. As Mayberry walked past Joey and down the hall to the elevators, Joey wondered to himself why he didn't just ask for help. Why didn't he ask if he could go into Mayberry's room and steal a bathrobe, or at least a towel?

Click, flash, click. By the time Joey turned back toward the stairwell to see that the same kid had popped out and taken another picture it was too late. The kid was already headed back down the stairs.

"Hey!" Joey yelled after him and started toward the stairwell before realizing he didn't want to chase after some kid through the entire hotel while in his underwear.

Another click from down the hall. Was there normally this much activity on the 14th floor?

"Everything alright out here Joey?" It was Raptor, a cruiserweight from the undercard, leaning out from his doorway down the hall.

Now was the time to ask for help, Joey thought.

Click, click. Jesus Christ, was there some public gathering out here this morning?

Deep Six and Safire appeared from behind the two doors opposite Jade's room. Safire laughed.

"What's going on out here?" she said.

Click. From the other side. Joey turned slowly to see who else was joining the party. It was Jade. Thank God.

"Oh nothing," Joey said to Safire, beyond the point of pretending this wasn't a total nightmare. Joey went to Jade, who looked at him with a mix of pity and surprise. With Raptor, Deep Six, and Safire all watching, Joey went into Jade's room and closed the door behind him.

"Shit," he said as he dropped onto the sofa.

Jade stood where she was, her eyes still adjusting to being awake.

"What was that all about?" she said.

"That was about me making an ass of myself and probably you too."

Jade took the middle seat of the sofa and sat cross-legged, facing Joey. Joey told her the story, starting with him reaching for the newspaper, including the kid with the camera and all the wrestlers who'd seen him come back here in his underwear.

"Maybe it's for the best," she said.

A memory of Joey's mother appeared in his head. She was comforting him after a neighbor kid had punched his lights out.

"How could that be for the best? I got locked out in my underwear, Mayberry didn't offer to help me, Safire laughed at me, and some kid took pictures of the whole thing."

"Well, now we don't have to worry about keeping last night a secret." Jade's voice was quiet and morose. She didn't believe a word of her own optimism.

"Actually, somehow, the secret got out even before my little display."

"What do you mean?"

"Duke called this morning. He called here. I answered, which was fine because he was looking for me anyway. But somehow he already knew I was here."

Jade turned to face forward on the couch, then leaned back against the cushion. She took a breath in an obvious effort to contain herself. "Someone up here must have spied on us and reported to him. Why would anyone do that?" she said.

"I was actually thinking it was that kid with the camera."

Jade's eyes brightened. "I forgot about that kid," she said.

"You almost sound excited that it might be him," said Joey.

"Yes, I am. I'd much rather it be some Internet site than someone in the company spying on me and reporting to the boss. What did Duke say?"

"He wants me to stay in Houston and meet with him for lunch at noon."

"Well, aren't you the big shot?"

Joey shook his head. It was true. He was the big shot. Only the major players got private meetings with Duke. He was the big shot who would be all over the Internet looking like a dork in his skivvies.

"What are your plans for today?" Joey asked.

"I was going to drive to Dallas to hang with my sister tonight and tomorrow."

"Was going to? Does that mean you could change your plans?"

Jade smiled.

"Why don't you stay in Houston with me? Hell, it's not like there's any reason to be discrete."

"Joey, are you sure you want to do this? Maybe we should see what's on the Internet before—"

"Nonsense. You should stay with me in Houston and travel with me to Denver. To hell with the Internet clowns."

Jade sat still for a moment. "If you're sure," she said.

"I'm sure."

"You should get dressed. It's eleven thirty."

Joey kissed her before standing up. "I'm in room 809. You should check out of here and move your stuff in there. I'll head back there after I'm done with Duke."

"Okay," said Jade.

Joey felt a buzz in his chest as he left the room. He realized that, for the first time since high school, he had a girlfriend.

CHAPTER 17

▼

Joey stepped out of the elevator at floor 22. Arrows on the wall pointed him to the presidential suite. He knocked twice.

Duke opened the door and flashed the same gold-toothed grin that two weeks ago told Joey he was going to become the GWA champion. The presidential suite was a small house of luxury rooms. Duke led Joey through the entrance room, which featured a fountain of marble and granite that gurgled four feet above the hardwood floor. To Joey's right was a sitting area surrounding a flatscreen TV. To his left was a kitchen, separated from the main room by a mahogany counter. At the back of the entrance room, Duke and Joey sat at an oak breakfast table, between french doors and a picture window. The doors led to a small balcony, on which two potted trees filtered the incoming sun. Duke scooted his chair until he was directly opposite Joey, then handed him a lunch menu.

"Tell me what you want and I'll call it in," said Duke.

Joey didn't know if the luxury treatment was typical for Duke's guests or if he was being buttered up for a beating. Either way, he pointed out what looked best (pasta with vegetables and chicken) and Duke called it in. Two minutes later a waitress appeared with a bottle of Merlot, two glasses of water, and a basket of bread, and told them their lunch would be served in ten minutes.

Duke swirled his wine and smelled it before taking a long drag. When he put his glass down, he exhaled audibly, as if what he was about to say disgusted him.

"Joey, when I was your age, this business was about fooling the public," he said, speaking slowly and looking out to the balcony.

"Our number one goal when putting on a show was to get the people to believe the crap we were selling them. We thought, as long as they believed it was real, they'd be entertained. They came to see a real fight and we'd give it to them, at least in their minds.

"Now it's different. Now everyone knows our secrets. So instead of selling them sport, we sell them sex, stories, athleticism, and a little bit of fighting. We don't try to fool them anymore."

Joey nodded and took a bite of bread. He had no idea where Duke was going, but knew that Duke expected his guests to patiently listen to his tales. Duke continued.

"That's what's so puzzling about your situation after last night. Everything went wrong, people broke character, the fans were confused. It was almost like the old days, and I gotta tell you, it felt good to me. It felt fresh. For once, the fans weren't onto us. They didn't know if we were for real or not. By god, we had them mixed up, and I'll be a weasel in the henhouse if I said I didn't like it. That's the way it should be, Joey. That's what this business is supposed to be about. We're not fucking Broadway, or the fucking soap operas, we're wrestling, dammit. We're our own kettle of fish. And we've forgotten our roots. Our job is to put on a show that the fans believe is real. Wrestling was better when the fans thought it was real. And we're going to take what started on Monday night and continue it. We're going to be one step ahead of the fans again, Joey. It'll be great."

Joey said nothing. He was more confused than ever, and was starting to feel uncomfortable. He didn't really know what he expected from this meeting, but he knew this was not it.

The waitress rolled a food service tray into the room and to their table. Joey's pasta looked decent, but not worth twenty three dollars. Duke ordered a burger and fries, which seemed quaint for the fancy setting and service, and a little odd to be eating with expensive wine.

The waitress stood for an instant, in a practiced attempt at a tip, but got nothing from Duke. As she rolled out of the room, Duke said, "Eighteen percent gratuity included in the bill, don't know why they expect me to give more on top."

Joey smiled and nodded in agreement. In his mind, he could see himself looking like a kiss-ass.

"So, Joey, what do you think so far?"

"I'm with you so far." He was lost.

"Good. Here's what I've got planned. I think you're gonna love it." Duke inhaled a huge bite of his burger, so much so that his cheeks expanded as he tried to chew. Joey looked down at his plate. This meeting had become uncomfortable.

"What I'm thinking," Duke mumbled through a mouthful of hamburger, "is that we include Goliath's very real injury in our story, but do it like it was just another wrestling angle." Duke uncapped the ketchup bottle, turned it upside down over his plate, and smacked it repeatedly as he continued. "I want our fans to argue with each other about whether or not Goliath is really hurt, as I understand they're already doing. It will be the beginning of a new era, where once again the fans are out of the loop of what we're doing, as it should be."

Joey nodded again. He realized he had said almost nothing since he sat down, and hoped that was how Duke wanted it.

"So the story will be the World Title is now vacant. It will remain vacant until you and Goliath finish your match, meaning we won't have a champion until Goliath is well enough to return. In the meantime, the story is, everyone wants a shot at you since there's no title to shoot for. Every week you're going to go up against someone from the roster who's sure as hell they can beat you because you're just a little kid who got a fluke win, and if they can beat you, they'll prove they deserve a world title shot. Week by week you'll get win after win until Goliath comes back, and then your match with him will be a barnburner and no one will know who's going to win. It'll headline a pay per view and we'll make a killing."

"Okay," Joey said, almost against his own will.

"Okay? It's great my boy! Show some hutzpah! You're going to get a massive push!"

Duke was particularly ugly with food between his gold teeth.

Joey smiled, then realized he needed more 'hutzpah' and smiled bigger. 'Okay,' he told himself, 'you're still being pushed. Just keep your head up and maybe this will all turn out fine.'

Joey and Duke finished their lunch with only small talk between them. Joey felt like Duke wanted him to say more, to be his friend. Maybe Duke was looking for a new friend now that Goliath was out of action for awhile. If you were smart, Joey told himself, you'd grab this opportunity and do some serious butt-kissing. Duke was practically begging Joey to be his right-hand guy, and Joey couldn't come through.

It wasn't that he didn't want to kiss up. Hell, any chance Joey had of being popular in the locker room was already gone. Might as well buddy up to the boss and let people say what they want—they were going to say it anyway.

But Joey had no idea what to say or how to say it. What do you say to the most notorious wrestling promoter in history? Do you flatter him? Do you get him to talk about himself?

And before Joey could decide, it was already time to leave. Duke had another appointment. He shook Joey's hand and walked him to the door.

"One other thing, Joey," Duke said as he stood at the doorway. "Do you know what you're doing with Jade?"

Shit. Here was the bomb. What was the answer to this one?

"Yes," Joey said. Yes what? What did Joey just answer?

"Not that it's any of my business, but I want to make sure you know what you're doing. I'm sure you're already aware of what's out there on the Internet."

"Yes, I'm aware," said Joey, a total lie. What the hell was out there? What was Duke talking about?

"So you know what kind of trouble this sort of thing can cause. If I can be so bold, Joey, you need to end whatever you've started and cut your losses. If you and Jade become an item you're toast to those Internet kids. They'll crucify you both. Every time they talk about you, they'll make a snide remark about her. I've seen it happen before. This business just isn't meant for romance. You get me?"

"I don't know," Joey said cautiously.

Duke looked frustrated, like a father trying to scold his teenage son. "Come back inside for a minute," he said.

Joey followed Duke back into the suite and to the sitting area off the main room.

"Have a seat," Duke said, gesturing toward a black leather recliner. Joey sat. Duke remained standing, and paced among the furniture as he spoke.

"Joey, I'm sorry I wasn't being clear a minute ago. Sometimes I expect people to read my mind. It's a bad habit of mine. Anyway, what I was trying to say is, if we're going to pull the plug on this push, I need you to end whatever you've got going on with Jade."

"How come?" said Joey. He wanted to say, 'No way,' or, 'That's ridiculous,' but only got out the benign question.

"Joey, I hate that I have to do this to you, but Jade has a lot of history with this company, with our wrestlers, with our fans. I can't have…let me put it this way. If you insist on being with her I won't be able to go ahead with your push. I can't have two of my high profile stars…I can't—"

"Is it because Goliath has a history with her?" Joey was growing displeased with himself that he hadn't put a stop to this already. He wished he had it in him to jump up from his chair and tell off the boss for even suggesting this.

"In part, it's, more than that, it's complicated," said Duke. Duke's voice was careful but firm. There was nothing apologetic about it. Joey could tell that, even with his difficulty finding the right words, Duke wasn't going to accept an answer of no.

"What if Jade and I kept our relationship a secret? What if we kept a lower profile? I know I botched it last night and we were seen, but last night was crazy, with Goliath's injury and all."

"No, Joey, it's more than that. Okay, look, I'm beating around the bush here. Joey, you can't see Jade. You can't be friends with Jade. If you want to get this push, if you want to make it in this business, you'll need to go back to your room this afternoon and if she calls you you'll need to give her the cold shoulder. It's that simple. Jade has some troubles, some troubles of her own to work out, and some troubles with this company. We've got her signed to a long, large contract, and I need to keep her around and get what money I can out of her, but I can tell you, and believe me, she knows this, that when her contract's up in a little over a year, she's out of here.

"Trust me, Joey. This is a favor I'm doing for you. You don't want to be involved with her. I know it seems fine right now, but, Lord, listen to me, as your elder, as someone who knows this business better than anyone. If you want to make it, you can't get involved with someone like her. And don't forget that you're getting the offer of a lifetime here. I'm planning on putting you over every star on my roster, including the world champion. By the time we're done here Joey, you can have any woman in the world. I just need you to do this one thing for me. For yourself too."

"Duke, I'm sorry, I still don't understand what the big deal—"

"I can't believe you're even thinking about this!" Duke's face had turned bright red, and frightening. "Joey, I'm telling you to do something for me. Do this for me, and I'll do something for you. It's that simple. If you want to become the biggest wrestling star in the world, you have to do this for me. So, what's it going to be?"

Joey sunk a little in his chair. Why was this all so hard? He was a good wrestler. He just wanted to wrestle. Why did every step involve these personality conflicts?

"No," he said. "Duke, I can't do what you're asking."

Duke leaned against the back of the couch and sighed. "Okay, I can appreciate that," he said. "You want to do the right thing. You're a man with a conscience. I am too. I can appreciate that. I'll tell you what. You take some more time to think about it. Our next show isn't for a few days. You take a few days to figure out what you're gonna do. I'll see you on Friday, in Albuquerque. You can tell me then."

Duke started walking to the door. Joey stood up and followed him.

"Joey, if you confront Jade about all of this, she's going to tell you her side of the story, or maybe she'll just dump you like a sack of potatoes, who knows with that woman, but it's going to be your choice. Just remember that I know everything she's going to tell you, and my stance is unchanged. You can't be with her if you want to be my world champion."

"Duke, my answer's not going to change," Joey said as he stepped across the threshold.

"Just think about it," said Duke. "See you on Friday," and the door closed.

Joey took a step back, then stood for a few seconds, looking at the closed door to the presidential suite. So many things he should have said. Go to hell. Fuck you, this isn't any of your business. I don't need your fucking push or your fucking world title. He took a step toward the door and raised his hand as if to knock.

But he didn't knock. Feeling like he had no control over what he did, he left. He went down the hall and got on the elevator. His room was on the eighth floor. He pushed the button for the lobby. His reflection was in the mirrored walls on three sides of him. He didn't want to look at himself, so he looked at the red carpet on the floor. The elevator stopped three times on the way down to pick up and drop off other guests.

When they reached the lobby, he was the first one off, leaving an elderly couple and a man with two suitcases behind him. He went out the front doors into the swamp of the Houston afternoon and began to walk. He hadn't even turned the first corner before two preteens ran up to him and asked for his autograph. He signed one for each, then turned around and went back into the hotel.

Forty seconds later he slid his key card into the slot on the door of room 809 and pushed it open. Jade was lying on the bed watching television.

"Hey Handsome," she said as he entered.

"Where can we get Internet access?" Joey said, foregoing any attempt to hide his panic.

"Well, there are hookups in every room if you have a laptop—"

"I don't have a laptop, where else can we go?"

"Easy there Tiger. What's going on?"

It struck Joey that Jade was wearing a gray T-shirt that he'd picked up in Jacksonville. She had to open his suitcase to get that T-shirt out.

"I really want to know what's out there about my match last night and, anything else."

Jade looked at him with such curiosity that he wanted to hide. "Did Duke say something about us?" she said.

"No," said Joey. A stiffness raced through his shoulders with the realization that this would be the first of a string of lies. "He only wanted to talk about what happened in my match last night. It was…nothing."

Jade squished her mouth to the left side of her face and squeezed her eyebrows in bewilderment. "If you really want to see what those kids are saying out there, we can go downstairs to the business center and get a computer terminal. I think it costs like ten dollars an hour or something nutty."

"I'm not worried about the cost," Joey said, and then realized that Jade probably wasn't worried about the cost either. Neither of them were hurting for cash. Her hesitation was more about what they might see.

"Alright," she said resignedly. "Let me get some shoes on and we can go surf the Internet."

She said the last three words with more than a hint of disdain for the phrase.

"Thanks Jade. I'm sorry. I know I shouldn't be so concerned about this."

"No, no, Sweetie, it's okay. Celebrity's still new to you. And you're gonna see this crap one way or another. You can't escape it. I just hope you're ready. I'm sure they've skewered us both like yesterday's kill."

CHAPTER 18

▼

Vicky Archuleta had only been a member of Revolution Wrestling's creative team for three months, but in that time she had made herself indispensable. Trained in the jungles of Hollywood studios, Vicky knew well how the game was played, and by her second week on the job, had already booked herself on a two-day trip to Aruba with Max Zeffer on his private jet. From that point on, even though she was a woman in her early thirties with no experience in the wrestling world, even though former wrestlers and wrestling promoters made up the rest of the creative staff, even though she was loathed by the company and its fans, her voice was one of the most powerful on the team.

And this morning her voice was saying one thing: turn Lucifer heel.

The idea had come to her last night, as she sat on the plane, typing a screenplay on her laptop. The screenplay, a crime thriller set in Hollywood, had been her obsession for three years. She had begun it, certain that it would be her masterpiece, her ticket out of the annals of television and into the world of New York penthouse parties and personal profiles on cable TV. Three years and thirty rejection letters later (her agent had proclaimed he would drop her if she tried to push one more draft on him), she was certain that if she could just find the right motivation for her main character, Clint Shadow (she imagined Tom Cruise playing the lead) the screenplay would come together and the Oscars would follow.

As she thought about Clint Shadow, FBI-agent extraordinaire, chasing arch-fiend Dirk Hitler through the dark streets of Hollywood, and wondered what drove him to do what he did, she realized that Lucifer, the centerpiece of the television show she was supposed to be writing, was boring. Lucifer beat people up, he won championships, he apparently was very skilled at "submission holds" (why these wrestlers were so hung up on these human pretzel maneuvers was beyond her—it seemed to her that if they were to imitate real fighting there should be more punching and kicking), but no one knew why he did it. Why did he care about the World Title? Why did he put his body through such torture to win these silly matches?

And the answer was simple: he didn't know why, he just did it. He was just a violent person. Hence, the "heel turn." It was brilliant.

In her short time in the wrestling business, she had taken it upon herself to learn the lingo. Heels, Babyfaces, Heat, Pops, Get Over, Get Under (was Get Under a term?), Workrate, Shoot, she had it down. Of the established universe of the wrestling business, by far the most interesting concept was that of heels and babyfaces. She was shocked at how little the others on the creative team understood the storytelling power of heels and babyfaces. Good Guy/Bad Guy; Black/White; that dichotomy was perfect for storytelling to the masses, and the sole reason professional wrestling survived as a form of entertainment.

The problem with these wrestling promoters was that they wanted their biggest stars to play the good guy. Didn't they understand that the villain was the most interesting role in entertainment? The fans understood it. They always cheered for the bad guys, well, sometimes they did.

The fans would love a heel turn for Lucifer right now. It would be a big surprise. It would add depth to his character. It would give him motivation.

"I don't think so," said Gene. Gene Harold was one of five men sitting at the round wooden table with her. To the left of Gene's obscenely large belly was Patrick Childers, the production manager. Patrick was useless in these meetings. He just got in the way. On Patrick's left was Max, who was next to Vicky. On Vicky's right was Larry Jenkins, the Talent Manager, and next to him was Walt Thompson, an elderly former wrestler who now served as road agent and general lackey to Max.

"Why don't you think so, Gene?" said Vicky.

"We know where we're going with Lucifer, we don't need to make any changes to his character. He's the freshest thing in wrestling right now. It's a terrible idea. Let's move on to something else, please."

God, Gene was an asshole. As Head Booker, he clashed with Vicky on every one of her ideas. She didn't understand what his purpose was. She had been brought in as Head Writer, a position she had held for a daytime soap opera and a prime time drama, and she certainly didn't need any other chefs in the kitchen. She wished Max would fire Gene. If this creative team were to be effective, step one would be to give full creative control to her, and Gene's job would just be to figure out how the stories play out in the wrestling ring. All the storylines, dialogue, backstage sketches, and character development should be hers.

Alas, it didn't work that way. The truth was, Gene had control over most of the storylines, and her job was to write the dialogue for the backstage sketches and contribute ideas to these meetings. And were it not for her rendezvous with Max and the promise of another one, she might not even have that much.

"I don't think we're ready to move on to something else yet," she said. "Hear me out. This heel turn is a great idea. Lucifer's character needs motivation."

"He has a motivation. He wants to be the World Champion," said Gene.

"But why? It's just a piece of costume jewelry—"

"Just a piece of costume jewelry! Good God, can we please move on to something else?" said Gene.

"No. Now, what do the rest of you think?" said Vicky.

Gene looked to Max for help. Vicky was pleased that Max provided none.

"Well, we know where Gene stands," said Max, calmly. "How about you Larry?"

This is what she loved about Max. He was fearless. Larry and Gene made it a point to always disagree with each other on everything. With Larry on her side, the discussion would get interesting.

"I'm afraid I have to agree with Gene on this one," said Larry. "While Ms. Archuleta's arguments sound smart and thought out, I don't understand them. It doesn't make any sense to me to just turn our number one hero at the height of his popularity."

Bastard. They're all jealous little bastards, and they're scared to death of me.

"Okay," said Max. "Walt?"

"I'm with the guys."

Of course Walt was with the guys now. There was no point in even asking him, the spineless little slug.

"Patrick?"

"Max, I'm also with Gene."

"Alright then. It's decided. Lucifer will not turn heel, at least not now. But, frankly, I'm disappointed in this group. I brought Vicky in to give us a fresh perspective from a talented writer with a proven track record. Turning Lucifer heel when no one expects it is precisely the type of innovation that can turn Revolution from a great wrestling promotion into a great entertainment company. You gentlemen are all so immersed in the artificial rules of the wrestling world that you're horrified to think of trying something different. But if we're ever to increase our audience, we have to expand our vision. The market is saturated with fans who know how a heel and a babyface should behave. To bring in new fans, we need characters who behave outside the norms of the established wrestling universe."

"So what are you saying Max?" said Gene with resignation. "Are we or aren't we turning Lucifer? I'm ready to move on."

"I've already told you. You guys said no, so the answer is no, for now. Besides, we need to finish the program between Lucifer and Scott Rollins that we have planned. After that's done, we will revisit this issue, and when we do, I expect you all to come to this meeting with an open mind. I want this group to be leading the way not just for the wrestling business, but the entire entertainment industry. To do that, we need to think outside the confines of the wrestling world of the past fifty years."

"Okay then, moving on," said Gene, who then led the meeting in a new direction, discussing booking ideas for the ongoing feud between Flash Martin and Miguel Cervantes for the American Title, a feud about which Vicky had nothing to say. She'd write up the dialogue after these men had figured out whatever they had to figure out. No doubt whatever they came up with would be crap, but she knew to choose her battles carefully. She'd lost today, but Max was in her pocket on the Lucifer turn, and with all these goons against her, when they did flip the switch on her idea and the ratings lit up and the company made a fortune and *TV Guide* wanted to interview the brilliant writers for *Revolution Riot*, she'd be alone on the podium, and Gene Harold, the fat fartknocker, would be that much closer to being out of her way, and she and Max could turn *Revolution Riot* into a real TV show.

But that would all have to wait. For now, it was more cheesy wrestling dialogue and another month of evenings with Clint Shadow and Dirk Hitler.

CHAPTER 19

▼

"Steve, honey, someone's at the door for you."

Steve rolled over and looked at his watch. It was two o' clock. He had been asleep for four hours.

"Coming Mom," he said. Who was here to see him? His friends all worked during the day.

Steve stood up and looked in the mirror. His hair was comical. His mouth tasted awful. A headache was brewing behind his eyes.

Wearing the sweats, T-shirt, and socks that had been on since mid-day yesterday, Steve left his room and headed to the stairs. The world wasn't quite right. He was in the half-reality that always followed his mid-afternoon naps. He had to pee.

It was probably Sam Dawson, wondering if Steve would mow his lawn and trim his hedges for third world sweatshop wages. What excuse could he tell Sam that wouldn't filter back to Mom and bite him in the ass? Maybe he just needed to tell Sam that he no longer wished to do yardwork. He was really busy with his web site.

At the bottom of the stairs, Steve saw that it wasn't Sam Dawson. It was someone he didn't know. And before he was ready, this someone, a young guy in an expensive suit, a slicker as his Grandpa would say, was approaching him, practically charging at him. Steve glanced over at his mom for help. Her face had a look of motherly fear, of powerlessness. And then, before a word was spoken, the slicker was shoving a paper at Steve. It was folded in three, ready to be put in an envelope. Steve took the paper.

"Steve Garcia, you have been served with a cease and desist order from the 8th circuit court of the state of Illinois," the slicker said. "Good day." And the slicker turned and walked out the still open front door.

Steve's mother closed the door behind the intruder and turned to Steve.

"What was that all about?" she said in a mix of pity and anger.

Steve unfolded the paper.

"I don't know," he said. He headed into the living room area and took a seat on the sofa. As soon as his butt hit the cushion he was attacked by his yellow labrador.

"Not now Lady," Steve said, pushing the dog away and getting a handful of slobber in the process.

Lady made a circle around the coffee table before squatting down at Steve's feet. After wiping his hand on the armrest, Steve began reading the paper.

Court Ordered Injunction

The 8th Circuit Court of the State of Illinois hereby orders Steve Garcia, being a legal resident of Rosemont, Illinois, to cease and desist all libelous activity regarding the actions of the Family Television Group, Incorporated in the state of Vermont, L.L.C. This order includes but is not limited to all written communications on the website, "http://www.wrestlinghotline.com" posted on or before the date of this injunction.

The document had three signatures on it and a notarization.

"Looks like someone's upset about the content on my web site," Steve said.

"What did you put on your web site?" his mother asked, or better, accused.

"Lots of stuff. This is about my investigation of the Family Television Group."

"Your investigation? What are you now? A journalist? Steve, maybe this is a sign that now's a good time to quit horsing around and get a real job."

Flames arose from deep in Steve's beer-bellied gut. This was a never-ending sore spot; of course she'd use this as an opportunity to bring up her disdain for Steve's career choice. Steve's mother didn't have the courage to ask Steve to move out and fend for himself, but she carefully piled on the guilt in doses large enough to make herself a martyr but small enough that Steve never changed. If only he'd quit this silliness, get a real job, move out of his mother's house, get married, and live the normal life of a young adult—it was a constant undercurrent in their relationship, and it never ceased to irritate Steve that he had no choice but to deal with the guilt, since, after all, he was a twenty-four-year-old, perfectly capable, college-educated white male who lived with his mom because he chose not to work in any traditional sense.

"Mom, it's not a big deal. I'll handle this. Don't worry about it."

"It's not a big deal? You just got served notice from a court of law Steve! You could go to jail!"

"Don't be ridiculous. I'm not going to jail. I just need to call a lawyer and I'll get everything straightened out."

"Call a lawyer? Why do you need to call a lawyer? You just need to do whatever it is they're asking. You don't need to call a lawyer."

"I can't just do what they're asking mom. They have no right to ask this."

Steve's mom looked at him like he had grown a second head.

"Steve, I can't believe what you're saying. You can't fight these people. People like this will chew you up and spit you out."

"Mom, you don't even know who these people are."

"I know enough to know what's smart. They just served you papers."

"Mom, do you even know what 'served you papers' means? I'm going to call a lawyer, if for nothing else, just to see what my rights are."

"And how are you going to pay for a lawyer?"

Ouch. There was the rub. Steve hadn't thought about that. Here was his mom telling him that he absolutely was not to call a lawyer, and here he was, apparently assuming she'd sign the check. Steve was so used to her providing money whenever he needed it that he had forgotten he needed her on his side.

"I'll find a way," he said. Now the game began.

"But you won't find a way, Steve. You'll call the first name in the yellow pages, you won't know what you're doing, he'll keep you on the phone for an hour, you'll be no better off than you are now, but you'll have a bill for a thousand dollars that you can't pay and I will have to bail you out."

"I've got some money."

"Steve, we're not talking about this. I forbid you to contact a lawyer. You will do exactly what those papers say and that's final."

She couldn't do that. He was twenty-four years old for Christ's sake. He opened his mouth to express this opinion, but then realized she could do that. His website was maintained from a room that belonged to his mother, with an Internet account his mother paid for, on a computer his mother bought. Not to mention the fact that his mother paid for Steve to eat and be clothed. She had never used this arrangement to put Steve in his place, but the opportunity had always been there. Now his mom was calling in her favors.

"Can we talk about this again later, after I've had some time to research this?"

"Yes, we can and we will talk about this again later." Her tone was now one of total frustration. The message beneath her voice was, 'Where did I go wrong?'

Clutching the court document, Steve went upstairs. As he left his mother in the living room, he knew he was acting like a little kid throwing a temper tantrum. He was left with no choice. His mother had told him what to do, he didn't want to do it, but he had to.

He stopped in the bathroom to take an overdue piss. The mirror caught him on the way in. He was wearing sweats and a ratty T-shirt. His hair was an unkempt mess. He was out of shape and had pasty skin. It was after two on a weekday afternoon and he hadn't showered and was contemplating going back to bed. He had no job, no money, no girlfriend, no prospects, and his only ambition was to watch and write about professional wrestling.

Maybe his mom was right. Maybe this court order was a sign, a clear reminder that he had chosen the life of a loser.

He peed for at least a minute, flushed the toilet, and left the bathroom without washing his hands. He opened the door to his room and was hit with the smell, the stench, of dirty clothes, dirty sheets, and an unshowered man. Ignoring it all, he sat down at his computer and fired up his email. Two hundred and sixteen messages. He sorted them by subject line and immediately noticed a pattern.

"Joey and Jade"

"RE: Joey Mayhem Spends Night With Jade Sleek"

"FW: Joey in Underwear After Romp With Jade"

Hundreds of messages with similar subject lines.

Steven opened his web browser and went to www.wrestlingdailytribune.com. The splash picture on the front page showed Joey Mayhem, wearing only white briefs, standing in a hallway with a look on his face like he'd just been caught.

> The Internet is abuzz this afternoon with a new twist to add to the story of last night's taping of *GWA Burn*. It seems that despite his disastrous World Title Match with Goliath, Joey Mayhem got lucky last night with the first woman of wrestling, Jade Sleek. More...

Steve clicked on the link to read the rest of the story on his competitor's web site. The story began with a re-cap of last night's wrestling action, then went to Houston General, where Joey and Jade were spotted and photographed together, then went to the Green Dragon coffeehouse, where Joey and Jade were photographed again, then to the Hyatt, where Joey was spotted entering Jade's room and not exiting until morning, at which point he was photographed in his underwear.

Still not a mention of Goliath's mysterious transfer to Houston Medical Center even though Steve had reported it nearly five hours ago. Either Steve had gotten some bad information or nobody cared about Goliath's hospital transfer. He suspected the latter based on the number of Joey/Jade emails in his box.

Oh well, all the better. Per his publicly stated policy, Steve paid little attention to gossipy stories like this one. Chandler Dresby and his minions at Wrestlingdailytribune.com could have Joey and Jade's romance all to themselves. Steve's little visit from the Illinois Circuit Court this morning was proof that he was onto something much bigger.

Finishing up the story on Joey and Jade, Steve went back to his own web site. He did a search for stories currently posted that referenced the Family Television Group. References to the FTG in his last three columns, a feature story on the history of the FTG, a long-winded opinion column about the hypocrisy of the FTG's morals, and of course, the Andrew Smith pages.

Steve realized he couldn't just take all of this down without raising a maelstrom in the Internet Wrestling Community. And he didn't want to post anything describing the court order he just received, lest he unknowingly say something in violation of his order.

What he needed was for someone else to spread the word for him.

He opened a new email message.

To: chandlerdresby@wrestlingdailytribune.com
From: steve@wrestlinghotline.com

Chandler,

Hey. What's up?

Thought you might be interested to hear. The FTG just put a gag order on me. I'm not allowed to mention them on my web site at all. Seeing as how I have no money to get a lawyer, I have no choice but to do what they say. So, I guess it's up to you guys to keep the fight alive. Let me know if there's anything I can do to help. I'd love to expose these goons for the hypocrites that they are.

Later.

Steve

He clicked Send. Chandler would read that message and weep. Wrestlingdailytribune loved that Steve had decided to take on the FTG in an all-out Internet crusade. The topic was boring for a lot of wrestling fans, and Steve's traffic had decreased as a result. Chandler Dresby had authored an editorial, claiming, among other things, that Steve had an overinflated sense of importance for thinking he stood a chance of making a difference in the GWA's fight with the FTG. He'd gone on to say that Steve should leave well enough alone, that maybe the FTG had a point. After all, didn't most Internet wrestling fans hate the way women were treated on *Burn* anyway? Wouldn't most Internet wrestling fans like to see the GWA go back to a pure wrestling show, without all the crap that the FTG railed on in the first place?

Steve had declined to dignify that editorial with a response, but no doubt there would be another. Chandler had probably just finished reading the email, and was already drafting an "I-told-you-so" editorial about Wrestlinghotline's failed attempt to take on the FTG.

And that would be just fine.

Steve began the arduous and slightly heartbreaking process of taking down all the references to the FTG from his web site. An hour later, Wrestlinghotline.com was FTG free.

Not that this was over. He opened another email message and addressed it to "Anti-FTG" an address list of his six most loyal supporters in the campaign.

To: Anti-FTG
From: steve@wrestlinghotline.com

Hey guys.

As you are sure to hear soon on Wrestlingdailytribune, this morning I was served with a court order to cease and desist all my ranting on the Family Television Group from my web site. As such, you'll notice that all the FTG stuff is now gone.

Before you guys get all belligerent on me for caving so easy, just hear me out. This is not bad news. The campaign's started, and it doesn't have to stop. There are enough of us to keep this thing going without me ranting all over the web. The fact that the FTG has taken such a keen interest in what we're doing is the most exciting thing that's ever happened to Wrestlinghotline. It's proof that they have something to hide.

So, I need you all to help. Someone else needs to spearhead the information campaign, as I am now legally restricted. Set up anonymous web sites, post on bulletin boards, do whatever you can do.

We can do this. We have to do this. What happened to me today is proof that we have the power to do this!

Call me for more info. I'm totally stoked about what we're onto here.

Peace,

Steve

He clicked send and stood up. It was time for a shower. Maybe after his shower he'd go downstairs and make peace with his mom. She'd be happy to hear that he was doing just what the court order requested.

CHAPTER 20

▼

There is a specific silence to the open road that comes about after one's brain has assimilated the hum of the engine and the beats of the tires on the asphalt. The air conditioner, the radio, the blast of wind from an open window—they all become a part of this silence that is immune to every attempt at covering it, save one, companionship.

Joey's world as a traveler, a showman on the move, was exquisitely changed with the addition of Jade to his passenger seat. Traveling alone for a year in the Southeast Wrestling League and a month in the GWA had given Joey much more solitude than his disposition required. Now, driving a rented Ford Expedition on Highway 187 through West Texas, into the purple of the fading sunset, with open prairie on either side and no taillights obstructing the view in front of him, Joey felt profoundly different about his place in the wrestling world, and wished he had taken on a traveling partner sooner.

They had spent the rest of Tuesday relaxing in and around the Hyatt in Houston. They had surfed the Internet for over an hour, finding pictures and articles about their tryst on virtually every wrestling web site. Wrestlingdailytribune.com was particularly brutal. The kid in the trench coat who had followed Joey to the hotel apparently worked for this virtual rag, as it was the one that showed a full splash of pictures of Joey in his underwear. The captions pointed out that Joey was standing in front of the room registered to Jade Wilcox, where he had spent the night. The little snoops had successfully re-created Joey and Jade's entire Monday night, showing pictures of them leaving the arena, waiting in front of the hospital, talking at the coffee shop, and entering the hotel together.

Jade was entirely unfazed by the photo spreads. She told Joey it was part of being a star, and he should be flattered. She told him that she had been aware that this sort of attention was a possibility, but wanted to spend the night with him anyway.

The web sites were most fascinated that Joey was sleeping with Goliath's ex on the same night that he laid him out in the ring. More than one webmaster had opined that Joey's kick was purposeful, and that there was backstage friction between him and Goliath, centered around Jade. A notably horrendous site called Thefigurefive.com was covered in stories about backstage confrontations between Joey and Goliath dating back two weeks, each story beginning with the ominous, "Sources say…"

Another interesting take was that everything, from Goliath's injury to Joey and Jade's tryst, was an elaborate "work," which, in wrestling lingo, meant that the company was pretending all this was real when in fact it was scripted. The rationale behind this theory was that the GWA wanted to set up a storyline involving Joey, Goliath, and Jade. As Joey read the fervor with which this hypothesis was proclaimed, he wondered if it wasn't such a bad idea. Wouldn't that get people talking, if all of this were just an angle, right up to the backstage relationship between Joey and Jade?

If only Duke could be persuaded that Jade should become part of his main event angle. Sadly, Joey knew that Duke would hear nothing of it. For whatever reason, Duke was very clear that Jade wasn't to be involved with Joey at all, in real life or on television.

Joey had not mentioned Duke's orders regarding his relationship with Jade. Everything he told Jade about his conversation with Duke was grayed in a web of half-truths. He told her Duke was considering turning Goliath's injury into part of the story. He also told her that Duke was considering an end to Joey's push altogether.

Both these stories were true, but didn't make any sense to Jade. How, she asked, could Duke consider ending Joey's push at the same time he was pondering a main event storyline for him? Joey said he didn't know, a lie. Duke's commandment to Joey, his insistence that Joey not speak to Jade, was the missing piece. Joey tried carefully to cover its absence while still telling as much of the truth as possible. He envisioned a scenario in his mind whereby Jade would never find out the whole story.

The scenario required Joey to continue hinting at the possibility that Duke might end Joey's push out of sheer disgust at the whole Goliath fiasco. After this seed had been planted in Jade's mind, Joey would return to work on Friday, with

Jade at his side. When Duke saw Joey and Jade still together, in defiance of his order, Joey's push would end. Jade, and the rest of the wrestling world, would believe that Joey's mistake on Monday night, combined with his shrinking status backstage, spelled the end for his push. Only Joey and Duke would ever have to know the real story.

There was some relief in those thoughts for Joey. Even if he wallowed at the bottom of the card for the rest of his contract, it was only for a year. Maybe at this time next year he'd be wrestling for Revolution. Maybe Jade would join him there, and all this crap would be in the past. The Goliath fiasco would be forgotten, there would be new rookies to take the brunt of the backstage jealousy, and Joey would be free to do what he loved, free to wrestle.

"Why did you get into this business?" he asked Jade. She smiled at him, perhaps surprised at the question, perhaps surprised that this was the first time it had been asked. She sat quietly for a minute, too relaxed to just leap into an answer of such importance. She had rolled back into the passenger seat, her bare feet on the dash, her thighs spilling from her denim shorts. As she prepared to speak, she sat up.

"My dad and I watched wrestling together when I was a kid," she said. "It was our thing. Actually, it was his thing, I didn't really get it. But I knew he liked it, and I knew he liked it that I watched with him. I didn't realize it at the time, but he needed me to watch with him and to talk to him about it. In the eighties, wrestling was practically a kid's show. If I didn't watch it with him, he didn't have any excuse. I don't have any brothers."

A lone car approached them going the other way. Jade paused as it passed, its lights briefly invading their private space.

"So it was our Saturday thing," she continued. "And he loved to talk about it. When he talked to me about wrestling, he talked to me like I was his equal. He had to. I loved it when we talked about wrestling. He never acted like I was a little kid who couldn't understand that it was staged. He'd get really critical of the booking and the writing and really excited about things he liked and I'd just listen. I don't know if he ever knew how wonderful it was for me that he trusted me to listen to all his opinions." She trailed off, her eyes out on the road, lost in some memory.

"Who was his favorite wrestler?" Joey asked.

"Barry Wayne," she said without hesitation. "Dad loved the Shoulderbuster."

"Definitely a classic," Joey said, thinking of Barry Wayne's signature move, an impressive piledriver-like maneuver in which he used his knee to crush his opponent's shoulder. The move was outlawed in every North American promotion now—less than perfect execution and the recipient's neck gets snapped—but back in the day, when Barry Wayne swung some unfortunate soul upside down, the crowd went nuts.

"When I was in fifth grade, Dad and I went to The Cottonwood Theater in North Dallas to watch the 1986 GWA Championship Series on closed circuit TV. I remember he had to pay twenty bucks for our two tickets, which seemed like a fortune to me to pay for wrestling. Do you know the '86 Championship Series?"

"Oh yeah," said Joey.

"Well, we had told my mom that we were going to the zoo. She didn't care much for wrestling, and definitely wouldn't have approved of Dad taking me to see it on the big screen and spending twenty bucks.

"I don't know what you think of the 86 Series, but it's my favorite pay per view of all time. Shane Walker versus Tank Willis, Red Jackson versus Barry Wayne, The Lyon Brothers versus Havoc—that was just a great show. And my dad was so happy, so at home to be watching it with all the other fans, cheering for the same good guys, talking to each other about the booking. I was really proud that day. I felt like I was at least partly responsible for giving this to him."

"That's just awesome," said Joey. He imagined how thrilling it must have been to watch the 86 Championship Series live when it happened. That show truly was one of the all-time greats. The match between Red Jackson and Barry Wayne was a thirty-minute masterpiece that Joey had watched so many times he had it memorized.

"On the way home, Dad and I got our stories straight for Mom," said Jade. "We planned out what we'd say about all the different animals at the zoo to make sure the lie was genuine. Looking back, it almost sounds kind of dysfunctional, but it was so important at the time. I can't even begin to describe how special it was to me that Dad and I were breaking the house rules together."

"So you decided then that you wanted to be a wrestler?" asked Joey.

"You know, I don't remember making a decision. I don't remember a moment when I said, 'Okay, I'm going to be a wrestler.' But at some point after that day, I knew. By the time I was in high school I was already making plans."

"Wow. So you knew for a long time that this was what you were meant to do. That's great. Were you just, totally certain? Did you ever think of doing anything else?"

"Well, there was a time, in high school, when I learned that I needed to keep my plans secret from my mother if they were ever going to happen. When I was a freshman I signed up for gymnastics and track and basketball and volleyball one after the other, and my mom asked me if maybe I shouldn't slow down some, and I told her I needed to get in shape and learn how to be physical because I wanted to be a wrestler. She laughed it off and told me I was dreaming, but that night after I went to bed, I heard her giving my dad hell. She was telling him that it was time for him and me both to quit watching wrestling. She said it had gone too far, and we were both too old for it, and it embarrassed her, and she wanted it to end. After that it was never quite the same. My dad was always busy with something on Saturday mornings and I'd watch alone, or he'd find something for the whole family to do and I wouldn't watch at all. That was pretty much how it was for the rest of my time in high school. But I can't remember ever thinking that I didn't want to be a wrestler, that I didn't still love wrestling."

Joey nodded as he listened. Jade spoke so matter-of-factly about her past. It was obvious that she was meant for this business, and that was why she was such a success. "Then you went to Texas Star," he said, continuing her story for her. He knew from his days as a fan that Jade attended wrestling school at Texas Star in San Antonio. She was the first woman ever to go through the prestigious program there.

"That's right," said Jade. "I went there right after high school. As you might imagine, there was all sorts of shit in the house over that one, but in the end, my dad won out. He told my mom that if I could get in and pay my own way, then there was no reason I couldn't go.

"You paid your own way?" said Joey. Texas Star was the most expensive wrestling school in the world; it had turned out more superstars than anywhere. Goliath, Deep Six, Lord Mayberry, Flash Martin, Bret Stevens, Butterfly Johnny Grace, and Jade were the current crop of major stars who were graduates of the school. The Star's legendary training regimen was just two years of instruction and practice, but it was brutal. Those few who made it all the way to the end were guaranteed a spot in one of the major promotions.

"I paid my own way with a lot of work and a lot of debt," said Jade. "I worked at Macy's every summer in high school and saved every penny. That paid for the first year. The second year I scammed a bank into giving me a student loan. I was so proud of myself at the time, but it turned into a nightmare. I applied and got into UT San Antonio, applied for and got a student loan at Bank South, used the check to pay for wrestling school, and disenrolled from the university. When the bank found out that I wasn't going to UT, they started applying this jacked up interest rate right away. I was a big dummy who hadn't read the contract very carefully and certainly hadn't thought everything through. I had to take a night job at a call center to make the payments, and even then I was using credit cards and borrowing from friends and not eating just to hold everything together. Had I not gotten a job with GWA right after I finished at Star, I would have had to declare bankruptcy."

"Gosh," said Joey. "So you really got lucky?" He was amazed that every wrestler, no matter how rich and famous, at some point in their past, had been flat broke.

"You could say I was lucky. I signed on with Duke because he offered me a huge signing bonus. At the time, I also had an offer from Max Zeffer, who didn't even have a promotion yet. He had the bold idea of assembling a core group of wrestlers around whom he would center his new promotion. He wanted me and Crystal Waters to be the first two in his women's division. She signed on. I didn't. She got stock options when the company went public and is now a millionaire a hundred times over, plus she's wrestled in some of the greatest women's matches ever. I'm a magazine centerfold with a hundred bra and panties matches in my book. Man, if Crystal and I were in the same promotion, touring the country, wrestling…we'd change women's wrestling forever. We'd put it on the map."

"So, it's not too late," said Joey. "You both are still young."

"She's not going anywhere, and I'm stuck here for another two years on the damned contract I signed when I wasn't thinking straight."

Joey wanted to tell her that it didn't have to be this way, that there must be some way out. It was crazy to him that Duke, for whatever reason, didn't want her to work here, and she didn't want to be here, but they both were slaves to this contract they could end if they'd only talk to each other. For just an instant, Joey considered telling Jade everything Duke had said. All of a sudden it wasn't fair for him to hold back this info that Duke had something against her, something so strong that he was going to end Joey's push just for being with her. She was too good at what she did, too meant for greatness, to be stuck working for someone who didn't appreciate her. And why the hell didn't Duke like her? It didn't make any sense. She was the greatest women's wrestler in the world, and had been for six years now. She had the look, the microphone skills, the mat skills, the fans loved her. Was it her thing with Goliath last year? Was there more to this story that he didn't know?

"Jade, can I ask you something?" he said.

"Of course."

That's right. Of course he could. They had slept together all week. They were traveling together to the next show. Why was he afraid to talk to her?

"I need to preface this by saying that I know it's none of my business, and this is not at all motivated by jealousy, at least not consciously—"

"You want to hear the scoop about me and Goliath," she interrupted. There was bemusement in her voice. She was so confident in herself. No wonder the world was in love with her. "Of course you realize what it means if I tell you all this."

"I promise I won't tell a soul. What you say in here stays between us."

"No, you goober. I know you won't tell anyone any of this shit. What I was going to say is that, if I tell you, it means you and I are for real."

Joey turned his head to look at her. His face must have been confused because she elaborated.

"Joey, when you asked me out a couple weeks ago, I assumed you were just another wide-eyed rookie who hadn't figured out yet that you're my colleague now and not my fan. It happens all the time, and I always say no. I have no idea why I said yes to you, but I did, and here we are.

"Anyway, you're ten years younger than me, you've got a huge future in this business, you and I have already caused some waves with what we've done, I just want to make sure you know what you're doing."

"Of course I know what I'm doing," said Joey, with some legitimate frustration in his voice. If only she knew how much he was willing to give up for her.

"I'm just saying…there's stuff about Goliath that I wouldn't tell to just anyone, but I want to tell you. I don't want to have secrets from you, and frankly that's a little scary to me."

"Why's it scary?" Joey knew the answer; he felt the same way about the secret he was holding.

"It's scary because telling secrets is what people in real relationships do, and I know very well that this business isn't a friendly one for people who want real relationships. I tell you my secrets, and then you tell me yours and before we even get to Albuquerque we're in love and we want to watch out for each other. Then one of us gets hammered in some backstage political powerplay of the week and the other one of us gets involved because we won't stand for our lover getting hammered and before you know it it's us against the world. Then one or both of us gets de-pushed or fired. Then we grow resentful because wrestling was our lives and we gave our lives up for each other and found out we miss wrestling. By the time we're done, we hate each other with a passion, and it all started because I told you my secrets."

"Do you want to tell me?" said Joey.

Jade furrowed her brow in displeasure at the question. "Of course I want to tell you."

"Then you should tell me."

She took a deep breath, as if steadying herself for a big story. A personal story. Then she began.

"He was so huge, so instantly over with the fans. He had it. He was just like you—" Jade stopped short, her face showing surprise. "Wow. He was just like you. I didn't realize that until now. Does that scare you?"

"Why would it scare me?" said Joey.

"Because, I must have a type. You and Goliath are my type."

"Your type is wrestlers who are over?"

"I guess so—what are you laughing at?"

"Jade, you're so worried about everything being right. You have this vision in your head of what a functional relationship is like—"

"And this isn't it? You're right. I never thought I'd be into a guy ten years younger than me who's wrapped up in this tabloid conflict with my ex-boy-friend."

Joey laughed again. "It's not just that," he said. "You're scared to tell me any-thing personal because you think we'll get too close too soon—"

"I've told you all sorts of personal things tonight."

"Okay, you have, I'm sorry. I was thinking of how you didn't want to tell me about your relationship with Goliath. By the way, you still haven't."

"Well, that's because you interrupted me."

"I didn't interrupt you. You stopped to ask me if I was scared that you had a type."

Jade grinned and looked down at her lap. "Oh yeah," she said, playfully, then sat silently for a minute.

"Well…" urged Joey.

"Are you sure you want to hear all this?" said Jade.

"Oh come on. Yes, I want to hear it."

"Okay." She took another second to compose herself. "Well, unlike you, Goli-ath didn't come onto me."

Joey considered disputing whether he'd come on to her, but decided not to interrupt.

"I was married to Jonathan at the time. That was a flop. We both knew it was a flop. He was hanging around because I had just signed on with Playboy for a ton of money.

"I was just into Goliath. It was obvious he was going to be the World Cham-pion, like I said, he had it. I don't know why, I just wanted to be near it. I started talking to him backstage, then I started hanging around with him after shows. I bummed a ride off him from Tacoma to Sacramento. That night, I went to his hotel room, uninvited, let myself in, and the shit started." She shook her head and stopped talking.

"That's what you're so worked up about telling me?" said Joey. "I could have guessed something like that. It happens. Your marriage wasn't working, you were on the road—"

"It's more than that, Joey. It's…I really wanted it to be real, and I've never told that to anyone."

Far from it, Joey thought. Jade and Goliath both had gone out of their way to portray their affair to the media as a horrible lapse in judgment on both their parts, and the few times Joey had seen them interact with each other were miserable affairs of anger and denial. "So you really liked him?" he said.

"Yeah, or, I thought I did. It was a really bad time, and now I look back and see that I was mixed up. It's a terrible thing to screw up a marriage, at least for a woman. I felt like I'd failed at the most important decision of my life. I felt like I was letting my parents down."

"What happened? It sounds like your marriage went really wrong really quickly."

"It did. I had barely been married a year when I made a pass at Goliath. It was like, I knew, even when I was in my wedding dress saying my vows, I knew that this was horribly wrong. I said the vows anyway. We honeymooned in Greece, and literally on the first day, on the plane, we got in a fight. It was just…I don't know. Have you ever jumped into something even though you knew it wasn't going to work out?"

"I have," said Joey, thinking of his mindset when he started wrestling school. He was ready to give it a shot, fail, and then get a real job. Now, two years later, he was a headliner for the GWA.

"So you know what I'm talking about," said Jade. "I guess what it all boils down to is I had a hard time adjusting to fame. Maybe I still do. When things really started to blow up, and I was on talk shows and in tabloids, I got scared, and I think that's why I jumped into a bad marriage. I was just desperate for something secure and private, you know?"

"Sure," said Joey. "I'm starting to see what being famous does to your personal life. Everything changes."

"You're right, everything changes. And I think that's also why I allowed myself to get involved with Goliath. It was a huge mistake, but, I just didn't know what I was doing." Jade seemed extremely pleased to have a listener who understood her so well.

"Do you feel different now, like you know more about how to be famous?"

"Yeah, well…no." Jade laughed at herself. "I guess I know more about how to deal, personally. I know how to protect myself, how to keep it from getting to me. But I don't know how I should behave, how to keep the negative spotlight off me. Just look at the mess I've gotten you into."

"Oh no," said Joey. "The only mess I'm in is my own doing. I'm the one who screwed up that match with Goliath. The stuff with you and me would just be idle gossip if I hadn't knocked out the champ, who just happens to be your ex-boyfriend."

"Well, I still feel bad."

Joey wanted to tell her to forget it, that it was all his doing, that he was the one who had dragged her into the muck. But it wouldn't be honest. Something about her, about her past with Duke, was dragging Joey down, better, was going to drag Joey down.

"I hate to be nosy," Joey said, "but I want to hear more about you and Goliath. I feel like I still haven't heard these secrets you're so nervous about telling."

"My goodness Joey Hamilton, aren't you the bold one? I've already told you the big secret. Maybe it's not as shocking as I think it is, so you didn't even notice."

"I guess I didn't. It's all been pretty tame."

"Well, maybe that's a good thing, I don't know. The big secret is that I thought I was in love with Goliath, for real. There was a time that I thought my relationship with him was the real deal. And when it ended, even though I ended it, I was hurt. And here I am, with you, in a relationship, are we in a relationship?"

"I think so," said Joey. "We're driving between shows together, and I'm hoping that we'll keep on driving between shows together. I think that's a relationship."

"Okay then, I do too." Jade laughed at the awkward turn the conversation had taken. Joey laughed with her. "Anyway, onward."

"Onward," Joey agreed.

"What I'm trying to say is," Jade laughed again, nervously, "I guess…I don't want to get hurt again."

"Okay. That's fair," said Joey.

"And, I guess I'm nervous to talk to you about this because…well, I can see myself getting hurt again."

"What are you saying? Do you think I would hurt you? Because I guarantee you my intentions—"

"No, it's not that I think your intentions are bad, or that you'd ever want to hurt me. It's that, if things don't work out with us, for whatever reason, and I admit I'm nervous about the way things have started, what with our pictures all over the Internet," she paused, and exhaled, as if tired. "If things don't work out," she said, "I think I'm going to get hurt, because I really like you."

Her sincerity was brutal. It was a blameless indictment of Joey and his secret conversation with Duke. "I like you too," he said.

An awkward silence took them a few miles before the conversation started again. This time the conversation was about impersonal things, like crummy jobs they'd held before wrestling and stories about their friends. They talked until they reached Albuquerque, four hours later. They checked into the Wyndham Hotel near the airport, where the GWA travel office had reserved rooms for them.

"I show two rooms, one for Joseph Hamilton and one for Jade Wilcox," said the receptionist.

"Just one room for us both," said Joey, remembering how Duke had found him in Jade's room on Tuesday morning. "Is there a way to get both our names on the room?" Joey asked.

"Sure, if you'd like," said the receptionist.

"We would," said Joey.

CHAPTER 21

▼

To: Steve Garcia
From: ntaylor@powervolt.net

Steve,

Sorry, I don't have anything new for you on the FTG. Honestly, I didn't spend any time this week looking.

I gotta tell ya Steve, I think you're laying too many eggs out on this one. No one's really interested. Well, we're all interested, but not enough to be a part of this big campaign. I admit, I thought it was cool when they got the lawyers on your ass, like we'd found something, but then I thought about it some more, and it's obvious that we haven't found anything, and we're not going to. They're probably not hiding anything. They just don't want their donors' names posted on the web. It's bad PR.

If you ask me, I think you should consider dropping this whole FTG thing. I don't think it's good for your column or your site. Just get back to commenting on the wrestling, man. It's what you're good at.

Nick

Steve closed the email. He wouldn't reply. This just sucked.

Nick was his most reliable email resource for tips and tidbits. If Nick wasn't interested then no one was.

Only four days had passed since Steve had been served by the 8th Circuit Court of Illinois, and already his campaign against the FTG was dead. He had sent an email to his most loyal supporters on Tuesday morning, begging them for whatever info they could gather on the FTG, and had received a resounding nothing. Nick, reliable Nick from Long Beach, who owned the largest collection of Indie Wrestling Bootlegs in America, was the only one to respond.

Steve slouched in his chair. The fat on his belly rolled out from under his T-shirt like a balloon being squeezed. What the hell was he doing?

In high school, Steve was an honor student. He graduated thirteenth in a class of four hundred. He could have been number one if he'd wanted it. His only B's were in his senior year, when he had discovered ditching and apathy.

He went to Northeastern Illinois University on a presidential scholarship, which he lost in his sophomore year, after two semesters on academic probation and his fourth change of major (Engineering to Business to Economics to Communications). His remaining three years at NIU were financed out of his mother's checking account, which was filled mostly with child support payments from his father.

Steve's parents divorced when he was twelve. His father, a certified financial planner, had decided to replace his current wife with a client he had been sleeping with for two years. As an only child, Steve suffered the feelings of responsibility and guilt that might be expected. As a very intelligent only child, he used those feelings to exploit his father for a loot. Between the finalization of the divorce and Steve's thirteenth birthday, his father bought him a bicycle, a Bowie knife, a twenty-inch television, a VCR, a Nintendo, eleven Nintendo games, and a set of golf clubs. The next year saw a Super Nintendo, a 3-wheel all-terrain vehicle, and a computer. As the years passed, and Steve became increasingly belligerent toward his father, the presents became even more extravagant. On Steve's sixteenth birthday, his father took him to the Ford dealership and told him to pick a truck. Steve picked an Explorer. When he wrecked the Explorer a year later (he ran a stop sign and found a Chevy Caprice in his passenger seat), his father bought him another one.

Steve lived at home during college, and upon graduation decided to take a summer off before venturing out into the real world. Two years later, that summer still hadn't ended.

At twenty-four, Steve was no longer eligible to be the object of legally enforced child support payments, but the money kept coming. Steve's father had a lifetime of guilt and a pile of money. Steve's mother didn't mind getting the checks at all.

Sometimes Steve wondered if his mother wanted him to remain a loser because she liked that he was a disappointment to his father.

Steve's five-year high school reunion had just passed. He hadn't attended. Many of those people had kids by now. They all had real jobs. Some of them probably had good jobs.

At one time Steve had a good group of friends. They were all misfits and nerds, but they stuck together and had fun. Kyle, Austin, Andrew, Zack, and Irene were their names. The group had formed in middle school by default, the six least popular kids, and had remained close through their senior year. They played *Dungeons and Dragons* at lunchtime; they went to movies together; they talked about books, video games, and television. College broke the group apart, sending them all over the country, and Steve had lost touch with all of them.

Sometimes he thought about looking them up, especially Irene. Irene, what a waste. Irene had been confined to thick glasses since childhood, and was scourged with acne in adolescence, but was brilliant, and nice. Looking back, Steve could safely say that he had loved her since seventh grade. But he had never said anything. Back then, it wasn't even an option. Social misfits aren't allowed to date until college, when their peers are finally adult enough to let them lead normal lives.

College was too late. Irene went away to Carnegie Mellon to study computer science. Steve never made an effort to stay in touch. No doubt she had found someone already. Someone worthy of her. Someone who had a job.

Steve opened his Internet browser and went to a popular jobs search site. He did a search on "All Jobs" in "Greater Chicago". Twenty-nine thousand matches came up. Out of twenty-nine thousand there should be at least one good job.

Telemarketing, receptionist, truck driver, telemarketing, telemarketing, home-based business (read email spammer), commission based sales, telemarketing, telemarketing, what would Irene think of him if he took one of these jobs? What the fuck was he qualified for anyway? His resume was blank.

Maybe it was time to go back to school. Maybe graduate school. Maybe he could become a professor. Maybe he could write a screenplay.

The futility of these thoughts was more than Steve could bear. His heart started racing. Maybe it was time to take a nap.

The email icon appeared in the corner of his screen. Thank God.

Steve opened his email.

To: Steve Garcia
From: Anonymous98@freemailforu.org

Dear Steve,

Keep digging into the backgrounds of the FTG's donors. This is where you'll find the good stuff. Trust me.

Anonymous

Steve clicked on "Reply."

To: anonymous98@freemailforu.org
From: Steve Garcia

Dear Anonymous,

Do you have anything more to add?

He clicked on send. Probably one of his readers just yanking his chain. Nick was right, this FTG crusade was ruining Steve's reputation on the Internet. It was time to bag it. Hell, it was time to bag the whole thing.

He thought about the self-help gurus on TV, who all had some story about hitting rock bottom before they turned their lives around and made a fortune. Maybe this was Steve's time. Maybe this was rock bottom. He could drop the column, and the life associated with it right now. He could just stop, no explanation, no apology, no warning, just stop the column, quit watching wrestling, get a job, move out, get in shape, get a girlfriend, get married, have kids, live a normal life. It wasn't too late. By the time he was thirty, he could be caught up with the rest of his generation.

Another email icon appeared in the corner of the screen.

To: Steve Garcia
From: anonymous98@freemailforu.org

Dear Steve,

Here's something to whet your appetite.

Check it out.

Anonymous

Attached was a PDF file named Saxon Fund Prospectus.

Steve double-clicked to open the file. It was a 30-page document. The design was Spartan, with black text on a white background, and no graphics or font highlights to assist in the reading. The document was amateur, nothing like one would expect from a corporation, who would at least put their logo on the front page. Mr. Anonymous was definitely someone fucking around with him.

The table of contents wasn't even in hypertext. He'd have to go page by page to sort through this thing.

Page One was headed, "About the Fund."

> The Saxon Fund was created in 1999 to serve high-end, invitation-only clients. The Fund is managed by Payne Shaiman and seeks out the strongest growth investments for—

Blah, blah that was enough of that. Why did he get this? This was the most boring prank Steve had ever heard of. Page Two was headed, "Investments". It was a slew of financial gobbledy-gook. Risk/Reward ratios, Earning Per Share requirements, stocks, bonds, commercial paper. Steve scanned through the next five pages, seeing nothing of interest. Page Seven was headed with "Clients".

> The Saxon Fund serves high-end investors who seek a low-risk environment for long-term growth and wish to partner with respected investment strategists

Steve's eyes involuntarily shot to the middle of the page. Andrew Smith. Jonathan Taylor. Jeremy Washington. Peter Jackson. These four names were listed sequentially in the middle of a long list. These four names were burned into his brain. He had typed each of them into every search engine on the web, in every combination and advanced search algorithm he could think of, and had found nothing. Andrew Smith and Jonathan Taylor were the founders of Americans For Productive & Responsible Entertainment & Media. Jeremy Washington and Peter Jackson were behind The Betsy Piper Foundation. These were the largest donors to the Family Television Group.

How could this be the first time he had seen this? The names were right in a row. Surely one of the search engines would have seen…

"Wait a minute," Steve said aloud. He rolled his eyes and shook his head. Of course. A hastily thrown-together site. An anonymous email. Someone had put a lot of effort into this prank.

Steve opened a new browser window and went to www.fwyn.com, his favorite search engine. The "Find What You Need" logo was decked out in Mexican garb to celebrate Cinco de Mayo. Steve typed in "Andrew Smith Jonathan Taylor Jeremy Washington Peter Jackson" and clicked search.

"No documents found."

He knew that would be the case. He had done that search before. He typed in "The Saxon Fund" and clicked search.

"No documents found."

This had to be a hoax. What kind of investment fund doesn't have a web site? A fund that has something to hide.

Steve went back to the email from Mr. Anonymous. He clicked Reply.

To: anonymous98@freemailforu.org
From: Steve Garcia

Dear Anonymous,

I've gone through this document and believe I've found what I'm supposed to see. Can you tell me more?

Steve Garcia

He clicked Send, then went back to the Saxon Fund document for a thorough reading of the whole thing.

CHAPTER 22

─────────────── ▼ ───────────────

Friday night's house show was at The Pit in Albuquerque. Joey and Jade had arrived together. They entered on the south side and walked together to the locker rooms, where Duke spotted them.

Duke was standing in front of the entrance to the Visitors' Locker Room, talking to Mike Clarke, a GWA road agent. He eyed Joey and Jade as they passed, but didn't say anything to them. It's done, Joey told himself. He hoped that would be the extent of his contact with the boss that night.

Two hours later, Duke was in his face. The pop guitar riff of Jade's music was audible through the walls—she had just entered the arena for her match. Duke had found Joey alone, pacing in the back of the locker room.

"Do you realize what you're giving up for that woman?" said Duke. He was standing a foot away, looking up. Joey had never realized Duke was so short.

"Yes, I've thought about what I'm giving up, and frankly, I was ticked that you'd even asked. I made my decision. To hell with my push." Joey was amazed that he was speaking this way to this man.

"To hell with your push? Kid, this is your one and only chance. We're talking about superstardom or jobber obscurity. What the hell? Are you in love?" Duke said love like it was the most childish notion he'd ever heard of.

"I'm not talking about this," said Joey. "You do what you need to. I'm not talking about my personal life with my boss." Joey started to leave. Duke grabbed his arm and pulled him back.

"Alright then. Tonight, you were to go over Raptor. Switch that. Put him over. Go find him right now and tell him that you're putting him over on my orders. You two work out the match. Make it good. You are now a jobber, Joey

Mayhem. If you want to continue working for me, you'll make my stars look good as they kick your ass."

"Fine," said Joey, and again turned to leave. This time he got two steps away before Duke called after him.

"Another thing, Joey. The gossip about you and Jade on the Internet isn't good for my business. Consider yourself gagged. I don't want you saying a word to anyone in the real press or on the Internet about anything regarding this company. I also don't want you talking to anyone within the company about any of our recent conversations, including this one. That includes your girlfriend."

"Fine." But it wasn't fine. It was ridiculous. Where did Duke get off telling him what he could and couldn't say to Jade? No matter. Revolution wouldn't want him to be a jobber. He'd do as he pleased and if he was fired so be it. "Anything else?"

"That's it. Get out of here. Find Raptor. Work out a good match. You're on soon." Duke waved him away like a housefly. Joey felt like he was being thrown out of the locker room.

He found Raptor sitting with a group of wrestlers in a makeshift common area just before the arena entrance. Raptor, whose real name was Eduardo Baca, had been a huge star in Mexico before signing with GWA for much more money than he was worth. Unlike most wrestlers in Mexico, Raptor wasn't a skilled acrobat. He got over with the fans due to his charisma, which hadn't translated well in America, mostly due to his poor English.

As Joey approached, all the conversation in the common area stopped.

"Raptor, I need to talk to you about our match," said Joey.

"Okay."

"In private," said Joey.

Half an hour later, after a brutal conversation about re-working the match (Raptor barely understood what Joey was asking him to do, much less why), Joey did the job for Raptor in front of fifteen thousand fans. They reacted worse than Joey expected. Raptor was popular in New Mexico, but not popular enough to go over Joey Mayhem. The boos were extraordinary.

The displeasure of the fans brought about a slurry of questions when Joey returned to the backstage area. Why did they get booed? Did Raptor go over? Was that planned? Joey refused to answer anyone, which only made everyone more curious, including Jade.

"What's going on?" she asked, following him to the locker room. She had to run to keep up, he was moving so fast.

"I can't talk about it now," he said.

Joey expected her to protest, or ask why he couldn't talk about it, but she didn't.

"Do you want to leave?" she said.

"Yeah, let me just…ah fuck it, I'll take a shower at the hotel." Joey ran into the locker room and came out with his bag. Still wearing only his tights and boots, Joey walked out of the arena. Jade followed him to her car.

"I'll drive," she said.

"Thank you," said Joey.

She let Joey in the passenger seat, closed the door after him, ran around the front of the car to the driver's side, and hurriedly drove out. They came to a red light and cars pulled up on either side of them. Joey slouched in his seat.

"They can't see you," said Jade. "I got these windows tinted in Arizona because that's the only state where it's legal to have them this dark."

"Are you serious?" said Joey.

"Yes, I'm serious," she said. Joey laughed, quietly.

The Wyndam Hotel was only three minutes from the arena. It took most of the drive for Joey to find and put on a T-shirt from his bag. They said nothing as they arrived, walked through the lobby, rode the elevator, and entered the room.

"Do you need the bathroom before I shower," said Joey.

Jade shook her head. "Honey, are you okay?" she asked.

"Let me take a shower, then we'll talk about it."

Joey smiled at her before shutting the bathroom door. He sat on the toilet seat and began unlacing his boots. The phone rang.

"Hello," he heard Jade answer. "May I ask who's calling?" she said. Shit, it was for him. If it was Duke, he'd tear this room apart. "Why don't you give me your number, and if he wants to talk to you he can call you back," she said. She wouldn't say that to Duke. He finished unlacing both boots and took them off. The smell of feet, or wrestling locker rooms, filled the bathroom. He heard Jade hang up the phone.

"Who was that?" he called out.

"Some kid from Pro Wrestling Newsletter. He wanted to talk to you about your match tonight."

Great, he thought. Since when do wrestling journalists give a shit about what happens at the house shows. Doing the job to Raptor, even at a house show, was big news, and Duke knew it. That's probably why Joey wasn't supposed to talk to anyone.

He opened the door and walked out into the room. "Well, even if I wanted to talk to him, which I don't, I'm not allowed."

"What do you mean?" asked Jade. She was sitting on the bed, having kicked her shoes off and let her hair down.

"Tonight Duke told me I wasn't allowed to talk to anyone about anything, including you."

"Is that why you've been so quiet?" she said.

Joey laughed. "Hell no. I just wasn't in the mood to talk, I'm so pissed. I'm going to talk to you about whatever the hell I want. Duke can kiss my ass."

Jade's eyebrows shot up. "What happened tonight, Joey?" she said.

Joey sat down in an easy chair by the bed. "I'm being de-pushed."

Jade sat quietly for a minute, then said, "Is it because of your match with Goliath?"

Joey thought for a minute before answering. He could continue the lie, or come clean. Jade's question would force him to choose.

"Well, no," he said. "It's because Duke told me to do something, and I didn't do it. That's why I'm in the doghouse. But I don't know why he told me to do it."

Jade's face was overcome with the horror of recognition. "What did he tell you to do?" she asked, obviously anticipating a particular answer.

"He told me to stop seeing you," Joey said.

She stood up from the bed, and looked around in a fury, as if ready to kill something, if only she knew what it was. She grabbed the phone off the night-stand, ripped it away from the wall, and threw it across the room as she screamed, "God Dammit!" The phone collided with the bottom of the entertainment center in a muddle of bells and clatter. Jade fell back on the bed, this time flat on her back. "I knew it. I knew he'd pull something like this. He told you on Tuesday, right? At your lunch meeting."

"Yes," said Joey, wondering if she'd known the whole time that he had been lying.

She sat up and looked at him. Her eyes were filling with tears. "Why didn't you tell me?"

"Well, I thought I'd just take what was coming and tell you I was being de-pushed because of my screwup with Goliath. I didn't figure I'd get this pissed about it. Now I want to tell you everything just because Duke told me not to."

"Joey, you can't do this to yourself. You need to go to Duke tomorrow and tell him you'll do whatever he wants."

"Like hell I'll do that! He has no right to ask, and even if he did…am I that unimportant to you?"

"No Joey, you're not unimportant. It's that you're giving up so much. I don't want to be responsible for that. You're on your way to being the biggest wrestler in the world. You're talking about fame, and money, big money, hundreds of millions of dollars over time—you can't give that up for me."

"It's not what I wanted. This whole thing isn't what I wanted. I wanted to make it to the top, but I didn't want to do it with everyone in the locker room hating me, and my promoter telling me who I can and can't be with. If this is what it takes to be on top—"

"Joey, this is what it takes to be on top. I'm sorry to be the one to tell you that. You'll never make it in this business if you don't play the game. There's never been a World Champion who wasn't envied by every has-been in the locker room. And there's never been a World Champion who didn't do what Duke asked. That's his way. He only gives you what you want if he gets what he wants."

"Well what he wants is stupid. Who cares if there's some gossip on the Internet about us? It doesn't mean I should have to stop seeing you."

"It's more than the gossip on the Internet, Joey. A lot more." Jade was slouched on the edge of the bed, looking down at her feet, tears now running down her face.

"What, is it something to do with you and Goliath?"

Jade sat silently for a minute before saying, "No, it's not about me and Goliath."

"Jade? What is it?"

Jade tensed up, as if Joey's question were a threat. Her cheeks reddened, and she looked around the room, her eyes stopping in several places other than on Joey. Finally, she looked down at the floor again and began speaking.

"Last year, after my shit with Goliath went sour for everyone, Jumbo started…I had this thing…with Jumbo. It started with him following me around. He acted like I needed an escort, like he would protect me from Goliath or anyone else who happened to look at me. And I didn't know what to say. My relationship with Goliath had ended badly, and, well you know, Goliath isn't a totally safe person. It didn't seem so bad that the biggest guy in the company wanted to be my bodyguard.

"I was stupid. Any girl could see what he wanted, where this was headed. God, I was stupid. Anyway, one night after a big show, the Storm pay per view in New Orleans, Jumbo tried to come into my room with me. He wouldn't take no for an answer, and before I knew it, he was pushing me into my own hotel room, closing the door behind him, and forcing himself on me. I screamed bloody murder as loud as I could before he covered my mouth. Thankfully some guy in the hotel heard and started banging on the door and asking if everything was alright. That distracted Jumbo enough for me to scream some more. I yelled to the guy at the door that I was being raped and he should call the police. Even a dolt like Jumbo could figure out he was had. So he got off me, and left. I locked the door behind him. The guy who was banging on the door, I don't even know who he was, but he stuck around even after seeing Jumbo leave, can you imagine seeing this seven foot tall monster come out? But the guy stayed at the door and asked if I was alright. I told him I was, and thanked him, and told him everything was fine and he could leave. I wish I'd let him call the cops. Everything might have been different.

"The next morning I called Duke and told him everything. He told me to meet him in his suite to talk about it in private. I was sure he was going to listen and he was going to make things right and fire Jumbo.

"But he didn't make things right. I remember his fat face and his fucking gold teeth that afternoon. He asked me if anybody knew, and I said no, not yet, and he said to keep it that way for now while he figured out how to handle it. He told me he'd make it right but I had to promise to keep my mouth shut while he worked things out.

"Then nothing happened for two weeks. Jumbo left me alone, but I could tell nothing had happened, he hadn't even been talked to, so I called Duke again and we had another meeting. This time he told me that since technically nothing happened, since someone banged on the door and Jumbo got off me before anything happened, that he didn't have cause to do anything to anyone. I told him that was bull shit. Then he, Jesus Christ, I'll never forget what that fat fuck said to me. He said, 'If the public should come to know of this the company and I will not stand beside you.' Then he said, 'It's best for all of us if this stays quiet.' He said if word got out he'd personally make sure I never worked again."

Joey felt like the walls were closing in on them. Unable to continue standing, he sat on the bed next to Jade.

"Oh my God," he said to her. "Jumbo tried to rape you, and Duke just let it go?"

"Just a minute," she said, then stood up and went to the bathroom to blow her nose. She came out with a handful of tissue, sat down, and sighed, trying to compose herself.

"Yes, Joey, Duke just let it go, and I've been shit ever since. I haven't wrestled a real match since then, just Duke's crap fests. He's squeezing every dollar he can get out of me, all the while trashing my name and my character so when I leave this godforsaken shithole of a company I won't be even remotely over. And that's why you're not allowed to be with me. It's not because of the gossip on the Internet, or my past with Goliath. It's because I have this shitty secret to keep and he can't make you his top star if he thinks you'd side with me."

Joey put his arm around Jade and kissed her forehead. "Thank you for telling me," he said.

"Joey, I know it's going to be hard for you, but it's really important to me that this information stays between us. If I've learned anything in this business, it's that you can't make it if you rock the boat. And I'm the dumb one who signed a long contract I'm still stuck in. When it's up, I'm out of here. There's still time for me to have the career I wanted."

"I understand," said Joey. "I'm out of here as soon as my contract's up too."

Jade turned so she was facing him. "Joey, are you sure this is what you want?" she said.

"What do you mean?"

"I mean, I'll understand if you go to Duke and tell him you'll do whatever he asks. You're throwing away an opportunity—"

"No way. We're not even talking about that anymore. I'm glad my push is over. Now that I know the whole story, I don't want to rise in this company. This company can go down the crapper as far as I'm concerned."

Jade leaned back, nodding in agreement. "Me too," she said.

They faded into a relaxed silence. Joey realized that they both had unveiled their biggest secrets in a matter of minutes. It was somehow tiring.

"I'm going to take a shower now. I'm overdue," he said. He kissed her before standing up. He felt like they were rebels, the only two who understood what Duke and his business were really about and would take it down from the inside if they had to. He felt comfortable. For the first time since his landmark match with Jumbo on *Burn*, Joey felt like he could face the locker room without shame.

Jade was asleep when Joey came out of the shower. She was lying on top of the comforter, still in her clothes. Joey slipped her shoes off, turned off the lights and lay beside her.

The phone woke Joey seven hours later, playing the elevator music of a hotel wake-up call.

They ate breakfast at the hotel buffet, then checked out and hit the road. Saturday's show was six hours north, in Denver. Joey was surprised that they didn't need to speak further about the previous night's revelations. During the drive, they spoke of other things, the dialogue drifting across their interests and desires with the ease that can only exist among people who are completely honest with each other.

The Denver show was at the Uptown Center. Joey did the job to Raptor again, and again the crowd was livid. Jade wrestled in a mixed tag match with Gordy Goodnow, Safire, and Lord Mayberry. During her match, Joey was approached by Mike Clarke, a production assistant.

"Phone call for you Joey," said Mike, handing Joey a cell phone.

Joey took the phone, fearful of who was on the other end.

"Hello," he said.

"Joey, this is Duke."

Of course. The bastard wasn't even at the show tonight and he still managed to get hold of Joey at the one time Jade wouldn't be around.

"Hello," Joey said again.

"Listen Joey, we've been working out Monday's show in light of what you and I have talked about, and, anyway, you're going to be in the main event on Monday."

The main event on *Burn*? This didn't sound like a de-push.

"You'll be doing the job to Jumbo in the main event. I'll need you to really give him some heat too. We're talking about putting the strap on him while we wait for Goliath to get well."

Great. Joey had been avoiding Jumbo tonight, and hoped to do so from here on out, lest he lose his cool. Now he had to do a program with him.

"Are you there?" said Duke.

"Yeah, I can hear you," said Joey.

"Okay, good. Well, to prepare for Monday's bout, I'm going to have you and Jumbo work together tomorrow in Las Vegas. I'll be there to talk further with you guys. Just wanted to let you know."

"Okay."

"Alright then. See you tomorrow. Can you put Mike back on?"

Joey handed the phone back to Mike. A few minutes later Jade came backstage.

"How was your match?" Joey asked her.

"Good enough, I guess," she said.

"Good. I just got off the phone. Duke had some news for me, and he conveniently delivered it while you wrestling."

CHAPTER 23

▼

To: Steve Garcia
From: <u>anonymous98@freemailforu.org</u>

Dear Steve,

These people may not be real, but the money obviously is. Find out where the money came from.

Anonymous

The email had come ten minutes ago, and Steve had read it at least fifty times already. He read it slowly, quickly, aloud, word by word, phrase by phrase. Able to recite it from memory, Steve was confident he had deciphered all there was to get from the email.

It was Saturday, five minutes before noon. Steve had been awake since seven. He had spent the past five hours surfing the Internet. He was wearing black sweat pants and a Chicago Bears T-shirt. He was unshowered and unshaven.

Spring winds were banging an elm branch against his window. The smell of pending rain seeped into his room through the air ducts.

Steve took a sip of lukewarm coffee and re-read the email. Two sentences. Eighteen words. He needed more.

He had spent most of Thursday and all of Friday at the William Scott Business and Law Library at Northeastern Illinois University, trying to find information on The Saxon Fund, the mysterious entity (and still potentially just an elaborate prank) sent by an Anonymous source.

Steve knew that, if real, The Saxon Fund was some financial outfit from Canada that was somehow related to the four largest donors to The Family Television Group, the activist group that was attacking The Global Wrestling Association.

But that was all he knew. After two days of researching, he had found nothing. No references to The Saxon Fund on the Internet, nothing in the library's database, nothing in the business press, nothing on microfiche.

So on Friday night, Steve sent an email to Mr. Anonymous.

To: <u>anonymous98@freemailforu.org</u>
From: Steve Garcia

Dear Anonymous,

I have spent the past two days digging, and have found nothing. Do you have any more information? What is The Saxon Fund? Are these people for real? Who are they?

Steve Garcia

Fourteen hours later Mr. Anonymous sent his cryptic return message. "These people may not be real…" He obviously knew more than he was divulging.

"…but the money obviously is." That part was fluff. Of course the money was real. Steve had watched with the rest of the wrestling world as the Family Television Group had used the money to great effect, getting major GWA sponsors to fall one by one, getting real and implied commitments from both wrestling promotions to clean up their acts, getting Imagine Television Network to wring its hands over the ruckus *GWA Burn* was causing.

And "Find out where the money came from" was a no-brainer. That had been the point all along. The trick was, until this email, Steve had assumed the money came from Andrew Smith, Jonathan Taylor, Jeremy Washington, and Peter Jackson. Those names, found in his first search for info, then verified in the mysterious Saxon Fund document from Mr. Anonymous, were the centerpiece of Steve's developing story, whatever it might be. Those names were presents from Mr.

Anonymous, who, like Steve, seemed to have a gripe with the FTG. If Mr. Anonymous said those people weren't real, then, for all Steve was concerned, they weren't real.

Who was this Anonymous guy? A whistleblower from inside the FTG? It would make sense. The FTG, although outwardly supporting only "Family-friendly" television, had an obvious Christian bent to it. Someone inside the company might note the apparent disconnect between strong Christian morals and illegally funneling money around to increase the power of your message.

And why Steve? Why was he involved? More importantly, he thought, can I get anything for this discovery? What's available to an Internet investigative journalist who uncovers a television scandal? Maybe a job with the GWA, digging up dirt on its enemies for a living? Maybe a job as a real journalist? Maybe a profitable web site?

Steve thought about Matt Drudge, and his little web site that blew up when he discovered the president was getting wanked by an intern. Then he thought about Watergate, and *All The President's Men*. Were best-selling books and mega movie deals in his own future?

He opened his word processor and typed, *It was a hot afternoon in May when I got served.* Not a bad opening sentence for a future Pulitzer Prize winning book. Hundreds of pages to be filled…Steve realized he needed to uncover much more of this story before he could write a book, or even a column.

He went back to Mr. Anonymous's email, and clicked reply.

To: anonymous98@freemailforu.org
From: Steve Garcia

Dear Anonymous,

Do you have any more information? If not, do you have any suggestions of where to look? I'd love to help you get to the bottom of this story, but I need more. Please.

Thanks.

Steve Garcia

He clicked Send, then toggled his computer back to his open word processor document. He wrote another sentence. *The man who served me my court papers wore sunglasses, like he had the coolest job this side of the Potomac.*

Steve sat at his desk for another minute, wondering about a third sentence, and about The Saxon Fund, and Andrew Smith and company, and the FTG.

He left his chair and plopped onto his bed. Staring at the ceiling, he fantasized about book tours, television interviews, riches, fame, a house, and a girlfriend.

Ten minutes later, he was asleep.

CHAPTER 24

▼

The drive from Denver to Las Vegas was six hours. The road was a gentle downward slope the entire stretch. The trees, grass, and hills of Colorado gave way to the sand, cactus, and space of Nevada. Every mile was lower and hotter than the last one. By three o' clock, the sun had become a booger in Joey's eyes, stuck at the end of the highway, a fiery ball of hell that awaited at the bottom of the road.

Over the six hours, Joey and Jade talked about their years in high school, their political opinions (Joey thought he was a liberal until Jade convinced him he was more a libertarian), their hopes for the future, and even a little about where their relationship might be headed. The more they talked, the more Joey seethed. His match in Vegas was with Jumbo. How could he quietly do a job in the ring with the man who tried to rape his girlfriend? How could he even be in the same room with such a man without trying to kill him?

He had to bury those thoughts. He had agreed to behave. The first time the topic came up, Jade asked him to do the job, lay low, and pretend he knew nothing of her incident with Jumbo. She pointed out that nothing good could come from making a scene. He was still a professional, she said, in spite of all that had happened, and a professional did the job when he was asked to, even if the job was shitty.

She reminded him how wonderful things could be at this time next year, when he was free from his GWA contract, and wrestling for Revolution. She pointed out that Revolution might not be interested in him if he developed a reputation as a troublemaker.

So Joey agreed to do the job that night, exactly as he was told. He agreed to say nothing to Jumbo or anyone else about what he now knew. He agreed to keep his mouth shut and his fists open if the urge to defend his woman's honor overcame him. He agreed to all of this because his woman had asked him to.

But he wasn't happy about it.

They arrived at the Grand Garden Arena in Las Vegas at five Mountain time. Joey had never wrestled in an arena as elegant as the Grand Garden. His first view of the inside was from the parking garage, where the pillars were made of red brick, the ground floor of shiny cobblestones, and valet parking for performers was free. Luckily, Jade knew how much to tip. At the performers' entrance a red carpet began, which led them to the backstage corridors, all of which were carpeted and adorned with potted ferns and trees.

Catering was in a ballroom, rather than the usual section of the loading dock. Joey and Jade picked at the fresh fruit from the buffet table, then went to their separate locker rooms.

The men's locker room was spacious and cool. A shiny oak bench ran a circle in front of the lockers, which stood above a carpeted floor. Being early, Joey had the room to himself, and leisurely changed into his wrestling attire, then sat on the floor to stretch.

Twenty minutes later, the locker room had filled with wrestlers who had plenty to say to each other but nothing to Joey, so he left, and began meandering through the halls, hoping to run into Jade, and trying to look purposeful to anyone who saw him. The corridors were less like those of a locker room area and more like those of an office, with doors and windows into meeting rooms lining the walls.

It was from behind one of these doors that Duke appeared, and asked Joey to join him. On the other side of the door was a small meeting room, with a circular table and four chairs. Jumbo sat against the far wall, dwarfing the furniture and giving the room an Alice-In-Wonderland feel.

On Duke's invitation, Joey sat down, without a greeting or even an acknowledgment of Jumbo's presence. He had only promised to keep what he knew to himself; he hadn't promised to be civil to Jade's assailant.

"I wanted to talk to you both about your program on TV tomorrow. Tonight's match is meant to be a warm-up for you both," said Duke.

He knew. Joey could tell. Duke's smug tone of voice gave him away. Duke knew that Jade had confided in Joey. Duke knew he had scheduled a match between a rapist and a protective boyfriend. What kind of sick freak was Joey working for?

The match was to be a squash, Duke explained. Joey would get in no offense at all. "That is, until the ref bump," said Duke. "Try whatever works for the ref bump," he continued. "Tonight's match is to prepare you for tomorrow on television. I want you guys to feel free to be creative out there so we can come up with something good for TV. I'll tell Rodney to work with you."

Rodney Mustaine would be the referee tonight and tomorrow. Rodney was the ultimate company man, and was unpopular with the wrestlers, as he was downright pushy. When wrestling matches go awry, as they often do, it is the job of the referee, who is connected to Duke via headpiece, to work things out. A good referee will ask questions, give advice, and relay information backstage, but will leave the actual improvisation to the wrestlers. Rodney wasn't like that. Rodney would get information from backstage and immediately start barking out commands. He was used when Duke didn't trust the wrestlers to carry themselves through the match.

"After the ref bump," Duke said, "Joey gets in a low blow, maybe two low blows. Let's try that Joey. Two, no, three, low blows. Jumbo will fall after the third. That will be great. Then Joey, you go get a weapon, bring it in, and hammer the snot out of Jumbo."

Joey nodded. This was the strangest booking he'd ever heard. Joey, the most over face in the company, would be acting the part of the heel. The crowd would probably cheer anyway. Jumbo looked mildly confused. Dumb bastard, Joey thought. He hadn't put it together that Joey was being de-pushed, starting tonight, and step one was getting Jumbo all the heat back that he'd lost two weeks ago.

"When you're done with your weapon Joey, throw it out of the ring and cover Jumbo. Rodney will wake up and do a slow count. Jumbo, you'll kick out at two. Joey, you'll be amazed that he kicked out, and you'll take a second to vent your frustration around the ring, stomping your feet, you know, whatever. Then you'll pick up Jumbo and swing him to the ropes. Jumbo, you'll hit him with a mammoth shoulder block. Now this is important. Joey, you've swung him to the ropes, planning on a clothesline or a kick, but you immediately see that it's not going to work. Show some fear before you take that shoulder block, then bump the hell out of it. I want you to smack against the mat like a pancake. After he splats down, Jumbo, you'll cover him for three and the win. And that's it guys. Any questions?"

Jumbo probably had a slew of questions, but wisely withheld them. He was going to come out of this match looking like gold. Joey couldn't imagine a more one-sided squash than this one. The booking was so malicious that the crowd would see right through it. Joey gets squashed, then resorts to cheating and still can't get the upper hand, finally to be pinned after a shoulder block, of all moves.

What kind of match ends with a shoulder block? When they performed this match on TV tomorrow night, the whole world would know that Joey Mayhem was in the doghouse with Duke.

They opened the show. Normally, a match of this magnitude would be the main event, but Duke knew this crowd wouldn't tolerate a squash as the last match of the night. Joey came out first. The crowd, hot for the opener, gave Joey the loudest pop he'd ever heard. Joey entered the ring and stood against the closest ringpost on the second rope, giving a section of the crowd the chance to cheer for him. He took his time, thinking that the sound director would let him showboat for the fans for as long as they could keep this ovation going. He was wrong. Jumbo's music started before he'd even stepped down from the first corner.

"Duke wants you guys to get some action started right away," Rodney said to Joey as they watched Jumbo approach the ring.

"Okay," said Joey, and as soon as Jumbo was through the ropes, Joey was up in his face in a lockup.

"Throw me down," said Joey.

Jumbo pushed and Joey fell back, hitting the ground and doing a backwards somersault across the ring. He jumped up and ran right back at Jumbo.

"Throw me down again," said Joey.

"I'm calling this match kid," said Jumbo. "To the corner."

Joey considered rebelling. It was bad form for someone to disagree with the spot you called. But, it was also bad form for Joey to call the spot in the first place. The GWA convention was for whomever was on offense (usually the heel in the early going) to call the match. Since this was a squash, Jumbo would be calling the whole thing.

Joey did as he was told and allowed Jumbo to push him into the nearest corner. Jumbo then threw punches at Joey's gut and face. Joey curled up in his wimpiest pose until Rodney stepped between them. Joey stumbled out of the corner, hamming up the damage done as he prepared for the next spot.

Jumbo grabbed Joey by the hair, then pulled him into a side headlock. From there, he lifted Joey into a vertical suplex, holding him aloft for five seconds. The standing vertical suplex, a wrestling classic, was one of Jumbo's signature moves. He showed off his strength by holding his opponent upside down for several seconds before falling backwards. Although difficult, the move was part of every wrestler's repertoire, and was taught to first-year wrestling students across the country.

The move was so commonplace that Joey was surprised that Jumbo was ignoring one of it's most fundamental mechanics. Jumbo needed to hold onto Joey's tights to support him in the stationary headstand. He wasn't. Consequently, Joey had to use all his abdominal strength and balance to remain upright. Jumbo further complicated the move by turning his body while holding Joey upside down. Joey had never felt so vulnerable. Jumbo was breaking the cardinal rule in professional wrestling: protect your opponent. Unable to communicate verbally, Joey slapped the back of Jumbo's thigh, hoping to let him know that it was time to end this move if it wasn't going to be done properly. The slap must have caught Jumbo off-guard, because his whole leg buckled in surprise, and the house of cards that was Joey and Jumbo came tumbling down in a sloppy heap. Joey landed on the back of his neck. His body folded at his upper abdomen and then fell to the side. Brimming with pain and dizziness, he moved his fingers and then his legs to make sure he wasn't paralyzed. The crowd booed at the obvious mistake, then broke into the obligatory, "YOU FUCKED UP!" chant.

Both men on the floor, Jumbo rolled over to whisper something to Joey. It was hard to hear over the crowd, but it sounded like Jumbo said, "What the fuck?"

What the fuck? Joey wanted to jump up, get in Jumbo's face, and throw down right here, right now. The sharp pain in his upper back eased that idea, and instead he stretched out on the floor and tried to get his bearings.

"One...two..." Rodney was giving a slow count. Both men were down, and had until ten to get up. Jumbo got up first and was greeted by a plastic cup of beer that soared into the ring and splashed across his face. The crowd cheered for whatever rebel from the front row had successfully lobbed the missile.

"Jesus Christ," Joey heard Jumbo say. Jumbo picked Joey up by the hair and threw him into a chinlock. "God help the little shit who screws up a spot with me," Jumbo said, then tightened the chinlock to very real proportions. With the last breath he could squeeze in, Joey smelled sweat and beer. He could think of only one thing to do. A vintage wrestling spot, time-tested and approved for years as a way out of a straight chinlock. The mule kick.

The mule kick was a staple of wrestling villains for generations. When the ref wasn't looking, the villain would kick backwards and nail his opponent in the groin. Wrestling fans were so accustomed to the mule kick that even it's obvious forgery (the foot always missed the actually groin by six inches at least) meant little. Perhaps that's why the crowd gasped, then cheered hysterically, when Joey's heel hit Jumbo's privates as square as a carpenter's hammer on a doornail.

Jumbo broke the chinlock immediately, then fell back to the floor, groaning. The crowd was now in a frenzy of joy at Joey's mischief. Rodney signaled for the bell, ending the match, then grabbed Joey by the arm.

"Get backstage immediately," he said.

Joey looked at him as if to say, 'Who the hell are you to tell me what to do?'

"Duke's in my ear right now Joey. Don't wait for your music or the announcement, get backstage now."

Confused, Joey stepped through the ropes and hopped down from the ring.

"Ladies and gentlemen," Melissa Marcus, the ring announcer, began, "the referee has ruled that tonight's winner, as a result of a disqualification, is Jumbo Sanders!"

The crowd jeered at Melissa's announcement. Not only did the good guy lose, but the match sucked.

As Joey headed up the ramp, individual fans broke from the chorus of boos to give him goodwill.

"Kick him in the balls Joey! Yeah!"

"You rock Joey!"

When Joey reached the top of the ramp, Jumbo's music started playing, further incensing the crowd. Joey looked at the black curtain, and wondered what would happen on the other side. Would he be fired? Suspended? He imagined himself explaining to Duke how Jumbo botched a suplex, blamed Joey for it, then tried to choke his lights out. The groin kick was totally justified. Would anybody care? Did he care? Maybe getting fired or suspended wouldn't be such a bad thing.

The first person to greet him on the other side of the curtain was Martha Tanner, the stage manager.

"Real classy Joey," she said with disdain as she handed him a bottle of water.

Deep Six, Lord Mayberry, Raptor, and Gordy Goodnow were standing off to the side. They seemed mostly uninterested in Joey's appearance.

"What happened out there?" said Deep Six. "Was that match supposed to be a DQ?"

At the non-televised events, the wrestlers backstage could hear what was happening, but couldn't see it unless they went to the curtain and watched. These guys heard the ring announcer call the match a disqualification, but had no idea what had just happened.

"Long story," said Joey, and continued walking. He was looking for Jade. He found Duke.

"What the hell is going on?" Duke yelled as he came running at Joey. At house shows, if Duke attended at all, he watched the matches from the press box. Joey looked with disgust at the little man, who was winded from running down a flight of stairs.

"I'll tell you what's going on," said Joey. "Jumbo got careless on that vertical suplex and dropped me on my head. Then he went nuts and choked me out. That's why he got kicked."

"In this company, we have ways of dealing with wrestling mistakes, Joey. Why didn't you get Rodney involved? All you had to do was let Rodney know that Jumbo was out of hand and he would have taken charge. Instead, you fucking ruined my opener and now we've got to put on eleven matches to a crowd that's already sour to us."

"They were going to be sour anyway with the shit you'd booked for me tonight," said Joey. He could see that a crowd of spectators had formed around him and Duke. This display probably didn't look good for him a week after he knocked out the champ.

"Why, you little punk," said Duke, anger boiling up from under his tight Armani collar. "In case you didn't know, people don't question my booking decisions here. I've been a promoter for 30 years. I was booking million dollar matches ten years before you were born you little shit. It was my booking that made you popular with the fans, but I can see it's gone to your head."

"What are you going to do, end my push? It's a little late for that."

The tension in Duke's face was almost comical. It reminded Joey of Yosemite Sam. "You impetuous snot," he said quietly, almost in a whisper. "You overbearing brat. You think you can talk to me like this—"

"Clear the way! I'm gonna kill that fucker!" It was Jumbo, having just come through the curtain. He was practically running at Joey and Duke.

"Stop him!" Duke yelled at the crowd of wrestlers who had gathered to watch the drama.

Deep Six and Lord Mayberry ran up to Jumbo and tried to talk him down. Jumbo pushed them aside. Raptor, Gordy Goodnow, and Mike Clarke ran to help, Raptor and Gordy each grabbing an arm, Mike pushing on Jumbo from the front. Deep Six and Lord Mayberry recovered to help them. The five of them slowed Jumbo to a stop in time for Duke to address everyone.

"So help me," Duke yelled, "if either of the two of you lay a finger on the other tonight you're fired. On the spot, no questions asked, just fired. You two will stay away from each other for the rest of the night and you'll cool off and you will wrestle again tomorrow night. I don't pay petty little babies to get in personal feuds that disrupt my programming, and I will have my main even tomorrow night on TV! Tomorrow night you will wrestle the match you were supposed to wrestle tonight, you will get it right, you will not break character or work off script, you will not work each other stiff, and if either of you fuck up or disobey me I'll fire your ass and make sure you never work in this industry again and if you don't think I can do that then try me! Jumbo, is that clear? I said, is that clear!"

Jumbo slung a look of fire at Joey, then answered Duke. "Yes sir, it's clear."

"Joey?" said Duke.

Was it clear? Did he care? Joey considered saying Fuck You. If he was done with professional wrestling, so be it. It would be worth it just to say Fuck You to Duke right now.

But among the crowd who had gathered, standing next to no one, with genuine sadness in her eyes, was Jade. This wasn't her fault at all, but she probably thought it was. He'd have to explain to her that tonight's melee with Jumbo wasn't her doing. He needed to get this situation under control.

"It's clear," said Joey.

"Good. I'll see you both tomorrow night," said Duke. He took a second to give one more glare to Joey, then turned around to go back to the press box. Joey remained where he was as the crowd began to disperse. Jumbo scowled at Joey as he walked past, going toward the locker room. Joey stood still, and returned Jumbo's gaze.

After Jumbo had passed, Jade came forward and handed Joey his T-shirt and shorts, then put her arm across his back.

"Are you doing okay?" she asked.

"Yeah, I'll be fine." He wanted to ask her how she was, but decided it was best not to imply that she was somehow involved in this incident. "Your match is coming up soon," he said with forced composure.

"Yes. I'll need to check in with Martha in just a minute. Hey, do you know about the viewing area here?"

"I don't think so."

"Come with me. I think this will be a fine place for you to be while we wait for this night to end."

Jade led Joey out of the foyer and down an unlit corridor. They passed a trophy case, an equipment room, and a conference room. All were dark and deserted.

"The Grand Garden is my favorite arena," she said. "There are all sorts of surprises back here."

Jade grabbed his hand as she continued to lead him through empty, unlit hallways. Realizing they were going someplace where he apparently could wait out the night in peace, Joey wondered if he would be able to find his way back.

They came to a door marked, "Authorized Personnel Only." Jade opened it, leading them into a narrow hallway with concrete floors and white brick walls. To their right was Stephen Shepney, a rookie who wrestled as Stevie Sikes. Stevie was standing at a door at the end of the hallway, looking out a narrow window, where he had a clear view into the arena, all the way to the ring.

"Mind some company Stephen?" said Jade.

"No, no. Come in," he said, as if this dark hallway were his home.

"I'll see you later Honey," said Jade, "I'm going to go get ready for my match."

"Alright, I'll meet up with you backstage," said Joey. Jade kissed him and then left. Joey nodded his head at Stephen and came into the hallway. He was glad that it was only Stephen here, or else he'd have to find another place to hang out. Stephen, a rookie with a great physique but only a modicum of talent, was one of the few people who never showed any animosity towards Joey. Stephen got into the GWA through family connections. His father, Martin Shepney, was a World Champion in the early seventies who wrestled as Barbarian Bill Strong. Stephen was well-liked in the locker room, but even he knew that he wasn't going anywhere, and was only on the roster because Duke owed his dad a favor.

"That was an interesting match you had out there Joey," said Stephen.

"Not nearly as interesting as the aftermath backstage," said Joey.

"Oh yeah? What happened?"

"Oh, Duke was unhappy with how things went, as I'm sure you can imagine. He got into my face a little, then Jumbo came tearing in and wanted to beat the shit out of me. I'm sure you'll hear about it."

"I'm sure I will," said Stephen. "Do you mind if I ask—"

"What happened out there? I'd love to tell you. At least I can tell someone, before Jumbo's version becomes the historical record. Jumbo botched that vertical suplex—"

"I saw that. Why was he holding you with only one arm?"

"I have no idea, but he dropped me. Then his next move was a choke. I don't get that guy. He drops me, then he gets all pissed off, like it was my fault."

Stephen shook his head, "Sucks, man."

Beyond the window, in the arena, Safire was introduced to a minor fan reaction.

"It does suck," said Joey. "Now I'm supposed to wrestle Jumbo again tomorrow night on TV. We're supposed to keep our cool. I swear, if that asshole screws up even once, I'm all over him."

In the arena, Jade came out next. The fans roared. Despite all the company had done to hold her back, she was still the most over with the fans of any woman on the roster.

"I don't understand why the Women's Title isn't hers," said Stephen.

"There's a lot of history and shit behind the scenes," said Joey.

"Really? What sort of history?"

Joey wished he hadn't said anything. Stephen's voice had an eagerness to hear some gossip. Although Joey trusted Stephen more than most people in the company, he didn't trust him to keep Jade's secret.

"I don't know everything, and what I do know I shouldn't say. Let's just say that in the past few weeks I've learned that political skill is more important than wrestling skill in this company."

"See, I don't think so," said Stephen. "I think politics and who you know can get your foot in the door, but it's what you know that will get you up to the top."

Jade and Safire were wrestling a solid match. Jade was working on Safire's left leg, first with a chop block, then a series of elbow drops. Now she was trying to work Safire into a figure four leglock.

"Well, you keep thinking that," said Joey. "I don't want to burst your bubble. I look at this match going on here, and see one woman who has mastered her craft, putting on a great show and carrying her opponent, and I see another one who has a pretty face and a willingness to kiss ass but doesn't know what she's doing. Take a guess which one will get more camera time tomorrow night."

"I don't think that's a respectable thing to say about Safire," said Stephen. "She's very competent as a wrestler and isn't a kiss-ass."

Joey shrugged. He needed not to get into this argument with one of the few people willing to talk to him.

"Joey, here's some advice," said Stephen. "I can tell that your push is over. Everyone can. I can also tell you that you're wrong about whatever politicking you think is behind it. You knocked out the champion. It wouldn't be right for you to take his place."

Another ally down, thought Joey.

"Well, I disagree, but you're certainly entitled to think whatever you'd like," he said.

The two of them stood in silence for the remainder of Jade's match, both looking through the small window in the door. The match finished with Safire pinning Jade after landing an elbow off the top rope. Without a word to Stephen, Joey left the viewing room and found himself in a maze of unlit hallways. It took several tries and nearly ten minutes to find the path to the backstage area.

"There you are," said Jade. "Are you ready?" She was still in wrestling attire, unshowered, with her gym bag hanging over her shoulder. Joey caught a strong odor when he got near her, and smiled to himself. His girlfriend, an international sex symbol, stunk.

"Yes, I'm ready," he said. "Let's get out of here."

On the way to the car, Joey complimented Jade on her match. He talked with her about what he saw as the storyline they were creating and how he thought it worked. Jade was pleased with his assessment. She noted that the match would have worked even better if Safire had sold more of her offense.

Joey took the driver's side in Jade's Expedition to take them on the short jaunt from the parking garage at the Grand Garden to their hotel room at the MGM. They were 40 seconds into their journey when Jade said what Joey had been thinking.

"Does something stink?" she said. "I've been smelling it since the parking lot."

Joey didn't want to tell her he'd assumed it was her, given that she had just wrestled a twelve-minute match. "I don't know if I smell anything," he lied.

Jade lifted her arms and smelled underneath. "It's not me," she said, surprising Joey. How could it not be her? Was it him? As if reading his mind, Jade leaned over and stuck her nose under his shoulder. "It's not you either," she said. She took a few more deep breaths through her nose. "You can't smell that?"

Joey breathed deeply. He definitely could smell something.

"Maybe there's an animal carcass on the road," he said, but knew that couldn't be it, because he'd first noticed the smell back at the arena. It was a light but encompassing odor. It reminded Joey of his grandparents house. It almost smelled like someone was cooking lima beans.

"I think it's something in the car," said Jade.

Jade had unbuckled her seatbelt and was now rummaging through the back-seat, sniffing things.

"It's my," she sniffed twice more, "what the?" Jade pulled her gym bag to the front seat. "It's my bag," she said in disbelief. Her tone was one of fear, as if a whole world of manners had fallen apart. She was visibly embarrassed that her bag smelled so foul.

Jade unzipped the leather bag and the stench exploded inside the car. It was unmistakable now. It was the smell of piss.

"Holy shit," Jade said quietly, then pushed the bag and the blinding smell away from her face.

"What's going on?" said Joey.

"Stop the car," she said.

They were in the left lane on Grand Avenue, a three-lane busy street. Joey drifted two lanes to the right and pulled into a McDonald's parking lot.

"There's a dumpster over there," said Jade, pointing.

Joey drove around the near side of the restaurant, and to the dumpster at the back of the parking lot. Jade had the door open before the car was fully stopped, triggering the dome light inside the cab. In the light, Joey could see that Jade was crying.

Jade tore out of the car, lofted her bag into the dumpster, then, with surprising violence, kicked the dumpster's front face.

Joey put the car in park and undid his seatbelt. He was preparing to go out and hug her, but she stopped him.

"No, no," she said. "I'm done." She got back in the car and slammed the door. "Pull up to the restaurant. I want to go wash my hands."

Joey said nothing and did what she asked. As soon as he stopped the car at the entrance, she hopped out and ran inside. Joey was a few seconds behind her, taking time to put on the brake and turn off the engine. Jade's despondency and the shock of the smell had left Joey unable to think, but as he followed her into the restaurant, he realized his initial instinct about what had happened was the only possible explanation. After his match with Joey and the backstage confrontation with Duke, Jumbo had pissed in Jade's gym bag.

Joey entered the McDonald's and was greeted like the President. The entire restaurant was looking at him. The sounds of cooking machinery beeped and hummed, but not a word was spoken. No doubt Jade, still in her black leather wrestling attire, had garnered some looks as she stormed in and ran to the bathroom. Now Joey, a bona fide celebrity, had entered right behind her, wearing a T-shirt, shorts, and his wrestling boots.

Nothing conscious prompted what Joey did next. His consciousness was only a spectator, like these parasites at McDonald's who wanted a piece of him to make themselves and their worthless lives more complete, whose chronic desire to be larger than what they were had created the high-stakes, high-money world where simple human decency was a worthless microbe in a tidal wave of ambition that turned a man into an animal who pissed to mark his territory.

"What! What are you looking at?" Joey shouted at the restaurant. "Can't a man walk into a McDonald's? Can't you for once just give me some mother fucking privacy?"

"Joey, let's go." It was Jade. Somehow she had appeared at his side without his noticing, and was now pulling on his arm with wet hands as he gazed at a terrified old lady at the ketchup dispenser who certainly had no idea who he was.

"Fuck," said Joey, then followed Jade out the door.

"Give me the keys, I'll drive," she said, heading toward the driver's side.

"I'll drive," Joey retorted.

Jade stopped walking and looked back at Joey. Her face was filled with anguish and exhaustion. What was happening? Joey felt so out of control he wanted to march back into McDonald's and hit someone.

"Okay," she said, and walked around to the passenger side.

Joey drove them out of the parking lot and turned left onto the street.

"Where are you going?" asked Jade.

"Back to the arena," said Joey.

"Joey, what's going on? What was all that about in there?" she said. "I was washing my hands and then I heard you screaming. It scared the hell out of me."

"It was about me completely losing my cool. It was just…shit!" Joey slapped the steering wheel in frustration that he had missed a traffic light and now would have to wait. It occurred to him that he had never been this angry before.

"Joey, what's the matter? Why are we going back to the arena?" Jade was practically yelling, as if trying to control the situation with her voice.

"We're going back to the arena so I can find Jumbo and kick his ass. I'm sure he's still there, hanging around with his buddies, making plans to find some groupies tonight. When I'm done with him the only bag he'll piss into will be on the other end of a catheter."

"Joey that isn't funny. You don't need to do this. You don't need to protect my honor or any other macho shit. If you confront Jumbo you'll be fighting Deep Six and Lord Mayberry too, and there won't be anyone to back you up except me. And he outweighs you by a hundred pounds."

"He's a fat fuck and he won't touch me. Even if he does I don't care. I'm not leaving Las Vegas until I find him and this is done."

The stoplight changed and Joey ripped out of the intersection.

"Joey, think about what you're doing. This sort of shit happens in this business. I can deal with it. But I can't deal with you fighting with half the locker room. Please don't do this."

Joey wanted to yell at her to shut up, that this was happening and she wasn't going to stop him. But instead he said nothing and kept driving.

"Joey? Joey, are you listening to me?" Jade fell back into her chair. "Shit," she said under her breath.

Twenty seconds later they were in the parking garage. Joey threw the car in park, and hopped out.

"Welcome back, sir," said the valet. Joey ignored him, storming out of the car and into the arena. Jade followed him through the glass doors that led to the backstage area.

CHAPTER 25

▼

They found Jumbo in the center foyer, an open space of concrete floor and fluorescent light just past the arena entrance. He was amidst a group of wrestlers and entourage, all sitting against the far wall in the steel chairs that were so prevalent in the wrestling world. He was talking to two wrestlers and his wife. A handful of other people were scattered through the room. Jumbo stopped speaking to his listeners, seemingly in mid-sentence, and stood up when he saw Joey approaching. It was clear that Jumbo knew what was coming and why.

Joey surveyed the room as he continued his approach. Everyone had turned their attention to the pending conflict between Joey and Jumbo. By now, word had surely spread throughout the locker room of their botched match earlier in the night. Jumbo's wife, Rashann, stood up. As if experienced in this sort of scene, she took three steps away from her husband, clearing the path to his assailant.

To Jumbo's right sat Lamar Thomas, Deep Six, and Lord Mayberry. They glared at Joey with active skepticism, as if all three were eager to be involved in whatever was forthcoming. To Jumbo's left were Raptor and Pit Bull. Their faces expressed more concern. If this grew out of hand, they might get involved.

Ten or more others were dispersed among the room, mostly along the walls. In the perimeter of his vision, Joey saw Mike Sanders with his daughter, Gordy Goodnow with his boyfriend, and Martha Tanner. It occurred to Joey that Martha would call Duke through her headset soon, if she hadn't already.

But the focus of Joey's vision was Jumbo, who was now standing directly in front of him, less than six feet away, prepared to fight. Jumbo wore only blue jeans and wrestling boots. He stood nearly a foot taller than Joey.

"Do you have a problem?" said Jumbo.

"Someone pissed in Jade's bag, and I think it was you," said Joey.

Some mumblings and whispers immediately circled around the room. Joey could now hear Martha speaking into her headset. He needed to get this started and finished quickly.

"What the fuck you punk," said Jumbo. "I didn't piss in nobody's bag."

Joey continued to approach, albeit slowly. He wished he hadn't said anything, and instead had run in and thrown a punch. This wasn't an argument that needed to be settled. He didn't need any proof. Jumbo's denial meant nothing except that he was a coward.

"Where is your little woman?" said Jumbo, now looking over Joey's shoulder. "If she's so sure it was me, why doesn't she tell me to my face?"

You fucking coward, Joey thought, and maybe said, he couldn't remember, it wasn't clear. In the midst of that thought, he charged and threw a punch. A solid right hook, that started at his waist and swung through the air too fast for Jumbo to dodge it, landed right underneath Jumbo's left eye.

Jumbo stumbled back two steps and then fell. He put his hand to his face for just a second, before jumping back to his feet and lunging at Joey. He threw his shoulder into Joey's stomach and tackled him to the ground. Joey's head whipped backward and slapped into the concrete.

Then the room erupted. Pit Bull and Raptor jumped on Jumbo from the side, knocking him off Joey before he could land a punch. When Jumbo tried to shake them off, Mike Sanders and Gordy Goodnow assisted. The four of them held Jumbo back while Joey rolled around on the floor, holding the back of his head.

"You fucking pussy!" Jumbo yelled over the heads of his restrainers. "Next time I'll kill you!"

Jumbo's screaming brought about everyone else in the area to see what was going on. While Joey continued rolling around on the floor, the foyer filled with crew members and other wrestlers.

"Joey, are you okay?"

It was Jade. This fight apparently was over.

Was he okay? His job required him to get beat up every night, sometimes taking steel chairs to his head, but nothing had ever hurt like this. He was dizzy, and nauseous.

Joey rolled to his back, and tried to sit up. The room was blurry, and the light hurt his eyes.

"I'll be fine," he grunted. He flailed his arms around him to stave off the crowd of would-be helpers.

"Well you don't look fine," Jade said. "Somebody get the doctor in here," she called out.

The room was now a buzz of conversation and movement. Through the blur, Joey could see several concerned faces looking at him. He tried to focus on Jade's. He lost her face when the doctor's hand appeared.

"Joey, how many fingers am I holding up?" the doctor asked.

Joey pushed the hand away. "I'm fine," he said, then tried to stand up. It was as if the room stood up with him. Nothing was right. His knees didn't work, the walls weren't straight, and before he knew it, he was back down on the ground.

"We should call an ambulance."

"Duke's gonna be pissed," someone said.

"I'm fine," said Joey. "I just..." He wanted to say, 'I just need a minute,' but the sentence didn't come out. He started it, but he lost control of the end of it. Then he turned his head to the side and vomited on the concrete.

Such a nice arena to make such a mess, he thought. Then he blacked out.

CHAPTER 26

▼

Joey woke up in a fog of sickness. He vaguely remembered a dream about discovering a parasite in his intestines. The plot and visuals of the dream had dimmed, but the feeling of nausea deep in his gut sharpened as he rejoined the waking world. A churning somewhere in his bowels provoked a pathetic moan that came out of his mouth in a weak voice that didn't seem his own.

There was a clear tube hanging across his torso. His eyes followed it to its source, a blue box on a metal stand next to his bed. He decided he was in a hospital room. Instantly, memories of yesterday started piecing together, and through a haze of medication, Joey came to fathom what had happened.

He had fought with Jumbo. He had wretched on the concrete. He had ridden in an ambulance. There was a hospital bed, doctors, an IV, shots, a CT scan, he remembered all of this, but not as he might normally remember something. The memories were faded, like they had been stored in his brain twenty years ago and were only now coming forth. And they didn't fit with the current reality. The hospital room, with the rolling and dripping sounds of the IV, the ticking of the clock, the humming of some generic machine, the light through the blinds on the window, seemed unrelated to the haste and fury of the montage he recalled.

"Good morning," said a voice. Joey knew the voice. It was Jade. He tried to roll his head toward it, but it didn't quite work right. Had he forgotten how to turn his head?

"Good morning," he said. His tongue was thick and slow. He needed some water.

"Do you know where you are?" the voice said. He had to turn to it. He had to see her. He had a vision of using his hands to turn his head; that would work. But where were his hands?

"Easy there," said the voice. Then she appeared. His line of sight unchanged, she appeared in it, and the static became a clear picture. She was so beautiful. Was he drunk?

Now she was holding his hand, no, his wrist. She was laying it at his side.

"Best not to move much, I think," she said. "How do you feel?"

"I feel funny," Joey said. And he sounded funny too.

"How so?" she said. And then she was gone from sight again. This time he would turn his head and look at her, dammit. It was like moving a brick with his chin, but he did it. He turned his head, and the room spun with the movement, but he could see her. How did he ever get so lucky to have someone so beautiful in his room?

She smiled at him. Was he smiling at her?

"Are you okay?" she said. Her voice was cutesy, like they were being mischievous. Maybe he was drunk.

"Yes, I...just feel funny."

She laughed, nervously. "How so?" she said.

And then he realized the joke. They had been over this already. He says he feels funny, she asks how so. He laughed. It was a breathy laugh, the best he had. He wanted her to know he understood what was funny. But apparently she didn't. She looked at him like he was speaking Chinese.

"I'll be right back Sweetie," she said.

No, wait, don't go. But she was already gone. She could move so quickly. Ah well. No big deal. He'd just go back to sleep.

*   *   *   *

"Mr. Hamilton." The voice was not Jade's. It was the troll's.

He opened his eyes. She was leering over him. Two hundred pounds of face with stringy red hair and a wart on her cheek. The troll.

"Good morning Mr. Hamilton," said the troll.

"Good morning," he said.

"Your girlfriend told me you were up. That's good. So tell me, how do you feel?"

He almost started laughing again. Would the troll understand the joke?

"I feel funny," he said.

"I bet you do," said the troll. "You're on some heavy-duty painkillers. We're going to go ahead and turn those off this morning to see how you do."

"Okay," said Joey. None of this was making any sense. "I have to pee," he said.

"Alrighty," said the troll. "Do you think you can sit up?"

Joey tried to lift his legs. It seemed they would have to move first if he were to sit up. The brick was back, though, and now it was tied to his ankles.

"I'm having some trouble moving properly," he said.

"Okay. Well here, let me help you." The troll reached around Joey to fiddle with something and the bed started moving. The back of the bed began arching upward, taking Joey with it. The movement made him wheezy. He closed his eyes and waited for it to end.

"Okay, let's try again," said the troll.

Joey opened his eyes and took a big breath. He was sitting up now. And he was dizzy.

"Okay, and, let's just get you going here." The troll had lifted the sheets off Joey and moved his legs over the side of the bed.

"Sweetie, can you help me?" said the troll to someone else. It was Jade. She was here again. The troll put one of Joey's arms over her own shoulder and Jade took the other.

"Okay, one, two, three," Jade and the troll lifted Joey right out of the bed. His legs were wobbly. The room was now spinning out of control. He felt like he was going to throw up.

"Help us out here Joey," said Jade.

Okay, thought Joey. Anything for you. He managed to get his feet planted and his legs stiffened. He was standing. He felt like he'd accomplished something huge by standing. Then it occurred to him that standing used to be something that was easy. What the hell was wrong with him?

"Okay honey, one foot in front of the other," said the troll.

"Maybe we should just use a bedpan," said Jade.

"No, he's good to make it to the other end of the room. We need to get him up today. His head will clear faster if we can get him out of bed a few times this morning."

Somewhere on the other side of the world, after an eternity of encouragement, steps, missteps, spinning, more steps, more encouragement, Joey was in the bathroom. Jade had dropped him off at the door, leaving only the troll to help him with the big work. Joey had envisioned a standing group of three at the toilet with him in the center, but the troll wanted him to sit, and come to think of it, that wasn't a bad idea. Joey sat on the toilet and the world calmed for a minute.

"Okay honey, I'm gonna leave the door open a smidge, but I think you're good to go on your own. I'll help you up when you're done." And the troll left. Joey was alone on the toilet.

To his left was a mirror. To his right was a shower. He looked in the mirror.

He was wearing a white hospital gown. His skin was pale. His hair was matted.

The room was spinning. What was he doing here? Peeing. Yes, peeing. That happened without issue, thankfully.

He didn't remember leaving the toilet, flushing, going back to the bed, or going to sleep. But he woke up in the bed several hours later. His nausea had subsided. His head was more clear. He was aware of his surroundings some, and had a better grasp of what was going on. And he hurt. His head, neck, shoulder, back, stomach, and sides all hurt like hell.

"Good morning again." It was Jade.

He turned his head. It hurt, but it worked.

"Good morning again," said Joey.

"You look better," she said.

"I feel worse."

"How do you feel? And don't say you feel funny."

"I hurt. My head, and my shoulders," he lifted his arms to point out where he hurt, but lifting them revealed new sources of hurt in his chest and his hands.

"What happened?" he said. "Did Jumbo totally kick my ass or something?"

"No. Well, maybe. I guess you are the one who's in the hospital."

Joey looked at her for more clarification. She got out of her chair and approached his bed. She stroked his hair, then leaned in and kissed his forehead.

"My memory of yesterday is all screwed up," he said.

"Maybe it will come back. If not, I'll make up something pleasant for you."

Jade's presence soothed Joey to the point of lessening the pain. She was calm. She was more calm than he'd ever seen her.

"So what happened? Where am I?" he said.

"You're at Presbyterian Hospital in Las Vegas. It's Tuesday morning. Actually, now it's Tuesday afternoon. Yesterday you bravely defended my honor backstage at the Grand Garden. Jumbo tackled you, you hit your head on the concrete and suffered a bad concussion. You blacked out and an ambulance took you here. The doctor thinks you're going to be okay, but may suffer from concussion syndrome for awhile."

"Why do I hurt so much?"

"I don't know, Honey. You're getting a full-body MRI in a few hours. We'll learn everything that's wrong with you then. If that checks out okay, you'll be discharged tonight."

Joey relaxed his shoulders and closed his eyes for a second. The aching in his neck was really uncomfortable.

"Painkillers? Do I get any painkillers?"

"You've had a slew already. Your nurse is weaning you off them today to see how you do. This morning you were drugged up and loopy. Do you remember any of that?"

"You mean earlier? Yeah. I remember, sort of. You all helped me to the bathroom."

"Mm-hm."

Jade went back to her chair and sat down.

"So I'm not going to wrestle tonight?" said Joey, as if he needed to ask.

Jade shook her head. "Neither will Jumbo; neither will I."

"Why aren't you going to wrestle?"

"I told Duke I was going to the hospital with you, and I wouldn't be performing."

"What did he say?"

"We can talk about that later."

Joey closed his eyes. He wanted to jump out of the bed and run out of here. He wanted to run away from the murky pain, the headache, last night. What had he done? He'd screwed up the whole TV show for tonight. This wasn't going to make him any more popular backstage.

"I really hope you're not going to be in trouble," said Joey.

"Joey, we're both in trouble."

She said it like it wasn't a big deal. Maybe it wasn't. Duke already knew about what Jumbo tried to do to Jade last year. Maybe as soon as he knew that Jumbo pissed in her bag too—Joey had done the right thing, even if it had turned out sour.

"What's going to happen to Jumbo?" he asked.

"I have no idea, and I really don't care."

"Well, does Duke know that Jumbo pissed in your bag?"

"I don't know."

"I'll call him. I'll let him know. He'll want to talk to me anyway." Joey reached for the phone, but a sharp sting in his neck shut down that idea.

"Honey, please don't try to call Duke. I don't think he wants to talk to either of us today. Sweetie, I need to tell you something."

Her voice was sullen, like a warning to Joey to prepare for bad news. He worked through the pain of moving his neck to get a good look at her face so she'd know he was listening.

"What is it?" he said. For some reason he was sure she was going to say she was pregnant.

"Joey, we're going to be suspended."

"What do you mean?"

"I mean we're not going to be allowed to wrestle for awhile."

That was strange news. Fights had broken out backstage before. Sometimes they resulted in fines or de-pushes. Never suspensions. Suspensions were reserved for drug offenders, and even then only if the company chose to notice. It just wasn't good business to keep someone off the card when he might put some asses in the seats.

"Why are you being suspended?" Joey asked.

"Technically, I don't know for sure that either of us is going to be suspended. It's not official yet, but I talked to Duke, and, well, I know how he is, I know how this locker room works, and I know this business."

"That doesn't mean anything. What did Duke say?"

"He said things are going to have to change around here, and to tell you that he's very disappointed in you. He said he's very disappointed in both of us, and that I should never have gotten involved with you."

"What the fuck does that mean? It's his business now what we do outside of the company?"

"Joey, I know this isn't what you want to hear, and I can only tell you I'm sorry. I'm sorry I made things so complicated. I'm sorry I got you involved. I'm sorry I've ended your…"

"What are you apologizing for? This doesn't make any sense. You've done nothing wrong. Hell, I've done nothing wrong. If anyone should be suspended, it should be Jumbo. More than suspended, he should be fired. And we need to talk to Duke and talk to the others backstage and talk to the journalists if we have to until something is done because this isn't fair." In his anger, Joey grew light-headed. He had to lean back into his pillow and close his eyes. He wondered if this was what it was going to be like to be old.

"It doesn't have to be fair, Joey. Tonight three of the company's biggest stars are going to miss their scheduled appearances on TV in our second largest market—"

"Well it doesn't make any sense for you to be suspended. You didn't do anything."

"Yes I did, Joey. I refused to perform tonight. I came over here instead. And beyond that, I instigated the whole thing."

"What are you talking about? Somebody pissed in your bag a year after he tried to rape you. I picked a fight with him, against your will, landed one punch, and you instigated the whole thing?"

"Jumbo's still denying that he's the one who peed in my bag. He never admitted that he tried to rape me. I'm just a little girl causing trouble."

"But you know that's a bunch of bull shit! We know it was him. I could see on his face yesterday when he stood up that he was guilty. He was ready for me to start shit the minute he saw me. The fact that he denies it just makes him a coward. Man, that guy is such a bastard."

"Joey, we don't need to be talking about all this. It won't help anything. I need you to accept that we're not going to win this fight."

"I can't accept that. I'm not going to accept that."

"Well you need to. For me. For me, you need to say that life's not fair and shit happens and you'll give up this stupid fight I got you in. You need to accept it before your whole career is washed down the tubes because of me, if it isn't already."

Jade turned away to hide her tears.

"Jade, honey, it doesn't have to be like—"

"Yes it does!" She stamped her foot as she turned back around. "It does have to be like that! It's the way this fucked up business works, and nobody knows it better than me. People treat you like dirt and you take it because they're in the loop and you're out. It's just the way it is, Joey, and if you can learn it now you might still make it, and please learn it now so at least you'll get something out of this shitty week you've spent with me."

Joey lay quietly, with lots to say, but little courage to say it. "I don't think it was a shitty week," was what came out.

"I'm sorry," she said. "We don't have to talk about all of this now. You're in a hospital bed for Christ's sake."

"Okay," said Joey.

An hour later the troll came back and took Joey out of the room on a wheelchair. He got the dreaded full-body MRI. Forty minutes of stillness in a tiny chamber.

Three hours later, back in the hospital room, Joey's doctor, a balding, overweight man who didn't look the part of "health care provider" went over the

MRI with Joey and Jade. Some evidence of concussion and some bruising near the rib cage, but otherwise, things looked good. The prognosis: no wrestling for at least a week, watch for signs of concussion syndrome, visit a doctor again in seven days for reevaluation. Joey was discharged at five that evening, able to walk out on his own. The shrieking pain of the morning had turned to general aching in the evening, and by the time he walked out, he felt less like he'd been tossed to the concrete, and more like he'd just been through a ringer of a match.

CHAPTER 27

▼

Max approached James with the idea on Saturday.

Apparently, Scott Rollins, currently playing a heel but getting face pops (the fans were still happy to see him since he was newly stolen from the competition's roster), would "turn" on Monday's *Riot*. The notion of "turning" was a creation unique to professional wrestling. In no other form of storytelling did an arch villain so easily become a hero, or vice versa. In wrestling, fifteen years' worth of dastardly deeds could be forgotten with one act of kindness. Similarly, a career of heroism was often discarded and erased from the historical record if the fans lost interest in a character.

The Scott Rollins turn was to be executed in the most cliched of fashions, with a surprise run-in. In the main event, a match between Lucifer and Tony Campbell, Jerry Senika would interfere, ruining the match, then Senika and Campbell (two of the company's most established heels) would beat Lucifer with chairs, belts, ring bells, and sledgehammers. Scott Rollins would then appear from backstage and come to Lucifer's rescue, clearing the ring of the villains. Then Rollins and Lucifer would shake hands and walk to the back together with a newfound mutual respect.

James could imagine the fans responding well to this idea, but it was fraught with problems. One, Lucifer didn't have friends. It was crucial to his character. Allowing him to get buddy-buddy with Rollins would add a human dimension to Lucifer that might make him more popular with the female viewers, but didn't make any sense based on his history. Two, Lucifer and Rollins had a hot feud going. Why change it? Yes, Rollins was getting cheers, but he was a fresh face. His character was already established as a heel and should remain that way to protect the integrity of the story. So what if the fans were cheering for him? Let them cheer for the villain. Allowing the mood of the crowd to dictate the storylines was a bad tactic. James had always thought Max understood this.

On Sunday morning, James called Gene Harold to talk about this new storyline development.

"This is news to me," said Gene, after sighing with despondence. "I've heard nothing of this change for Scott. I was pleased with how things were going. It doesn't make any sense, even against the silly things that are down the pipe. In fact, just this week Vicky was tossing out..."

Gene's voice trailed off, as if he didn't want to finish his sentence.

"What is it Gene?"

"Well, James, this week, at our meeting on Thursday, there was discussion of turning your character heel."

"Turning Lucifer heel? That's—"

"Ridiculous. That's what I said. I thought the idea was closed. But this...well, I don't like where this is going."

"I don't either," said James. Not at all, in fact. Seen with this new information, the Rollins turn made sense, in a bad way. If they wanted to turn Lucifer heel, they first needed someone for him to turn on. As a loner, he effectively played neither heel nor face, just someone out for himself who happened to be a fan favorite. But if they gave him a best buddy—why hadn't he seen this before? In modern wrestling, the only purpose at all of "best buddies" is to have one betray the other.

"Why do they want to turn me heel?" James asked.

"I don't know," said Gene. "Vicky was spouting off some claptrap about the character lacking motivation and some other Hollywood garbage."

"I'll call Max and see what he says," said James.

"Let me know. I'm sure I'll have a few words for him myself."

Max wasn't home, and didn't return phone calls. James left a message with Max's secretary at the office anyway.

Monday night's taping of *Riot* was in Cleveland. Max was not in attendance. Larry Jenkins ran the show in his absence.

The opening segment went well, with Lucifer, Rollins, Campbell, and Senika all cutting solid promos. They hyped a main event between Lucifer and Campbell later in the night. They laid out the framework for the eventual Rollins face turn.

The first hour built to a steel cage match between Flash Martin and Miguel Cervantes, which featured some great spots and a nice storyline going into their scheduled ladder match at the pay per view. The second hour was also effective, with three decent matches and steady reminders of the pending main event.

And when Rollins's face turn happened in the main event, the crowd was into it. James couldn't deny that Max and his team of writers and bookers knew how to take an idea and run with it. If only they valued the integrity of the idea itself.

That was what few in the wrestling world understood, the integrity of the ideas, the human story that must be told underneath the costumes and the characters. Wrestling is a unique dramatic art that zeroes in on the driver of all storytelling, conflict. Gene and Larry were the only two bookers James had worked with who began to understand the responsibility that came with presenting this art form at this level. Max certainly didn't. Neither did his floozy. His floozy was uniquely dangerous.

James had only met Vicky once, but once was enough. With only one look James knew she neither understood nor cared for professional wrestling. She was on board to cash in. She just as easily could have been writing for a soap opera.

The idea of turning Lucifer heel, certainly hers and hers alone, capsulated everything that was wrong with the presentation of modern professional wrestling. Shock over story. Caricature over character. Convenience over realism. The fans warmed up to Chapter One of this story, presented tonight with Rollins's face turn. And they might accept Lucifer as a heel when it happened. But at what cost? The creation of the Lucifer character, with each word and gesture carefully considered and planned, would go down the tubes in one trite storytelling ploy. The fans took to Lucifer because he was real. Yes, he was larger than life, but he was real. His actions, his motivations, and his persona were all tightly woven into one consistent character who was interesting because he represented reality, and in doing so, allowed his admirers to project their own dreams upon him. Those dreams were of athletic achievement, macho bravado, and intimidating strength. They were the universal masculine dreams of our age. Those dreams, rather than pulp storytelling, are what wrestling is about.

Still, James would do what he was told. Yes, he was an idealist, but he was a wrestler first, and wrestling doesn't work if there are too many storytellers. One day he would run his own promotion, and it would be done properly. Until then, he would follow the instructions of his booking team. He would do his best to prepare the Lucifer character for a heel turn.

CHAPTER 28

▼

Taken from www.wrestlinghotline.com

Greetings slugs.

Today is Tuesday, May 9th, and this is your Tuesday Morning Hangover, where we show up to give you what you need regardless of how f*#$&d up we are.

Today we're going to skip the pleasantries and get right into the overnight ratings report:

GWA Burn pulled an overall 3.3, with a 3.9 in the first hour, a 3.1 in the second hour, and a 2.9 in the overrun. This is officially the worst rating in the history of *GWA Burn*. Those (few) of you who watched the show last night know why. More later.

Revolution Riot reaped the benefits of *Burn*'s sucktitude. *Riot* got an overall of 5.2, with a 4.4 in the first hour, a 5.4 in the second, and a 5.5 in the overrun. Ladies and gentlemen, that is the highest rating in *Riot*'s history, and the highest overnight rating ever pulled by a wrestling program.

It's safe to say the worm has turned.

Onto…

The News:
Slugs, I know I'm getting creamed by the competition these days. They're scooping me left and right, they're hits are rising, mine are falling, they're reputation is improving, mine is declining, etc. I've gotta tell ya…STAY TUNED. Yours truly

is working on something that is getting hot as a Montreal crowd at a Philip Marcel match. I can't divulge anything yet, but…

Steve pulled his hands from the keyboard and gritted his teeth. Should he be saying this? He didn't have anything publishable yet, just an intriguing connection between the Family Television Group and some investment fund in Canada. He also had an Anonymous source who apparently had some real dirt to dish, and wanted Steve to dish it, but was yet to give him something substantive.

This was not enough to publish anything. In fact, anything Steve did publish that referenced the FTG would be in violation of his court order. Perhaps it wasn't wise to put this teaser paragraph in the Hangover, since it was entirely possible that Mr. Anonymous's goose chase could lead nowhere.

But he needed something. His readership was dwindling, and with good cause. His work wasn't up to snuff. The wrestling world was having a killer month of major stories and Steve was missing all of them. Last week Wrestlingdailytribune.com had been all over the Joey Mayhem/Jade Sleek affair, and WrestlingHotline.com hadn't mentioned it. This weekend there was a brawl backstage at a GWA house show. Wrestlingdailytribune.com had broken the story and had already covered it thoroughly. Steve was yet to mention it. Updates on Goliath's condition? The competition was nosing around backstage with ears open and pen in hand. Steve had done nothing. Chandler Dresby was reporting that Revolution was planning to turn Lucifer heel, news that was a complete surprise to Steve.

These stories all would have been cake for Steve even a few weeks ago. His network of email and bulletin board informants had recently been second-to-none. But the FTG crusade had hurt him dearly. No one had been interested in digging up dirt on these people. No one had cared.

And the court order was an embarrassment. It made Steve look like the second-rate journalist he was. Anyone who had been on board had seen their work disappear, as Steve wasn't allowed to publish it and none of the other sites gave a damn.

Still, the opportunities were there. The same source that gave Wrestlingdailytribune the scoop on Revolution's future plans had given the word to Steve, but he had never read the email. Hundreds of emails were deleted unopened or read too late because Steve had spent all his free time following these shoddy clues regarding the Saxon Fund and its potential relationship to the sponsors of the FTG.

Steve erased the teaser paragraph. If he was going to play investigative journalist, he was going to do it right. Mr. Anonymous might hush up if Steve got too opportunistic. And if this inquisition into the Saxon Fund and its beneficiaries led nowhere, then so be it. He would recover. The potential reward for uncovering something meaningful and doing it properly were worth the risk.

He started The News section again:

As has been reported on several other sites already, there was a backstage fight between Joey Mayhem and Jumbo Sanders at the GWA house show in Las Vegas on Sunday night. The fight left Jumbo with a severely swollen black eye, and put Joey Mayhem in the hospital. Obviously, neither was able to perform last night on *Burn*. Jade Sleek, whose name keeps getting attached to this story, was also absent from *Burn*.

The truth on this story may or may not be buried within the piles of speculation all over the Internet. The closest thing to fact we have so far is from an interview Pit Bull did on the Bobby Franken radio show out of San Diego last night:

> "Joey made some accusations; Jumbo denied them. They got in an argument, and then Joey threw a punch. Jumbo came back with a tackle and Joey smashed into the floor with Jumbo on top of him. We got the fight broken up after that."

The rumors coming from backstage seem to confirm Pit Bull's testimony. The general storyline floating around the Internet is that the fight was short and broken up by Pit Bull, Raptor, Deep Six, and Lamar Thomas, all of whom were witness to the spectacle.

Notably, the GWA is yet to comment on this incident at all. They'll have to say something soon. Their ship is sinking. Need proof? Let's take stock of the GWA main event scene:

Goliath—World Champion—out indefinitely with injury. The latest word from Wrestlingdailytribune.com is that Goliath is suffering from concussion syndrome. This condition can clear up in a week, or go on for years or the rest of his life. Until there's some certainty, the GWA needs to put the strap on somebody else. But who?

Crusader?—gone. Now wrestling for the competition.

Joey Mayhem?—suspended. The sense I get from the gossip around the net is that Joey's suspension will be long, maybe permanent. The locker room really hates this chap. Can you blame them? His first time on TV, he winked at his opponent, breaking character on camera. His second time on TV, he went over a company veteran who jumped ship the next week. His third time on TV he knocked out the champion. His fourth time never happened because he refused to follow the script at a house show, and got in a fight backstage.

Jack Branson?—out for 6-8 months with a torn thigh muscle. And who knows what kind of shape he'll be in when he returns?

That leaves us with Jumbo and Deep Six, maybe Lord Mayberry and Zombie could be elevated. That's a thin bunch up at the top. Time to create some new stars, quickly.

Burn fans, you're show's in trouble.

Speaking of which…

The High Points:
GWA Burn—None. A total snoozer. I've seen tapes of backyard wrestling that were more organized and coherent. The show opened with an embarrassing interview segment with Duke, Gordy Goodnow, Lord Mayberry, and Deep Six, none of whom are great on the mic. It immediately became apparent that they were improvising, without any idea of where they were going. Truly the most gut-wrenching twenty minutes I have ever seen on wrestling television. I'm not the only one who hated it. The ratings speak for themselves. EVERYONE abandoned the show within the first half hour. I don't know how they're going to recover from this mess.

Revolution Riot—A face turn for Scott Rollins? Interesting. I guess Max grew weary of him playing a heel and always getting face pops. What makes this extra-intriguing is that it looks like they're going to pair up Rollins and Lucifer as on-screen allies. This would be a first for the Lucifer character. Here's hoping they don't weaken the strongest character in wrestling.

The Big Picture:
You know, as I watch Rollins perform in Revolution, and get over, I can't help but wonder why GWA held onto the ridiculous name "Crusader" for so long.

With every week, it becomes more clear that Revolution has their shit together and the GWA does not. GWA can't even keep its locker room under control.

Whatever happened between Joey and Jumbo on Sunday night has been a long time coming. Duke has created and allowed for an unacceptable level of conflict among his top wrestlers, vying for the number one spot in the company. He pushed Joey Mayhem to the moon when he wasn't ready, then didn't give him any support when the Internet wolves tore him apart.

That brings me to another point, and this one's for you, Slugs. Why in God's name was there so much interest in Joey and Jade's personal life last week? Why was the Internet flooded with pictures of the two of them at the hospital, pictures of the two of them drinking coffee, pictures of the two of them getting into a car, pictures of Joey in his underwear! These are real people with real lives for Christ's sake! Treating them like circus freaks no doubt puts tremendous strain on their own well-being, strain that plays out in dangerous backstage brawls. Joey Mayhem was a promising young star who grew too bright too fast. He was in over his head and made all sorts of mistakes. But the potential was there. I hope there's still a future for him in this industry.

Okay. Enough ranting.

Until next time, this is Steve Garcia. Peace.

CHAPTER 29

▼

"Honey, it's starting," Jade called from downstairs.

Joey was in the master bedroom, watching a tape of Red Jackson vs. Lucifer from a broadcast of *Revolution Riot* a month ago. He found the remote control and pressed pause.

"Coming," he yelled back. As he descended the hardwood stairs, he wondered if the happiness of this past week was meant to last, or if it was just a byproduct of the fresh surroundings. He had spent the week with Jade, at her house in Dallas, effectively on vacation. Now, one week removed from his hospital stay in Las Vegas, he was leaving a wrestling tape in one room to watch a live wrestling broadcast in another.

Joey found Jade in the den, sitting on a leather sofa, facing a flatscreen TV hung on the opposite wall. She had tuned in to *Revolution Riot*, but had *GWA Burn* in the lower corner using the split screen function.

Joey plopped down next to her. There was a bowl of popcorn on the glass coffee table in front of them, a bottle of water on the end table next to Joey, and surround sound emanating from the speakers built into the ceiling. Truly, this was a wrestling fan's dream.

"Not so bad being a fan again, is it?" said Jade.

"Not bad at all," said Joey.

He knew he couldn't stay away from performing forever without missing it, but that didn't stop him from reveling in the current bliss. In the past week, he had swam in Jade's indoor pool every morning, taken a nap every afternoon, and gone out for a fancy dinner with Jade every evening. His body was thankful for the rest. It took only four days off for the pain to heal, the pain not only from his fight with Jumbo, but also from his accumulated wrestling wounds over the past three years, during which he had never taken a vacation. He had grown so accustomed to small pains in his knees and large pains in his shoulders that he had forgotten how enabling it was to be free of injury. There was a playfulness of the healthy body that was only now solidifying after being dissolved in a bath of back bumps and body slams. It was almost as if the abused body of the wrestler had adapted so fiercely to mistreatment that it became inhumanly strong when left alone.

Jade felt it too, Joey could tell. Her normally pleasant demeanor had evolved into a floodlight of joy. It was impossible not to be happy around her. It was one of those weeks that they both would remember with fondness.

Revolution Riot opened with a video package of the feud between Flash Martin and Miguel Cervantes.

"We'd never open with a package for the mid-carders," said Jade, referring to *Burn*'s unstated policy of always opening and closing the show with whomever was feuding for the title belt.

"I know it," said Joey with regret, a sentiment they shared. Featuring the mid and lower card in prominent spots during the TV broadcast was necessary in order to create new stars, ease locker room politics, and keep the show fresh. Duke didn't understand this at all, hence his locker room was a quagmire of power-mongering.

Ten seconds into the broadcast it was already apparent they had been wrestling for the wrong promotion. *Riot*'s production was cleaner than *Burn*'s. *Riot*'s opening package had more drama. Their announcers had more energy. Their fans were louder.

Furthering the distinction, using their "picture in picture" mode, they simultaneously saw that *Burn* was opening its broadcast with Jumbo, Deep Six, and Duke in the ring doing an interview segment. With Goliath and Branson out with injuries, Joey suspended, and Crusader gone, Jumbo and Deep Six were all that was left of the main event scene. Despite the fact that they both played heels (and both were not over with the fans) they would have to carry the show.

The crowd was cheering for something going on in the *Burn* broadcast in the lower corner. Jade lifted the remote and punched a button which swapped the screens, so *Burn* occupied the bulk of the frame, with *Riot* relegated to a small corner.

"Oh my God," she said in response to the television. A very tall, slightly chubby man with long black hair and a braided black beard was standing atop the entrance ramp.

"Who the hell is that?" said Joey.

"That, my friend, is Zeke Thunder," said Jade, "and his arrival means we got out just in time."

Joey looked closely. He had seen Zeke Thunder on GWA television a long time ago. He didn't look at all like this out of shape wannabe biker.

"This clown just won't die. He thinks he's worth a million bucks. Look at his belly." Jade seemed overjoyed. "Have you ever worked with this guy Joey?"

"No. I barely even remember him."

"He's been holding out, thinking that one of the two promotions would give him a good contract. They didn't. Until now, I guess. Duke must be really desperate. This joker wanted a guaranteed million annually and a reduced house show schedule. Plus, he's total poison backstage. Lazy, whiny, son of a bitch. I can't believe they signed him."

In the bottom corner, *Riot* had segued from the video package into a match between Flash Martin and Butterfly Johnny Grace. Jade switched the TV back to *Riot*, saying, "Now I've seen everything, I think."

Joey watched *Riot* intently. He had worked with Flash Martin briefly in the SWL before Revolution signed him, and was impressed with the guy's skills. And Butterfly Johnny Grace had always been a hell of a worker.

"See, this is much more interesting than anything we've been doing," said Jade. "Butterfly Johnny Grace is a main-eventer, but they're having him wrestle against their mid-card champion. If Flash Martin goes over, then his match at their pay per view instantly becomes much more interesting."

"I totally agree," said Joey.

The entire evening was full of these revelations. Whereas *Burn* carefully booked its matches with run-ins, disqualifications, and a slew of ref bumps, *Riot*'s matches ended with clear winners. *Burn*'s strategy was a feeble attempt to please everyone backstage (thus pleasing no one), with no wrestlers losing any heat, and the stories going nowhere. *Riot*'s strategy was much more far-sighted. The matches meant something, so even though someone had to lose, the fans had a reason to watch. When Flash Martin defeated Butterfly Johnny Grace, after a solid twenty minute match with no interference and no cheating, Flash Martin was elevated, his character ready to move forward in the storylines, and his pending match with Miguel Cervantes at the pay per view that much more important. By contrast, *Burn*'s first match of the night featured Gordy Goodnow losing to Bret Stevens, with illegal help from Pit Bull. Nothing proven there, except that Bret and Pit Bull were cheaters, a fact established more than two years ago.

The main event of *Burn* featured Deep Six vs. Jumbo's wife Rashann. Somewhere during the two hours when Joey wasn't paying attention, *Burn* had set up this match and was going to play Jumbo as a face. Right before the match started, Zeke Thunder laid out Jumbo with a 2 x 4. The whole thing was ridiculous.

Riot's main event was Scott Rollins vs. Red Jackson. Jackson went over, but Rollins put on a great match, and was established as a big-time player in his new role, suitable to be in storylines with Lucifer at the upcoming pay per view.

At ten o'clock, with both shows finished, Joey felt a strong sense of satisfaction. In taking a stand against Jumbo and Duke, he had earned an indefinite suspension, likely to be followed with walking papers for both himself and his girlfriend. He had turned his back on the entire locker room, placing himself ahead of the promotion, the ultimate taboo in professional wrestling. Watching the embarrassment of *GWA Burn* when compared to the smooth machine of *Revolution Riot*, it was clear that the promotion deserved nothing. A few months down the road, Joey's contract with GWA would be expired, and he'd be free to wrestle for the competition. He couldn't wait.

CHAPTER 30

▼

Steve finished watching the tape of *GWA Burn* at 11:30. He had fast-forwarded through much of the show, violating a personal rule and marking the first time he would sit down to write a Tuesday Hangover without having watched both shows in their entirety.

Burn was too awful to sit through. He'd mention that in the column.

He had another reason to fast forward. His mind wasn't altogether on his column. At six, two hours before *Riot* started, Steve got another email from Anonymous, the first in over a week.

To: Steve Garcia
From: anonymous98@freemailforu.org

Dear Steve,

You asked for more information. Here's a clue for you. Calgary Financial Telegram, Volume 8. Issue 3.

Anonymous

This was the most mind-numbing email yet from Mr. Anonymous. The Calgary Financial Telegram?

Unfortunately, the Internet was no help in deciphering the email. The Calgary Financial Telegram was not online, and the few references to it on the Internet led nowhere.

He would have to wait until the next morning to go to the university business library which was now closed. Hopefully, they would have this issue of what he assumed was a newspaper or newsletter. Until then, he would have to sit on what might be a good scoop.

"A damned good scoop," Steve mumbled to himself with indignation. His feelings towards Mr. Anonymous tonight were mixed. While he had been trying to track down the mysterious Calgary Financial Telegram, he had ignored an important email from Nick Taylor, one of his most reliable sources.

To: Steve Garcia
From: ntaylor@powervolt.net

Steve,

Major scoop for you. I just got off the phone with my friend Monty Warren, whose friend's brother is at the GWA show tonight in Sacramento. He was sitting out back, spying on the wrestlers as they came in, and he said that he saw Zeke Thunder enter the arena! GWA must have signed him!

As far as I know, nobody has this up yet. Give me a shout-out when you post this, k?

Happy reporting!

Nick

The email had arrived at six thirty. Steve remembered the email icon popping up around then. He had ignored it, drowning in his fruitless search for this Financial Telegram.

At eight, when *Burn* started, Steve was as surprised as anyone to see Zeke Thunder, the ever-elusive free agent holdout, show up on *Burn*. He got on the web and saw that Wrestlingdailytribune.com had reported it at seven forty. An hour later, during a commercial break on *Riot*, Steve checked his email, and saw the letter from Nick. Had he read it when it came in, he would have been the first to report the story. Instead, he missed a major scoop. He probably also lost a major source. These guys who sent the goods didn't do it for free. They wanted their names posted with credit for their finds. Had Nick sent his letter to Wrestlingtribune, he would have received his coveted "Shout-Out." Since he sent it to Steve, of late the sloppiest wrestling journalist on the Net, it went nowhere, and Nick was certain to be pissed.

Steve opened a new email and began typing:

To: anonymous98@freemailforu.org
From: Steve Garcia

Dear Anonymous,

Thank you for the tip about the Calgary Financial Telegram. I am yet to find anything on it yet. Do you have more information?

I appreciate your assistance, but, honestly, if you're only going to give me cryptic one-liners, spaced weeks apart, I will have to assume that you are not serious. If you are a prankster who is messing with me, you've done a good job. I had the scoop on Zeke Thunder's return tonight, but lost it because I wasted the evening looking for this Calgary Financial Telegram thing (again, I found NOTHING).

Please send me something concrete, or explain to me why you have to write in riddles, or else I will abandon this project and attempt to regain the credibility I've lost while on this wild goose chase.

Steve Garcia

Steve clicked send, then fired up his word processor and began typing up the Tuesday Hangover. He had nothing original to say. Like everyone, he was displeased with *Burn* tonight, which brought in a new face but still couldn't put together a good show. GWA was hurting, and neither Zeke Thunder nor Jumbo nor Jumbo's wife nor Deep Six were the answer. He'd mention all that.

And hopefully soon he would have some original, ground-breaking things about the FTG to mention as well.

CHAPTER 31

▼

Steve's alarm woke him at nine in the morning, three hours earlier than normal for a Tuesday. The business library at Northeastern Illinois opened at ten, and he intended to be there when the door was unlocked.

He had posted his most uninspired Tuesday Hangover in memory a little before midnight and gone to bed. Usually, he posted the column just before dawn, after an entire night of crashing the bulletin boards, watching the tapes, writing and re-writing. Last night he threw together one draft of generic opinion in less than an hour and didn't bother to re-read it before posting. It probably was riddled with errors, but Steve didn't want to know. He put it up for the world to judge, and decided to get on with it. He had already committed himself to Mr. Anonymous's scavenger hunt. If it led nowhere, so be it. The damage was already done. Might as well let it all hang out and hope to get lucky.

There was a new email:

To: Steve Garcia
From: anonymous98@freemailforu.org

Dear Steve,

The story you are following is much bigger than any of these other 'scoops' you're missing. Here's another tidbit to keep you motivated. Dr.

Harold Claven in Houston recently moved. His old address was 628 Amherst Drive. His new address is 4853 Ledgestone Court.

Anonymous

Steve had printed the email but forced himself not to dwell on it yet. One thing at a time. He had never heard of Dr. Harold Claven. The information was so random, in fact, that thinking about it led him closer to believing again that this was all an elaborate hoax, which was too painful to consider. At least Mr. Anonymous had acknowledged Steve's anger that he'd missed out on the Zeke Thunder story.

Parking at Northeastern was a bitch. Three laps around a massive campus, only to find a metered space a good ten minutes from the library. Steve put four dollars into the meter, buying himself two hours. After a trek across two parking lots and a courtyard, he entered the library with a ratty backpack strewn over his left shoulder.

His previous jaunts to the library had taught him how to find what he was looking for. He went down one flight of stairs and across an array of bookcases to reach the periodicals. Six computer terminals arranged in a semicircle faced him in front of the book stacks. He sat at one and opened the library's search software. He typed "Calgary Financial Telegram," and reached his first dead end. "Not in subscription database." The publication was too obscure for this library.

Undaunted, Steve grabbed a scrap piece of paper, wrote down "Calgary Financial Telegram," hiked back to the first floor and approached the information desk. A teenage boy with horn-rimmed glasses and matted hair sighed as he pulled his head out of a hardback copy of *Dune*.

"Can I help you?" he said.

"I'm looking for an issue of a financial newsletter that isn't in your subscription base," said Steve, showing the boy his scrap of paper.

"Calgary Financial Telegram," the boy read to himself, then shook his head. "You say it's a newsletter? I don't think you're going to find it."

A slacker himself, Steve recognized that the boy only wanted to get rid him. "Well where else can I try?"

"I don't know. Have you checked the Internet?"

"Yes," said Steve. "Listen, I really, really need to get my hands on a copy of this newsletter. Is there somewhere else I can look?"

The boy blew air out of the corner of his mouth. His breathe smelled like coffee. "Just a second," he said, then picked up a phone on the edge of the desk.

"Mary, hi, this is Paul. There's a guy here who's looking for a copy of a really obscure financial newsletter that we don't subscribe to and isn't on the Internet. Is there any other place he might find it? Mm-hmm. Alright. Thanks Mary."

"Okay, come on," the boy, Paul, said as he stood up. Paul led Steve across several aisles of bound periodicals to a bay of computer terminals.

"Double-click on that icon that says Ilib," said Paul, pointing to a square icon on the screen. Steve clicked on the icon.

"This is the library system of all the state universities of Illinois," said Paul. "If you can't find your newsletter here, you won't find it anywhere."

"Thanks," said Steve. He waited for coffee-breath Paul to leave, then entered a search for "Calgary Financial Telegram".

The hard drive spun. A task bar appeared, and said, "Searching…" Steve sat back in his chair. He waited. And waited.

Ten minutes later, the screen turned blue, and said:

1 of 1 documents found

Calgary Financial Telegram, Calgary Investors Bureau

Steve hit enter. The task status bar returned. Steve leaned back in his chair and waited it out. This time it took close to fifteen minutes.

120 of 120 documents found

The screen listed 120 different issues of the newsletter. Steve used the arrow keys to scroll through them, until he found Volume 8, Issue 3. He hit enter. Two minutes later a pop-up window said, "Print? Y/N"

"Paul, could you come help me?" Steve called out in a breach of library etiquette. He could hear Paul sigh from across the book stacks.

"Yes?" Paul said.

"Does it cost me anything to print this?"

Paul appeared from behind the bookstacks, looking severely inconvenienced.

"Ten cents a page and I need to see your student ID," said Paul.

"Oh. Well, I'm not a student…anymore," said Steve. Paul looked displeased, so Steve added, "I'm alumni."

"Sorry dude. If you're not a student, I can't let you print."

"Well, can I print to the screen?"

"Nope. Ilib only lets you print hard copies. Ten cents a page for students with ID."

"What if I just print this, and pay you ten cents a page, and we just pretend I had my student ID?" said Steve, grinning at Paul like they were old friends.

"Nope. Sorry man. University policy. I could get fired."

Whatever, Steve thought.

"Listen Paul, I really need to see this document. I'm just going to go ahead and print it and pay you ten cents a page."

"No way Dude. I'll turn off the printer."

Was this a bad dream? So close to being a real journalist, only to be thwarted by Paul, the teenage geek with a warped sense of duty.

"Maybe it'd be best if you left, Dude," said Paul. "I don't want any trouble."

"No, no. I won't cause any trouble," Steve held his hands up like they were potential printing weapons. He was about to stand up and leave, thinking that if this system was in every library for state universities, he'd just go to Champagne and print it out. But right before he stood, he saw his reflection in Paul's glasses. His face was chubby and covered with stubble. Here he was, mid-twenties, trying to be a journalist, and his first attempt at a real story was going to be shut down by an 18-year-old slacker.

"Paul. I need this document. I can make it worth your while."

Paul laughed nervously. "What?" he said.

"How about ten bucks? Ten bucks, plus ten cents a page, and you just pretend I showed you my ID."

"I don't think so Dude. Maybe you'd better—"

"Twenty bucks," said Steve, with confidence in his voice. Paul was beginning to crack.

"I don't think so," said Paul.

"Fifty bucks Paul. I'm dead serious. I need this document."

Paul looked at Steve to judge his earnestness. Then he looked around to see if anyone else was listening.

"Really? Fifty bucks?"

"I need this Paul."

Paul took one more look around the area, then leaned over Steve's shoulder and hit the Y key, initiating the print job.

"It'll print out over there," said Paul, pointing to a printer next to the far terminal. Steve walked over, and grabbed the pages as they printed. The first page was labeled, "Calgary Financial Telegram, Volume 8, Issue 3." Steve glanced at it quickly, not sure what he was looking for. He picked up Pages Two, Three, Four, and Five. He hadn't seen anything yet, but there was no time to look now. He put the pages in his backpack.

"See you later Paul," he said, and headed toward the stairs.

"Hey!" Paul caught himself yelling, "hey," he whispered as he chased after Steve.

"My fifty bucks please."

Steve kept on walking.

"Forget it Paul. I'm not paying."

"Then I won't let you walk out of here. I'll tell the front desk you have library property."

"Go ahead. I dare you." Steve kept on walking. Paul followed him up the first flight of stairs, then stopped.

"Asshole," Paul said as he turned around.

Steve walked out the front door of the library without incident. He felt like a king.

*   *   *   *

It began to rain shortly before Steve made it home. He parked in the driveway, taking his mother's vacant spot, and covered his head with his backpack as he ran to the front porch.

Once inside, he darted up the stairs and shut himself in his room. He emptied his backpack on his bed, spread the print-outs across the mattress, and plopped down in front of them.

The Calgary Financial Telegram was apparently circulated among exceedingly honest and boring Canadian Investors. Page One was filled with a dreary article about "gold funds" as a "deflation hedge." Page Two had a smarmy "Letter From The Editor" behooving Canadian Investors to learn from the mistakes of their neighbors to the south, who insisted on losing their shirts in market fads. Pages three through six were splattered with tidbits, little paragraphs about selected industries and financial sectors. Steve tried to read each one, certain for some reason that the info he wanted was cloaked somehow, not unlike Mr. Anonymous's emails. The content was so dry he couldn't help skipping along the paragraph headers. "Pullman Bearish On Bonds"; "British Columbia Utilities Bought Out"; "Skyler Holding To Reorganize"; "Bacon Futures Sizzling"—Steve's eyes jumped back. Buried in the small text was a word he recognized, "Saxon." He skimmed the sentence, "…liquidated assets will be reorganized under the new parent company, The Saxon Fund." His eyes darted to the top of the paragraph:

Skyler Holding To Reorganize

On December first, Skyler Holding, LLC, will begin liquidation of its North American assets, following the buyout of all secondary partners. Founded in 2002, the holding company for seven commercial real estate interests intends to sell all properties at appraised values. The liquidated assets will be reorganized under the new parent company, The Saxon Fund, LLC.

What the hell did that mean? Steve went to his computer, brought up a search engine on the Internet, and searched for "Skyler Holding."

"3 documents found."

Steve clicked on the first one, "History of Ashwood Park."

The site was for a business campus in Calgary, apparently "constructed in 1992" and "home to three of Canada's most exciting companies." Steve hit control-F, and typed "Skyler Holding" into the "Find:" window that appeared. The page automatically scrolled halfway down and highlighted "Skyler Holding" in the middle of a sentence. Steve found the sentence's beginning: "The property is owned by Corinth Realtors, a subsidiary of Skyler Holding."

Steve went back to the search engine. He typed "Corinth Realtors."

"0 active documents found. 1 cached document found."

Steve clicked on the cached document, a web page that was no longer visible on the Internet except through the search engines that saved old web pages on their servers.

The document took him to what apparently used to be the home page for Corinth Realtors, a "commercial real estate development company founded—"

Steve's eyes dashed down the page involuntarily. His peripheral vision had seen a name so familiar to him that it jumped out from the field of words like one's own name in a buzz of conversation.

Steve read the name, two words, and everything came together. If that name was on this page then it all made sense. Mr. Anonymous, Skyler Holding, The Saxon Fund, even his court-ordered silence, they were all part of one story, one mega-story.

And it was his. It was his scoop.

He hoped.

Steve typed "www.wrestlingdailytribune.com" into his web browser to check in on the competition.

"Oh my God," he whispered as their front page came up. Steve clicked on the entrance link to the main story and then read intently. As far as he could tell, the competition wasn't on to his story. Unfortunately, they had scooped him on something else.

CHAPTER 32

▼

Wrestlingdailytribune.com is proud to be the first to present you with this story, potentially the biggest in wrestling history. We have just confirmed that, as of tomorrow morning, The Global Wrestling Association will no longer exist, its name and all its property having been purchased by Revolution Wrestling. The deal will be announced on Revolution.com later today, with a press conference at Revolution Wrestling World Headquarters in New York City tomorrow morning.

The terms of the deal are as follows:

- *For an undisclosed amount, Revolution Wrestling has purchased the Global Wrestling Association.*

- *This purchase is complete and unconditional.*

- *Revolution Wrestling will receive full rights to the Global Wrestling Association name, all its trademarks, its entire library of video footage, its entire inventory, and negotiating rights to the contracts of all its employees.*

- *All employees of the Global Wrestling Association will be allowed to renegotiate their contracts with Revolution Wrestling.*

Further details about this breaking story will be posted on Revolution.com in one hour (8pm eastern). These details will include an announcement regarding the final broadcast of GWA Burn and what we can expect to see.

"Holy shit," Joey said quietly.

"I know," said Jade.

They sat in silence, staring at the computer screen, taking in the monumental news.

"Well Baby, it looks like we're going back to work," Joey said.

"Maybe," said Jade.

"What? You don't think we'll get a call?" said Joey.

"It says Duke is expected to have an important role in the new organization. I don't like the sound of that."

"Yeah, it's too bad he'll still be around, but I think things will be different. I can't imagine him having any sway with Max Zeffer."

"We'll see. I wonder what's going to happen to everyone. Revolution can't roll over everybody's contracts."

"I know," said Joey, feeling a twinge of guilt. Despite his anger toward the promotion, its president, and its veteran wrestlers, Joey still felt guilty for the recent demise of the GWA. There was no question that he would be blamed. First he kicked the world champion in the head, then he created a mess in the locker room, then he dropped the torch he was given to carry. In just over a month, the GWA had lost its biggest stars and its creative direction.

But his guilt wasn't caused by any loyalty to the current incarnation of the GWA. Two weeks away from that septic tank had taught him one thing. It deserved to die. And good riddance.

Furthermore, Joey was convinced that the promotion was headed for failure sooner rather than later. He had just sped it on its way.

Still, the guilt was there, and it came from a deep, hurtful place. It was rooted in his childhood and his memories of what the GWA once was. Growing up, Joey had watched the GWA every Saturday morning, admiring stars like Shane Walker and Red Jackson. He admired the crafty storylines of Gene Harold and Larry Jenkins, and although he didn't know it at the time, he admired the locker room discipline Duke had instilled.

All of that was dead now. Maybe it had died long ago.

"Sweetie, you know this isn't your fault, right?" said Jade, reading Joey's feelings exactly.

"I know, well, it's a little bit my fault," he said.

"It's not your fault at all Joey. There is much, much more here than Goliath getting injured."

"Well, yeah. There's also Crusader leaving, Jumbo and I missing a prime time show, the locker room in chaos. All of that is my fault."

"Stop it. Crusader was asked to do the job to a future star. It's tradition. It's part of the business. If he can't handle it, then he doesn't deserve to be doing this. And your incident with Jumbo started well before you were even working here. You just finished what he started."

Joey laughed, thinking it was ridiculous to say he finished anything. He landed one punch before getting knocked out cold and sent to the hospital.

"I'm serious, Joey. The GWA was doomed when Gene Harold and Larry Jenkins went to Revolution. Our storylines went to shit and Revolution's became great. Then Shane Walker retired and Red Jackson went to the competition. They got replaced with egomaniacs like Goliath and Crusader. Then a little clique of veteran wrestlers started running the locker room like their own little racket. Joey, you've got to admit, our company was a mess."

Joey nodded silently. Of course Jade was right. The GWA was falling apart well before he arrived. If only he'd known when he joined. Had he started in Revolution things would be completely different.

He thought back to the time when the choice was his to make. Wrestling for the Southeast Wrestling League, it was obvious to him and everyone around him, that it wouldn't be long before the big boys came calling. He should have decided back then to weigh both promotions against each other, and hold out for the offer from the better one. Two years ago, it wasn't as obvious that Revolution was going to take over the wrestling world. They were an upstart promotion wrestling in small arenas who had won a television contract through the force of Max Zeffer's wallet. The GWA was still the ultimate goal. Bigger arenas, bigger names, a long, prestigious history.

But it took only a month before Revolution had Gene and Larry. Soon the Internet declared Revolution the more interesting promotion. Then Lucifer came onto the scene. But Joey was young, and the GWA came calling first. Duke himself showed up at an event in Nashville and found Joey backstage after the show. Duke Correlli, the most powerful name in wrestling, walked right up to Joey at an indy show and offered him a contract.

And then it all went haywire almost right away. Two months in the development territories, one dark match before *Burn* and it was already time to do a program with Jumbo on television. Of course the locker room would hate him. Of course the promotion would rip apart at the seams.

But if he hadn't gone to work for GWA, he would never have met Jade.

They spent the rest of the morning in the throes of the news. Slowly, all the other wrestling web sites began posting the story that had broken on Wrestlingdailytribune.com. At half past ten, Revolution.com put up a press release, confirming the story and all the details. All GWA contracts would be up for renewal with the new company.

At noon, GWA.com posted an open letter from Duke to the fans:

To the loyal fans of the GWA,

It is with mixed emotions that I announce the end of The Global Wrestling Association. On the one hand, I feel sadness at the end of an era. I founded the GWA in 1971, raising it from the ashes of the Philadelphia Wrestling League. We offered a new kind of wrestling, specifically marketed for television with a nationwide strategy. We were the first to win a nationwide contract on cable television in 1981. Between 1981 and 1983, we bought out six regional promotions to quickly become the single dominant force in professional wrestling. Thinking back on this time, the challenges, the risks, the exhilaration, I am sad that it has to end.

The 1980s and the 1990s belonged exclusively to the GWA. Many upstarts tried and failed to catch us. During this time, we were the very first organization to put on a nationwide pay per view television event. We sold out arenas across the country. GWA Burn became the number one rated show on cable television. Our hard-knocks, unforgiving style of entertainment forever changed the landscape of cable TV.

But quietly, when we weren't looking, things changed. A new game in town, under the tutelage of a young and focused financier, landed its own television contract. With courage and tenacity that remind me of myself twenty years ago, Max Zeffer systematically assembled the most talented people in the business to finally offer a suitable alternative to my own product.

And now, at age sixty-two, I must concede defeat. Revolution Wrestling is the new home of cutting edge wrestling entertainment. Therefore, I have sold the rights to the GWA name, library, and talent to my vanquisher.

To all the long-time fans of the GWA, thank you. Thank you for letting me entertain you like no one else has. Our current journey ends here, but I'm certain a new one will begin before the ref calls for the bell.

Sincerely,

Michael "Duke" Correlli

At twelve thirty, the phone rang. Joey and Jade were on her front porch, eating turkey sandwiches she had prepared. Jade rested her plate on her chair before going inside to answer the phone, which had been ringing all morning. Family and friends of them both were eager to hear their take on the day's big news. When Jade came back outside with the cordless receiver in her hand, her eyes were wide with anticipation.

"It's for you," she said, handing Joey the phone.

"Who is it?" Joey mouthed as he took the phone.

Jade didn't say, answering only with a hand wave that indicated Joey was to get on the phone immediately and find out.

"Hello?" Joey said into the receiver.

"Hello, Joey. This is Max Zeffer."

▼

Cats, everywhere. How could one town have so many cats?

Joey sat alone in the rear of a black Lincoln Town Car with maroon plush interior. In the front seat, the driver, an obese, bald, white man who wore gaudy rings on every finger, continually fiddled with the air conditioner but said nothing. They were traveling toward the ocean.

"Joey, I want to meet you in person and discuss your contract," Max had said the day before. On the phone, Max's voice was tame and soothing, a far cry from the tyrannical persona he presented to the world. "Can you come to my house in Key West tomorrow?"

"Tomorrow?" Joey had said.

"Yes, if you're available. I'd like to move on this quickly. My assistant can give you your flight information and instructions for when you land. I look forward to seeing you tomorrow." The conversation with Max had lasted less than five minutes, during which time Joey had agreed to talk about a new contract with Revolution and visit Max in person right away. Max's assistant, a woman with a syrupy "May-I-help-you?" voice, came on the phone and gave Joey a series of confirmation numbers and flight information. She knew which gate he needed to be at and at what time. She was prepared to arrange transportation for Joey to and from the Dallas/Fort Worth airport if need be. When Joey hung up he realized these tickets had been purchased before Max had made the phone call. People apparently didn't say no to this man.

"So, what did he say?" Jade asked.

Joey recounted the entire conversation for her. She was excited for him. They talked about what Joey should expect, what he should demand (they agreed he should take whatever he was offered), and what life might be like wrestling for Revolution. Through all of this, they didn't talk about the fact that Max had not acknowledged Jade. In Joey's mind, it was only a matter of time. Jade was too important in the wrestling world not to get a contract with Revolution, regardless of her history with Duke, Jumbo, and Goliath. Besides, if Joey had his foot in the door, he could swing it open for her.

Twenty hours removed from the phone call, and Joey was in Key West, having been picked up at the airport by this big bald fellow who drove him in comfort through this island city of cats.

"Are there always so many cats out?" Joey asked the driver.

"People say it was Earnest Hemingway brought them cats. More of them than people in Key West." The driver had a shrill accent that reminded Joey of his days in the Southeast Wrestling League.

Joey believed it. He had been surprised to see a stray cat meandering about the baggage claim at the airport, and equally surprised to see that everyone ignored it. But the real shock didn't happen until the driver led him out the front door of the airport. Cats in every garbage can. Cats under your feet. Cats chasing birds in the medians. Cat carcasses on the road. Calicos, Tabbies, Black Cats, Persian Cats, Siamese Cats, even Hairless Cats.

Ten minutes in the car, and Joey felt like he knew Key West. Trees, ocean, condos, and cats. Despite the latter, this was a nice place. The weather was breezy and temperate, with the salty mist of oceanfront property. It was a suitable place for Max Zeffer's vacation home.

The driver pulled into the driveway of a two-story house that backed into an ocean cliff. The house was one of four along the overlook, each separated by a near-jungle of underbrush and palms, each worth millions.

The driver opened Joey's door for him. Standing up, Joey could see behind the house, where a steep hill of rock and sand led directly to the beach.

"I'm to wait here, Sir. You go on ahead. I'll see you when you're done," said the driver.

Joey wondered if he was supposed to tip him. He reached into his pocket.

"Mr. Zeffer has it all covered, Sir." The driver gently nodded his head as he spoke. "You just go on ahead."

"Thanks," said Joey. A flagstone path led from the driveway to the front porch, which was held up by two marble pillars. A crystal chandelier hung above the stoop. A wall of glass surrounded the mahogany front door. Joey exhaled before he reached for the doorbell, realizing that, even though he was a media superstar, this sort of big money still intimidated him.

A young woman dressed in black answered the door. She had olive skin, dark hair, deep blue eyes, and breasts that most certainly belonged in the world of pro wrestling.

"Hello, Joey. We've been expecting you," she said. "Please, come in."

"Thank you," said Joey as he entered the first room and consciously forced himself not to gape. The giant picture windows on the front wall were matched on the opposite side of the house, allowing a full view of the ocean from just inside the front door. The front room was completely open space, broken only by a winding staircase that lead to a loft and a catwalk, likely leading off to the bedrooms.

"I'm Vicky," said the woman. "I'm a writer for Revolution."

Joey shook her hand. "Nice to meet you," he said.

"Max is in the office," said Vicky. "Follow me."

Joey followed with pleasure, for when Vicky turned to lead the way, it became apparent why this writer for the company was with Max at his beach mansion. Vicky's legs, long, bronze, muscular works of art, were the type of genetic gift that made life downright unfair. As Joey followed those legs, visible in their entirety between a short black skirt and diamond-studded black pumps, stomping on the hardwood floor in a gait that belonged on a Paris runway, he guessed that Vicky was probably as skilled a writer as he was a lion tamer.

The office was a converted bedroom at the end of the hall off the main room. Max was sitting in a leather chair at the back of the room, behind a round table with a black marble top. Two identical chairs to the one he sat in occupied the table's perimeter. A small pile of papers and two ballpoint pens were on the table-top. Max's chair was turned to face away from the room. He was talking on the phone.

"No, no. The Internet leak was my idea," he said to someone. "We're going to start giving out useful information to whichever of those kids is doing the most for us...I know it's odd, but listen, you'll find we think differently around here. Anyway, we'll talk more on this later. I have an appointment waiting...Alright...Bye."

Max hung up the phone and turned in his chair.

"Max, this is Joey Hamilton," Vicky announced.

Max stood up and shook Joey's hand. "Joey Mayhem," he said, correcting Vicky. "It's good to meet you in person, Joey. Please sit down."

Joey sat in one of the empty chairs. From his seat, the ocean was visible out the window. The motion of the surf behind Max's head made for a creepy serenity.

"Vicky, our guest has nothing to drink," said Max.

"Oh, gracious…I'm so sorry Joey. Can I get you something?"

"No thank you, I'm just fine," said Joey.

"Nonsense," said Max. "Vicky, bring us two glasses and a pitcher of iced tea."

"Where do I get a pitcher of iced tea?" she said nervously. Joey wanted to tell them both he really didn't want anything to drink, that Vicky was fine and could go, but he thought it best to remain silent.

"There's a pitcher in the cupboard, a tea-maker on the counter by the stove, and there should be tea bags in the pantry," said Max, his voice a warning that she was not to ask anymore questions.

"I really don't need anything to drink thank—"

"No, no, you're my guest, Joey. Vicky doesn't mind at all."

As if in concurrence, Vicky was already clopping down the hallway. Joey could tell just by listening to her gait that she wasn't the type of person who normally played hostess. 'None of my business,' he thought to himself.

"Well, Joey, how was your flight?" said Max.

"It was fine," said Joey.

"And the drive in? Bobby got you here okay?"

"The drive in was fine."

"How about the neighborhood? Not a bad place to come for a meeting, huh?"

"It's certainly very nice. You have a very beautiful house."

"Thank you. I own all four of these houses on the strip. This one's mine. The other three are available to my wrestlers. I believe we all need a nice play to go and get away, especially in our business. Hell, you know what it can be like as a celebrity. Sometimes you just need some privacy."

"Certainly," said Joey.

"Well Joey, as we've discussed, I'd like you to wrestle for me. The lawyers have the contract all written up. I'd like to go over it with you." Max pushed the pile of papers from the center of the table toward Joey.

Joey looked at page one. "This contract serves to bind the undersigned…" His mind raced back three months to his contract signing with the GWA. That signing took place in Philadelphia in a small office on the third floor of GWA headquarters. The office had been packed with lawyers and clerks. Duke smoked a cigar the entire time, filling the cramped space with a dirty mist. By the end of that meeting, Joey was ready to accept whatever Duke offered, just to get out of the stuffy room.

"You'll notice this isn't standard, Joey. Today you're only signing up for your first gig," said Max.

"Mr first gig?" Joey wondered if he needed an agent here with him.

"That's right." Max flipped over the first page of the contract. "This is how we're handling everyone coming over from the GWA. Think of it as a short audition for the starring role, no strings attached. I want you to do some promo work for me on Monday night, some production work during the week, and then wrestle for me next weekend in Montreal. After that show's done, we'll sit down again, with the lawyers and agents and whatnot, and sign you to your long-term contract."

"Okay," said Joey, with hesitation. It seemed odd that he was flown all the way to Florida—

"I can tell you think this is weird," said Max. "This doesn't seem standard to you, and you think it's strange that I'd bring you here just to talk about one show."

"Yeah, I guess," said Joey.

Max opened his mouth to speak, but closed it again. Vicky's clomping feet signaled her return. She came in and placed two glasses on the table. She put a pitcher of ice water between them. Max looked at the water, then looked at Vicky.

"Your tea machine doesn't work," she said.

"It does so," said Max.

"Thank you Vicky. This will be fine," said Joey.

Max curled up his lips and furrowed his brow. He looked like he was pondering the fate of the world. Then he released whatever was held in his mind with a sigh and a waving of his hand, as if brushing off Vicky's failure to bring tea as the cruel hand that fate had dealt him.

"You're welcome," Vicky whispered to Joey as she left.

Max shook his head, then refocused on the contract.

"Anyway, Joey, let me alleviate your concerns," he said. "First off, like I said, we've decided to do this with everyone from the GWA. Everyone gets a short-term contract, six months or less, some day-to-day. The idea is that we're bringing in lots of new people all at once, and we know that some of them aren't going to work out. Plus, some of them are going to deserve to be on the pay scale with our top performers. But we won't know that until we've worked with them for a bit.

"In your case, I'm very confident that things are going to work out marvelously. I am certain you'll fit in perfectly with our company and do great things here. I want you to wrestle my next pay per view, Apocalypse, in Montreal, then we'll sit down and get you a contract. Of all the GWA wrestlers, you're the one I'd feel confident signing right away. But, to be fair to everyone, you get an audition like everyone else. It's in part to protect you. Unlike your former employer, here we're very sensitive to the politics of the wrestling locker room. I watch out for my guys, Joey. I see you as my World Champ some day, but not until I've got the locker room ready to accept you, and the first step in getting the locker room to accept you is to treat you the same as everyone else."

"Okay," said Joey, nodding his head, still hesitant, but pleased with what Max was saying.

"And it's not like this first contract is going to be small potatoes either. You'll be wrestling at our next pay per view, which I expect to be the most successful in wrestling history to date. Our ratings are up, the wrestling world is buzzing with news of our buyout, and everyone is going to be pumped to see GWA wrestlers and Revolution wrestlers on the same show. I fully expect your payout on the Apocalypse show to be six figures if you sign this contract."

Joey made sure to contain himself. He didn't want an errant smile or wide-eyed twitch to give away his excitement. A six-figure payout was the kind of real money he had expected (but never made) when the GWA signed him. And perhaps this would just be the first of many. It took only a second for Joey's mind to race through pictures of a new house, a new car, a new wardrobe, financial help for his brother, a retirement-fund...

"Alright, let's go through this," Joey said.

For the next half-hour Max and Joey read through the contract. Max explained the language, pointed to where Joey needed to initial, and solicited questions. Joey initialed sections covering liability of Revolution if he was hurt while performing, the nature of the agreement between Revolution and him, his willingness to follow the instructions of performance to the best of what can reasonably be expected, and his financial payout. Joey would do some production work for Revolution for a promotional package that would appear on *Riot*, he would show up on *Riot* to hype his upcoming pay per view match, and he would wrestle at *Apocalypse*. He was guaranteed at least ten thousand dollars for performing at *Apocalypse*. His likely take would be far greater. He would get one percent of the gross TV revenue, and two percent of the gross gate sales.

"I'm not lying Joey when I say that we can expect at least 800,000 buys on this pay per view and a sold out arena. Obviously, that's not guaranteed in the contract, but I'm being square with you, that's what we're looking at. At forty dollars a pay per view buy, and fifty dollars a ticket, your take would be close to half a million dollars."

Half a million dollars for one night's work. Clearly, this was the company to be working for. Joey could have expected to make the big money in the GWA some day, but never half a million dollars in one night. The highest-paid GWA wrestler, Goliath, made between two and three million dollars a year, half of that from merchandise sales. The rest of that money was earned in a grueling, four nights a week, fifty-one weeks a year schedule of wrestling across the country, covering your own expenses.

"Why do you expect so many people to buy this pay per view?" said Joey.

"Well Joey, how long have you been waiting for GWA stars and Revolution stars to land on the same show?" said Max.

He was right. This was an attraction that had been a long time coming. But there was only a week to hype and build for it. How could anyone be prepared? How could they build up a card for the fans? What would be the main event?

"Who would I be wrestling?" Joey asked.

"Ah, the big question," said Max. "Let's finish up this contract and then we'll talk about what's planned for you. In honesty, it's not finalized yet. The card depends greatly on you signing a contract with me. If I have you locked up for the night, I've got a super-card in mind. If I don't have you, well, I'd have to go with Plan B."

Max turned to the last page. "So, here we are. The print on this page just explains what your signature means. It is the final seal on everything you've initialed. It's your final agreement that the contract is solid, as written. Basically, this last page is your last chance to think it over. You've initialed your understanding of everything. Now you just need to sign."

Max drew an X on the first line, where Joey was to put his signature.

Joey put his pen to the page. The ballpoint pressed against the papyrus. Smooth black marble was directly underneath this last, solitary page. Half a million dollars awaited his signature.

He lifted the pen without signing.

"I'd really like to know who I'm wrestling," said Joey.

Max drew back and inhaled, his impatience palpable.

"Like I said Joey. The decision isn't made yet. The minute you sign this, I'll be ready to put together the card."

"You said you have a super-card in mind. Who's in mind for me to wrestle? There are so many options between the two companies."

"Joey. I'd like you to sign before we discuss any of that. Show me you'll do what we ask of you here. Sign the contract. Remember, I'm offering you hundreds of thousands of dollars for one night."

Joey put the pen back on the paper to sign. It seemed strange that Max wouldn't even divulge a clue. But what was there to hide? It was wrestling. For a half million dollars, Joey would do anything he asked.

So why wouldn't Max just tell him what it was? Max had to know that Joey would sign even if the work was undesirable. The money was just too much.

"I'm sorry Max," he said, putting the pen down. "I'm not signing until I know what's planned."

Max sighed.

"Alright Joey," he said. "I'll tell you what I have in mind. Better then that, I'll show you. Follow me."

Max stood up, grabbed the last page of the contract, and walked out of the office. Joey followed. They walked through the hall, through the main room, and out the front door. As they hit the open air, Joey felt a rush of panic. What was Max doing? Why couldn't he just say what was going on? They walked past the Lincoln in the driveway (a black cat bolted from underneath the car as they passed) to the sidewalk, turning left. Max said nothing as they crossed his house, then the large expanse of foliage, and then up the path to the house next door.

As they approached Max's second mansion, Joey's hands grew cold and his shoulders tightened. He had just been offered half a million dollars and a chance to revive his career, and he had held it up over a detail. The largesse of Max's homes were a reminder of what awaited Joey if he signed the contract.

"Your opponent at *Apocalypse* signed his contract with me this morning," said Max as they came upon the front porch of the house. This one was smaller than the house they left, but still shamefully extravagant. "As one of my employees, he's now living the good life. He is my guest in this house for as long as he wishes to stay." Max rang the doorbell, then looked right at Joey as they waited for an answer.

Silence for two seconds, then the sound of footsteps on the other side of the door. Maybe it was the pattern of the footsteps, or maybe it all made too much sense, but Joey knew who was going to answer the door before it opened.

Like Max's residence, this house had a tall mahogany door at the front porch. It opened slowly and quietly. Standing inside, wearing shorts and a muscle shirt, was Goliath.

CHAPTER 34

▼

"Good evening Max, Joey," said Goliath. "Come in."

Like the house Joey had come from, this home was designed to give the maximum view of the beach. It too had a loft, a winding staircase, and a hallway to the left that led to a greater expanse of space. What separated this house from Max's was the decoration. Whereas Max's house was exquisitely kempt, with expensive furniture and art, this house was plain.

"It's good to see you Joey," said Goliath, shaking Joey's hand.

Goliath's hand felt clammy, like a ghost's. This was the first time Joey had seen him since their match. Joey had no idea what to say to him.

"May we sit down Patrick," said Max, "Joey had some questions of me that led us here."

Goliath hesitated for a minute, then said, "Of course, of course." In the GWA, Goliath would never let anyone call him Patrick. He must have been humbled by Max's money.

Goliath sat in an upright wooden chair. Joey and Max sat to his right on a sofa. Max put the last page of Joey's contract, carried over here from the other house, on a small coffee table in front of the sofa.

"Patrick, Joey and I were going over his contract, and a sticking point came up before he'd sign. Joey wanted to know about his program. I have a policy of never giving out any of that sort of information before the papers are signed, but considering the delicate nature of the program I want you two to perform, plus the enormous draw we've got if we do this right, I thought I'd make an exception."

Goliath nodded his head. Joey's mind shot back to the meeting in Lubbock, with Goliath and Duke, where Joey was told he was going to be the world champion. At that meeting, Joey's future seemed bright as the sun. A few weeks later, everything had gone to hell and the GWA had folded.

"Joey," said Max, turning to face him, "you and Patrick are going to wrestle in my main event. You're going to do the job. You guys will get twenty minutes or more to put on the match of lifetime.

"Like I said, I don't ever give out this sort of information before a contract's signed, but we all know this is different. A few weeks ago, you two had a match that shook up the whole wrestling world. Joey, I know that after that match, your life in the GWA locker room was a living hell. I want you to feel comfortable that here, in my company, things are different. And I want you to feel comfortable with your opponent. This morning, Patrick and I had a long talk, and, well," he turned to Goliath, "maybe you should tell Joey what we talked about."

"Joey," said Goliath, leaning forward, "I haven't had the chance to tell you, or even to say to the media, that I have no hard feelings about what happened in our match. It's just something that happens in wrestling sometimes. Normally, when I take a superkick, I lean with it to make sure it's safe. In our match, I didn't position myself well, and I wasn't ready when the kick came. Anyway, I just want you to know that I feel perfectly safe with you in the ring and I have no hard feelings about what happened in our match."

"Thank you," said Joey. "I appreciate that." And he did. He felt like he could let go of an anchor he'd been dragging since that night in Houston. He could feel his whole body expanding with the freedom that it wasn't entirely his fault, that Max Zeffer, and apparently even Goliath, still thought he was not only a good wrestler, but a major draw at the biggest pay per view of all time. Joey realized that some day Goliath would tell the world what he had just told Joey, that it wasn't all Joey's fault. He also realized that wrestling a second match with Goliath, a great match, would go a long way toward erasing people's memory of that failed superkick and the ensuing fiasco.

"Joey, do you know why I won the Monday Night Battle?" said Max.

Was this a trick question? Was Joey now supposed to kiss up to his new boss? Or was Joey the answer to this question? Did Max want Joey to tell him that his failed superkick won the Monday Night Battle for him?

"Well, there are lots of reasons, I guess, but I don't know if I know the full story," said Joey.

"The reason I won, Joey, is because I am a businessman. I seek out opportunity, and create it if it isn't there. When I started Revolution Wrestling, there was no demand for a second national promotion. There was no niche for it. I created that niche. In doing so, I expanded the wrestling audience. It wasn't just about guys in underwear settling their differences in the ring. Now it was about two competing products, and the real drama of competition between them. GWA and Revolution both benefited from that. Wrestling benefited from that. And when the time was right, I pulled the plug and let it all hang out. I made my product the very best one out there, so it could be the only one out there. Opportunity, Joey. I saw it and I grabbed it.

"There's opportunity in your story. Joey Mayhem, the exciting upstart, earns a shot at Goliath, the champ, and blows it. A superkick goes sour, the champ goes down, the match is a non-finish, and the kid's life becomes hell backstage. Joey, that's fucking Shakespearian. It's a killer story. We're gonna tell it, and we're gonna finish it. Are you with me so far?"

"I think so," said Joey.

"Joey, on Monday night, *Riot*'s going to open with a video package of your now famous match with Goliath. It's going to be in black and white. Your voice is going to narrate what we see, from your perspective. You're going to say things like, 'I was so excited to be in my first title match, it was such a thrill, but everything went wrong,' then boom! We show the superkick. We show Goliath laid out on the mat. We listen to Clive Silver say his piece about how sometimes things go wrong. Then you say something about how you were scared, about how you were horrified that it went so wrong.

"Then we'll cut to footage of Goliath laid out in a hospital bed. He'll start narrating about how he wondered if he'd ever get better. He wondered if he'd ever wrestle again. He was pissed off, but he felt bad for you.

"The music changes. We cut to footage from our press conference yesterday afternoon, where I announced the purchase of the GWA. Then your voice comes back on, and says, 'I just want another chance to show the world what I can do.' Then Goliath comes on and says, 'I want to do that match again, and this time I want to finish it right.' Then text flashes on the screen, 'Goliath vs. Joey Mayhem, Apocalypse, May 15th.' Joey, the audience is going to piss their pants. More importantly, they're going to call their friends. By the time you and Patrick come out for your promo at the end of the show to give the final sell, we're gonna have the highest rated show in cable TV history."

Max reached forward and dropped a pen on top of the last page of the contract, then he slid both page and pen across the coffee table, putting them directly in front of Joey.

"Joey, this is potentially the biggest night in wrestling. I've violated my own policy of secrecy because I need to have you. Now you know, my estimate of 800,000 pay per view buys is conservative. We may well do over a million. Joey, I know life was shit for you in the GWA. I know that Duke didn't handle you or your situation well. I promise you, things will be different here. I'm going to make you a megastar, and I'm going to make the locker room love you, because you're going to help make us all rich. Sign this contract for me, Joey. Become a millionaire. Save your career in one night. Turn everything around. Joey, the disaster of your life in the GWA is our opportunity to make you a permanent star, and for all of us to make a shitload of money."

Joey leaned forward to sign. There was no question, he was sold. Hearing Goliath's forgiveness for the travesty of the Houston show was enough to convince him that life in Revolution would be far better than life in the GWA.

But there was something else. A new hangup. As Joey lifted the pen to sign, he couldn't help but wonder, should he ask for more? Yes, he was going to make a bundle, but only because his story would bring millions of dollars to the company. Max needed him. Goliath needed him. He would be a fool not to ask for more.

And there was something he wanted.

"Max," he began, leaning up from the contract.

"What is it?" Max could hardly contain his anxiety that Joey hadn't signed yet.

"I was wondering…" Could he ask for this? Goliath was sitting right here. Goliath had been more than gracious tonight. Goliath was willing to leave the past in the past, and here was Joey about to bring the past screeching into the present. Joey was about to ask if Jade would get a contract as well.

"What is it Joey?" said Max, speaking like a policeman to a terrorist, as if Joey had deadly potential in his hands.

Joey's mind raced through the possibilities. He could ask, Max could say yes, Goliath could get mad. He could ask, Max could say no, Joey's chance could be shot. He could ask, Max could say yes, Goliath could be fine.

"Nothing, never mind," said Joey, then leaned forward, put the pen to the paper, and signed his name. There would be another time, a time when Goliath wasn't here. Max was offering Joey a chance to undo his greatest mistake, and get rich in the process. It was a gift, and it would be rude to ask for more.

"Excellent," said Max, clapping his hands together once and grinning like a kid in front of his birthday cake. "Gentlemen, tomorrow we get to work on the video package that's going to go down in wrestling history. But today we celebrate. I have a bottle of '68 Dom Perignon next door. Let's go open it."

CHAPTER 35

▼

Following champagne at Max's beach house, Max, Vicky, Goliath, and Joey had dinner on a chartered yacht, complete with chef, waiter, and violinist. Over dinner, they planned out the next week and a half. On Saturday, Joey and Goliath were to meet Max in New York City to record their parts for the video package. They would carry recording over into Sunday if necessary. While in New York, they would be briefed on their performance for Monday's taping of *Riot*, and would be flown direct to Toronto on Sunday evening. After the taping on Monday, Goliath and Joey were welcome to stay in Toronto as long as they felt necessary in order to work out their match for the pay per view.

They also talked about the GWA, and what went wrong. Goliath spoke about the lack of discipline from the top down through the entire locker room that had permeated the company since Gene Harold had left. Max assured them that everything was different in Revolution. Joey looked at the exquisite dinner on his plate, the beautiful ocean around him, and the focus in Max's eyes, and he believed him.

On the way back, Max offered Joey one of the beach houses for relaxation until it was time to go to New York. Joey declined. He wanted to go back to Jade and tell her everything.

"Alright then, we'll get you on the next flight out," said Max.

And so, a little after eight o clock, Joey said goodbye to his new friends, got back into the Lincoln Continental, where Bobby the driver had been waiting for more than eight hours, and was taken to the airport. His flight left at ten thirty. He arrived in Dallas a little before midnight central time and took a cab to Jade's house.

The lights were off and she was asleep when he arrived. She woke up briefly when he crawled into bed, and asked, "How was your trip?"

"It was good," he said. "I'll tell you about it tomorrow."

*　　　　*　　　　*　　　　*

"Joey, I don't feel good about this," said Jade. Unlike Joey, she was completely dressed, having been up since dawn. Joey had awakened at nine, gone downstairs in his briefs, and leisurely told her all about his trip to Key West from the kitchen table, with a glass of juice and two slices of toast in front of him.

"I know it sounds weird, but I'm telling you, Goliath is fine with everything," he said. "We had a wonderful conversation over dinner. I honestly think the guy is excited that things turned out this way because we stand to make so much money."

"It just doesn't sound like him," said Jade. She was leaning against the kitchen counter, sipping on a glass of ice water. "He's the proudest person I've ever met. I was sure he was going to be pissed when he finally came around. This was the first major injury he's had in his career. And with all the shit that went down, I just...wow. You think you know someone."

"I know. I was shocked too. But the more I think about it, the more it makes sense. It's like Max said. It's almost like Shakespeare in its tragedy. What started as a little mistake, me kicking Goliath in the head, turned into this huge wrestling empire quickly falling apart. By that last taping of *Burn*, well you know, we watched it, the whole company had gone to hell. Now we're going to finish that fight that started all of this, and we're going to tell the story that happened in between. The fans will eat it up, and we'll make a shitload. Goliath might be pissed that I kicked him in the head, but he's perfectly willing to forget about it since my little mistake is going to make us each half a million dollars."

Jade raised her eyebrows and shook her head. "Gosh," she whispered. "Who ever would have predicted this?"

"It's crazy, I know," said Joey.

"So what else is going to happen at this pay per view?" said Jade.

"I have no idea. On Saturday, I'm going to get a script for my promo on *Riot*. Maybe I'll learn more then."

"A script? As in, someone is actually going to plan out a little bit of the show before it happens? That'll be a change." Jade had a hint of sarcasm in her voice. It was true that towards the end, *Burn* was going on the air with little or no advance planning.

"Jade," said Joey, "I thought of something when I signed that contract. I ultimately didn't do anything, but I bet I could."

"What is it Honey?" She could tell something substantive was on his mind.

"Do you want me to push for a spot for you in this company, or would you rather wait for them to call you?"

She smiled, then took a drink from her glass. "You're so sweet," she said.

Joey was relieved she didn't seem patronized by the question.

"Honey, I've been thinking." Jade pulled back a chair and sat with Joey at the table. "Maybe I don't want to go back to wrestling just yet."

"Okay, sure," said Joey, doing his best to empathize. He could immediately see where she was going. Their last few weeks in the GWA, particularly Jumbo's piss, had to leave her sour toward the business.

"I don't know, maybe…" she looked out the window behind Joey as if to gather the words, "maybe I don't want to go back ever."

"Okay," said Joey. He wondered if he should get up and put his arm around her or something.

"It's just…I don't know…it's hard for me," she said. "I have enough money to live on until I'm old. This house is paid for. And these past two weeks, just being here, in one place, with you, they've been…wonderful. Have you enjoyed yourself?"

"Of course I have," said Joey. It was true. He was as happy as he had ever been.

"Well, I'll certainly have to give it some more thought, but I think I really am ready to hang up the boots. I mean, wrestling's really important to me. Hell, it's been my life. It's what I've always wanted. But it's also been shit. Even when I was at the top it was shit. And I don't think that's going to change for me, even in a new company. There are people, ruthless sharks of people, who'll do anything to get to the top, including ruining your life. And I'm not bitter, well, okay, I am bitter, but I'm not speaking from a bitter place here. It's just true."

"I understand," said Joey. "You've got to do what makes you happy."

"Yes, I do. We both do. That brings me to what I really want to talk about."

"What's that?" said Joey.

"Us."

Uh-oh. 'Talk about us.' It was always the start of something bad.

"Sure, sure," he said. "What do you want to talk about?"

"Well, I'm older than you."

"Yes."

"And even though we do great together, I wonder if we're in the same place in our lives."

Joey didn't like how this sounded at all.

"Anyway, Joey, I'm ready to settle down. I'm ready to stop traveling for 300 days out of the year. I want something real."

Joey's face must have conveyed the fear he felt, because Jade's tone quickly switched to reassure him.

"It's okay, you don't need to be scared. All I'm saying is…well, if you're going to be wrestling and traveling, and I'm not, is this still going to work? I just wonder. I think we started this thing between us when we were in one place in our lives, both of us traveling together and living the life, and now we're someplace else, or at least I am. I want to know where you are."

"I'm…right here," said Joey, totally flustered.

Jade laughed. "I'm sorry. Maybe this isn't the right time to talk about this. You've got big things going on."

"No, no, I'm the one who's sorry," said Joey. "I'm ready to talk—"

"Honey. It's okay. You're not ready to talk about this, so you shouldn't have to."

✳   ✳   ✳   ✳

Joey's flight left at seven on Saturday morning. It was nonstop to JFK in New York, arriving shortly before one in the afternoon.

Upon entering the baggage claim area, Joey was pleased to see his name on one of the white posters being held up in the line of chauffeurs. His driver, a tall black man in his fifties who didn't give his name, took Joey to Centersound studios in Brooklyn.

A man Joey recognized greeted him at the front door.

"Good afternoon Joey. I trust your flight in was okay."

"It was fine, thanks. Asher, right?" Joey said as he shook the man's hand.

"That's right Joey. You probably remember me as Nero Caligula from the 80s. Now I'm the project coordinator for Revolution's production department."

"Excellent. It's a pleasure," said Joey. He of course remembered Nero Caligula, real name Asher Mulrooney, the comic wrestler of the 80s who always came to the ring in a toga.

"Come on back Joey. We're going to get you started right away on your voiceovers. When those are done, we'll get you in makeup and film some scenes."

The next twenty-four hours were a blur of excitement. The first six were spent recording the footage for the video package. With every take, and every playback, it became increasingly apparent that the video package would be everything Max had promised it to be. The world of wrestling would change forever with the telling of this story. When Joey and Goliath went back to their hotel on Saturday night, they were giddy with anticipation of what they would soon present to the world.

Sunday began with breakfast in Max's suite at the Waldorf. Max presented Joey and Goliath with their scripts for Monday's show. Joey would cut a promo toward the end of the show, interrupted by Goliath. They would further the story from their video package. The crowd was certain to go apeshit.

Then it was back to Centersound studios for video shoots. They recorded closeups, head-shots, and silhouettes to be shown on *Riot*, as well as two television commercials. After lunch, they did a photo shoot for the newest *Apocalypse* poster and T-shirt.

Every minute was planned and organized. This was a far cry from the publicity tour he did in Houston for GWA. Max Zeffer was a man who left nothing to chance. It was exhilarating to work with him.

The flight to Toronto left at six on Monday morning. From the airport, Joey and Goliath were picked up and taken directly to the arena. Their driver took them through a side entrance to the parking garage and pulled right to the performer's entrance. As soon as the car stopped, a slim black man appeared out of nowhere and opened the door for them.

"Good morning gentlemen," said the man. "I'm Sam. I'm your travel buddy for today."

"What's a travel buddy?" said Joey.

"On the day of every show, you'll be assigned a travel buddy when you arrive at the arena. There are six of us. There's me, Claudia, Daniel, Aaron, and Naomi. Today you're both on my list. It's my job to answer your questions, keep you on schedule, and be your gopher."

Joey and Goliath looked at each other in surprise.

"You'll get used to it," said Sam. "Follow me please. You two have first crack at the ring today."

They followed Sam into the arena and through the backstage area. It wasn't yet eight in the morning, and the place was already brimming with activity. Cameramen were running lighting checks, electricians were inspecting power strips with Ohm meters, set builders were erecting wooden scaffolding.

"You two are the first performers here today," said Sam, leading them up a short stairwell and into the arena.

"Wow," said Joey, in awe of what they had done to this place.

"It's something, isn't it?" said Sam. "Tonight's show is going to be huge."

Indeed, thought Joey. He had seen *Revolution Riot*'s set, and this wasn't it. This far surpassed anything he had ever seen. The entrance ramp was made of glass, underneath which were massive lighting rigs. From the rafters hung two giant sculptures of wrestlers, idealized in form, as if flying at each other over the ring on the floor. Above the ring entrance was the largest teletron he had ever seen, easily forty feet in height. That alone must have been worth tens of millions of dollars.

"Joey, Goliath, what do you think?" It was Max, who had been talking to two other men by the ring. He was now approaching the ramp to talk to them.

"This is fucking amazing," said Goliath.

"Better be," said Max. "Cost twenty times as much as the old set."

"Well it's…impressive," said Joey.

"Glad you dig it. We need something special to establish the new Revolution Brand Name, now that we own the old GWA."

"Gentlemen, I'm going to turn you over to Max now. I'll be back at ten to answer any questions you have about your schedules for the day," said Sam.

"Thanks Sam," said Max. "So guys," he said to Joey and Goliath, "you're here to run our sound checks and practice your promos. You wanna get started?"

✳   ✳   ✳   ✳

Ten hours later, *Riot* went on the air.

Joey saw the completed video package for the first time when it aired. It was a work of art. Joey was proud to be a part of it.

Perhaps that was the theme of the night for Joey, maybe for everyone who had come from the GWA, Revolution was a company they could be proud to work for.

Everyone arrived on time, which was an hour before the first dark match. Everyone gathered together for a company meeting, complete with a briefing by Gene Harold and a motivational speech from Max. Everyone had a screenplay in their hands, which they studied carefully. Everyone had a schedule, which was mirrored on a whiteboard at the performer's entrance. Everyone sat together during the taping, and watched the broadcast on a television outside of the locker rooms. The "travel buddies" kept everyone on track, and made Joey feel like he could relax, because they wouldn't let him miss his cue.

After the video package, which received applause from the spectators in the locker room, and a fury of emotion from the crowd, Max Zeffer came to the ring.

"My friends, welcome to a new era," he said to the audience. He went on to talk about the history of The Monday Night Battles, the history of the GWA, the history of Revolution, and the significance of the merger. "But before we begin on our new course, in a new company, old business must be settled. My friends, before we can arrange for the Titanic struggle between the GWA Champion and the Revolution Champion, a struggle to create the first ever undisputed World Champion, we must settle an important point. Who is the GWA Champion? This Sunday you'll find out. This Sunday, Goliath makes his return, to finish what was started in Houston a month ago. This Sunday. Montreal. Apocalypse. Joey Mayhem vs. Goliath to determine the GWA World Champion. The winner faces Lucifer in the dream match of the century!"

The crowd, of course, ate this up like a final meal. Even Joey, watching from television backstage, knowing what Max was going to say before he said it, couldn't help but feel a swell of excitement, the wrestling fan within him thrilled at this present Max Zeffer was giving.

"But tonight we celebrate. Tonight I present to you the first ever match between a GWA superstar and a Revolution superstar, as Deep Six takes on Jerry Senika. Tonight I present to you Lucifer, Goliath, and Red Jackson in one arena, on one show. Tonight I present to you the new *Revolution Riot*, the greatest show on earth!"

Riot went to commercial as Max left the ring to a standing ovation.

CHAPTER 36

▼

By Tuesday afternoon, it was apparent that *Revolution Riot* had been a smash. Joey checked a few wrestling web sites from a computer terminal in the business center at his Toronto hotel. He had never seen such a high level of excitement from the fans.

The opening video package was everyone's favorite part. A close second was Joey and Goliath's promo which closed the show. "If you screw up this time I'll make sure you never wrestle again," Goliath's closing line in the segment, was quoted on every web site, and the Internet kids couldn't help but gush with enthusiasm over the line's shoot/work entendre.

Best of all, the overnight ratings numbers were in, and were phenomenal. The show got a 7.2. If that number held when the final ratings were released later in the week, last night's broadcast of *Riot* would be the highest rated television program in cable TV history.

Joey closed the web browser and went back to his room. He shaved and took a shower.

In a startling sign of the seriousness of their short relationship, he and Jade had agreed over the phone that she needed to fly up and stay with him during the week, turning his free time into a short Canadian holiday for them both. She arrived at the hotel via taxi just after five. Joey took her to dinner at Michelle's, a French restaurant recommended by Max.

"So, are you nervous?" she said.

"Not really. I know that Goliath and I can put on a killer match. It felt like that when we wrestled the first time. Even he admitted that the accident was partly his fault."

"That still blows my mind. It's so unlike him."

"I know it. Listen, Jade, before I left, we started to have a conversation, and we didn't finish it. I think I'm ready to finish it now."

"Okay," she said. Her eyes were so welcoming, Joey wondered why there was ever any doubt.

"Honey, before I left, you wanted to talk about us, and where this was going. I was scared to talk about it, because, well, you know how the last month has been. It's been horrifying how out of control everything suddenly got around us. And even though you were the only constant thing for me, it was still scary to think about promising you something, only to have the world change all around, in a way I didn't expect, and all of a sudden I couldn't keep my promise. Anyway, what I'm trying to say is, I'm not afraid of all that anymore. It's so amazing to see how things can just turn around in a good way too. Everything that's happened over the past few days, it's like everything's fair, and maybe it was always fair, and I just had to wait to find out. And I don't mean to say that I could only commit to you if my career was good, I just mean to say...I—"

"I think I understand, Joey."

She smiled at him in a way that made him feel more adored than any mob of screaming fans could.

"So the thing is, I think last week when we started to talk about us, you wanted to ask me if we could still do this, even if I was traveling and you weren't. And the answer is yes. I still want to do this, no matter what. I want to do this more than anything else."

Jade reached across the table and took Joey's hand in hers. "Thank you," she said. "I want to do this too."

*   *   *   *

There was a knock on their door at nine the next morning.

"Can you come back later?" Joey called out from bed, hardly stirring at the noise. Conversations through the door with hotel housekeeping were a daily part of his life.

An hour later, after room service had delivered breakfast, another knock came.

"Housekeeping," a woman called from the other side.

"Jesus Christ they want to clean this room," Joey said to Jade. "Please come back later," he yelled at the door.

"Ok, sorry," the woman said back.

Another hour passed. Joey and Jade had both showered and dressed. Jade was applying makeup. They were talking over a possible sightseeing jaunt through Toronto, when another knock came on the door.

"I don't fucking believe this," said Joey. He went to the door and opened it, preparing a polite but forceful statement to the maid about when to come back.

But it wasn't a maid standing at the door. It was a young man. He was short, pudgy, and ugly. Joey had flashbacks to the Hyatt in Houston, when a similar-looking geek took his picture in the hallway wearing only his skivvies. This new geek had a black leather satchel thrown over his shoulder. Probably had his laptop or some video game shit inside it.

"Mr. Hamilton, Joey, my name is Steve—"

"I don't care who you are. Listen up. You're not getting any further. Neither of us is going to talk to you. Now you can leave or I can call security."

"But Mr. Hamilton, Joey—"

"I'm going to close the door now," Joey was almost yelling to make sure he spoke over whatever the geek wanted to say. "The next time I open it, you'd better be gone." Joey slammed the door shut. He looked through the peephole and watched the geek turn away to leave, only to stop after one step. The geek took a big breath, as if steeling his resolve, and came back to the door. He was about to knock again. Before he could get his hand on the wood, Joey opened the door.

"You've got a lot of nerve. You Internet geeks have made my life miserable and I've got a good mind to break you in half."

"Goliath faked his injury," the geek blurted out. "I have proof. Please give me a minute of your time. I've been chasing this story for more than a month. You'll want to hear it."

The geek crouched backwards and contorted his face in a pathetic smush, as if he were preparing for a beating. Joey suddenly felt very sorry for him. He probably had no friends. He probably never had a girlfriend. All he had was wrestling and whatever else occupied his time, and here he was, having found Joey Mayhem and Jade Sleek in a hotel in Toronto, risking bodily harm to present something.

"Okay. I'm listening. But here's the deal. As soon as I think you're bullshitting me or I get tired of your story, you're leaving."

"I understand. Thanks Mr. Hamilton."

"Call me Joey."

"Okay, great, Joey. So, my investigation started when I learned that Goliath was transferred from Houston General to Houston Medical Center. Did you know about that?"

"Yes, I knew."

"Okay, great. So, I learned that and thought it was weird that no one paid any mind to this hospital transfer in the middle of the night." The geek looked at Joey for acceptance of this inference.

"Go on," said Joey. "What did you say your name was?"

"Steve Garcia," the geek said, and thrust his hand out. Joey reluctantly shook it. "Have you ever visited my web site, www.wrestlinghotline.com?"

"Can't say I have Steve. I rarely read what you guys are writing."

"Well, anyway, just so you know, I never engage in gossip stories, and my site refused to get caught up in the shit that they were putting out there about you and Jade."

"I appreciate that, Steve. Is there any more to this Goliath thing?"

"Yes, there is. You see, well, this is where it gets complicated. I've been investigating the Family Television Group from my web site, ya know, to find out if there's any dirt on them I could use to discredit their anti-wrestling campaign."

"That's very noble of you Steve."

"Thanks. So, I found out that all the big donors to the FTG are in Canada, and—"

"You're losing me Steve."

"I know this sounds far-fetched, but it's related. Would it be okay if we went inside and sat down? I've got all these documents that I need to show you." Steve patted his satchel. "They'll make things more clear."

Joey thought for a second. Deep down, he was sure that this was all baloney, but something about the geek, his humbleness maybe, kept Joey interested.

"Okay, sure. Come in."

"Thanks so much Mr. Hamilton—I mean...Joey."

Joey closed the door behind Steve.

"Hello Ms. Wilcox," Steve said to Jade.

Jade, still sitting in front of a make-up mirror, looked at Steve warily, then gave Joey a look as if to say, 'Have you lost your mind?'

Maybe he had. Joey shrugged his shoulders.

"Have a seat," Joey said, pointing Steve to the small table in the corner.

"Thank you," said Steve, placing his satchel on the table as he sat down. Joey sat in the chair opposite Steve at the table. Jade left her chair at the vanity and sat on the bed, close to the table, as if preparing to shut down this conversation between Joey and Steve as soon as it took a wrong turn.

"So, Steve," said Joey, "you left off with the Family Television Group."

"Right," he said, then started rifling through his satchel, pulling out manila folders full of paper. One at a time, he pulled them out and dropped them on the table, until six were in front of him. Each folder had big, sloppy handwriting on the front, written in blue ball point pen. One said, "Houston Medical Records." Another said, "FTG donor info."

"So, anyway, I found out that the FTG has all these donors from Canada. I compiled a list and tried to figure out who they were and what sort of dirt I could get on them."

Jade put an exaggerated look of confusion on her face.

"Let's just hear him out, Honey," said Joey. "He says it's all going to make sense." But it couldn't. This geek was going all over the map already. How could this possibly relate to his match with Goliath? And why was he so anxious to hear this news? He and Goliath had made amends. He had a half-million dollar match on Sunday.

"It will, yeah," said Steve. "So, just days after I got started with this project, this man shows up at my house and serves me with a court order, saying I have to cease and desist all my writings about the FTG and their donors on the web. It was so screwed up, but it told me I was onto something big. So I kept researching, only I did it in secret and didn't publish anything.

"It was right around this time also that I started getting emails from this anonymous guy who was telling me to keep on going, because I was onto something huge. So I kept on digging. And I found out that all these donors to the FTG from Canada were tied to this group called The Saxon Fund."

Steve opened up one of the folders marked, "Saxon Fund Stuff." He pulled out a wad of papers and brochures and spread them in front of him. From the mess, he grabbed a booklet of plain white paper that was clipped together.

"This is the business filing of The Saxon Fund for the Province of Quebec," said Steve. "On page two it says," he began reading, "The mission of the Saxon Fund is to seek out safe growth investments in International Markets for a select group of founding partners." Steve flipped to the back page and held it up for Joey and Jade to see. "And then back here it gives a list of employees of the fund. Andrew Smith, Jonathan Taylor, Jeremy Washington, Peter Jackson."

Steve put the book down in the pile of papers, then grabbed another manila folder labeled, "FTG Donors." He pulled out a single sheet of paper from the folder.

"Andrew Smith, Jonathan Taylor, Jeremy Washington, and Peter Jackson are the four largest donors to the FTG last year," Steve said with excitement.

"I've got to tell you Steve," said Joey. "You're getting a long way from Goliath faking an injury. Where is this going?"

"It's all connected, I swear. If you'll just give me a few more minutes, I'll show you how it all fits together. Are you following me so far?"

"No Steve," said Jade, who was now lying back in the bed, on her elbows, having lost interest in this whole charade. "I'm not following you at all."

"Okay, so we've got this business in Canada, The Saxon Fund, that has only four employees, and these four employees just happen to be largest supporters of the FTG, by far." Steve looked back at the paper in his hand. "Listen to this," he said. "Here are last year's contributions to the FTG. Andrew Smith, three hundred thirty thousand and forty dollars. Jonathan Taylor, forty four thousand dollars. Jeremy Washington, eighteen thousand dollars. Peter Jackson, ninety two thousand three hundred and twenty dollars. Everyone else who donated to the FTG last year combined, eleven thousand dollars. These four men gave the FTG virtually all its money last year!

"And here's the kicker. These four men don't exist! My friends and I dug up information on every Andrew Smith, Jonathan Taylor, Jeremy Washington, and Peter Jackson in Montreal, and none of them gave or even could have afforded to give these sorts of donations.

"So I knew I was onto something really strange here and I emailed the information to this anonymous guy. He wrote back," Steve grabbed another manila folder labeled "Important Emails" and started flipping through the papers. He pulled one out. "Here's what he said: Dear Steve. These people may not be real, but the money obviously is. Find out where the money came from and you'll really be onto something."

Steve took a big breath. Joey could tell this little presentation was a huge deal to him. Whoever this fellow was, he was very thorough.

"Well, around this time," Steve continued, "all the big news in wrestling started unfolding. You and Jumbo got in a fight. You two got suspended. Revolution bought GWA. I was so wrapped up in all this money chasing and government record searching that I missed all these stories, and my web site has suffered for it. I was pissed, and I began to think this anonymous fellow either needed to get to the point or expose the story himself, and I told him so in an email. He wrote back with this whopper." Steve pulled another paper out of the "Emails" folder and began reading it aloud:

"Dear Steve. The story you're following is much, much bigger than any of these other 'scoops' you're missing. Here's another tidbit to keep you motivated. Dr. Harold Claven in Houston recently moved. His old address was 628

Amherst Drive. His new address is 4853 Ledgestone Court. See what your Houston people can tell you about that."

"This is where Goliath gets involved Joey." Steve was so excited he was breathing heavily. "Dr. Harold Claven works at Methodist Hospital in Houston Medical Center. He performed Goliath's MRI. A week after he performed the MRI, he moved to River Oaks, the richest part of Houston."

Joey looked at Steve with bewilderment, then looked to Jade. Her face was agape. She had obviously figured out whatever Joey was missing. "Did Goliath ever get an MRI at Houston General?" Jade asked Steve.

"No," Steve said with the excitement that only good gossip can bring. He pulled out the file marked "Medical Records."

"Goliath's official medical records are confidential, but his insurance claims aren't." Steve flipped through the papers in the folder as he continued talking. "Goliath, like you all, and most everyone in your business, is self-insured, so it was easy to follow this paper trail." Steve pulled out a wrinkled paper that looked like a business invoice and laid it on the table. He pointed to figures as he spoke. "Goliath paid nine hundred dollars to Houston General. He paid twenty six hundred to Houston Medical Center. He must have a huge deductible. A full-body MRI costs a minimum of two thousand dollars. Goliath never had one at Houston General."

"I don't see where we're going," said Joey.

"I do," said Jade. "The ambulance took Goliath to the nearest hospital to the arena, Houston General. By the time we got there, he had been discharged. Then some Internet photographer snapped a shot of him going into Houston Medical Center."

"Yeah…and?" Joey was frustrated that everyone except him understood the significance of all this trivia.

"And," said Steve, "after Dr. Claven at Houston Medical Center performed the MRI, suddenly he could afford a new house worth millions of dollars. Goliath paid off this doctor to tell the GWA that Goliath had concussion syndrome!"

"So the results were faked?" said Joey.

"Why else would Goliath go to so much trouble to see this one doctor who suddenly becomes super rich?" said Steve.

"But why?" said Joey. "It doesn't make any sense for the world champion to fake an injury and disappear for a month."

"To find that out, we have to go back to the FTG and the money trail," said Steve. "So, if you'll recall, we've got these four employees of the Saxon Fund in

Canada, all of whom are fictitious people, supporting the FTG. Following Mr. Anonymous's advice, I tried to follow the money back to its real source."

Steve went back to his paper booklet from which he had read the names of The Saxon Fund employees. "Now, according to this, Mr. Andrew Smith is the president of Saxon LLP, meaning he should be the one who ultimately provided all the money. But since he doesn't exist, I decided to chase down the money that actually made up The Saxon Fund. Canadian Law requires a fund like this to disclose its investments, but not its investors, which made it difficult. On this one, I just got lucky. A library search and a tip from Mr. Anonymous turned up this gem."

Steve went back to the "Saxon Fund" folder and pulled out the one remaining sheet of paper. "This is from an issue of the Financial Times dated January 14th," Steve said, then began reading. "Skyler Holding To Liquidate North American Assets. On January twentieth, Skyler Holding will begin liquidation of its North American assets. The liquidated assets will be reorganized under the new parent company, The Saxon Fund."

Steve looked at Jade and Joey as if he'd just given them the world. "Have you ever heard of Skyler Holding Company?" Steve asked them.

They both shook their heads.

"Skyler Holding used to buy and sell corporations. It had to reorganize earlier this year after it bit off more than it could chew. It was named after the daughter of one of the wealthiest men in the world."

Once again Jade's face conveyed understanding before Joey had solved the riddle.

"Spit it out man," said Joey, impatiently.

"Skyler Holding was Max Zeffer's company," said Steve.

"What does that mean?" asked Joey, fearing where this was going.

"What it means is that the Saxon Fund and all its money belongs to Max Zeffer. What it means is that Max Zeffer was the one who was giving money to the Family Television Group. He was laundering hundreds of thousands of dollars through a Canadian investment fund so the wrestling world wouldn't see that he was bankrolling the anti-wrestling activists!"

"Oh my God," said Jade, quietly, obviously aware of why Steve was so excited.

Joey still didn't understand. Why would Max Zeffer support an anti-wrestling group?

"But there's more," said Steve. "Yesterday, Mr. Anonymous sent me an email with an attachment." Steve grabbed the last manila folder. It was labeled "Next Year's Prospectus."

"Every year, investment funds like The Saxon Fund have to present a prospectus for public record, even if the fund is closed to new investors," said Steve. "Mr. Anonymous sent me the most recent prospectus for the Saxon Fund. Buried on the second to last page, in small type, is the list of employees. Our four fictitious fellows who gave to the FTG are still on there, as are two new names. Harold Claven and Patrick French, or as we know them, Goliath's doctor and Goliath."

Joey took the booklet from Steve and looked at the name in disbelief. There it was, Patrick French, also known as Goliath, employee of this strange Canadian company that this Internet geek had dug up.

"What does this mean?" Joey asked with hesitation.

"It means that Max Zeffer can pay Goliath and the doctor who performed Goliath's MRI whatever amount of money he wants, and the wrestling world will never know about it."

"Jesus Christ," said Joey. "Is that legal?"

"I have no idea," said Steve. "What I do know, without a shadow of a doubt, is that Max Zeffer paid Goliath to take a dive in your match."

"And in doing so wreck whatever was left of the GWA," said Jade.

"That's correct," said Steve. "Max attacked from two fronts. From the outside, Max paid the Family Television Group to come after the GWA and its advertisers with a ton of money. From the inside, Max paid the GWA's biggest star to sit out with a phony injury. It worked. The ratings tanked and Duke panicked. With the advertisers fleeing and the ratings in the toilet, Duke knew he had to sell the company before the network officially canned the show and the stock price plummeted. Now Max Zeffer is the only major promoter left in professional wrestling."

Joey sat in stunned silence, having finally put it all together. Here, in front of him, was documented proof that Goliath had faked his injury, an injury that had ruined Joey's reputation. Here was proof that all the crap Joey took backstage and on the Internet was unwarranted, that the last month of politicking and heartache were unnecessary. Joey had been nothing but a game piece in an elaborate scam for Max Zeffer to become the sole promoter of North American wrestling. Joey grimaced as he thought about how schmaltzy and fake both Max Zeffer and Goliath had been when they told him of their plan to resurrect Joey's failing career, a career that they had destroyed.

"So what are you going to do?" Jade asked Steve.

"Well, I was going to put together a piece to go on my web site. I've already written a lot of it. But apparently, there's even more to this story. That's why I'm here. Are you ready to hear more?"

At this point, Steve could have told Joey and Jade that he had pictures of Bigfoot and they would have listened.

"Go ahead," said Joey.

Steve went back to the folder labeled "Emails" and pulled out another sheet of paper. He handed it to Joey.

"I got this email from Mr. Anonymous yesterday," said Steve.

Joey began to read.

To: Steve Garcia
From: Anonymous

No doubt you've figured everything out by now. But there's more to come. Revolution has hired Joey Mayhem to a short-term contract, with his purpose being a blowout feud with Goliath at the Apocalypse pay per view.

Joey is going to get screwed again. He will be asked to do the job to Goliath, and will be released shortly thereafter. This will be the final payoff to Goliath from Max Zeffer. Getting rid of Joey Mayhem clears the roster of the only person who might be a legitimate challenge to Goliath's spot on the roster. Somebody has to fight Lucifer in the big blowout match. The fans want Joey Mayhem. But if Joey is gone, the fans will accept Goliath.

You would do well to inform Joey Mayhem that this is going to happen.

This is your last task before you run with your story. Tell Joey Mayhem that he is going to be screwed. Tell him that part of the deal was that if Goliath took the dive, Max Zeffer got rid of Joey Mayhem, clearing the way for Goliath to wrestle Lucifer, Champion vs. Champion, in the biggest match in wrestling history.

As proof of the credibility of this information, give Joey Mayhem this tidbit of news that is unknown to the world yet. In two days, Revolution will be announcing Duke Correlli as its "General Manager." This announcement will be made at 10 am eastern time on Revolution.com. When this comes to pass, Joey can be confident that the information in this email is coming from a well-connected source.

Well done figuring everything out Steve.

Your friend,

Anonymous

Joey passed the paper onto Jade. She read it, then looked up in disbelief. She obviously didn't know what to say. Joey didn't either.

"So, I guess the big question left is, who is Anonymous?" said Joey.

"That is the big question," said Steve. "And why has he been so concerned with helping? I've been thinking about that one for weeks. Here's what I've come up with.

"We know that Anonymous has got major inside access at Revolution, and has to be close to Max Zeffer. This narrows it down some. Gene Harold, the head booker; Larry Jenkins, the talent manager; Vicky Archuleta, the head writer; Patrick Childers, the production chief; or any of the front office.

"Of those people, I've been trying to think of who might have a motive for disclosing all this stuff, and that doesn't really get me anywhere. I have no idea why I'm privy to all this insider info."

"I don't either," said Joey. "I guess that makes me skeptical of the whole deal."

"That was me too when I started getting emails," said Steve. "But this Anonymous Guy is right on every time."

"Well, I guess we'll see," said Jade. "Tomorrow, if Duke gets named the General Manager of Revolution, whatever that means—"

"Even then, will we really know everything?" said Joey. "Yes, this guy's obviously got connections at the very top of Revolution, but can we really believe what he's saying about me getting screwed again if we don't know why he's saying it? Why was it so important that you had to come out here and find me?"

"I don't know," said Steve. "My best guess is that this guy doesn't want to see you get screwed again."

"But who would care?" asked Joey. "If he cared, why didn't he stop this whole charade from playing out before it started?"

"I don't know," said Steve.

"Well, we still have the question of what you're going to do, Steve," said Jade. "Joey now knows about everything and can decide for himself what he's going to do. But what are you going to do with all this information?"

"I guess I'm going to go home and write my story," said Steve. "Whatever you decide to do, Joey will just become part of the ending."

"Where do you live, Steve?" asked Jade.

"Chicago. My flight back leaves tonight at eight."

Jade was thinking about something. "What are you going to do until then?" she asked.

"I don't know. I guess I'll just hang around at the airport."

"You know what Steve, you should stay here for a bit. I've got a story to tell you. Since everyone in our business is going to be reading your web site soon anyway, you might as well have all the scoops."

"Oh, okay," said Steve. He reached into his satchel and pulled out an empty notebook and a pen. "What's the story?" he said.

"I think you should title this story, 'Why Jumbo Sanders is a Piece of Shit: An Exclusive Interview With Jade Sleek.'"

CHAPTER 37

▼

The announcement came at ten A.M. on the spot.

Joey and Jade had been in the hotel business center since nine in the morning, surfing the Net. There were three computer terminals in an otherwise empty room. Joey and Jade occupied two. The third was empty.

Joey was checking in on Revolution.com every few minutes. The opening screen had remained unchanged for an hour. There was a splash picture of Joey and Goliath standing in the ring, from the most recent broadcast of *Riot*, and a headline that read, "Re-Match at Apocalypse." When Joey checked Revolution.com at 9:59, the site was unchanged. When he checked again at 10:00, it was there. It was the first box of text underneath the banner logo.

"Revolution Wrestling Names Michael 'Duke' Correlli as General Manager."

Joey clicked on the link to read the story.

> Revolution Wrestling is proud to announce Michael "Duke" Correlli as its new General Manager. This announcement comes just four days after Revolution's groundbreaking acquisition of the Global Wrestling Alliance, of which Correlli was the president.
>
> "Duke and I have had many harsh words for each other over the years, but this week we sat down and buried the hatchet. Business is business, and hiring Duke is good business. He is the preeminent figure in professional wrestling, and we'd be a fool not to ask for his help as we create the greatest wrestling promotion in history," says Revolution President Max Zeffer.

"I ate my piece of humble pie on Thursday, and now I'm ready to get on with what I do best," said Correlli. "Revolution won the Monday Night Battle fair and square with a superior product. I couldn't beat them, so I'm ready to join them. I'm excited to be a part of what will truly be the greatest wrestling promotion of all time."

As General Manager, Correlli will assume a leadership role behind the scenes, as well as an on-air presence as the infamous "Duke Correlli" character made famous on *GWA Burn*. Look for him to make his inaugural appearance as a Revolution superstar this Monday night at 8 eastern on *Revolution Riot*.

"There it is," Joey said to Jade. She rolled her chair closer to him, and read over his shoulder.

"So what does this mean?" she asked.

"It means this Anonymous guy knows his shit. It means that what Steve said is going to happen is probably going to happen. I'm going to do the job to Goliath on Sunday night and them I'm out."

Jade stood up, stepped away from Joey and the computer, and began pacing around the room.

"I don't understand what you're supposed to do with this info," she said. "So, now you know you're getting screwed again. So what? Do you turn down the big money you're getting for the show?"

"I don't know. It's almost like this guy's playing with me."

"How so?"

"Well, knowing that Goliath faked his injury makes it hard enough to consider doing the job for him. Knowing that I'm gonna get let go afterwards...why would I do the job at all?

"Joey, it's okay if you don't want to work the show. We don't need the money. After Steve runs his piece, everyone would understand why you didn't want to work."

"It's not that I don't want to do the show. I really want to get in the ring with Goliath. I really want to get in the ring with him and give him a real concussion."

He was surprised at his own venom. In speaking his violent desire to Jade, he made it real. The thought had been in his mind since Steve presented his news the night before, but he hadn't allowed himself to consider the desire as real.

"Don't talk like that Joey," said Jade. "You don't need to be getting into any more fights. It's not worth it. Your little bout with Jumbo almost killed you."

"You don't think I can take Goliath?"

Jade looked at him with sympathy. "Honey, he's got fifty pounds of muscle on you."

"Fifty pounds of steroid muscle. Not that any of it would matter anyway. I was up all night thinking about what he did and what I'd like to do to him. He'd never know what hit him."

"I don't like the way you're talking at all, Baby. You're not seriously considering this are you?"

"Why not? It used to happen all the time in wrestling. The phony show turns into a real one. Just thinking about kicking his ass in front of the whole world right before everyone finds out what he did to me, what he did to all of us—"

"Joey, you can't do this. You can't do this to me. You're all fired up with rage and you're not thinking straight."

Joey stood up, carried by his own excitement. "I am thinking straight. This is a good idea. Steve's piece isn't running until Monday. No one will be expecting anything like this on Sunday night. I go out there, beat the shit out of him, go home, get fired, then the next day Steve tells the world everything. We're both vindicated and Goliath is left looking like a dupe."

He didn't know if he really believed what he was saying. Somewhere in the back of his mind was the reality that he would get paid half a million dollars just to put on a wrestling match. If he chose to do what he was saying, he would give that up.

And maybe that was the appeal. Picking a real fight with Goliath would be supremely rebellious, not only because Joey would be flouting years of convention, but because he would be giving up the biggest payout in wrestling history.

"Honey, please. This is crazy. Didn't you learn anything from your fight with Jumbo? You ended up in the hospital. You're lucky you didn't end up with brain damage. You're lucky you didn't get killed. Don't you think it would be more effective if you didn't show up at all? Don't you think that would make a stronger statement?"

"It's not just about making a statement. It's about revenge."

"You're going to get revenge, Joey! On Monday morning the whole world is going to know everything!"

Jade's eyes were filling with tears. Her face was flooded with desperation. Joey didn't care. How dare she suggest that Goliath could beat him in a fight, just because the scrap with Jumbo went awry. She certainly wouldn't be the only one who would think Goliath could take him. He would beat up Goliath and surprise the entire wrestling world. He would be the underdog, and he would be fighting for the right reasons. He had been wronged. He was about to get screwed. He was going to do this.

"I'm calling Steve," he said. "I've got an idea. Can I have your cell phone?"

"What? What's your idea?" She was crying now.

Joey hated the way she sounded. Her desperation made it clear that, in her mind, this wasn't just his decision. He had to ignore her now. He had to do this. If ever there was anything in his life that he had to do...

"Please, can I just...if you don't let me have your cell phone, I'm just going up to the room to call Steve," he said.

Jade looked at him, judged him, then gave up. Her desperation changed to resignation, and to anger. She shook her head as she pulled her cell phone from her purse.

"Fine, whatever you want," she whispered, handing over her phone.

"How do I get into the phone directory to dial his number?" Joey asked, remembering that Jade had programmed Steve's number into the phone the day before.

"Here, let me do it," she said, taking the phone from him.

She pressed some buttons, then handed the phone back to Joey, its display reading, "Calling STEVE."

"Honey, please. Tell me what you're doing," she said.

He held up his hand and nodded his head, in a feeble attempt to communicate that everything would be fine. Jade's face only became more intense.

"Hello, Steve, this is Joey." He walked past Jade, out of the business center and into the hotel lobby. She followed him.

"What is it Joey?" Steve said from the other end of the connection.

"Steve, I have another story for you to post on your web site. This one is good."

Jade was standing right in front of him. Behind her was a stone bench. Behind the bench was a decorative water fountain. Behind the water fountain were stairs leading to the hotel front desk, where a young blonde woman caught herself looking right at Joey, and turned away.

Joey looked back to Jade, who slowly sat on the bench, as if her nerves were too rampant to continue standing. Joey's instinct was to run away—he didn't want Jade to listen to this conversation—but he knew he couldn't keep his idea secret from her for long. Perhaps it was best if she heard it first.

"Okay, I'm listening," said Steve.

"Steve, on Sunday night I'm not going to lay down for Goliath. I'm going to shoot, and I'm going to try to pin him. What if, right before you post your story about the FTG and Goliath and everything else, I give you a piece to put up, explaining why I chose to shoot? You could post the story right as I do my ring entrance, so that a lot of the fans at home will know right away what's going on, but Goliath sure as hell won't. It will give me a chance to speak my piece, and to screw Goliath and Max before they get the chance to screw me again, and it'll give you another big story."

Jade exhaled heavily then dropped her head. Her hands gripped the front of the bench like she might fall forward.

"Wow, are you sure this is what you want to do?" said Steve.

"Oh yes, and I'll be doing it whether or not you post my piece. I just think it would turn out even better if I could tell the world why I wasn't going to lay down. Think about it Steve. Wouldn't it be amazing to have this news on your web site as I walk into the arena for my match?"

"Well Joey, I wasn't going to post any of the stories until Monday morning. I wouldn't want to put up your explanation of things before I got my story on the site."

"So, change your schedule! Steve, I'm giving you the scoop of a lifetime here! This is going to make you famous."

"Yeah, I guess this is quite a story. It's just that—"

"Steve, if you don't agree to run with this, I'll just find someone who will."

Jade lifted her head. The movement caught Joey's attention. She was looking at him like he had just kicked a dog. A drop of panic caught him. He wondered if all of this was getting out of hand.

"Joey, don't go to anyone else, please. I'll run your story. Give me just a bit to call you back to talk about it further."

"What's the problem here Steve?"

"It's just that…Mr. Anonymous had told me not to run anything until after the show. Let me just shoot him an email quickly, and tell him I want to run with the story on Monday night…just to clear it with him. His instructions were very specific."

"Why does he want you to wait until after the show?"

"He said he has his reasons, and he can't tell me."

"Well that sounds like a crock of shit to me. Steve, it's your web site. It's your story. Why do you have to do what he tells you?"

"Joey, I have to trust him. He's been right every time."

"Steve, you're not going to tell him about my plan are you?"

Jade was sitting on the edge of the bench now, thoroughly engrossed in the conversation. Hearing this spat with Steve, this potential snag, had given her new energy.

"I was…I won't say a word about this Joey, it sounds like you don't want me to, so I won't. I promise," said Steve.

"Okay...," Joey began, then was overcome with fear. This conversation, both with Steve and with Jade, wasn't going how he wanted it to. He wanted both of them to see what he saw. He saw the ultimate opportunity for revenge. It was so perfect in his mind. But Jade wasn't with him. Neither was Steve. Joey was losing control of the plan before it even started. If he couldn't control this conversation with Steve, how in the world was he going to control Goliath tomorrow night? "You know what?" Joey said to the phone, his voice running away from him. "No. No, Steve. I want you to agree with me right now that you're going to run this story right when my match starts. Fuck what Mr. Anonymous wants. I want you to promise that to me right now or I'm taking the story to someone else."

"Joey...I, this...I don't know—"

"Yes or no, Steve."

Silence on the other end of the line. Silence from Jade. Silence in the room, except for the gurgle of the fountain and the pounding of his heart. What in the world was he doing?

"Okay Joey. I'll run your story as you want. Send it to me over email. I'll post it right when your match starts, and I'll make it work with what I've got. I won't tell Mr. Anonymous a thing about it. We'll just run with it and see what happens."

"Excellent," said Joey, feeling tiny waves of contentment. It was a small victory, but victory was something he hadn't felt much of lately. His entire body calmed as he realized that, with just a little force, he got what he wanted.

Goliath would be next.

"You're making the right decision Steve. This will be the biggest story in the history of wrestling Steve. You're going to win the fucking Pulitzer Prize for this."

"Sure thing, Joey. You have my email?"

"I do. I'll have the story, my statement, to you by the end of the night."

"Okay then. We'll be in touch. Thanks for calling Joey."

"Thank you Steve."

Joey clicked the phone off and turned toward the business center. He had an email to write, an email that would be turned into a web page that would be read by hundreds of thousands of fans. Words were already forming in his mind. "Goliath faked his injury last time, but tonight I'm going to hurt him for real," or something like that. Before he took a step, he realized his conversation with Jade wasn't finished. She was still sitting on the stone bench, in front of the fountain. He turned toward her.

"Honey, I need to do this," he said.

Her face was an accusation. It accused him of ignoring her, and ignoring her wishes. It accused him of thinking only about himself. It accused him of hurting her.

"What was the trouble?" she said, softly. She had given up.

"The trouble?" Joey stepped closer to her. He thought of how he took control of the conversation with Steve and got what he wanted. He willed himself to walk right up to her. She ignored him. He put his arm around her. He would take control of this conversation too.

"It sounded like Steve was reluctant to run your story," she said.

"Yeah, this anonymous guy wanted him to wait until Monday. That's settled, though. Steve was just caught off guard. I think it took a minute for the significance of what I was offering him to set in."

"Honey. Aren't you worried that you're basing all of this on the word of some Internet kid and his anonymous friend? What if they're wrong? What if we're being played?"

"They're not wrong Jade. We're not being played."

"How do you know?"

"I know because I'm one hundred percent positive that I didn't mess up that kick. I know that Goliath faked that injury. I knew it the instant it happened, but I allowed myself to believe all this crap that's been said about me lately. I've done a superkick hundreds of times before, and I've missed a superkick once. I know what it's like to do it right, and I know what it feels like if you mess up. My heel barely touched Goliath's cheek. I just convinced myself that I messed up because it didn't make any sense otherwise. It didn't make any sense for him to fake an injury like that. Everyone believed that I botched it, because I'm Joey Mayhem, and I'm reckless in the ring. But I didn't botch it. And yesterday, when I was about to slam the door in Steve's face and he said to me, 'Goliath faked his injury,' I knew I needed to let him in and listen to what he had to say, because deep down inside, I knew it was true."

Jade stared straight ahead. In front of them was a revolving door surrounded by picture windows, through which the late morning sun was broken into the shadows of window panes and trees.

"Have you ever heard about Goliath's incident in Sydney?" she said, softly.

"Yes, I remember that I think." Joey's mind stuck on a conversation he had with a companion in wrestling school, a kid named Neil Crawford. Neil was always up-to-date on the latest gossip, and had mentioned Goliath causing a scene in Australia.

"Duke did a good job of covering the whole thing up," said Jade. Her voice was empty, like the words were being pulled from her without any effort on her part. "Today, any fans who hear about the Sydney incident think it's just gossip that may or may not be true."

Joey was frightened at where this was going.

"It's true," she said. "I was there."

Joey had lost control of this conversation. The uneasiness was back. Did he know what he was doing?

"We did a tour in Australia two years ago," Jade continued. "Duke didn't go. Neither did Shane. Martha Tanner came to run the backstage, but there was no one there to control the wrestlers. They turned into spoiled kids, frat boys on a drunken spree. It was awful. In every city there was some fight on the bus or on the plane. Rocky Preston and Flash Martin were both rookies with us on that trip, and they got hazed like you wouldn't believe.

"But the worst was in Sydney, after the show. A bunch of us went to a bar. Goliath and I were together at the time. He was still all 'roided out from his match, he got way too jacked up that night. Everyone else was drinking and having fun, but he was just stewing in this chemical shit, hardly saying anything to anyone, and his eyes. He was scary.

"And it was crowded, and some local guy bumped into him on accident. Goliath flipped out and punched the guy in the face. Instantly the whole bar blew up. I swear, I'm never going to a bar in Australia again, the men get drunk and they want to fight. And one by one Goliath beat the shit out of all of them. And it wasn't pretty. He was knocking people's teeth out and kicking them in the ribs. And he was yelling, "Who's next! Who's next!" Even the bouncers couldn't contain him. He had this rage in his eyes. It was horrifying. It took half the locker room to get him under control. The next morning, on the airplane, I told him I never wanted to speak to him again and then sat next to Jumbo for the rest of the trip, thinking it'd be smart to stay near the biggest guy in the locker room until I knew Goliath was safe."

Jade leaned forward, as if the story had exhausted her.

"Honey, I'm sorry you had to see that," said Joey. "I promise Sunday night won't be like that at all."

"You can't promise that. You can't..." She shook her head and let out an angry sigh.

"I can't what?" Joey knew he was being ruthless. She was drained, and now he was asking her to fight with him.

"I can't what, Jade? I can't protect myself? I can't win? Your story doesn't scare me, Jade."

"It wasn't meant—"

"It was meant to scare me!" He backed away from her, preparing to yell at the top of his lungs if he had to. "And I'm sorry that it doesn't scare me. I'm sorry that I have to do this, and I'm sorry you don't want me to. And I'm sorry that I can't guarantee that I won't get my ass kicked, because I might. But I have to do this!"

"Why? Why do you have to do this? It's stupid Joey. You're not proving anything."

"I am proving something. I'm proving that I can hang. I'm proving that I deserved my shot at the top. I'm proving that I didn't deserve all the shit I took from everyone in the GWA locker room from the minute I arrived. I'm proving that next time no one's going to push me around, no one's going to work me stiff, no one's going to talk shit about me—"

"Shootfighting Goliath doesn't prove any of that! You're a wrestler, Joey, not—"

"That's right. I'm a wrestler, not some drunken barfly who's easy pickings for Goliath's 'roid rage. This is what I do for a living."

"This is not what you do for a living! You pretend. We pretend to fight, Joey."

Her eyes were full of tears, dyed black from mascara. Joey turned around so he didn't have to see her. He looked out the revolving door and thought about storming outside. His mind was made up, and hers was too. This argument was nearing the point where the stakes would increase. Soon they wouldn't be arguing about what he should do, but why he should do it. Soon he would be asked if this fight was more important to him than their relationship.

"I'm sorry," he said.

She said nothing. A man in a suit, carrying a briefcase, walked through the revolving door. He nodded at Joey before heading to the front desk.

Joey turned around and looked at Jade. Drags of mascara now underlined her eyes. She was crouched forward on the bench like she was suffering from stomach cramps. He was hurting her. This had to stop.

"Honey?" he said, taking a small step towards her, looking to her for permission to come any closer.

"I'm sorry," he said. "I don't have to do this. I want to do this, but I don't have to."

She shuddered, from either a laugh or a cry, Joey couldn't tell.

"Jesus, Joey," she said. "I'm just...I don't want anything to happen to you. I love you."

He knelt before her, then kissed her. Her lips were salty and wet with tears. Her cheeks were cool from evaporation. He pulled away and cleaned her cheeks with his thumbs, then kissed her again. He stood up and pulled her into his chest, where he held her.

"I love you too," he said. "Give me the word, honey, and I'll call this off."

"Oh no," she said. She forced her way up, making Joey take a step back to allow her room. "I'm not making this decision. You go do whatever you want. I think this is a bad idea, but I'm not going to take the blame for your regret if you make the wrong choice."

"Okay," he said, containing a small and perhaps inappropriate joy. He had won. He and Jade were in a fight, which was now over, and he was going to get what he wanted.

And if he could win this fight, he could win his next one too.

"Why don't you go up to the room?" he said. "I'm going to the business center to write my email to Steve."

CHAPTER 38

▼

To my fans,

What you are reading was first posted on the web precisely when my name was announced for my title match with Goliath at Apocalypse. It is important to me that everyone understands that what I did (what I am about to do) was carefully planned and thought about over the course of several days.

If you are one of the lucky ones who is reading this soon after it has been posted, congratulations. You will be witness to wrestling history. What happens in my match with Goliath tonight will be talked about for years to come.

Tonight I am supposed to "do the job" for Goliath. I am supposed to lose. The plan is for the two of us to get approximately fifteen minutes to work a strong main event match, with many near-falls and lots of momentum changes. Near the end of the match, Goliath is supposed to gain control, then nail me with his finisher, The Thunderclap. Then he is supposed to pin me, getting a clean victory and going on to face Lucifer at next month's Pay Per View.

I have been told that doing the job is the right thing for me to do. I have been told that, since I carelessly injured Goliath in our title match and knocked him out of wrestling for a month that it is only fair for me to lay down for him tonight. I have been told that since the stakes are high at this *first pay per view of the new Revolution I should lose to a proven superstar in the Main Event. I have been told that the world wants to see Goliath vs. Lucifer, and that Goliath deserves this opportunity.*

But there is much more that I wasn't told, until I met an ambitious Internet wrestling columnist named Steve Garcia. Stay tuned to this web site for more details, for soon, very soon, Steve Garcia will be telling the entire world what he told me.

After you read that story, you will understand why I did not just lay down for Goliath tonight. You will understand why I came out and did not follow the script. Tonight I intend to pin Goliath for the 3-count. To do so, I will have to wrestle him, to fight with him, for real.

Tonight you won't see any clotheslines or Irish Whips. There won't be any bulldogs or slingshots. If steel chairs or ring bells or blood shows up tonight, the violence will be very real.

And I may lose. Despite my best efforts, I may still get pinned, or knocked out, or disqualified.

But I will not lie down. What happened to me and to professional wrestling is a disgrace, and I will not lie down.

Enjoy the show.

Sincerely,

Joseph Hamilton a.k.a. Joey Mayhem

Steve closed the email. He had now read it five times or more.

It was an impressive piece, if a little rough around the edges. Steve wanted to run it. He still hadn't decided.

He went back to his Inbox. There were still only three messages, nothing new. At the bottom was the message from Joey, sent on Jade Wilcox's email account. It had arrived at four thirty. Its subject line was "My Statement." Right above that were two emails from Anonymous, both titled "RE: Posting the Story." They were part of a chain that Steve had started right after reading Joey's statement.

To: Anonymous
From: Steve Garcia
Posing The Story

Mr. Anonymous,

There has been a new development. I need to post my story tomorrow night. It's very important that I post the story right away.

Steve

It had taken Anonymous all of two minutes to respond to that email. He had written back:

To: Steve Garcia
From: Anonymous
RE: Posting the Story

Steve,

What is this development?

Anonymous

That was it. Greeting and signature with one line in between. Right to the point. So, Steve sent a message right back to him:

To: Anonymous
From: Steve Garcia
RE: Posting the Story

I can't tell you about the development. There's been a new twist (a big twist) to the story, but I promised my source I'd protect him. Needless to say, the story has taken on even more urgency, and I MUST post my story tomorrow night. If you're still holding onto any information—I need to have it right away if you want it to show up. I will be posting the story, with or without your new information, tomorrow night.

Steve

As expected, Anonymous wrote back right away.

To: Steve Garcia
From: Anonymous
RE: Posting the Story

Steve,

You are a good journalist, and I can appreciate that you want to protect your sources.

I promise you that it is safe to tell me about this "development." Not only is it safe, it's extremely important. It would be a huge mistake to publish your story before you've heard from me. I'm the one who has led you to where you are, and I'm the one who knows everything that's going on. There is so much more at stake than you know, and if you don't follow my instructions, you jeopardize the story and your own well-being. I don't say this to intimidate you, just to remind you that you don't know everything and would do well to listen to me since I do.

Steve, I might be persuaded to have you run your story early, but I must know what this "development" is and how it fits into the scheme of things. Trust me Steve. You can trust me. You have to trust me.

Anonymous

That email had arrived a little under an hour ago. Since then, Steve had been paralyzed with indecision. There were lines in that email that were downright frightening. "You jeopardize the story, and your own well-being." "You have to trust me." In the midst of this story that had unfolded, of the facts that had fallen into his lap or revealed themselves like treasures for which only he had the map, of his meeting with Joey and Jade, and their interest in what he knew, of their willingness to use him and his web site to alter the course of wrestling history, Steve had forgotten that he was just an unemployed twenty-something who lived with his parents and was playing a high stakes game with some of the most powerful people in the world.

The answer was obvious. He needed to tell Mr. Anonymous everything and hope for the best. Yes, he had promised confidentiality to Joey, but he was in over his head. And his promise to Joey was ridiculous anyway. As soon as he posted

Joey's column, Mr. Anonymous would read it like everyone else. So what if Mr. Anonymous saw it a few hours early?

But that thinking only led to the other wall: Who was Mr. Anonymous and why did he care so much about any of this? Obviously, Mr. Anonymous was very well-connected with Max Zeffer and/or Goliath. This new email, its desperate tone, suggested that Mr. Anonymous was involved. He had fed Steve all this information with a purpose. For some reason, he wanted Steve to present the story as Mr. Anonymous knew it, on Mr. Anonymous's terms. Failure to follow these rules apparently was not acceptable. Mr. Anonymous had a lot at stake here.

And if he had a lot at stake here, he might have his own agenda regarding tomorrow's taping of *Riot*. He obviously didn't want any information to escape until after *Riot* had already aired. Perhaps something big was going to happen, something bigger than Joey's shoot fight.

And that led back to the first wall. Steve was trapped between his word to Joey and his fear of Mr. Anonymous.

He played out the two possible scenarios in his head.

Number One: He keeps his word to Joey. He would have to email Mr. Anonymous and tell him the story gets posted on Steve's terms, because it's Steve's story. If Mr. Anonymous wishes to help by providing whatever this last bit of information is, then fine. If not, so be it.

Instantly, Steve's mind swarmed with visions of men in suits and sunglasses greeting his mother at the front door, no, knocking the front door down and entering with guns. There was still a good twenty four hours between now and the start of Joey's match on *Riot*, plenty of time for Mr. Anonymous to do whatever he felt necessary to ensure things went according to his plan. "There is so much more at stake than you know, and if you don't follow my instructions, you jeopardize the story and your own well-being."

Of course, he could just remain silent, or better, tell Mr. Anonymous, "Forget it, there's no new development. I was just trying to get the story out of you early. I'll do it your way," only to post Joey's story as planned. Still, the men in suits might come. Now that the cat was out, Mr. Anonymous knew that Steve had something juicy, this game might continue until Steve spilled his guts, one way or another.

Okay, Scenario Number One didn't go anyplace happy. What about Number Two: He betrays his word to Joey and forwards Joey's statement to Mr. Anonymous. Mr. Anonymous could say, "Very interesting, go with what you were planning, here's my information too. Now we've got a killer of a killer story." Or, Mr. Anonymous could say, "Don't run this piece, this will muck everything up," and then do Lord knows what behind the scenes to destroy Joey's big moment. Or, Mr. Anonymous could say nothing to Steve, he could take the information and run with it, and whatever master plan Mr. Anonymous had in the first place could be adjusted to account for the new information.

Any way it played out, Scenario Number Two didn't involve men in suits visiting his mother's house. Clearly, Scenario Number Two was the superior choice.

Steve clicked on the Reply button to send a new email to Mr. Anonymous.

To: Anonymous
From: Steve Garcia
RE: Posting the Story

Dear Anonymous,

Okay. Attached to this email is "the development." A few hours after I returned home from my visit with Joey Mayhem, I received a phone call.

Steve thought about the phone call. Joey had been thrilled with his plan to shootfight Goliath. It was a way to restore his dignity after the wrestling world had screwed him. And he had chosen Steve. After everything Joey had learned about all the lies, Joey still blindly put his trust in someone. He put his trust in Steve.

Steve thought about his mother, about her constant harassment of him to get a real job. How she had never believed that this Internet "journalism" was worth a second of his time. How often she told him he was throwing his life away. How she thought her only son was a loser.

Steve deleted what he'd written and started over.

Dear Anonymous,

I will not divulge my information. I promised my source I wouldn't. I will post the story on my own terms. I thank you for your help. You are correct, you gave me this story, but it's still mine, unless you'd like to write and post it yourself.

If you'd like to give me your last bit of information in time for it to appear with the rest of the story, please send it right away.

Steve Garcia

He clicked the 'Send' button before he could change his mind.

CHAPTER 39

▼

Joey and Jade pulled into the parking lot of the Montreal Arena at six o' clock. They had both wrestled here before. But they had wrestled here for the GWA. Somehow, the new promotion changed everything. The yellow lines of the parking lot, the red bricks of the arena's outer walls, even the cool evening air of French Canada, were all the same, but were somehow different too, as if they had been lifted from the old, familiar world and put in a new place, where the changes couldn't be seen, only felt.

A man with a TV camera and a woman in a polyester suit rushed into Joey's face as soon as he stepped out of the car. Not remembering any mention of a parking lot taping, he stopped and waited for them to arrive, only to find out they were not with Revolution, but with a local television station.

"Excuse me, sir?" the woman said. "Are you with the wrestling show tonight?" Her voice lilted with the distinct bounce of a Quebecker.

Joey didn't know if he was relieved or insulted that she didn't recognize him. He looked to Jade for guidance. She said nothing, and began walking toward the arena. Joey followed. The cameraman mumbled a few words to the woman, one of which Joey could tell was "Mayhem."

"Sir? I understand you're Johnny Mayhem, the wrestler?" the woman said. She was fumbling with a nest of cords and papers that had been stored in each armpit. Joey and Jade continued walking.

"Sir? Mr. Mayhem?"

"No comment," Joey said, and continued walking.

"What about you, ma'am?" the woman said to Jade.

"No comment either," said Jade.

As they raced to get in the arena and away from the reporter, Joey realized just how foreign everything was tonight. In the past, he never would have turned down an opportunity to speak with a TV reporter. You just don't do that in the wrestling business. You're a wrestler—you're trying to get your character over. Television time, any television time, is golden.

But not tonight. Tonight was not about building for the future. Tonight was about avenging the past, and until the proverbial cat was out of the bag, Joey ached for privacy.

The performer's entrance was a white metal door. Upon its opening, a gust of cool wind poured out. Joey felt a finality as he stepped inside, like he was entering a battle zone, and would be profoundly changed before he left.

"Joey, Jade, hello, my name is Phillip Gaines, I'll be your stage manager for the evening." Phillip shook hands with both of them. He was wearing a maroon dress shirt and a tie. A headset was over his ears, but somehow not over his perfectly managed hair. "Joey, your locker room is down the east hallway and to the right. Jade, you're welcome to make yourself comfortable backstage. We have a TV viewing room with refreshments, or, if you'd prefer, I can arrange for box seating for you in the arena."

"I'll make do. Thanks," said Jade.

"Alright Honey, do you need anything?" said Jade.

"No. Thank you," said Joey. He didn't need anything. At least not anything she could provide.

"Okay. I'll be in the viewing room."

She kissed him quickly on the lips, then patted his hip once before turning to leave. Joey watched her follow the signs toward the viewing room, stopping to talk to no one on the way. As she walked out of the area, he thought about what he was doing to her. If it wasn't too late, if he hadn't already committed that statement to the web, he might have considered backing out, just so she wouldn't have to deal with tonight. Tonight was going to be hell for her. Joey walked up to the whiteboard to read the entire match listing. The card was a wrestling fan's dream.

The show opened with Flash Martin vs. Miguel Cervantes, then a tag team match between The Howlers and The Hanson Boys. Bruiser Franks vs. Deep Six would be the first match on the show between a Revolution Star and an old GWA star. The first hour would conclude with the Lucifer/Rollins vs. Jackson/Senika tag match. The second interpromotional match was a tag team event: Tyson Turner and Lord Mayberry vs. Butterfly Johnny Grace and Tony Campbell. Then Crystal Waters vs. Marian Mailor for the Women's Title. Finally, unassumingly, on the bottom of the board was written, "Main Event: Goliath vs. Joey Mayhem."

"Joey, how are you doing?" The voice was familiar. It brought about a quiver in Joey's neck.

"Hello Max," said Joey.

"You want to come back with me to the office?" said Max, as if there were a choice. "Goliath is there, so is Duke, and some other people I'd like you to meet."

"Sure thing," said Joey.

*   *   *   *

Joey wondered if anyone in the room could tell that he wasn't listening. Four people had been barraging him with final details about his match tonight and he had heard none of it. Now there was absolutely no turning back. Even if everything else went to hell, even if his fear was too great, Joey was now going into the biggest match of his life without a clue of what he was supposed to do.

It wasn't that he didn't want to listen. He wanted to know what the choreography was supposed to be, what Goliath was expecting, what the decision-makers backstage were expecting. But the facade was so prevalent, so thick in the air, that he couldn't pay attention. In the room with Joey were "The Big Four," the most important wrestling promoters of the past twenty years: Max Zeffer, Duke, Gene Harold, and Larry Jenkins. Every important wrestling promotion in North America was run by one of these people at one time. With the Big Four were Joey Mayhem and Goliath, the stars of what portended to be the biggest match of all time. These titans sat in a circle of folding chairs, in a small carpeted room with no windows, in the basement of a sports arena, under one banner of lies.

Those lies were what made it so hard to pay attention. Did Gene or Larry know what Goliath and Max knew? Were all of these people in on the sham that brought down the GWA? Now that Duke was officially among the top brass in the new company, what secrets was he aware of? What secrets had he already known?

And if Steve's guess was right, Mr. Anonymous might be sitting here with him right now. Gene Harold and Larry Jenkins were on the list of suspects. Neither of them gave anything away. They both participated in the discussion, assisting Max and Duke as they described the twists and turns of the match. Joey prayed that they didn't ask him to repeat the script back to them.

Of course, the biggest masquerade belonged to Goliath, who had to act out a complex character who had forgiven Joey for injuring him in a previous match, and understood that Joey would be more cautious this time. While Joey worked to conceal his intentions for tonight, Goliath worked to conceal the truth of the last two months.

The lie loomed over Goliath like an odor, and made it easier to sit in his physically intimidating presence. There was no doubt about it, Goliath was a huge, strong man you didn't pick a fight with. Goliath had been chosen among hundreds of eager hopefuls to play the part of the invincible monster whose physique was so frightening that crowds paid to see it in action. He had been chosen over professional football players, former bodybuilders, and amateur wrestling champions. The more Joey looked at him, the more he realized he probably wouldn't win his fight tonight. He probably would get trounced, made to submit in front of millions, with his overconfident statement posted on the Web for the world to see.

"Do you have any questions, Joey?" said Max. Joey had plenty of questions that couldn't be asked tonight.

"No sir, clear as a bell," said Joey.

"Well then," said Max, "I guess we're ready to get this show started."

CHAPTER 40

───────────── ▼ ─────────────

Joey found Jade sitting alone in "Viewing Room 2."

"How are you doing?" he asked.

"Scared. I've had to pee three times since we got here. How about you?"

He sat next to her. The "room" was an open space off one of the hallways, where someone had arranged 9 folding chairs in three rows of three, facing a twenty-five-inch television on a rolling cart. In the open space of concrete and brick, the sound from the television was so lost as to be inaudible.

"I'm scared too," said Joey. "I just met with Max, Goliath, Duke, Gene Harold, and Larry Jenkins."

"Goodness. That's quite an assortment."

"I know, it was...crazy. They gave me the details of the booking for my match."

"And..."

Joey looked around to ensure no one was within hearing distance.

"I can't really tell you. I was so petrified that I couldn't pay attention."

Jade turned away to look at the television.

"That's understandable," she said. "I certainly can't keep my head clear."

She looked like she had more to say, but two women came into the room. They were both young and striking.

"Hi, I'm Virginia, I'm married to John Taylor," said one.

"And I'm April, I'm with Miguel Cervantes," said the other.

Joey nodded a hello as the two wrestler's wives sat down next to Jade.

"It's a privilege to meet you Jade," said Virginia.

"Thank you," she said. She smiled graciously and shook hands with each woman. Joey couldn't bear to think about how many introductions like this she'd make tonight, only to have to face these people in shame at the end of the show after her boyfriend went ballistic in the main event.

"Do you mind if I turn the volume up? It's almost time," said April.

"Oh no, go right ahead," said Jade.

As April went to adjust the television, more people came in. Mid-carders with Revolution, bookers, agents, more wrestler's wives and girlfriends. By the time the show started, every chair was taken and the walls were lined with people.

As soon as the opening pyrotechnics finished, an 80s-style guitar riff lit through the arena, and seven seconds after the crowd erupted in a mix of cheers and boos, Max Zeffer appeared on the television of Viewing Room 2. As Max walked to the ring, the camera picked out relevant home-made signs held up by the fans. One said, "Max, you've conquered the world, now what?" Another said, "Mein Heil Max Zeffer!."

Once in the middle of the ring, Max lifted the microphone to his lips and began the interview.

"Ladies and Gentlemen, I, Max Zeffer, proudly present to you tonight, the greatest success story in wrestling history. The ultimate rise to power and glory, the greatest tale of triumph our industry has ever seen. The most influential, important, incredible, stupendous figure in the business. Me!"

The crowd gladly played along and booed. Max opened his arms, as if eagerly accepting their disdain.

"And tonight, I, Max Zeffer, present to you the greatest show on earth! And don't think that anyone but I could have brought it to you.

"It was I who changed the way our business was run. It was I who created a show that was edgy, modern, and new, that you wanted to see, that you needed to see every week. It was I who—"

Max was interrupted by a distinctive snap of brass instruments, leading into overblown pop music straight from a sixties spy movie. The crowd recognized the tune immediately, and cheered as Duke Correlli stepped into the arena. Duke waved his hands at the fans as they chanted, "Duke! Duke!" The scene was unusual for Joey to watch. In the GWA, Duke's character was despised as a heel. Just two weeks ago he stepped in front of a crowd in Denver and was greeted with loathing. But to fans of Revolution Wrestling, Duke was a fresh face who signified the birth of a new era. They couldn't help but cheer for him.

"Don't get too cocky, Max," said Duke, still standing at the top of the entrance ramp, far from the ring. The crowd loved it. For them, seeing Duke Correlli and Max Zeffer in the same arena was just too good to be true.

"Oh look," said Max. "It's my newest employee, Duke Correlli. For those of you who don't know him, this is the man who took me on and lost."

"For those of you who don't know me," Duke said, full of pride, "I'm the man who invented the style of television this man stole!"

"I only made it better, Duke. And by the way, I don't appreciate my employees talking to me like that. One word from me, and you're out on the street."

"You can't fire me, Max. You need me."

"I don't need you. You're history. I hired you for fans who were nostalgic, but as soon as you're a problem, which you already are, I'll fire your ass!"

The crowd booed at Max, eager to accept the villainous role he took on. Duke waited for the crowd to calm before taking his turn to speak again.

"Max, that's fine. Fire me if you want to. It's not like working for you is my dream come true. But just know that if you fire me, I take all of these people with me."

A host of wrestlers came out to join Duke. Deep Six, Raptor, Kevin Daniels, Skip Franklin, and Christopher Doom. The group had a common thread, they were all good guys, babyfaces, in the old GWA. In fact, with the exception of one wrestler, every major babyface from Duke's old promotion was now onstage. The one wrestler missing was Joey.

Joey and Jade exchanged glances. If he needed any more proof of where he was to be after tonight, it was right in front of him. It was all true. Everything Steve had said was undeniably true.

In calling a group of wrestlers to stand onstage with him while he argued with the boss, Duke was employing one of the most common storytelling devices in professional wrestling. Duke was creating a stable. This group of wrestlers would serve as the pawns in the burgeoning storyline of Duke vs. Max.

It made perfect sense. In the new promotion, where years of storytelling in two separate worlds needed to come together right away, every character could be quickly defined by his allegiance to either Duke or Max. Fans could choose sides; tag teams could be formed; rivalries could be put in place immediately. Every character would be given something to do.

But Joey wasn't out there. After tonight, after his planned loss to Goliath, there would be nothing for his character to do, and he would disappear from the wrestling universe.

The unequivocal truth of the matter welled inside Joey, and if ever there was a doubt about what he planned to do, it was gone. The powers that be wanted him to leave professional wrestling after tonight. He was going to take the old GWA World Title with him.

Duke spoke more about these five men who had gathered about him. He said they had pledged their loyalty to him, and if Max fired Duke, he would lose all these men. The crowd cheered. Max grimaced, as if Duke had pulled some impressive power play.

Duke went on to make a call to all the wrestlers in the locker room to join his faction. He said something unintelligible about quality of work and life and self-respect. He and Max quibbled for another few minutes, and the segment ended.

"Why weren't you out there?" Joanne said to Joey with a smile. Poor woman, she had no idea. But if she noticed Joey's absence from that segment was conspicuous, the viewers must have as well. Joey smiled back and said, "They have other plans for me."

The rest of the first hour was seamless. Four matches, each one a solid performance, each beautifully produced. Revolution ran a much tighter ship than the GWA. Performers were right on cue, backstage segments fit into the mix perfectly, and the backstage area was quiet and civil.

"I'm going to go get ready," Joey said to Jade.

"Would you like me to stay here?" said Jade.

"Yes, that would be great," said Joey. As great as anything could be tonight. There was no great place for Jade. When Joey's match started, she was going to be in a terribly awkward place. First the observers in Viewing Room 2 would ask her what was going on. Later, the top brass from Revolution would come find her for interrogating.

Joey had asked her to stay behind. She had refused. "You can't be alone tonight," she had said to him. "Someone needs to stand between you and the mob. Someone needs to have a car waiting for you. Someone needs to be there if you're taken away in an ambulance."

Joey stood up and left Viewing Room 2. No one said a word. They just watched him leave. That became the theme for the rest of the night. No one said a word to him as they passed him in the hall, where he was stretching his hamstrings and calves. No one stopped him to say hello or ask about his match as he paced up and down the hallway. Even Goliath walked past him without acknowledgement.

'So be it,' thought Joey. 'The silence will leave me focused.'

But it didn't. His mind was everywhere. He thought of submission holds he had learned in wrestling school. He thought of a 3rd grade schoolyard fight with the class bully. He thought of Goliath in a bar in Sydney. He imagined himself in that bar, fist-fighting a horde of drunk Australians. He thought about his superkick to Oscar Esquivel's chin in the Southeast Wrestling League. He imagined delivering that very kick to Goliath's head.

"Joey, are you ready for your entrance?" said Phillip Gaines, the stage manager.

Joey looked at Phillip, somehow confused. Was he ready? No. Would he ever be ready?

"Yes. Let's go do this."

CHAPTER 41

▼

"Ladies and gentlemen, the following match is scheduled for one fall, and is for the GWA World Heavyweight Title," said Mardi Carter, Revolution's ring announcer. "Introducing first, from Memphis Tennessee, weighing in at two-hundred and twenty pounds, Joey Mayhem!"

Joey stepped into the arena to a clamor of cheers. This crowd was thrilled to see him. If only they knew.

If all was going well on Steve's end, right now, with Joey's name having just been announced, the statement would be up on the web. Of course, most fans were watching the show, not surfing the net, but there would be a few who would see it soon. They would call their friends, who would look and then call their friends. In ten minutes, hundreds of thousands of fans would have read Joey's statement, "Why I Will Not Follow the Script Tonight."

There was no turning back now.

Joey walked quickly to the ring. It was important to get these introductions over and the match underway before anyone backstage saw or heard about what had just shown up on the web.

"And introducing second, from Los Angeles California, weighing in at two-hundred eighty pounds, Goliath!"

The house lights faded. Goliath's intimidating heavy metal guitar riff started. He entered the arena to a flash of pyrotechnics, then roared at the audience like a crazed animal. From a hundred feet away, Joey could see the craze in Goliath's eyes. His body was pumped more full of chemical enhancers than in their last match. As Goliath walked to the ring, under the guise of friendliness, Joey wanted to turn and run. When Goliath stepped through the ropes, and gave a pose to the crowd, muscles bulging out of his arms and chest, Joey had to turn away, or he would have lost his nerve.

"Gentlemen, approach the center of the ring," said Aaron Grant, the referee. Joey and Goliath approached, standing on either side of Grant, who held up the World Title Belt between them, in a show for the camera.

"Gentlemen, I want a clean fight," said Grant. "No closed-fist punches, no chokes, and no funny business. First pinfall or submission wins the title. Now go back to your corners and wait for the bell."

Joey rolled his head around his shoulders as he walked back to the corner. The rules normally were just part of the show. Tonight they were important. Once Grant figured out what Joey was doing, he would call backstage for instructions. Backstage, they would probably decide that Grant should find a way to disqualify Joey, meaning Joey would have to follow the rules carefully.

The bell rang. The two men strode to the center, then snapped into a head-collar lock up, the first planned spot.

"Ease up a bit Joey. I'm going to throw you into the corner," said Goliath, reminding Joey of the plan to start the match with Goliath winning the show of strength.

Now is the time, Joey thought to himself. Just get it started and it will be over soon.

"I'm not jobbing tonight," Joey said, feeling a rush of adrenalin as he voiced the words. "I know everything, Goliath.

From the confines of their lock-up, Joey could see the surprise on Goliath's face, but before Goliath could react, Joey rolled behind him, grabbing his left hand on the way and stretching it behind his back in a hammerlock.

The hammerlock was a standard spot in professional wrestling. The victim's arm is bent awkwardly behind his back and the victim pretends to yelp out in pain. Many matches began with this hold. No one ever submitted to it.

Tonight Joey hoped that convention would be different, for the hammerlock, perhaps the most simple hold in all of wrestling, was as painful as they came if applied for real. Joey stretched Goliath's arm much further than he would in a typical, scripted match. The pain Goliath was selling was undoubtedly real.

"What the fuck are you doing?" Goliath said between squeals.

"I know everything," Joey said quietly. "If you want to leave here with the belt, you'll have to pin me."

"Jesus Christ," said Goliath, then reached for the ropes with his good hand.

Goliath managed to touch the ropes with his right finger before Joey pulled him back away.

"Make him break the hold," Goliath said to Grant, then shrieked in more pain.

Grant, looking thoroughly confused, ran around Goliath and started yelling at Joey.

"Come on, he made it to the ropes. Break the hold," he yelled, then added in a whisper, "What the fuck's going on here?"

Joey kept the hammerlock on, squeezing tighter.

"Come on!" yelled Grant. "One…two…three…four…"

Joey broke the hold just before Grant reached five, the number at which Joey could be disqualified. As soon as Joey let go, Goliath whipped his right elbow back, nailing Joey in the face and sending him to the floor. Joey landed, dizzy, with numbness in his nose and teeth. He rolled himself up, preparing to stand, but only got to his knees before Goliath was on top of him, swallowing him in a front face lock.

Goliath squeezed around Joey's cheeks, the strength of a huge bicep and forearm pressing against his skull. It was easily the worst pain Joey had ever felt.

"If you want to do this, we'll do this, but it'll be short, and you'll be dead when it's done," Goliath said.

Not knowing if it would make a difference or not, Joey reached out with his left foot and found the bottom ring rope. Technically, with his foot on the rope, the ref would have to break the hold.

Through the squeezing on his ears, Joey could hear Grant counting, "One…two…"

At five, Goliath broke the hold. Grant immediately jumped between them, and pushed Goliath away from Joey.

The crowd booed. It wasn't normal for a ref to actively break up the fighting so early in a pro wrestling match.

Joey rolled into the corner, and used the turnbuckles to help him stand. He was dizzy. His nose was bleeding from the elbow to the face. It was probably broken. Grant had taken Goliath to the opposite corner, no doubt to ask him what was going on, and maybe to relay some instructions coming from Max backstage via Grant's headpiece. Maybe this match was going to get canned.

Leaving Goliath in the opposite corner, Grant walked up to Joey.

"Max wants me to tell you that if you don't follow the script, you get no money. It's in your contract," said Grant.

Exhausted, and feeling sick, Joey nodded. He would do whatever had to be done to keep this thing going. Max obviously wasn't aware yet of Joey's statement on the Internet. This wasn't about the money.

Eyeing Joey warily, Grant stepped out of the way so the match could continue. As soon as the path to Goliath was clear, Joey charged. He sprinted out five forward steps and buried his shoulder in Goliath's gut in a brutal tackle, sending both men to the ground in a heap.

Joey landed on top, and grabbed for whatever was there. A hand, Goliath pulled away. An arm. Goliath rolled through. A leg. Goliath kicked like a mule. He got hold of a foot.

Joey was now on his knees, holding Goliath's left foot, while Goliath lay on his back, far from the ropes. Joey had no idea if the ubiquitous ankle lock, a wrestling staple, had any basis in the real world. It had never been part of Joey's repertoire. But here he was, in a perfect spot to try it.

Apparently, he applied the ankle lock correctly. Goliath screamed right away. It was a shriek out of hell. Joey smiled, realizing this hold might win him the match.

Joey didn't know that the ankle lock, when applied in real shoot fights, was always done from a standing position, because kneeling or squatting leaves an opening for the victim. Since Joey remained on his knees, Goliath was able to use his free leg to heel-kick Joey in the back of the head. The crowd gasped at the brutality of the blow. Joey lost his grip on Goliath's ankle and fell forward. Face down on the mat, Joey realized his eyes were open but he couldn't see. Just as the horror of blindness set in, the blackness faded to a blurry haze, like an old television warming from darkness to picture.

He could feel the mat shake underneath him. Goliath had stood up. Under any normal circumstance, Joey would have given up here. He couldn't think straight. He was about to wretch. But some instinct, buried deeper than any rational thought, took over, and as Goliath reached down to put Joey in another front facelock, Joey's right hand shot upward, nailing Goliath's chin with the base of his palm. Goliath staggered back, and Joey rolled to the edge of the ring and under the bottom rope. He slid out of the ring, landing on the floor below in a quiet thud.

*   *   *   *

Max Zeffer watched the match from a booth backstage. The booth was an enclosed room just below the arena entrance, with makeshift walls made of two by fours and plexiglass, and a ceiling made of plywood. An open doorway sat next to Max Zeffer, from which anyone could come and go. Not that anyone ever did.

It was well known in the company that the occupants of the booth below the arena entrance were not to be disturbed when a show was on the air.

In the booth with Max were Gene Harold, Larry Jenkins, and (for the first time) Duke. The four men sat at a folding table. In front of each man was a television monitor. Each man wore and spoke into his own headset. Gene, Larry, and Duke's headsets were connected only to the television announcers, for whom they fed lines to ensure all the proper points were pushed to the television audience. Max's headset, in contrast, was attached to a four-station control knob that sat on top of his monitor. Station 1 on the control knob connected him to the television announcers. Station 2 connected him to the stage manager. Station 3 was an open line among all the technical directors, cameramen, and television producers. Station 4, where he was now connected, was rarely used. This station connected him to the referee, via a small headpiece over the referee's right ear. This was a one-way channel. Max could speak to the referee, but the ref could only respond with discrete hand signals into a television camera.

Early in the match, Aaron Grant waved a hand signal, a circular motion of his lower left arm, that had never before been used in Revolution Wrestling. This signal meant the match was off-script and out of control. It had been invented in the GWA in the eighties when a female wrestler named Pantagruel consistently lost her temper in her matches and abandoned the scripts to legitimately beat up her opponents.

Despite their friendly tidings over the past week, Joey and Goliath had not buried the hatchet over their tumultuous past together. Maybe somebody said something backstage. Maybe something happened during the week Max didn't know about. Maybe this had something to do with Jade Sleek.

Whatever it was, it was absurd. The largest pay per view audience in history had tuned in to see this match, and the men were blowing it. As far as Max could tell, it appeared that Joey Mayhem was the primary culprit in this farce.

"Max, I think you should look at this," said some junior production assistant. The kid had walked into the booth while the show was on the air, breaking an important company rule.

Max's panicked thoughts were interrupted long enough to look at the kid, a skinny white boy with bad skin and the beginnings of a goatee. Max had never seen him before.

"Not now, kid," said Max, brushing him away like a fly.

"Max, you'll really want to see this," said the kid.

He was trying to hand Max a piece of paper.

"Go away kid. This is a very bad time," said Max.

He could hear the kid exhale, almost with impatience. Who the fuck was this kid to get impatient with Max Zeffer? Especially right now.

"Max, I swear, you're gonna want to see—"

"Will someone get this kid out of here?" Max called out to whomever might listen. "Kid, you're fired."

The kid furrowed his brow and raised his shoulders, then took a deep breath and yelled at the most powerful man in wrestling. "Max, Joey Mayhem posted a statement on the Internet titled, 'Why I Won't Follow The Script Tonight!'"

Max took off his headset and turned away from his monitor, where Joey Mayhem and Goliath were both laid out, Goliath in the ring, Joey out of it. The ref was counting to ten, technically for a double countout. Max had instructed him to ensure that Goliath was up before he reached ten.

"What?" said Max.

Gene Harold, Larry Jenkins, and Duke, all took off their headsets and turned toward this kid, this teenager who was barely old enough to work, and was now handing Max a computer printout.

"Well I'll be God-damned," Max said quietly, as he read Joey's statement.

"This has been on Wrestling Hotline Dot Com for the past ten minutes. The entire Internet is talking about it," said the kid.

Max put his headset back on.

"Grant, stop the count," he said to the ref. Grant was on eight. He stopped counting. The crowd, who had been eagerly counting along, didn't notice and finished the count up to ten.

"You say the whole Internet is talking about this?" Max asked the kid.

"Yes. Every chat site and newsboard is flooded. Wrestling hotline must be getting swamped."

Max leaned his face into his hand, thinking.

"Max?" said Larry. "Max, Grant needs instructions. This match is dead out there."

The match was dead. Both men were still on the ground. The crowd was silent with confusion.

"Grant. We need to shut this thing down," Max spoke into his headset. "Find a way to declare Goliath…"

Max's eyes widened. He turned his head and smiled at the kid.

"You say the whole Internet is buzzing about this?" he asked.

"Yes sir. It spread like wildfire. Our web site got so swamped that it crashed. Emails are flooding in. Phones are ringing. Sir, the whole world is crazy over what's going on out there."

Max turned back to his monitor and spoke into his headset. "Grant, scratch that. Hold for instructions." Max covered his mouthpiece with his hand and leaned in to speak to the kid.

"Kid, you're re-hired. Take this paper out to Anson right away," he commanded, referring to Anson Buchanan, Revolution's television announcer.

The kid nodded, took the paper, and ran out to the arena entrance. As he left, Max changed the channel on his headset, then began speaking.

"Anson, this is Max. A production assistant is taking a document out to you. As soon as you get it, I want you to read it on the air. Introduce it as a statement that has just been posted on Wrestling Hotline Dot Com."

Max switched the channel on his headset again. "Okay Grant, new instructions. I need you to keep this thing going. Stall until both guys are back in the ring. This will continue to be a shoot. Do not let Joey Mayhem win. No matter what you have to do. I want this fight to continue until Goliath is the clear winner, even if you have to punch out Joey yourself."

Grant gave the slightest of nods into the camera, indicating that he understood.

*   *   *   *

Joey stood up first. As quickly as he could, he rolled back into the ring. Goliath was already on his knees, struggling to his feet. Joey fell into him, hoping to catch Goliath in some sort of hold before he had a chance to get up.

The two men collided, then thrashed to the floor, each attempting to lock in a wrestling hold. Joey succeeded first, getting Goliath in an armbar. Goliath groaned in pain, then realized where he was and grabbed the ropes.

"One…two…" Grant counted out.

Technically, Joey had a five-count to release the hold, but at two, Grant reached and broke the hold himself, prying Joey's hands free of Goliath's arm. The crowd, many of whom now recognized that this was a real fight, booed.

As soon as Grant broke the hold, Goliath whipped around and slapped Joey in a headlock, which gradually turned into a choke. Seeing that the ref was doing nothing, Joey reached with his foot for the rope, and got it.

Still nothing from the ref. He had clearly seen Joey's foot on the rope, but was pretending he hadn't.

The crowd went into a near panic. Hot dogs and plastic cups and crumpled program notes sailed into the ring. Grant raised his hands to count, "One."

After an unusually long pause, Grant counted, "Two."

Joey couldn't breathe at all, and the flow of blood to his brain had slowed to a trickle.

"Three."

He was dizzy. He was fading.

"Four."

His vision was failing. The world was breaking up, as if Joey's eyes were coated with frosted glass.

"Five."

Right before Grant voiced the five-count, Goliath broke the hold, and Joey flopped face-first into the mat. The crowd was silent.

Goliath rolled Joey onto his stomach, then pressed a hand on each of Joey's shoulders to pin him. Grant flew into position and slapped the mat.

He slapped the mat again. The crowd screamed "Two!" Joey lifted his foot and put it on the bottom rope. As soon as his boot crossed the invisible boundary at the ring ropes, the crowd erupted in elation, lest the ref didn't notice. The crowd's noise left Grant no choice but to point at Joey's foot and stop the count.

Undeterred, Goliath grabbed Joey by the hair and pulled. This spot, so common in worked wrestling matches, took on a new form in this shoot fight. Through his exhaustion, Joey had to hop to his feet and follow Goliath, or else have his hair pulled out of his head.

Once in the center of the ring, Goliath slapped Joey into a front face lock, both men standing and hunched over, Joey's head surrounded by Goliath's massive arm. Joey knew it was over. His attempt had been valiant, but it wasn't meant to be.

As if in agreement, Grant leaned his head in underneath Goliath to whisper to Joey, "This match is over Joey, you've just submitted."

Grant's words awakened something, something that was within Joey, hidden until now, but forcefully present, as if it had been waiting to be tapped Joey's entire life. It was a reserve of energy, unavailable before, but discovered in the anger. Joey was angry that after all this pain, all this effort, the match would end again with him getting screwed. Without even the dignity of submitting for real, Joey was going to lose this match because Grant was now on Goliath's side, and was going to call for the bell as if Joey had just submitted.

He couldn't tolerate it. And with the final strength left in his body, Joey reached forward and locked his arms around Goliath's right leg and pushed upward with his back. Continuing the motion, using only the muscles in his own abdomen, Joey snapped Goliath off the ground and through the air into a fisherman's suplex, instantly reversing the tide. When they landed, Goliath was on his back, shoulders down, and Joey was covering him, with the leg hooked, in a perfect bridge.

The crowd burst with joyful noise. Grant however, was deliberately slow to react, and had he begun the count in time, the match would have finished, with Joey winning by pinfall. As it were, Grant made it to a slow "Two," before Goliath was able to push Joey off of him. In a normal match, this sort of near fall would instantly deflate the crowd. In this match, however, the crowd responded with vehemence, booing loudly at the obvious cheating of the referee.

Both men stumbled to their knees, then their feet. Without great force, Goliath kicked Joey in the left side. Joey was too slow to block it. With slightly more force, Goliath kicked Joey's right side. Joey felt the air leave his lungs. The next one, whatever it was, would send him back to the mat, and he wouldn't be able to get up.

The next one was a closed-fist punch. Fortunately, Goliath was slow, and Joey was able to duck. Goliath's right arm swung over Joey's head, and his momentum swung him around half-way, enough for Joey to rush in behind him and snatch his left arm into another hammerlock, the same hold that opened the match.

Joey didn't have enough strength to press in the hammerlock completely, but Goliath didn't have enough strength to break out. Goliath fell to his knees in pain. The crowd cheered, sensing that victory for Joey, who had played the baby-face in this fight by virtue of the biased referee, was near.

✱   ✱   ✱   ✱

"Shit," said Max. "Grant, don't let Goliath submit. Tell him help is on the way."

Max took his headset off and yelled into the backstage area. "Somebody get me Scott Rollins, now!"

Five seconds later, Scott Rollins, formerly Crusader, was standing in front of Max Zeffer, the man who had saved him from a career putting over cocky young stars and given him his first legitimate shot at the main event.

"Scott, I need a favor," said Max.

In less than a minute, Scott Rollins was at the arena entrance, preparing to enter. Half the roster followed him to the entryway, wanting to get a view of whatever chaos was to come. Unseen in the excitement was Gene Harold, Revolution's Head Booker, leaving his post in Max's booth to go to the locker room.

*   *   *   *

Goliath was on his knees, in the middle of the ring, his left arm wrenched behind his back. Joey was going to win this match. The crowd was screaming beyond anything ever achieved in a wrestling event. Not one of the twenty-thousand was sitting; not one was silent.

Referee Aaron Grant squatted in front of Goliath, their faces inches apart. They had been that way for going on half a minute. To the audience, it appeared Grant was asking Goliath if he wanted to quit. Joey knew they were talking about something else, something he couldn't hear over the roar of the crowd.

Joey's ignorance didn't matter. It was only a matter of time before Goliath had to tap out, or verbally quit. Even wrestling's greatest monster couldn't resist the pain forever. Joey would let him go as soon as that submission, in whatever form it took, was visible to the television audience, and not before.

Impossibly, the noise in the arena grew. Something had the crowd excited. Perhaps Goliath's face betrayed signs of quitting. Joey looked down to the referee, hoping for the victory signal. It didn't come. With his free hand, Goliath palmed the ref's face like a basketball, then pushed him away. Grant, an experienced ref, turned the little shove into a massive attack, and he flopped against the ropes then fell on his face.

'Maintain the hold,' Joey told himself. Goliath, or maybe Max, was growing desperate, and the new plan apparently was for the ref to take a bump. No doubt this would lead to Goliath cheating to break the hold.

It didn't matter. Goliath couldn't break out of this hammerlock, even without rules. At some point he would have to tap out, and even though there would be no ref to call it, the world would see it.

Unless Goliath had help.

Joey couldn't finish the thought. An explosion of force, accompanied by a sickening thud, smashed into the back of his head. The impact of the blow pushed Joey forward. His feet entangled with Goliath's just as his strength began to leave, and he lost the hold. In that instant of clarity, right before the pain, Joey was able to turn his head and see the desperate eyes of Crusader, Scott Rollins, holding a steel chair with an imprint of Joey's skull in the seat. Joey fell to the mat, then lost himself in agony.

He didn't see Rollins face the crowd and hoist the chair, the weapon, over his head, to an onslaught of boos. He was too weak to resist when Goliath grabbed him by the ankles and dragged him to the center of the ring. Still dazed, he couldn't fathom why the resonant boos instantly changed to piercing screams and thundering cheers. Nearly unconscious, Joey could tell there was activity in the ring, but he couldn't open his eyes to see it. Whatever it was, the crowd adored it.

What was it? Joey felt the ring shake. He felt multiple sets of wrestling boots stomping around him. He heard a titanic splash, undoubtedly a heavyweight wrestler falling to the mat.

The crowd was ravenous. Joey still lay on his stomach. Blood was streaming into his head, bringing with it the sharpness of pain, but also a growing sense of clarity. He was going to be able to open his eyes soon. Then he would be able to stand. If he could just hold out for a few more seconds.

He felt more movement around him. Then a sound, a voice. It was Aaron Grant. "One," yelled Grant. "Two," yelled Grant, after a pause. On "Three," the crowd joined in. Someone was being counted out. It was him. Noise and blackness and pain were swept aside for just a second as Joey's brain contemplated what was going on. He was being counted out! He had to stand. He had to get up before ten.

Joey pushed against the mat with his hands, using his knees to help him crouch upright. Slowly and deliberately, fearful of dizziness, Joey lifted his head, and took in everything around him. Goliath was down, flat on his back, five paces from Joey. Grant was standing between them, holding up his hands as he yelled, "Four!" Scott Rollins was nowhere to be found.

Had he imagined Scott Rollins thwacking him with a chair? He couldn't have. The pain was too real. Perhaps he had been out cold for a long time. But if so, why was Grant only on count four? And why was Goliath down?

"Five!" Grant and the crowd yelled together. The count would stop when Joey and Goliath were standing. Goliath rolled onto his side; he was about to get up.

"Six!"

Joey lifted one foot, planted it on the floor, and turned his knee into a stoop from which he could push himself up. Goliath was now on his knees.

"Seven!"

Joey briefly made it to both feet, only to be overcome with dizziness which sent him reeling backward. He stumbled two steps back and fell into the ropes, sliding down to his knees, his arms both hung over the second rope.

"Eight!"

Goliath was preparing to stand. Unlike Joey, he was taking the time necessary to ensure he would stay on his feet. Joey breathed deeply, then pulled against the second rope, willing himself upward.

"Nine!"

With help from the ropes, Joey was now on his feet, and only slightly dazed. Goliath too was standing. Grant dropped his hands, stopping the ten-count.

Goliath was bleeding from the mouth. His eyes were unfocused. He looked delicate. Were Joey not equally weak, Goliath would be easy pickings.

The two men circled the inside edge of the ring, facing each other, each frightened to make the first move, uncertain because of their own frailty.

With each step, Joey felt his head growing clearer. Despite great pain in every joint, and bitter nausea in his gut, the will was there to finish this fight.

Goliath struck first, stumbling forward and swinging with closed fists at Joey's face. The right arm swung first, and was so slow that Joey, even in his debilitated state, was able to dodge it. The left arm swung next, and connected with Joey's jaw. The hit would have knocked Joey cold, except that Goliath's left arm was weak from the hammerlocks earlier, and the punch only registered as a hard push, a knock to the head that, if anything, helped wake Joey from his daze.

Staggering backward, Joey bounced off the ropes, then swung his arm at Goliath, in what would have been an ugly clothesline in a standard match. Goliath ducked, leaving Joey to swing like a weathervane. Goliath hurled a forearm at the twisting mass of Joey's body, and landed the blow to Joey's left kidney, knocking Joey backward, and forcing him to lurch his torso over in pain.

With his body slightly tilted, Joey was a lame duck for Goliath's favorite hold of the night, the front facelock. Goliath reached around Joey's head to lock it in. As the arm surrounded his ears in what was now a familiar position, Joey knew this would be the end if he didn't escape.

Without thinking, Joey put his arms on Goliath's torso and pushed. Goliath was too weak to resist, and he fell back, with his arm still locked around Joey's head. They both fell to the floor in an ugly pileup.

The instant they hit the floor, both men began flailing and flopping like fish out of water, simultaneously trying to put a hold on their opponent while avoiding their opponent's grasp. They rolled right to the center of the ring, where, by some providence or luck, Joey found himself on top of Goliath's back, able to reach his left hand.

Joey put in the hammerlock for the third time of the bout, this time in the center of the ring with Goliath face down on the mat. As soon as Joey locked it in he knew. The crowd did as well. They popped like twenty thousand balloons in elation at what they were seeing.

Goliath tapped out.

Grant hesitated, probably waiting for the okay from backstage, before signaling for the ring bell.

"Let him go, Joey. You won," said Grant.

Joey released Goliath's arm, then fell flat, facing the ceiling. He closed his eyes.

"Ladies and gentlemen, the winner of this bout, and the new GWA World Heavyweight Champion, Joey Mayhem!"

CHAPTER 42

▼

The trek up the ramp was surreal. Nauseous, aching, dizzy, exhausted, Joey was barely conscious for the post match ceremonials. With his entrance theme playing, and the GWA World Title belt hanging over his left shoulder, he lumbered out of the arena, into a mist of smoke and fuzzy vision, while Goliath was still strewn in the ring. All the while, twenty thousand Canadians exalted the match they had just seen.

Upon entering the backstage area, an open foyer of concrete right before the locker rooms, a nameless face tried to give Joey a bottle of water. A violent swipe knocked it out of his hand, sending the precious fluid flying across the room. Joey felt like a desert straggler having seen a mirage.

His eyes looked at the swiping hand, then up the tattooed arm and shoulder that connected the hand to the scowling face of Deep Six. "What the fuck did you do out there punk?" Deep Six said.

Joey ignored him, and instead watched with sadness as the water bottle flew away from him and landed sideways on the floor, where it gurgled out onto the concrete. He had no energy to fight anymore. He wondered if there was someplace he could sit down.

"Are you listening to me?"

"Hey man, cool it, that ain't how we work here," someone said to Deep Six.

"Fuck you!"

At once the entire room was chaos. Thirty professional athletes were about to riot. Joey didn't care. He pondered taking a seat on the floor where he stood. Maybe no one would notice.

An arm went around Joey's waist, and a shoulder lodged itself under his—blessed heaven he could rest his weight on this shoulder. Joey's vision was a cloud, but he knew by smell that this angel supporting him was Jade.

"Come on, we have to get out of here. Even if we need to take you back into the arena. Let's go," she said.

Jade started to turn Joey away from the riot.

"Stop it! Stop it! Shut up! Listen to me! Listen up you shits!" yelled a voice from the back of the foyer. The voice overruled the turmoil and became the room's focus. It belonged to Max Zeffer.

"No one else is fighting here tonight!" Max surveyed the room for dissenters. There were none. Money and fame, the prizes Max dealt, meant more to all of these men than any disputes.

"Joey, come with me," Max said.

"Honey, just follow me," said Jade. "We don't have to go anywhere but home."

The room was watching them. Jade led Joey forward, through the crowd of wrestlers, past Max Zeffer, towards the exit.

"If you leave you're a fucking coward!" yelled a raspy voice from the back of the room.

"Ignore it Joey," said Jade. "You've done what you came to do tonight. It's over."

Joey's mind was slow to sort all these suggestions, but he realized that the voice that had called him a coward belonged to Goliath, who must have just arrived backstage. Wrestling convention required the loser to exit second, when the television cameras are off, but the audience is still present. A long walk of shame up the ramp. Normally, it was just part of the act. For Goliath, the shame tonight was all too real.

"Honey, let's go back for a minute. We have to end this right," said Joey.

They stopped walking.

"Joey, you ended it right. It's over. You've done what you wanted to do. You need to go to a hospital."

He did need to go to a hospital. He really needed a drink of water.

Joey led Jade back around, facing the room, facing Goliath, facing Max.

"Can I please have a bottle of water?" Joey said to Max.

Max stared at him for a minute, then walked across the foyer and grabbed a bottle of water from a table. He walked back, twisting the cap off the bottle as he moved, then handed the water to Joey. The room watched as Joey took a long drag from the bottle, then another, gasping in between.

"Okay Max, let's go," said Joey. "Jade comes with me."

"Fine," said Max. "Goliath, this way."

Max led them out of the foyer, down a hall, and into a locker room, where Gene Harold, Larry Jenkins, Vicky Archuleta, Duke, and Lucifer were sitting in a spacious circle.

"Have a seat," Max said to the three new guests.

Joey grabbed an open space of bench and felt like he had gone to heaven. How wonderful it was to sit down. How fleeting the pleasure. As soon as he settled in, he wanted to lay down. Yes, to stretch across the floor and go to sleep. It took greater strength of will to remain upright than it had to resist submitting to Goliath's facelock. Joey leaned forward, his elbows on his knees and his face in his hands. That would do for now.

"So let's have it," said Max. "How long have you two been planning this?"

"Jade had nothing to do with it. This was my plan," said Joey.

"What the hell are you—why would I give a flying fuck about what your girlfriend had to do with this?" said Max.

Joey wondered if his head was playing tricks on him, if this conversation actually made perfect sense, and he just didn't know it. He looked to Jade for help.

"Lucifer and Joey have never spoken before tonight," Jade said to Max.

Lucifer? What did he have to do with anything? Why was he even here? Joey sat up and rubbed his eyes.

"Is this true?" Max said to Lucifer, now right up in his face.

"Yes," said Lucifer, neither flinching nor defensive to Max's intrusion of his personal space. The man seemed as if he had no fear.

"So why the fuck did you get involved?" said Max.

"It was the right thing to do," said Lucifer.

Max stepped away in exasperation, looking to the ceiling and shaking his head. He was about to go ballistic. As Joey watched the anger boil up inside the billionaire, the conversation came together with an unclear memory from the fight, and it all made sense. Scott Rollins had hit him over the head with a steel chair. He had been knocked to the mat, nearly unconscious. When he got up, Goliath was down, and Scott Rollins was gone. Lucifer must have come out to the arena and saved Joey. Lucifer must have taken out both Rollins and Goliath. Since the ref had been down, hiding his head, it was fair game for anyone to come interfere without disqualification.

But why?

"It was the right thing to do? The right thing to do?" screamed Max. "I made you, you son of a bitch! And you spit on me! The point of the match tonight was to set up you and Goliath for next month's pay per view. It was going to be the biggest match in wrestling history! We were all going to make a fortune!"

"So I wrestle Joey instead," said Lucifer.

The words, so calmly delivered, turned Max from angry to raging, and as if the proverbial steam inside him were pressurized in his right side, and his right arm was the barrel from which the bullet of his fist exploded in a bath of scalding water vapor, Max swung a knockout blow at Lucifer's face.

He connected with Lucifer's left forearm. With truly frightening speed, Lucifer had raised his left arm to block the punch and, with his right, landed a straight blow of his own with an open palm, right in Max's chest. Max flew off his feet, landing on his tailbone, then sliding backward half a yard. Lucifer remained seated, calmly looking at Max, the way one would look at a goldfish in a bowl.

Gasping for air, Max grabbed at his chest. His face went from anger to panic as he took his first few heaves, the breath clearly knocked out of his lungs. Vicky left her seat to tend to him. He waved her off, and the room sat quietly, listening to Max slowly regain control of his breathing.

Half a minute later, still gasping, Max managed to squeeze out the words, "You're fired."

Without saying anything, or even acknowledging Max with a nod or a scowl, Lucifer stood up and left the room.

Vicky helped Max to his feet. He brushed at his gray pants, tugged at his jacket until it was straight, then approached Joey.

"And you," Max wheezed. "I can't fire you, because I never hired you, but I can promise you that you'll never work in this business again. That title belt you're holding belongs to me. I'm giving it to this man." He pointed to Goliath. "You can either give it to him, or he can take it from you, and this time nobody's going to help you."

Goliath stood and walked toward Joey. He held out his hand. Joey looked down at the belt, the GWA World Championship, sitting in his lap. Three gold-plated shields, arranged on a leather belt. His dream since childhood. He was the GWA World Champion. He'd earned it. He was now going to experience his one and only title loss.

"It's too late gentlemen. The world already knows." The voice came from behind Max and Goliath. It was deep, and hoarse. It belonged to Gene Harold.

"What the hell are you talking about?" said Max.

"I'm talking about the scheme you two perpetrated on the wrestling world. I'm talking about the Family Television Group, The Saxon Fund, and Goliath's Injury in Houston," said Gene.

Joey and Jade looked at each other with the surprise of recognition. Their anonymous source was coming forward.

"Right now, the same kid who posted Joey's statement tonight is posting the complete story of the greatest scandal in the history of our business. The money trail, the payoffs, the evidence, the whole thing—it's on the web right now. And thanks to your brilliant idea to turn Joey's shoot fight into an angle, to have his statement read on the air, every wrestling fan in the world is reading the truth as we speak."

"Gene, I don't know what you're trying to pull," said Max, "but I eat guys like you for breakfast. If you think you can mess with me you'll be surprised when you find yourself in my stool. You're fired. You, Joey, and Lucifer can hit the welfare line together. You'll never work again."

Gene stood up. "Max, I've been in this business for 30 years. I'm not going away anytime soon."

"You might stay in the business, but starting tomorrow you're back to high school gyms and fly-by-night trailer park tours buddy." said Max.

"We'll see," said Gene. "Every generation, some hotshot like you comes into our business. And every one of them has failed, for the same reason you will. This is the dirtiest business in the world. You're not up to it."

Gene walked to the door, then stopped and held out his hand. "Joey, Jade, after you," he said.

Joey set down the GWA World Title belt on the floor, then stepped over it as he and Jade left the locker room.

CHAPTER 43

▼

No one said anything as Joey and Jade walked through the backstage foyer to the arena exit. Every wrestler on the card was present to look upon them with curiosity, but none was bold enough to interrogate them. The entire roster of Revolution Wrestling had just watched their champion, their superstar, who put the asses in the seats and the zeroes on the paychecks, march silently from the locker room to the exit. Now they watched these newcomers, who brought the chaos of the old GWA with them, proceeding along the same path. And behind the newcomers walked Gene Harold, the legendary booker and mastermind of all that had gone right for Revolution Wrestling in the past year. The silent procession was worthy of a funeral.

The exit from the backstage foyer led to the parking garage. Lucifer held the door open for Jade, Joey, and Gene. Joey stepped across the threshold, thinking about what he was leaving behind. The door closed behind Gene, and on Joey's life as a professional wrestler.

"Honey, wait up a second," he said to Jade. She stopped walking, and turned to him with concern. She wanted to take him to a doctor. He had to resolve the night first. With great effort, Joey turned around and spoke to Lucifer.

"Why did you do it?" Joey asked. His voice was weak, almost not his own.

"It was the right thing to do," said Lucifer. In the dull colors of the security light, his voice echoing off the cement ceiling, Lucifer seemed more spirit than man. Joey thought back to the lightening reflexes Lucifer showed when Max attacked him. Without question, this was the most intimidating presence Joey had ever met.

"Did you know everything?" Joey asked.

"I knew enough," said Lucifer.

"I told him enough to make his decision," said Gene as he approached the group.

"When did you two have time to talk?" Jade said to Gene.

Gene took a few more steps before answering, the uphill walk on his former wrestler's knees obviously straining him. "I snuck away from my spot in the booth for just a minute," said Gene, between breaths. "I didn't tell James the whole story, just that you were getting screwed Joey."

Joey looked at Lucifer. The man bulged with muscles and veins, was covered in tattoos, and carried himself like a deity, but in his eyes was a thoughtfulness more suited for a philosopher. Somehow he reminded Joey of a child, who saw the world only in right and wrong, and for whom the proper course was always evident.

"So, you came out to the arena, you gave up your career, because I was getting screwed?" Joey asked him.

"I trust Gene," said Lucifer. "He wouldn't have talked to me if it wasn't important. The integrity of this business means everything to Gene. It means everything to me also. It means nothing to Max. The decision was simple."

"And he hardly gave up his career," said Gene. "Neither did you, Joey."

Joey wanted to smile at Gene's faux optimism, but didn't have the energy. He let his head sag and exhaled.

"Joey, tonight's show was the beginning of a story," said Gene. "It was a story I played out in my head many times over the past three months, from the minute I stumbled onto what Max was doing with the Family Television Group. I'd like for you and James to continue that story, with me."

Gene wasn't finished, but needed a pause in order to catch his breath. Joey considered sitting down on the concrete floor.

"Joey, Lucifer," Gene continued, "I'm going to start a new wrestling promotion, and I'd like for you two gentlemen to anchor it."

Joey felt a shock to his system, forgetting for a minute that he was past his physical limit. He looked at Jade, hoping to see as much surprise on her face as he felt at the way this night was unfolding. He did. In addition to surprise, he saw understanding.

"You orchestrated this whole thing," said Jade, in a tone that was both indignant and appreciative.

"No, I just made sure everyone knew the truth before tonight's match happened," said Gene. "Wrestling off the book was Joey's decision. I must admit I had hoped he would make that decision, but nonetheless, he did it on his own.

"And, Joey," Gene continued, "I've gotta say, I'm impressed. You showed some real guts out there tonight. You come wrestle for me, and I'll make sure you take your proper place in history among the all-time greats. What do you say?"

"I...don't know," said Joey. He paused, trying to think of why he didn't know. His brain seemed to be crawling. There was so much to say, but Joey couldn't put the words together to say it. He wanted to tell Gene that he loved wrestling, that working for Gene Harold would be a dream come true, that he trusted him to do right, that he appreciated what Gene had orchestrated here tonight. But he also wanted to tell him that he hurt. His body hurt. He was tired of hurting. He just wanted to go home.

"The last few weeks have made me wary of the whole thing," he said. "I'll need to think about it."

Gene nodded. "That's fair. You've only seen the worst of our business, and that's too bad, because it's a great business. But you and I will be in touch, Joey. You're going to do great things, and I want to be a part of it.

"So what about you James?" Gene asked Lucifer.

Without hesitation, but also without haste, Lucifer nodded his head once. Joey was amazed at the power of the small gesture. With that nod of the head, Lucifer humbly proclaimed his trust in Gene Harold and his as-yet nonexistent wrestling promotion to properly handle the biggest star in the industry.

"Jade, I'd like you to wrestle for me as well," said Gene. "I know that you may not be ready to commit yet either. Just know that in my promotions the women are wrestlers, not porn stars, and you'll get the treatment a talent like yours deserves."

"Thanks Gene," said Jade. "I'm flattered, and I'll think about it."

Gene cracked a smile. Joey thought about what Gene had gone through tonight. When the evening began, Gene was the number two man in the business, having toiled in the trenches for thirty years to become the head booker of the only major promotion in North America. Now he was a nobody. But he had a vision for a new world of wrestling, and had the industry's hottest commodity already signed up. Joey and Jade would help him get things going, but he didn't need them. This night, and the carefully planned sequence of events that created it, were a wild success for Gene Harold.

"Well, you two should get going," said Gene. "Joey, you might consider seeing a doctor to make sure your head's alright."

"I'll make sure he's taken care of," said Jade.

"Gene, before you leave, one more question," said Joey. "How did you know so much?"

Gene took a deep breath, then licked his lips. "Max doesn't know the business," he said, shaking his head. "Max assumed Larry and I would be loyal as long as Revolution was number one. So he wasn't careful to hide his tracks. He was right about Larry; he was wrong about me. What Max didn't know is that some of us are in this business because we love it, not because we want to be rich and famous. Max will never understand why paying Goliath to fake a real injury is such a slap in the face to those of us who built this industry. Goliath doesn't understand it either. Neither does Duke. That's why, even though Revolution is the only game in town right now, they're already dead in the water. Not one person running that show truly understands professional wrestling."

Gene stopped speaking to breathe some more. The poor man was a middle-aged physical wreck. He had sacrificed his youth and his body for his love of wrestling. He truly believed that sacrifice would have been for nothing had he not sabotaged Max's big night. This was a man Joey could follow. Joey wouldn't commit anything to Gene tonight, but some day he would.

"Well guys, I guess now is the time for me to say thank you, especially to you Lucifer," Joey said.

"I only did what was right," said Lucifer. "You did too."

CHAPTER 44

▼

To: Steve Garcia
From: wrestleslut@renet.buzz.com

Steve,

Congratulations on your new job. What am I talking about? Come on.
Those of us who know wrestling know that this whole Joey-May-
hem-shootfight-statement thing is a work. How much is Revolution paying
you?

The Wrestle Slut

This was the most popular thread. Steve had more than a hundred emails so
far that accused him of being part of an elaborate hoax. Of course, Revolution's
on-air reading of Joey's statement did cloud the matter. Steve had to admire
Max's hutzpah. In reading Joey's statement live on the air, just minutes after
Steve had posted it, Max had defused the situation as well as he could. Why in
the world would Revolution point people directly to the web site if Joey's post
were legitimate? Shrewd wrestling fans, used to being played, immediately suspected that the whole thing was fishy.

But there was another group, a smaller group, that was more (or perhaps less) cynical. These people believed it was all for real. It would take time, perhaps months, before the entire wrestling community knew the real truth. Max would make sure of that. But for now, Steve would have to find comfort in emails from those people who were willing to believe that some things in wrestling aren't scripted.

To: Steve Garcia
From: brunostanton@fsgatwak.com

Steve,

Brilliant column. You've got an open and shut case that's going to change wrestling forever. This was an amazing night.

Bruno Stanton
New York

At one time, Steve received regular emails from Bruno Stanton. Bruno was a longtime reader of the Tuesday Hangover. But when Steve started the FTG crusade, Bruno, and a hundred people like him, disappeared. Seeing Bruno's name in his Inbox, couched among lots of familiar but long-absent names, brought about an unusual nostalgia in Steve. He was accustomed to thinking of the past few years as an unmitigated failure. Now he wondered, for the first time in memory, if that time was well-spent.

When Joey's statement was read on the air, traffic on Wrestlinghotline.com shot through the roof. Sensing a once in a lifetime opportunity, Steve immediately posted the story, the complete story, about Max Zeffer's payoffs to Goliath and the FTG. He opened the story with a new paragraph:

Greetings. It is now nine o'clock on Sunday night, and Joey Mayhem's statement, recently posted on this web site, has just been read live on the air to everyone watching *Apocalypse*.

Unfortunately for Max Zeffer, he made the decision to read Joey's statement without all the facts. Max must not have known or realized that someone knew the entire truth about Goliath's faked injury in his match with Joey Mayhem on *GWA Burn*. Max couldn't believe that I was preparing to post the entire sordid story of his payoff to Goliath, his payoff to the Family Television Group, and his money laundering through an investment fund in Canada.

Slugs, what you are about to read is entirely true, and comes from very credible sources. Be forewarned, for fans of Goliath or Max Zeffer, the truth isn't pretty.

The column went on for close to three thousand words, Steve's longest ever, with every detail included. Traffic on the web site increased steadily for the next three hours, as news of the shoot fight and accompanying expose on Wrestling-hotline spread to those who hadn't purchased the pay per view.

By Monday morning, it was safe to say that the entire wrestling community had read Joey's statement and Steve's column.

Now, on Monday afternoon, with traffic finally starting to slow down, Steve was ready to post his third and final shocker, his interview with Jade. Of all three columns, he was most proud of this one, entitled, "What You Never Knew About the GWA Locker Room: An Interview With Jade Sleek."

The column was written in Question/Answer format, beginning with the story of Jumbo's attempted rape of Jade and Duke's silence on the matter. In three devastating pages, Jade explained to the entire wrestling world how Duke first ignored her charge, then dropped her to the bottom of the roster. She explained how a group of veterans grew jealous and ultimately bitter at Joey Mayhem's success, culminating in Jumbo pissing in Jade's gym bag. She described in detail the backstage fight between Joey and Jumbo, and the aftermath. And she recounted the life of a woman wrestler in Duke's GWA, where bikini wrestling in horse manure was a job requirement.

Steve watched the file transfer run to completion, made a pass on the live site to ensure that the newest column had properly posted, then closed his web browser. He was done. He felt relief, but also sadness. He wondered if he would ever again experience exhilaration like that of the past few days.

Back to the email box, where Steve hoped to plow through all five hundred of his unread messages. His eyes immediately picked out one from the hundreds. He opened it.

To: Steve
From: Anonymous

Dear Steve,

Congratulations on your successful columns. The entire wrestling world is talking about you this morning.

I have recently left my long-time position as head booker for Revolution Wrestling. I am planning to start my own promotion. I'll be doing the booking, but I need a writer. I need someone young, who's in tune with what the fans want to see. I'd like you to have the job.

Let me know if you're interested.

Anonymous, aka Gene Harold

Steve clicked on reply. As he typed his response, an acceptance, he realized everything in his life was about to change.

He clicked Send. Then he pulled his hands from the keyboard and took a big breath through his mouth. In the past week he had flown to Canada to make a cold call on Joey Mayhem, a wrestling megastar, then boldly challenged his well-connected Anonymous source, then written and published a column that shook the entire foundation of North American wrestling, then watched in stunned surprise as it was read live on the air. Now he had just sent an email that would soon result in him moving out of his mother's house and living the life of his dreams.

But it was his next task that made him truly nervous.

Three hours earlier, he had done a search for Irene Maxwell, from Rosemont, Illinois, age 24, on a person locator web site. It cost him $4.95, and it found for him the address and phone number of the love of his life, the one that got away.

She lived in Philadelphia. Her address suggested she was in an apartment complex. She still had her original last name.

"You only live once," Steve said aloud as he picked up the phone.

It rang twice before a woman answered, a woman he hadn't spoken with since she was a girl, but whose voice was still familiar.

"Hello," she said.

"Hello, is this Irene?" Steve asked, knowing the answer.

"Yes, it is. Who's calling?"

"Hi Irene. This is Steve Garcia."

CHAPTER 45

▼

Joey landed flat. The powder blue ring mat clapped against his bare back.

These rings weren't the greatest. Constructed of plywood boards and tarp, they gave almost nothing to the poor wrestler who landed on them.

Such was life in an independent promotion.

A week after his infamous shoot fight with Goliath, Joey signed a contract with Gene Harold to become the newest member of The International Wrestling Consortium (the IWC), Gene's upstart promotion. Jade signed on as well. They both agreed to work for minimum wage plus a percentage of the gate.

Since then, they had been touring the Great White North. Gene correctly predicted that a promotion featuring Joey Mayhem, Lucifer, and Jade Sleek, would be an immediate draw in Canada's most active wrestling towns, with or without a television contract.

The IWC's premier show was in Vancouver, three weeks to the day from *Apocalypse*. They performed in front of five thousand fans at the New Johnson Arena. Following Steve's advice, Gene arranged for the show to be taped by a freelance recording crew, and then distributed for free on the Internet.

When the IWC put on its second show a week later in Winnipeg, they sold out the Queensbury Coliseum, selling eight thousand tickets. Again, the show was taped and the footage distributed for free over the Internet.

The next show was in Montreal; the week after in Toronto.

Tonight's show, in Edmonton, had gathered fifteen thousand in Alberta Memorial, a crowd worthy of a major promotion with a national TV contract. The main event would feature Lucifer versus newly signed Flash Martin, in the first ever IWC World Title bout.

Before that match could go on, the crowd needed to be warmed up. That was Joey's job tonight. He was wrestling against Matt Allen, a kid from Maryland whom Gene had been watching for over a year.

The kid had spunk, and the crowd was taking to him. Tonight, Joey wanted to give the kid a good rub before pinning him. Doing so required Joey to play the part of being in trouble. He had just fallen flat from his second straight back body drop. Matt followed up with an elbow to the sternum, then a knee drop to the face. Joey sold the moves like Matt was a seasoned veteran. The crowd's reaction was mixed. They enjoyed seeing the new guy get some offense, but most of them were marks for Joey Mayhem.

"Hit me with something off the whip," Matt whispered to Joey, before picking him up. Joey was impressed. His first match in a real promotion, and this kid was already calling spots. Joey followed the instructions, allowing himself to be whipped into the ropes. Joey bounced off the ropes and sprinted back towards Matt, whose left hook was too slow, allowing Joey to duck under. Joey ran to the opposite ropes, bounced off, and came flying back at Matt with a forearm. The crowd cheered at the change of pace.

Both men were now down on the mat. "Smack me off that exposed turnbuckle," Joey whispered to Matt.

In one of many revolutionary changes, Gene had instituted what he called a "night-long story in the ring." Gene promoted telling stories that continued from one match into the next, and the next after that. As such, the metal turnbuckle that was exposed from beneath its soft padding (a classic dastardly trick) by Reston Howard in the previous match, was still available for use in this bout.

Paying heed to his elder, Matt did what he was told, and, after stumbling to his feet, led Joey right to the corner, where he smashed Joey's forehead into the metal turnbuckle.

The poor kid was overexcited and smashed Joey too hard. The skin on Joey's forehead broke open and began bleeding profusely.

As Joey stumbled back to sell the injury, he saw a look of fear on Matt's face. Having spent the better part of the last year petrified of making a mistake in the big leagues, Joey understood the look in Matt's eyes, the look that said, "Oh no," and "I'm so sorry."

Knowing he shouldn't, knowing the Internet would jump all over it, Joey decided to communicate to Matt that everything was okay. Right before falling to the hard plywood mat, with blood gushing over his face in a crimson mask, Joey looked right in Matt's direction, and winked.

0-595-32675-7

THE ROUTLEDGE HISTORY
OF DISEASE

The Routledge History of Disease draws on innovative scholarship in the history of medicine to explore the challenges involved in writing about health and disease throughout the past and across the globe, presenting a varied range of case studies and perspectives on the patterns, technologies and narratives of disease that can be identified in the past and that continue to influence our present.

Organized thematically, chapters examine particular forms and conceptualizations of disease, covering subjects from leprosy in medieval Europe and cancer screening practices in twentieth-century USA to the ayurvedic tradition in ancient India and the pioneering studies of mental illness that took place in nineteenth-century Paris, as well as discussing the various sources and methods that can be used to understand the social and cultural contexts of disease. The book is divided into four sections, focusing in turn on historical models of disease, shifting temporal and geographical patterns of disease, the impact of new technologies on categorizing, diagnosing and treating disease, and the different ways in which patients and practitioners, as well as novelists and playwrights, have made sense of their experiences of disease in the past.

International in scope, chronologically wide-ranging and illustrated with images and maps, this comprehensive volume is essential reading for anyone interested in the history of health through the ages.

Mark Jackson is Professor of the History of Medicine at the University of Exeter. His publications include *The Age of Stress: Science and the Search for Stability* (2013), *The Oxford Handbook of the History of Medicine* (ed., 2011), *Asthma: The Biography* (2009), *Health and the Modern Home* (ed., 2007), *Allergy: The History of a Modern Malady* (2006), *Infanticide: Historical Perspectives on Child Murder and Concealment 1550–2000* (ed., 2002), *The Borderland of Imbecility* (2000), and *New-born Child Murder* (1996).

THE ROUTLEDGE HISTORIES

The Routledge Histories is a series of landmark books surveying some of the most important topics and themes in history today. Edited and written by an international team of world-renowned experts, they are the works against which all future books on their subjects will be judged.

THE ROUTLEDGE HISTORY OF
WOMEN IN EUROPE SINCE 1700
Edited by Deborah Simonton

THE ROUTLEDGE HISTORY OF
SLAVERY
Edited by Gad Heuman and Trevor Burnard

THE ROUTLEDGE HISTORY OF
THE HOLOCAUST
Edited by Jonathan C. Friedman

THE ROUTLEDGE HISTORY OF
CHILDHOOD IN THE WESTERN
WORLD
Edited by Paula S. Fass

THE ROUTLEDGE HISTORY OF
SEX AND THE BODY
Edited by Kate Fisher and Sarah Toulalan

THE ROUTLEDGE HISTORY OF
WESTERN EMPIRES
Edited by Robert Aldrich and Kirsten McKenzie

THE ROUTLEDGE HISTORY OF
FOOD
Edited by Carol Helstosky

THE ROUTLEDGE HISTORY OF
TERRORISM
Edited by Randall D. Law

THE ROUTLEDGE HISTORY OF
MEDIEVAL CHRISTIANITY
Edited by Robert Swanson

THE ROUTLEDGE HISTORY OF
GENOCIDE
Edited by Cathie Carmichael and Richard C. Maguire

THE ROUTLEDGE HISTORY OF
AMERICAN FOODWAYS
Edited by Michael Wise and Jennifer Jensen Wallach

THE ROUTLEDGE HISTORY OF
RURAL AMERICA
Edited by Pamela Riney-Kehrberg

THE ROUTLEDGE HISTORY OF
DISEASE
Edited by Mark Jackson

THE ROUTLEDGE HISTORY
OF DISEASE

Edited by Mark Jackson

Routledge
Taylor & Francis Group

LONDON AND NEW YORK

First published 2017
by Routledge

2 Park Square, Milton Park, Abingdon, Oxfordshire OX14 4RN
52 Vanderbilt Avenue, New York, NY 10017

Routledge is an imprint of the Taylor & Francis Group, an informa business

First issued in paperback 2019

British Library Cataloguing-in-Publication Data
A catalogue record for this book is available from the British Library

Library of Congress Cataloging-in-Publication Data
Names: Jackson, Mark, 1959- , editor.
Title: The Routledge history of disease / [edited by] Mark Jackson.
Other titles: Routledge histories.
Description: Abingdon, Oxon ; New York, NY : Routledge, 2016. |
Series: The Routledge histories | Includes bibliographical references
and index.
Identifiers: LCCN 2016004659| ISBN 9780415720014 (hardback :
alk. paper) | ISBN 9781315543420 (ebook)
Subjects: | MESH: Disease Outbreaks—history
Classification: LCC RA643 | NLM WA 11.1 | DDC 614.4/9—dc23
LC record available at http://lccn.loc.gov/2016004659

ISBN: 978-0-415-72001-4 (hbk)
ISBN: 978-0-367-86881-9 (pbk)

Typeset in Baskerville
by Swales & Willis Ltd, Exeter, Devon, UK